Down By the River

Down By the River

A SMOKY MOUNTAIN NOVEL

LIN STEPP

KENSINGTON BOOKS
www.kensingtonbooks.com

KENSINGTON BOOKS are published by

Kensington Publishing Corp.
119 West 40th Street
New York, NY 10018

All Kensington titles, imprints, and distributed lines are available at special quantity discounts for bulk purchases for sales promotion, premiums, fund-raising, educational, or institutional use.

Special book excerpts or customized printings can also be created to fit specific needs. For details, write or phone the office of the Kensington Special Sales Manager: Kensington Publishing Corp., 119 West 40th Street, New York, NY 10018. Attn. Special Sales Department. Phone: 1-800-221-2647.

Kensington and the K logo Reg. U.S. Pat. & TM Off.

ISBN-13: 978-1-61773-276-8
ISBN-10: 1-61773-276-1
First Kensington Trade Paperback Printing: June 2014

eISBN-13: 978-1-61773-277-5
eISBN-10: 1-61773-277-X
First Kensington Electronic Edition: June 2014

10 9 8 7 6 5 4 3 2

Printed in the United States of America

This book is dedicated to my childhood girlfriends on Chalmers Drive, all cherished friends in my life today—Trish Hartman Mills, Paula Ferrell Kerr, Janie L. Johnson, Myra McCammon Johnson, and Nancy Troutman Hall. My early years among these special friends and other loving neighbors in South Knoxville, Tennessee, taught me my first lessons in love, caring, and community that still linger in my memory and weave their ways into my books and stories.

ACKNOWLEDGMENTS

Special heartfelt thanks go to my editor at Kensington, Audrey LaFehr, for her enthusiasm and love for my Smoky Mountain novels, her ongoing encouragement, and her excellent editorial help.

Thanks, also, to Assistant Editor Martin Biro, Publicist Jane Nutter, Production Editor Paula Reedy, Copy Editor Debbie Roth Kane, Book Cover Art Director Kristine Mills, Book Cover Illustrator Judy York, and others at Kensington Publishing for their help in answering questions, and in planning, publicizing, and copyediting to make this book a happy success.

Closer to home—continuing gratitude goes out to my husband, business manager, traveling companion, and the first reader of all my books . . . J.L. Stepp. He's the best—and I love sharing my journey as an author with him.

Special acknowledgment, too, to our family graphics artist, my daughter Kate Stepp, for her ongoing help with my author's Web site, which you will find at: www.linstepp.com.

Check it out often for book tour information and new books coming out. And if you enjoy Facebook, look for my page and friend me at: www.facebook.com/lin.stepp

Finally . . . continuing thanks go to the Lord, who directs and guides my journey—ever encouraging and helping me in all I do.

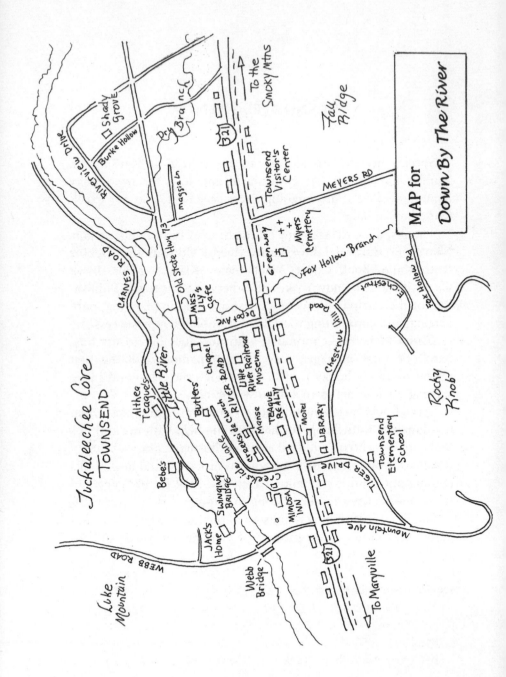

MAP for
Down By The River

Tuckaleechee Cove
TOWNSEND

CHAPTER 1

Grace Conley could hear that nagging little voice in her head again, chiding her with every step as she walked down the winding driveway from the mountain motel. "You're acting impulsively, Grace. Not being sensible."

"Oh, hush," she said at last. "I know I'm acting impulsively, but I don't care."

After all, what harm would it do to simply take a look at the old bed-and-breakfast for sale down by the river? Ever since she discovered it on her walk yesterday, she'd been dying to see inside of it. Still thinking about it when she woke this morning, Grace had even called the Realtor's phone number and made an appointment with the listing agent. In five minutes she'd meet with a man named Jack Teague.

Mr. Teague didn't need to know she wasn't a serious client—and was only curious to see inside the house. She didn't intend to tell him that, either.

Grace stuck her chin up, squared her shoulders with resolve, and skirted across scenic Townsend Highway 321 in front of the motel. Her family in Nashville could hardly offer an opinion or see what she was doing. She glanced behind her, grinning at the thought. And no one followed her taking notes to report to her family either. She was on her own and could do what she wanted today.

If Charlie were here, he'd say, "Let's do it, Grace." She and

Charlie had loved bed-and-breakfasts. Whenever they traveled, they'd searched the Internet to find charming inns or guesthouses to visit. Scrapbooks filled with pictures of their trips to bed-and-breakfasts lay stacked in a cabinet at home.

Slowing her pace, Grace glanced around in pleasure at the small businesses and quaint houses tucked beneath a shady canopy of trees along the narrow Creekside Lane in Townsend. With the day warm and balmy in early May, Grace saw no reason to drive the few blocks to the property. She knew the way and walked with a spring in her step down the quiet street off the highway. Seeing the mountain stream now, sparkling in the sun through the trees as it tumbled down the valley, Grace knew the inn lay only a short distance ahead.

Her mind drifted back to her daughter's call earlier at the motel. "What are you going to do today, Mother?" Margaret's voice had sounded young and bright.

"Well, I'm driving over to the college at nine to see your junior performance, of course, and after that, while you take your last final exam, I think I'll drive to Gatlinburg to poke around in the shops."

"That sounds like fun." Margaret had hesitated. "Could you come early to see me before I play? Maybe we could get a coffee." Grace could hear the edge of anxiety that always threaded through Margaret's voice before a major piano recital. "I hope I'll do well in the performance this morning, Mother. This recital is a part of my grade, and there are a lot of guests coming."

Grace had offered Margaret the assurance she needed. "Margaret Jane, you'll be wonderful. I love the piece you're playing. People will stand to their feet to applaud when you finish. You just wait and see. You are a gifted young pianist."

Margaret had sighed. "I hope so. Thank you, Mother, and I'm glad you're going to be there."

"I wouldn't miss it for anything. I've attended nearly every piano recital you've played in since you turned five years old." Grace had laughed to herself remembering Margaret in stumpy pigtails and a starched white dress, climbing on the piano bench at her first recital, her feet too short to touch the pedals or the floor. She and Charles had always been so proud of Margaret—and of all four of their children.

Switching to a new worry, Margaret had asked, "Do you think we can cram all my things in both our cars Saturday? I have more stuff now than when I moved into the dorm in the fall, especially with the new clothes and gifts I got at Christmas. . . ."

Grace had interrupted this string of concerns. "Margaret, you *always* have more stuff every year when it's time to go home. And we always get it crammed into our cars somehow. So don't worry."

"Okay." Margaret had paused and sighed again. "Well, I guess I need to start getting ready, Mother. I'll see you soon. Sit where you always do, if you can."

"Third row, right side. I'll be there. Knock 'em dead, darling."

Grace wished she'd heard a laugh or giggle at that last comment. But she hadn't. Margaret was such an intense child—always had been since only a small girl.

Smoothing the skirt of the silvery blue sundress she'd chosen to wear today, Grace's thoughts drifted backward. She really wished Charles's mother, Jane, hadn't put so much pressure on Margaret from an early age. Maybe that explained why Margaret was so intense about the piano. As soon as Margaret's talent emerged as a preschooler, Jane Conley all but pounced on her.

Grace supposed she couldn't really blame Jane in some ways. With Jane's own years on the concert stage past, and none of Grace's other three children showing even a snitch of musical talent, Jane naturally focused on Margaret. Jane desperately wanted to groom a protégé to follow in her footsteps. Fortunately, Margaret had always loved the piano. Even Jane's continual pressuring and aggressive expectations could never change that. Margaret was truly gifted in her own right. Grace was glad for that.

In fact, Margaret now attended Maryville College on a full music scholarship majoring in performance. Next year would be her senior year. Grace realized suddenly this would probably be Margaret's last summer at home.

She sighed at the thought. With her four active children grown, the big house in Nashville seemed all too quiet now. Since Charles had died two and a half years ago, the place felt even quieter. Grace had found herself discontented and restless this last year, too. She knew she needed to make some changes in her life, but wasn't sure what changes.

As she walked along in the sunshine, Grace smiled, remembering Margaret had received a standing ovation for her performance this morning. After hearing so many strident pieces performed earlier in the recital, the audience had loved the moody, lilting Bach concerto Margaret had played.

Starting around the bend in the road, Grace looked for the back driveway to the bed-and-breakfast she'd located yesterday. Of course, a main drive wound onto the property from off the Townsend highway, but Grace liked this back driveway that ambled under the trees by the old detached garage and around to the back of the inn.

Drawing closer to the house, Grace looked for the Realtor's car, but didn't see it. She checked her watch. He should be here by now. The Teague Realty office sat only a block or two away off the highway, a charming gray building behind a rock wall smothered in creeping phlox and white alyssum.

Perhaps he had walked over, too. Grace checked the doors and peeked in the windows, but found the house locked tight. And still no car in sight.

Grace frowned in annoyance, checking her watch again. She disliked people being late. She personally prided herself on always being prompt. It showed thoughtfulness and consideration of others' time. It also offered an indication of how well an individual managed his or her life.

Following the flagstone walk to the backyard to pass the time, Grace caught the sound of voices nearby—high childish voices accompanied by girlish giggles. She looked toward the sound to see two girls, eight or nine in age, walking across the swinging bridge spanning the Little River behind the bed-and-breakfast. The girls wore bright red swimsuits with loose, button-front shirts, and they pushed two huge yellow inner tubes along in front of them—the tubes almost as tall as the girls. Seeing Grace watching them, the girls waved and started up a worn pathway leading from the bridge through the backyard.

Obviously twins, Grace thought to herself as they drew closer. Identical short, brown hair, chocolate-brown eyes, and big smiles. Even matching flip-flops decorated with jeweled sparkles. Both cute as buttons, too.

"Are you the new owner?" one of the girls asked, dimples winking in her cheeks.

"No. I'm just looking at the house." Grace smiled back. "And who are you?"

"Morgan." The girl pointed to herself and then to her sister. "This is Meredith. We live across the river, and we're going to the Butlers' to tube with Daisy and Ruby."

"I see. I'm Grace Conley." She looked back in the direction the girls had come from, searching for an adult. They seemed young to be on their own.

Morgan picked up on her thoughts. "We have permission, Ms. Grace. Aunt Bebe talked to Daisy and Ruby's mother, and it's okay. She knows we're coming."

Grace nodded, satisfied. After all, a quiet, small town offered more relaxed rules for children than the city where she'd raised her own family.

"Want us to show you around the house before we walk down to the Butlers', Ms. Grace?" Morgan asked. "We know this house real well. We used to come here a lot to see the Oakleys, and our Aunt Bebe was super good friends with Mavis Oakley."

Grace decided to take the girls up on their offer for a few minutes since she still saw no sign of the Realtor's car. It would help pass the time. Besides, she liked the girls.

Pleased at Grace's interest, Morgan and Meredith leaned their tubes against the garage and began to skip along the flagstone path toward the front of the house, chattering and pointing.

"The lot's really big on this house and goes all the way out to the highway in front and then down to the river in the back," Morgan told her. "It's got three stories, a great porch in front, a screened porch in back, and a cool turret on the side."

"The turret makes it look like an old European castle, don't you think?" Meredith asked.

Grace nodded. "I do. It gives the house a romantic European look, and I love the dark green shutters and doors and the weathered slate roof."

Rounding the front of the house, they passed by flowering shrubs and flowers crowded in masses around the front porch stairs. A riot of blue and lavender morning glories twined up the porch railings, their blooms still partly open.

"Those morning glories will close up soon," Morgan announced, catching her gaze. "It's already late morning. They stayed open longer today than usual because the day started out cloudy without much sun."

Meredith walked closer to study a clump of blue morning glories by the porch steps. She looked up at Grace and offered that shy smile of hers again. "Did you know morning glory blossoms only live for one single day, Ms. Grace? After they bloom in the morning, they wither up and die forever. Isn't that sad?"

Morgan shrugged. "Yeah, but fresh flowers will bloom out again tomorrow."

"I know." Meredith sighed and reached out to touch a flower gently with her finger. "But it's still sad to think they only get to live one day. They're so beautiful."

Grace agreed with her. "That does seem sad, Meredith. "

Ready to get on with business, Morgan interrupted their discussion of morning glories. "This house is real old, Ms. Grace. I'm not sure how old. Mavis Oakley told me the first owner built it to be a fancy boardinghouse when Townsend first developed. They called it The Sweetbriar Inn. Next some rich people lived in it and then someone bought it and started a bed-and-breakfast. Last the Oakleys owned it. They lived here for as long as Meredith and I can remember. Then Mr. Carl, that's Mr. Oakley, had a heart attack and died three years ago. Ms. Mavis didn't want to keep running the Oakley by herself, and her daughter wanted her to move to Texas to live with her, so she left and went to Houston. That's why the place is for sale."

"I think the house is sad and lonely because it hasn't had anyone to live in it for three whole years." Meredith looked up at the house longingly.

Morgan frowned at her. "A house can't be sad, Mer."

Meredith lifted her chin. "I think houses can be sad. Don't you, Ms. Grace?"

Grace thought about her big colonial in Nashville and how forlorn and empty it felt these last two and a half years since Charlie died. "I think a house can be sad. My big house in Nashville misses my husband who used to live there and died like Mr. Oakley did. I also think my house misses the children who used to play in its yard and wade in its backyard fountain. I think it needs a family again."

"Can you cook good?" Morgan asked, interrupting Grace's thoughts.

Grace blinked in surprise. She'd forgotten how children tended to jump from one subject to another in their conversations. "Yes, I do cook well, Morgan. I used to entertain a lot in my big house in Nashville. Why do you ask?"

Morgan looked at Grace thoughtfully. "Well, maybe you should sell your big house in Nashville to a family with kids and come here and buy the Oakley. Then you could cook for people when they stay with you. And you can make this house happy again. We'd like to have someone living here, wouldn't we, Mer?"

"Yes, and you're *nice.*" Meredith drew out the last word with emphasis and then looked up at Grace with another sweet smile.

"Why, thank you, Meredith." Grace put a hand on Meredith's shoulder.

Morgan continued to study Grace, tucking her bottom lip under her front teeth. "Do you know how to lead Scouts?"

Grace wondered where this new thought might lead, already sensing that Morgan was the more aggressive and extroverted of the two twins. "Do you mean Girl Scouts, Morgan?"

"Yeah."

"Well, I served as the Scout leader for my daughter Elaine's troop and then later for my daughter Margaret's troop." Grace laughed. "Why do you ask, Morgan?"

"Were you good at it?"

Grace considered this candid question, which would probably be construed as rude among adults. She'd forgotten how refreshing and forthright children were, too. She smiled at Morgan. "Actually, Morgan, I think I made a very good Scout leader, and I helped to train other Scout leaders as well. In fact, I'm still on the Girl Scout Board of Directors in Nashville."

"Cool." Morgan grinned. "We need a Scout leader, too, Ms. Grace. None of the mothers want to do it since we left Brownies behind. And the Oakley would be a neat place for Scout meetings. The house is huge inside. There are lots of tables and a big kitchen and all kinds of neat stuff. There's even a real badminton court by the gazebo in the side yard and a rock patio down by the river with picnic tables and an outdoor grill. Plus this cool porch." Morgan gestured to the deep, shady porch, cluttered with old wicker furniture and spanning the front of the house.

"Aunt Bebe says people used to play croquet on the lawn here a long time ago," Meredith put in. "I like croquet, and our yard's too hilly for it."

"See, there's lots you could do here!" Morgan gave Grace a wide grin. "You could open the bed-and-breakfast and make the house happy again. You could lead our Scout troop and maybe even make stuff."

"Make stuff?" Grace tried to follow this remark, but couldn't.

Morgan shrugged. "Mr. Oakley built a little shop for himself in the old shed by the garage. He was real good at building things and made all kinds of neat stuff, like walking sticks, birdhouses, and picture frames."

"Oh," said Grace, beginning to understand. "He did wood crafts."

"Yeah, and Ms. Mavis just left all his stuff out there in the shed. She didn't even want it. Maybe you could do something with it. No one's hauled it off or anything. "

A small Volkswagen turned off the highway into the long

drive leading to the bed-and-breakfast. Morgan squinted to identify it.

"Ugh." She made a face. "We're out of here, Meredith. It's that icky Ashleigh Anne who helps at the realty." Morgan made a gagging gesture with one finger to Meredith, who giggled in return.

"We gotta go now," Morgan told Grace as the girls sprinted toward the side of the house where they'd left their tubes.

Meredith dashed back on impulse to take Grace's hand. "You come buy this place, okay, Ms. Grace? You're really nice, and I like you. And I don't want you to keep living in your house if it's sad."

She raced off again, waving a hand in the air, her final words trailing behind her. "Besides, we could be friends if you come. Having friends is nice."

Grace felt an odd lump form in her throat. However, before she could think further about the girls' comments, a young woman climbed out of the car and picked her way up the front walk to join Grace. Beneath a head of frizzy, permed hair, the young girl wore entirely too much makeup and an extremely tight, short skirt, barely covering her hips. A stretchy, tangerine halter top, with spaghetti straps, revealed all too clearly that she wore no bra.

"Obviously *not* Mr. Teague," Grace muttered to herself.

The girl smiled around the gum she smacked behind orange-painted lips. "Are you Mrs. Conley? I'm Ashleigh Anne Layton, and Jack sent me over here to meet you. He's running late and said for me to let you in the house so you could start looking around."

She glanced up toward the house and made a face. "You know, this place is really old and full of *totally* outdated furnishings. I don't know why you want to see it. Plus it's sat empty for three years now." She shrugged. "You might get really creeped out looking at it. There might be ghosts or spiders or something by now."

Grace stifled a smile while Ashleigh led the way up the steps to the porch.

Stopping to turn around at the door, the girl propped a hand on one hip. "Of course, you being older and all, you might like this place—even if it's old-fashioned." She gave Grace an appraising look up and down that revealed all too clearly she found Grace's appearance lacking. "Jack said you were, like, a widow or something."

Considering the source, Grace ignored her comments and appraisal. "Do you mind if I look around?"

"Well, yeah, sure. That's why I came. So you could." Ashleigh smiled at Grace and cracked her gum again. "Jack said for me to read you this description first, though."

Ashleigh pulled out a sheet of paper and started to read. "This house was built in the early 1900s as an inn for early travelers to the Smoky Mountains. It has been well maintained and has experienced several renovations. The last owners put in a new heat and air system, modernized the kitchen and baths, and put on a new roof. The house has a large parlor, which includes a half circle of windows in the turret area, a library with a wall of built-in bookshelves, original hardwood floors, a dining room with an antique chandelier, a large country kitchen, and a master bedroom and bath on the first floor."

At least the girl could read, Grace thought maliciously.

Ashleigh flipped the page. "On the second floor are four guest bedrooms, each with its own private bath. The bedrooms have floral themes, and each room has a plaque on the door to designate the name of the room. On the third floor, the two bedrooms with a sitting area and bath can be rented as a suite or used by the owners for family and friends who visit." She paused, scanning down the page. "The house has a three-acre lot, shade trees, outdoor porches, a patio, a gazebo, a two-car garage, a workshop, and two driveway entrances."

Grinning, Ashleigh looked up at Grace. "That's it. Except that Mr. Teague said to tell you Mavis Oakley left a lot of furniture in the house, all negotiable with the sale." She wrinkled her nose. "Although I can't imagine why anyone would want the furniture either. It's like *really* old, too."

Ashleigh's cell phone jumped to life, playing a popular rock song. She pulled it out of a chartreuse purse slung over her shoulder, turned it off, and checked the message.

"It's a call from the other place where I work at nights—the Shady Grove. I tend bar and sing with a band there." She offered Grace a self-important smile with this announcement. "I need to ring them back. It's probably about my work schedule."

She leaned over and unlocked the front door. "Can you look around by yourself while I make my call? I couldn't answer any big questions for you anyway." She shrugged indifferently. "I'm only temping at Jack's office today because his mother had a doctor's appointment. He'll be along in a little while. He got tied up in Wears Valley at a closing with Kendrick Lanier, his friend at Mountain View Realty."

The girl sent a Cheshire cat smile Grace's way. "I wish I'd been there with those two sexy, good-looking men at the closing. Wowy zowy. The pheromones off those two could heat up a whole room." She giggled and then looked somewhat disappointed at the lack of enthusiastic response from Grace.

Shrugging, Ashleigh flopped down in a wicker chair and propped her feet on the stool across from it. "You go on in and look around all you want. I'll sit out here, make my call to the Shady Grove, and watch for Jack."

Relieved to lose Ashleigh Layton as a tour guide, Grace let herself in the house. "Honestly!" she muttered, shutting the screen door behind her, but leaving the main door wide open. What sort of real estate agency would hire someone like that to represent them? She shook her head, annoyed, but then caught her breath as she looked to the right of the entry hall into the front parlor. It was stunning—like walking into a country garden.

Grace looked around in delight. The carpet in the parlor—a periwinkle blue scattered with a delicate floral design—partly covered the rich hardwood floors and set the tone perfectly for the room's decor. Wallpaper, curtains, and pillows echoed the floral theme, with the furniture upholstered in lush fabrics that repeated the rug's rich shades and created an eclectic but totally inviting room.

"Oh, my." The words slipped out as she turned around in

wonder. "Look at the lovely arched built-ins." Moving closer, she discovered the shelves filled with an array of collectibles, china and books, tastefully selected to promote the character of the room.

Grace caught her breath. "And look at that stunning piano!" Her eyes moved to the grand piano that perfectly fit the oval curve of the house's turret. Someone had shown very good taste in decorating here.

Having visited many bed-and-breakfasts over the years, Grace saw immediately that this one carried an individuality to make it well remembered by any guests who visited. What a shame this place was closed now! *I'd stay here every time I came to visit Margaret rather than in the motel on the highway,* she thought.

Eager to see the rest of the house, Grace wandered across the entry into a library decorated in a similar color scheme of blues, creams, and deep red, but in a more subdued tone. A broad antique desk sat under the front window, built-in bookshelves lined one entire wall, and inviting upholstered chairs sat tucked in the corners of the room, reading lamps situated beside them.

Ashleigh leaned her head in the door as Grace left the library to start down the hallway. "Are you all right in there, Mrs. Conley? If you're getting creeped out, I can walk around with you."

"I'm fine, Ashleigh. You don't need to accompany me."

"Oh, good." The girl blew out a breath of obvious relief. "Then I'll just stay out here and watch for Jack. If you have a problem, you holler, okay?"

"I'll do that," Grace replied, heading down the hall beside the front staircase. She passed a downstairs bath off the entry and then paused to glance into a gracious dining room with four guest tables and chairs. Arched built-ins held a mix of pale blue and floral dishes, and floral curtains and area rugs added cozy charm.

Wandering into the kitchen, she clasped her hands in pleasure, loving the huge space with all the white cabinetry, the big center island for preparing food for guests, and the way they'd painted the hardwood floors periwinkle blue with stenciled flowers to match the parlor carpeting. How charming.

She peeked through the wide French doors by the breakfast area into a shady screened porch simply crying out for guests. She could imagine them sitting out there, enjoying their morning coffee and listening to the sounds of the mountain river.

Wandering across the hallway to find the master bedroom and bath, Grace spotted more Waverly florals, creams, and sky blues in the wallpaper and curtains in the empty room. The color scheme ran throughout the entire downstairs of the inn, but the previous owner obviously had taken all the furniture from this bedroom. It looked bare after seeing the rest of the downstairs still furnished.

Upstairs, as Ashleigh had read from the specs earlier, Grace found four floral-themed guest rooms—the Iris Room, the Rose Room, the Azalea Room, and the Laurel Room. All the furniture, including bedspreads, sheets, and even towels in the adjoining baths remained. Although a little dusty from being shut up for three years, the rooms still looked ready to welcome overnight guests.

On the third floor, the color scheme grew more subdued. The area, named the Magnolia Suite, had two bedrooms, an ample bath, and a sunny sitting room with an expanse of windows looking out from the upper turret.

No furniture or anything here, Grace noticed, looking around. Except drapes and those botanical prints on the walls. Obviously, Mavis Oakley had taken these furnishings to her new home. But it was wonderful that she'd left the bulk of the furnishings behind in the rest of the house. They so defined the bed-and-breakfast's character. Grace found herself liking Mavis Oakley for that. She could have easily sold the furnishings at auction for profit. Probably could yet if a new owner didn't want them.

As Grace started back down the lovely staircase, she could hear Ashleigh's voice from out on the porch. That girl was probably still on the phone, Grace thought, but then she heard a deeper voice answering in reply. Well, well. Maybe Mr. Teague had finally decided to make an appearance. Grace paused to look at her watch. And over an hour late. Unbelievably rude.

Half way down the stairway, she paused. She could see Ashleigh standing in front of the open door talking to the Realtor, her back to Grace.

In embarrassment, Grace realized the words she could overhear Ashleigh speaking to Jack Teague were seductive ones, with nothing whatsoever to do with real estate. As Grace hesitated on the stairs, Ashleigh moved closer to Mr. Teague, plastering herself against him and arching one of her legs around him suggestively.

Frozen in place and horrified to be witnessing this intimate situation, Grace didn't know what to do. Should she clear her throat and speak out? Or slip back up the stairs?

She studied the Realtor through the door more closely. Certainly no young boy Ashleigh's age, but more a man Grace's own age or older, with salt and pepper hair and a roguish touch of a beard and mustache forming on his face. When he smiled, dimples flashed in his cheeks. Obviously a good-looking man, and from the way he acted—smug and relaxed—Grace thought she recognized the type, an aging playboy, still pursuing and charming the young girls. She frowned at the thought. Of course—to be fair—Grace could see Ashleigh Anne Layton was certainly contributing to the situation. The word *slut* came to mind, although Grace chastised herself for thinking it. Perhaps the girl was only flirting, seeing if she could gain the interest of an older man like Jack Teague.

Grace's eyes narrowed. He shouldn't be encouraging Ashleigh, regardless of the situation. She was practically a minor compared to him. Seeing Jack's hand reach around now to settle on Ashleigh's bottom, Grace found she'd seen quite enough.

She cleared her throat loudly, and saw Mr. Teague's eyes lift to hers in surprise. Ashleigh—with her back turned to Grace—didn't hear the sound, but Jack Teague did. To Grace's further shock, the man didn't immediately pull back from the girl. Instead, he shrugged with casual ease, winking at Grace and then letting his eyes rove over her with interest while Ashleigh continued to writhe against him. Unbelievable! Apparently, the man felt more or less indifferent to the girl's attentions. Grace found that even more disgusting somehow—that he could give Grace the once-over while this young girl still crawled around on him.

Grace scowled at him in annoyance and, amazingly, saw a charming smile spread over his face, which he directed straight at her. With nonchalance, he eased himself away from Ashleigh, patting her bottom fondly as he did so. He spoke to the girl, and she looked over her shoulder to see Grace.

"Whoops!" she said, giggling and starting to straighten her skirt.

Grace noticed Ashleigh didn't look either repentant or embarrassed, but instead looked positively smug.

"You run on back to the office," Jack Teague told her. "Roger's been covering for you on the phones, and he has an appointment. You need to get back."

"Okay." She eyed him flirtatiously. "Will you be back soon? I guess Roger will leave to meet his appointment. I'll be all by my lonesome over there."

Grace felt like making the same gagging gesture she'd seen Morgan make a little earlier. She suppressed a grin—remembering the little girl's gesture—and noticed Jack watched her do it. He smiled at her lazily as he sent Ashleigh on her way.

"Sorry I'm late." He let himself into the house and then stopped to lean casually against the newel post at the bottom of the stairs. Looking up to where she still stood rooted in place on the stairway, he let his eyes drift slowly up her legs, over her body, and finally to her face. Grace felt herself blush. How dare he assess her, the insufferable man! And after what she'd just witnessed, too.

Grace set her lips and started down the stairs. She'd make this meeting as brief as she could with Mr. Jack Teague, the Realtor. Spending any more time than absolutely necessary with this man did not sit high on her agenda today. It was all she could do to keep from telling him exactly what she thought of him. Especially when he obviously thought so well of himself!

Honestly! If she hadn't wanted to ask a few more questions about the inn, she'd simply walk out on him. Jack Teague was exactly the sort of man she always carefully avoided.

$\mathcal{C}$HAPTER 2

Jack Teague's day, before encountering Grace Conley, had started well. Earlier in the morning, he'd put together a good sale of two pieces of adjoining mountain lands over in Wears Valley with friend and Realtor Kendrick Lanier, helping the acreage go into the hands of a buyer who would wisely build on the land. They'd written land-protective conditions into the agreement, and the acreage high on Eagle Rock Mountain would now be protected from overdevelopment.

Jack had shaken hands with Kendrick as he left his friend's home office at his sprawling country house on Saddle Ridge. "We did well, friend," Jack had said, giving Kendrick a slap on the back along with his handshake. "It's a pleasure having you in the realty business over here in Wears Valley. I could never get any cooperation from the Inmans, who owned your realty business before, with any joint efforts to try to protect the environment."

"I want to do my part to preserve the beauty of this area," Kendrick had replied. "As does Rosalyn."

Jack had watched Kendrick's arm curl affectionately around his new wife's waist. He and the former Rosalyn McCreary had only been married a year now. It seemed a good match. Jack had always thought Rosalyn a fine, handsome woman, but he'd respected her husband Radnor McCreary's memory too much to make a pass at her when she'd been widowed. Besides, there had been the children. Jack drew the line at getting involved with women with young children. It wasn't right somehow.

As Jack left, he'd seen Kendrick and Rosalyn's pretty little daughter, Caroline, out in the yard working in a flower bed near his car. She had looked up at him and smiled as he came down the driveway. At thirteen, just budding, she was pretty as a picture, Jack thought.

"You're going to knock the boys dead soon, sweetheart." He'd stopped beside Caroline and leaned over to take her hand and kiss it. "You're turning into a lovely young woman."

She had blushed. "You said that at the wedding last year."

"Did I? Well, it was true then, and it's true now."

Caroline had bitten her lip and studied him. "Are you really a gigolo, Mr. Teague?"

Jack had bristled. "Who told you that?"

"Someone in the valley. It doesn't sound very flattering. I think it means you like the girls." She'd dropped her eyes.

"It doesn't mean that at all, but people use the word to mean that." He had considered whether to tell Caroline what the term meant.

She had a right to know if she planned to bandy the word about. "Technically, a gigolo is a man kept as a lover by a woman, Caroline. Usually a young man."

"Oh, well, that wouldn't be right about you at all," she'd said with candor. "I mean you're not kept. And, you're a father, too. Plus you're old . . . I mean older."

Jack had winced at her honesty.

"Well, whoever told you that term, you tell them what the word really means."

"I will." She'd nodded solemnly. "Nobody likes to be called names not polite or true."

"I agree." He had tweaked her cheek. "You and your brother come down and tube with my girls some day. The river runs right behind our house."

She'd brightened. "We will, Mr. Teague. Thanks."

Jack had left her to her weeding and started his drive down the mountain. He frowned, remembering her words. He'd been

called worse names in his time, he knew. Usually, he laughed
them off, but lately he hadn't been able to laugh things off so
easily. Maybe Caroline was right. Maybe he was getting old.
Hitting his fiftieth birthday last year had caused him to take a
second look at himself. His cousin Roger and all Jack's friends
had feted him with black balloons and an over-the-hill party.
Jack had gone along with the joke in good humor, of course, but
he'd hated it, too. Fifty, at one time, had sounded ancient to
him. And now it was his age.

   He looked at his watch. He was really late for his appointment with that lady, Grace Conley, at the Oakley Bed-and-
Breakfast. His mother had set the meeting up yesterday without
realizing how much time the closing with Lanier might take. He
knew no way to reach the woman once she'd left her motel either. She didn't provide a cell phone number. Jack tapped the
steering wheel in annoyance.

   In a goodwill effort, he'd sent Ashleigh to let the woman in at
the Oakley and to explain why he was running late. With his
mother at the doctor's, the only temp he'd found to cover the
phones this morning was Ashleigh Anne Layton. Jack grinned at
the memory of talking to her earlier. Cute little number who
worked the bar at the Shady Grove on Burke Hollow, but
hardly professional office material. Still, Ashleigh offered other
attributes. Jack whistled at the thought.

   Checking his watch again, Jack shrugged. That Conley
woman probably isn't a serious prospect anyway, he decided.
Ma said she was a widow with grown kids, over here from
Nashville to see one of them at a recital at the college. Most
likely one of those women who likes to look through houses
when she's bored.

   He glanced at his watch once more as he headed down the
highway toward the River Road. Already an hour late. She'd
probably left in a huff long ago. People seldom understood the
real estate business and why it wasn't always easy to be right on
time for an appointment. It was hard to judge how long each
appointment would take.

   Pulling into the driveway that wound down to the Oakley,

Jack saw Ashleigh's little Volkswagen, but no other car. He blew out a frustrated breath. Ah, well. Maybe if the woman was halfway serious she would call back. He'd like to turn over the Oakley place for Mavis Oakley. It had sat on the market for over three years now. A pricey property on the river, and a bed-and-breakfast at that, it would take a special kind of client to buy it. The place needed a new business owner. It would hardly suit a family.

Jack saw Ashleigh Anne waiting for him on the porch as he pulled up to the house. She waved at him with two fingers and sent him a blatantly invitational look. That girl was a cute little trick and well knew it. She wore a short skirt today that barely covered the bottom of her hips.

"I guess our client isn't here now." Jack sighed and started up the porch steps.

"Not right now." Ashleigh rose languidly to her feet and then strolled over to stand close to him with a suggestive smile. "It looks like it's just you and me here right now, Jack Teague."

She looked up at him provocatively, knowing he could see right down the front of her tight little shirt. The girl proved hard to ignore, and that was a fact.

"You haven't dropped by the Shady Grove to see me lately, Jack." She moved closer and ran a finger down the v of Jack's shirt, fiddling with the top button. "I've missed you." She nipped at his chin with her little teeth, stirring up his blood.

Delighted at his obvious reaction to her, she pressed closer to him, hoisting one of her legs to wrap it around his. Jack sucked in his breath. Ashleigh was never a girl to beat around the bush. Perhaps he wasn't so old, after all. He grinned. Ashleigh certainly didn't seem to think so.

Jack reached around to catch Ashleigh's firm little fanny in his palm, and then heard an intake of breath. Looking through the screen door into the house, he saw a vision of a woman on the stairway.

Mercy, but she was a knockout. And classy to boot. She wore some sort of floaty, silky blue dress that swirled around her knees, her legs long and shapely beneath. The dress, a shirtwaist in style and cinched around her waist with a matching belt, fitted snugly around her well-rounded breasts like a glove. Jack's eyes roved upward to her face, a classic oval with full lips painted a shimmering coral, her silvery blue eyes almost a perfect match to her dress. Some sort of dangly earrings danced below her ears, and a long chain with a milky gemstone fell to a tantalizing spot between her breasts. A natural blond, the woman had bound her fair hair up in some sort of loose bun that left little tendrils of hair to drift around the sides of her face.

Jack sighed; he liked women. He'd always liked and appreciated women. And this was one fine, beautiful woman standing poised on the Oakley's staircase. Wonder if she was the widow he'd been scheduled to meet?

She frowned at him, and Jack suddenly realized he still had Ashleigh Anne sliding up against him with his hand on her bottom. He sent the woman on the stairs a charming smile and eased his way away from Ashleigh, giving her a pat as he did so.

"I thought you said the widow left," he groused under his breath to Ashleigh. "Apparently, she's still here."

Ashleigh made some silly reply and then whispered back saucily, "I never said she wasn't here, Jack Teague. I just said she wasn't here *right now.*"

After dodging a few suggestive remarks, Jack finally got Ashleigh out of the way. Then he opened the screen door and let himself in. The vision still stood poised on the stairway. When his eyes slid over her again, Jack watched a blush steal over her neck and cheeks at his appraisal. She was obviously aware of him.

Definitely elegant material, too, and when she started walking down the stairs, she did it regally, like a queen or a model coming down a runway. Jack hadn't seen anyone like this woman around Townsend in a long time.

He gave her one of his knock-'em-dead smiles. "You must be Grace Conley." He held out a hand to take hers as she came to the bottom of the stairs.

She ignored the gesture and fixed him with an irritated glance. "And you must be Jack Teague. You are an hour late."

Now that she stood closer, Jack could see her eyes were a silvery, greenish blue, and the gemstones in her ears, the pendant around her neck, and the stones in the rings on her fingers were milky opals with a complementary bluish caste. She smelled like expensive, sultry cologne. Jack let the scent flow up his nostrils. It had floral notes mixed with a rich, earthy base. He knew a lot of women's scents as soon as he came near them, but not this one.

"Have you had a chance to see the house?" he asked, making an effort to be professional now. "It's a beautiful property."

She offered a feigned smile. "Yes, it is a beautiful place, and I already looked through all the rooms. It's charming."

Jack felt a prickle of annoyance. Did she think his little encounter with Ashleigh a big deal? Surely she knew the kind of girl Ashleigh was and how men acted around girls like that.

"Did Ashleigh Anne read you the specs about the house?"

She nodded as she walked down the last of the stairs to the entry to join him.

"So, what can I tell you about the Oakley Bed-and-Breakfast?" he queried.

Surprisingly, she asked him several intelligent questions about the profit base of the inn and about how many clients the Oakleys usually hosted each year. Jack needed to study the specs and the paperwork, retrieved from Ashleigh, to give her the answers she wanted.

Jack propped a foot on the stairs. "I doubt Mavis would have sold the place if Carl hadn't died. They did pretty well here. Carl was retired military when they bought the inn. The couple had a nice nest egg, and they didn't need a big profit base to get by."

Provoked a little at Grace Conley's continuing cool appraisal, Jack said, "You know, this is a rather expensive property, Mrs. Conley. I'm not sure if you are aware of that. If I recall from my mother's conversation with you, you still own a home in Nashville, and your family lives there. This is a business property, not a little vacation house, and Townsend, Tennessee, is a long way from the big city of Nashville."

Grace sent him a steely look and asked him the sales price.

Jack gave it to her.

She shrugged, casually adjusting one of her earrings. "I could easily afford that amount if I wanted to buy the place, Mr. Teague. Does that fact make you feel better about giving me a few minutes of your time?" Her tone dripped with sarcasm.

Refusing to let her bait him, Jack offered her yet another smile. "It's always a pleasure to give time to a beautiful woman."

Jack saw that little flush rise up her neck again, even though she frowned at his comment. She wasn't immune to him—he could sense that—and a tantalizing little swirl of emotions played between them as well. More than Jack was used to feeling and whispering of more than simply lust. He knew the difference. Grace Conley was an intriguing woman with a lot of layers. It would be fun to peel some of them back if she'd quit being so prickly.

"What caused you to be interested in the Oakley?" he asked, moving back to a more professional approach.

"I saw it when out walking yesterday. My husband and I always enjoyed bed-and-breakfasts, and I was curious about this one."

Jack raised his eyebrows then. Only there out of curiosity like he'd thought?

Seeming to read his mind, she lifted her chin. "I've been widowed for almost three years. It seemed like a good time to explore some new options. The house I own in Nashville is too large for me now, and I want something to do with my time."

He let his eyes drift over her again. "Have you ever run a bed-and-breakfast before?"

She shook her head, and something about her expression alerted him to words she didn't say.

"Have you ever worked at all, Grace Conley?" A faint smile played on his lips.

She gave him an annoyed glance. "I worked before I married, Mr. Teague. Then my time grew to be largely consumed with raising four children, helping with aspects of my husband's business, and working in charities and civic groups. Charles and I were very active in the Nashville community, important roles given his position."

Jack raised his eyebrows again. "What did Charles do?"

"The Conley family owns several fine carpet stores in the Nashville area, Mr. Teague. Perhaps you've heard of them."

He shook his head. "We deal with manufacturers nearer to home or drive to Dalton, Georgia, for our carpet, Mrs. Conley. I don't get to Nashville much."

Jack began to realize he probably wouldn't gain a sale for the Oakley Bed-and-Breakfast from Grace Conley. She'd been what he and Roger called a "kept woman" most of her life—a beautiful woman a man of prestige and power married as a statement of who he was. Seldom did those men want the little woman to work outside the home.

"What did you do before you married?" he asked casually.

"I worked in retail for several years and as a model while in college." She smiled as she mentioned the latter, and Jack liked the way an authentic smile lit her face. "But I married young, before I finished school. Later, around raising the children, I went back and finished my degree."

Jack's suspicions gained full confirmation now. He was dealing with a woman looking at a pretty property on a whim. She knew as little about running a bed-and-breakfast—or any other kind of business—as he did about walking down a modeling runway.

He smiled at her. No use in being rude. He'd waltz around in her pretty company for a while today, and tomorrow she'd head back to her fine big house in Nashville.

"Would you like to go outside and look around a little since you already had an opportunity to see the interior of the house? I could tell you about a few features of the property and the history of the place before I need to leave for my next appointment."

Frankly, Jack loved the Oakley place and always enjoyed showing it. The inn had a proud history and stood out as a truly unique house in the community. Jack figured Grace would enjoy seeing the old, hexagonal gazebo on the side yard, and he led her in that direction.

They walked under oaks, maples, and a multitude of mimosas not yet in summer bloom as they made their way around the house. The gazebo sat beside the badminton court to the left of the bed-and-breakfast, situated in the middle of a neatly manicured flower garden.

"I thought this old gazebo might appeal to you." Jack gestured toward it. "The original owners built it in the early 1900s. It fell into disrepair, but Carl Oakley restored it back to its original state while he lived here. Carl could fix anything, and Mavis had all the domestic arts in spades. Both of them loved people, and they enjoyed opening up their home and entertaining guests. We miss them around here."

Grace looked at the gazebo in pleasure. "I didn't notice this when I walked around the house before."

"Well, it's set back a little toward the side of the property. It's easy to miss. The Oakley sits on a large acreage, and land here on the river goes high now. But the right owner will come along in time. All of us hope to see the old place brimming with life again soon."

Jack watched Grace walk up into the gazebo—enjoyed looking at her long legs flirting beneath her skirt again. She was tall and still shapely for a woman with grown children. Jack didn't mind the fuller hips and rounded abdomen revealed under her clothes, and he liked her small but rounded bust more than the pendulous breasts so many older women had. He regarded her with interest, appreciating what he saw. He thought too many young girls today looked as thin as pencils, with too little softness to them. Jack liked his women with a little curve and cushion. Grace said she'd modeled in her younger years, and she still possessed the walk and stance of a model.

Continuing to watch her, Jack decided "Grace" seemed a good name for her, too. She moved with grace. And she was obviously a graceful lady.

As she started down the steps of the gazebo, she glanced up and caught his candid gaze on her. Their eyes locked, and a surge of feeling passed between them before she could shut it down. Rattled, she dropped her eyes, stepped down too rapidly from the gazebo, and then tripped. Jack tried to catch her in his arms to keep her from falling flat on her face, but her weight proved too much for him. They both went tumbling down onto the grass, Grace sprawling on top of Jack, her breath almost knocked out of her.

Arms still around her, Jack blew out a breath and looked up at her. "Are you all right?"

She nodded, still startled and trying to catch her breath.

Enjoying the feel of her warm body pressed into his, Jack wondered then if she'd orchestrated this situation. She might have. Women did stuff like this all the time around him.

Jack lifted Grace's chin with one hand and looked into her eyes. Her pupils dilated, and her breath escalated as he did. Sweet, he thought. And he kissed her.

She tasted delightful, like butterscotch candy. He only had a moment to savor her and to drop his hands to cup those full hips of hers, before she began sputtering and jerking herself away from him. She rolled herself to a sitting position on top of him as she did, which only aroused Jack more. He tried to pull her back down on him once again, but she scrambled her way off him and into the grass beside them, her skirt yanked up and her pretty thighs showing.

"How dare you!" he heard her say now.

Jack sat up beside her, only to feel her slap his face. Jack winced and put a hand to his chin. Then he got up and pulled Grace to her feet.

"You let me go!" she fumed, jerking her hand away from his. "How dare you attack me like that?!"

Her eyes flashed fury, while she brushed off her dress with frantic strokes. She was really upset.

Jack frowned. "Listen, it was you who tripped and fell on me, Mrs. Grace Conley. After that I thought you gave me signals you wanted me to pursue the moment."

"Well, you were wrong!" She gave him an enraged look. "And how dare you suggest I encouraged you."

Jack rubbed his chin again. "A lot of women trip to get a little attention from a man. How could I know that wasn't what happened with you?"

She marched over to the gazebo and pointed down at the

step. "See that nail? That's what I tripped over, that big nail sticking up. It made the step loose and wobbly. I lost my balance."

Jack went over to look at it. "Well, I can see the problem." He looked at her and grinned. "Honest mistake."

"I doubt that." Grace's eyes snapped as she glared at him. "I can easily imagine you take advantage of women with little provocation all the time from what I saw earlier today."

Jack laughed and shook his head. "Grace Conley, if you knew me better, you'd know I've never needed to take advantage of a woman in my entire life."

"Very cute. You're telling me women simply throw themselves at you all the time, is that it?" She put her hands on her hips as she spoke.

Jack stopped to consider her comment, scratching his chin. "Yeah. I guess that's about it. Women have always liked me."

She shook a finger at him like she might at a naughty child. "Well, let this day be an exception for you, Mr. Teague. I can tell you of a certainty that I do *not* like you at all right now. And I think I've had just about enough of you for one day, too."

She turned and started toward the driveway in a huff.

Jack grinned at her back. "Have a good trip home to Nashville, Grace Conley. It was sure nice meeting you."

She strutted off around the corner without looking back. Jack laughed and then started toward the house to lock up, whistling as he walked along. It had been a long time since a woman slapped him. All in all—a rather exciting day.

CHAPTER 3

Grace stormed out of the backyard of the Oakley Bed-and-Breakfast and down the River Road to her hotel. Fortunately, she could find her way to her room, situated on the side of the motel, without going through the lobby. She hated to think anyone would see her like this—a run in her hose, her dress grass-stained, and her hair falling down out of its bun. Good grief!

Shutting the door to her room at last, Grace leaned against the door to catch her breath and burst into tears. How dare that man treat her like some sort of trollop and kiss her out in the open yard! Anyone could have been watching. It was humiliating.

Grace dropped onto the side of the bed, trying to settle her emotions. She poured herself a glass of water and then moved to sit at the mirrored dresser to fix her hair. One look at her face started her crying all over again. Her lips looked like those of a woman thoroughly kissed, her face still flushed.

Gracious! What sort of man was Jack Teague to flirt with that young girl like she saw him do and then make a pass at her not thirty minutes later! The nerve of him. Grace sighed and shook her head at herself. Even more despicable was that she'd responded to him. She hated to admit it, but it was true. When she fell and got caught off guard, and when he looked at her with those deep brown eyes, she'd felt a quickening deep within and a rush of desire she hadn't experienced since young college days.

Grace got up to pace around the room and weep some more,

trying to analyze her feelings and reactions. "Oh, Grace, how foolish can you be. Jack Teague is obviously an aging playboy. Didn't you see that from the first with that young girl crawling all over him? And him enjoying it, too."

She heaved a sigh. Mr. Jack Teague was not the type of man she should admire or be attracted to. Where was her good sense? She'd purposely stayed clear of the Jack Teague types all her life. And for good reason. They were nothing but trouble. What was she thinking—responding to a man like that? How could she even find him attractive?

Grace shook her head, beginning to calm down a little. Lord, the two years she'd been widowed must really be getting to her.

Grace's eyes moved to the list of questions she'd meant to ask about the Oakley Bed-and-Breakfast still lying on the side of the dresser. She'd hardly get the answers to those questions now. And she certainly would *not* call Jack Teague to ask them. She sighed. No, the best thing was to get this whole thing off her mind. She'd acted impulsively to even go see that place, and now look at the trouble her impulse had caused.

Pulling her practical self to the forefront, Grace stripped off her blue dress, her hose, and her shoes, and got into the shower. The hot water felt like a balm to her frayed nerves. After getting out, redoing her hair and makeup, and dressing in a casual Capri set, Grace felt more like herself again. Squaring her shoulders, she took off for the afternoon in Gatlinburg she'd promised herself. Besides, Margaret would ask her about her day later on, and she wanted to be able to give her a cheerful and honest account. She certainly had *not* told Margaret she planned to look at the bed-and-breakfast down by the river this morning. Nor did she intend to.

She squared her shoulders before picking up her purse to head to the door. "Furthermore, I'll be switched-and-twitted before I allow some impulsive man to spoil my whole day," she said, starting for the car.

Grace soon drove through Townsend and into the beauty of the Great Smoky Mountains, heading for Gatlinburg on the Little River Road. The scenic two-lane highway wound in and out along mountain streams and over a high ridgeline to finally descend softly into the backside of Gatlinburg. It was a beautiful May day, and Grace rolled down the window of the town car so she could feel the clean mountain air on her face and hear the stream cascading merrily over the rocks as it rushed along its way.

She parked near the Laurel Mountain Village Mall at the west end of Gatlinburg, lunched at the Garden Café restaurant behind the mall, and then proceeded to explore the colorful mall shops. Grace bought mountain taffy and jars of candy sticks for her children and grandchildren at the Smokyland candy store. At the Book Nook, she found a new mystery for Thea Greene, the high-school girl who house-sat and cared for Grace's dogs in Nashville when Grace went away.

Grace's mood improved as the day progressed, and she felt more like herself by the time she started to explore a cute shop in the mall called Nature's Corner. She even indulged herself with a beautiful floral paperweight she found on sale.

The store's owner, who introduced herself as Zola Devon, smiled when Grace brought her treasure up to the counter. "I like that one especially," Zola said, reaching out to take the item from Grace's hands to wrap it up. "I ordered several boxes of those floral paperweights from abroad, each with different flowers in them. They've sold really well in the shop. . . ." Her voice trailed off.

Glancing up, Grace found the dark-haired girl staring at her with an odd expression. "Is something wrong?" Grace asked.

The girl studied her with a furrow in her brow. "I'm not sure. You bought a paperweight with a rose in the center, but I suddenly see you surrounded by mimosas. Pink mimosas. At your inn." She smiled. "Oh. Now I see it. You own a bed-and-breakfast called the Mimosa Inn, don't you?"

"I beg your pardon?" Grace stepped back, feeling disquieted by Zola's remarks.

Zola shook her head, looking puzzled at Grace's response. "Don't you own a bed-and-breakfast? Sometimes I see things about people." A frown wrinkled her brow. "Usually they're right."

"Well, actually, I looked at a bed-and-breakfast this morning with a Realtor," Grace admitted, not sure how far to continue with this strange conversation. "And I did see mimosa trees in the yard—lots of them, if I recall correctly. Although none of them were in bloom yet. Maybe that's what you picked up on."

"That's it!" Zola snapped her fingers in the air and then stopped to look thoughtful once more, as though listening to a voice only she could hear.

She leaned across the counter to look at Grace earnestly. "You're supposed to buy that Mimosa Inn. You've experienced doubts about whether you should or not, but I believe I received this little message to help you know of a certainty you should buy it."

Grace took a step back, studying the girl's gypsy looks. "Are you a fortune-teller or something?"

"Absolutely not." Zola looked deeply shocked. "I'm only a simple Christian woman who sometimes hears a little word from God for people. Like a Biblical seer."

Grace raised an eyebrow.

"You aren't a believer?" Zola asked, surprised. "I usually don't get things except for believers. Usually God is very careful about that."

"Of course, I'm a believer," Grace said, purposely not adding any more. She certainly didn't meet shop owners like Zola Devon every day and wasn't quite sure how much personal information about herself she wanted to reveal. However, the girl did know about the inn she had looked at earlier and about the mimosa trees in the yard.

Grace thought over the girl's words. "The bed-and-breakfast I looked at was called the Oakley Bed-and-Breakfast after the former owners, and not the Mimosa Inn," she said at last.

The girl smiled brilliantly at her. "But you'll change the name, of course."

Grace stood there somewhat speechless for a moment.

Meanwhile, Zola wrapped the paperweight and packed it into a neat white box before looking up at Grace again. "You see, the Lord knew you were struggling, trying to make a hard decision about a change in your life. He used me to help you know what to do. God's good like that. After all, you have been praying about making a change in your life, haven't you? And wondering what you should do?"

Grace nodded, hesitant to say more.

"Well, you see? This is your little nudge to help you decide." She looked at Grace with a sweet expression. "However, you still need to know in your own heart this is right for you, of course. You mustn't make a big life decision based only on a word from another believer."

Not concerned that Grace offered no ready response, Zola smiled at her kindly and reached over to pat her arm. "You know, I think that deep down inside, you knew as soon as you saw that bed-and-breakfast, it was for you. Didn't you? You just worry there will be resistance of some kind if you buy the inn. But the Father says for you to take courage. He will help you."

Grace felt goose bumps on her arms then. She certainly wasn't used to encounters like this, but admitted it uncanny this stranger knew so much about the inn and about her.

Zola rang up the sale and packed Grace's box into a green Nature's Corner bag, passing it across to Grace. "You come back to see me often since you'll soon be living in the area. And when you move into the inn and throw an open house, perhaps you'll invite me to come see it."

Grace walked out of the store, feeling shaken but determined to do a little more shopping and not think about Zola Devon's words to her. However, she found that resolution easier to say than do. How could that girl know what Grace had done this morning? And how could she know Grace had prayed for over a year for direction about what kind of changes to make in her life?

Driving back to Townsend later, Grace couldn't help but think what an odd day this had been for her. First, she had set an appointment to see the Oakley, which—admittedly—had called to her from the moment she saw it like no place before. Then she'd met those little twins, who had reached out to her with such sweet friendship and warmth, really touching her heart and wanting her to make the old house happy again.

Grace smiled, remembering the girls. And now, she'd received this odd prophetic word from a shop owner in Gatlinburg she had never met or seen before today. She didn't even think that sort of thing still happened like in the Bible stories. It was so peculiar—all of it.

A cloud passed over Grace's thoughts, making her sigh. The only real negative of the day was that embarrassing episode with Jack Teague.

She thought back on the encounter with a calmer perspective now. In all honesty, perhaps even that unpleasant episode held a touch of revelation in its own way. Grace paused, hating to admit her next thought, even to herself. Truthfully, she hadn't felt physically stirred as a woman in a long time—it was definitely a new experience—even if a man like Jack Teague had brought it on.

She smiled. It was nice, in a silly way, to discover all her juices still alive and well in that area and to realize they hadn't died with Charles. Grace had often wondered if she'd ever feel attraction for a man again with Charles gone. So, perhaps even a little good had come from meeting the irritating Mr. Teague.

After parking her car at the motel, Grace found herself walking back to the Oakley again. With all that had happened, she wanted to see the place once more. To think about it prayerfully. She felt drawn to the house; she admitted. She had even told Charles once if she could live another life, she'd like to run a bed-and-breakfast. He had told her she'd be marvelous at it. But then he'd leaned over to kiss her, telling her he needed her to run his own home. Had told her how efficiently she ran their household, how creatively she handled everything. Always sweet like that.

Not seeing a car at the Oakley, Grace walked around the house at leisure, looking at the old inn, enchanted once more with every aspect of it. She peeked through the dusty windows of the garage and peered into Carl Oakley's little shop, then explored the patio down by the river and walked out on the swinging bridge to look at the view up the mountain stream. Leaving the bridge, she walked through the grounds from front to back and noticed, more than at the other times here, how many mimosa trees were planted on the property. They would create a show of fuchsia pink when summer came.

Finally, Grace walked down the quiet little street that stretched east behind the Oakley, the road the girls had started down earlier heading to the Butlers'. The sign read Creekside Lane, and Grace noticed the inn's mailbox situated on that side road. The building closest to the Oakley, a picturesque, white country church with a high bell tower, sat on a large corner property between Creekside Lane and the River Road. It was a pretty church, larger than it appeared at first glance, with several attached wings. Beside it stood a white gabled house in the same style, probably the church manse, set back from the street behind a neat row of green hedges. Several other homes lay along the narrow lane, their shady yards and back porches looking out on the Little River, their front lawns facing the broader River Road. Grace could hear the sound of the mountain stream as she walked along—rushing along in small rapids and quiet swells behind the unpaved road.

It was a peaceful place, and Grace soon settled down on a stone bench by the river to rest and watch the water flow by. She'd sat there for only a short time when a golden retriever bounded up beside her, nudging his nose against her leg and wagging his tail in a sociable way. As she reached out to pet him, she heard footsteps behind her.

"Joel's a friendly guy. So don't worry," a man's voice said.

"I won't." Still petting the dog, Grace turned to see a tall young man walking across the street toward her. He held a leash draped over his arm.

"We just started out the back door to take our walk, and I guess Joel felt it his duty to come say hello first."

"It's okay." Grace stroked the retriever's head with pleasure. "I'm fond of dogs. I own two myself."

As the young man drew closer, Grace could see he was striking in appearance, tall and well built with almost white-blond hair above a tanned, square face. A dimple flashed in his lower chin, but his eyes showed a maturity and intensity beyond his obviously young years. He was dressed in khaki cargo shorts and a striped golf shirt and wore no socks with his worn dock shoes.

"What kind of dogs do you have?' he asked, coming closer to Grace now and propping one foot casually on the stone bench beside her.

"Welsh corgis, a brother and sister team. Almost three years old now."

"Cute dogs, corgis. I read they're intelligent and even-tempered, too."

"Mine are." Grace smiled.

"You live around here?"

"No. I live in Nashville. I'm only visiting the area." Grace held out her hand. "I'm Grace Conley."

The young man took it. "I should have introduced myself first. I'm Vincent Westbrooke."

Grace felt the young man's palm grow warm in hers. He placed his other hand over their clasped ones, looking thoughtful. "We were supposed to meet today, Grace Conley. There's a connection between our lives in some way." He smiled. "Did you feel the heat?"

"Yes," she answered tentatively, thinking this day was becoming more and more peculiar, like a scene from an *Alice in Wonderland* book.

Vincent dropped Grace's hand then and grinned at her in an easy manner. "I always get heat like that when I meet someone I'm meant to experience a connection with. It helps me a lot in the ministry."

Grace looked up in surprise. "You're a minister?"

He smiled and gestured to the church behind them. "The minister of Creekside Independent Presbyterian Church. I guess I look more official when I clean up and wear a suit."

"It's only that you're rather young."

"Twenty-five." He grinned. "Graduated Warren Wilson College at twenty-one and Louisville Presbyterian Theological Seminary at twenty-three. Then spent two years back at Montreat, North Carolina, as a conference director in the Young Adult Ministry Program before I came here. This is my first church."

"I see. And is it going well?"

"Very well. I grew up in the Blue Ridge Mountains of North Carolina at Montreat, so it seems like coming home to work in a mountain community like this. And the people welcomed me with love and warmth."

"You live in the manse house?"

"I do. Nice perk. Mostly furnished, too. Good for a bachelor like me."

Grace looked down at her hand again. "What you said about your hands, Vincent. What did you mean by that?"

He shrugged. "I'm not sure at this point what it means in relationship to you. I guess the Lord will show me in time. Are you planning on moving here?"

Grace found herself telling him about looking at the Oakley Bed-and-Breakfast, about her attraction to it, about meeting the girls, and about getting the odd word from Zola.

"Ahhh. Zola Devon."

"You know her?"

"Once you live around here for a while you start to hear tales about Zola."

"Do you think she really does hear from God?"

"I guess my question back is to ask why we experience so much trouble as Christians believing someone *could* hear from God in ways that help others. Most of my congregation would get real steamed and mad if someone questioned any of the Biblical accounts that speak of the miraculous. But when the gifts of God are manifested right here in our midst, rather than in a book, we get more squirrelly about the idea. Funny, huh?"

Grace laughed. "Yes. I suppose so."

"Yet, despite our doubts and feelings, the Bible tells us God doesn't change—that He's the same yesterday, today, and forevermore. It shouldn't surprise us so much when He works in our midst and uses people as He wills."

"No. I guess not. So what do you suppose the warmth of your hand means about me, Vincent?"

He scratched his head thoughtfully. "Well, perhaps I'm your third confirmation. In seminary, one of my professors said when God gives you a message through another, He often confirms it three times to give it validity. You said some little girls touched your heart earlier and told you they thought you should buy the Oakley. Next, you said Zola saw you owning the Oakley. And, third, I got the witness we're meant to have a lasting connection. The Oakley is next door to my church. Perhaps I'm your third confirmation."

"Maybe." Grace glanced back toward the old inn longingly.

"Why are you so hesitant when you obviously love the place, Grace? And when you've prayed for direction about the next step in your life?"

"Well, I have a rather strong-willed family in Nashville, and I think they entertain other plans for me."

"Are their plans ones that you want, Grace?"

"No. They're not. That's the problem. But my family means well."

Vincent smiled and clipped the leash on Joel. "Then you'll need to trust God to help you with it all, Grace Conley. And He will."

"I hope so." She looked thoughtfully out over the river, sparkling brightly in the sun. "Because I think I know what I want to do now."

"Perhaps I'll see you later?"

"I think so," Grace replied, giving him a smile.

Vincent glanced back as he and Joel started up Creekside Lane. "I'll be praying for you, Grace Conley."

"I appreciate that," she answered. "I will certainly need it."

CHAPTER 4

Jack Teague looked at his watch as he pulled into the parking lot of Teague Realty. Already two o'clock. Unbelievable. Saturday was often a busy day with realty showings, and today had proved no exception. As summer neared, people always began to buzz around the summer cabins and homes for sale near the Smoky Mountains. Most all day today and yesterday, Jack had showed mountain properties.

His family's business, Teague Realty, was located in a renovated house right on Highway 321. It had a nice ambience, painted dark gray, trimmed in white, and set back on a green lawn with dogwoods and shade trees framing the structure. Ivy climbed an old rock chimney on the front of the building, and Jack often held client meetings and closings on the large screened porch that spread to the right of the house. Over the front door, a dark blue awning added a distinctive touch, and Jack walked under that now, with a jaunty step, before pushing open the front door.

He grinned to see his mother back again at the entry desk. Jack had missed getting by the office yesterday to even check in with her.

"Hey, Ma. Good to see you back." Jack breezed by his mother to walk down the hall and drop a pile of papers in his office. Then he brought the bag of sandwiches he'd picked up back into the front office.

He buzzed his mother on the cheek as he passed by. "Had any lunch yet? I picked up some sandwiches and pie at the Lemon Tree on my way in."

"No. It's been too busy," his mother said. "I grabbed a piece of fruit, but I've been too swamped with work here to get back to the kitchen to fix more."

Jack grinned and passed a sandwich over to his mother as he sat down in the chair across from her desk. "Well, then, it's your lucky day. Here's one of Myrtle Kirkpatrick's famous, home-made ham-salad sandwiches. Complete with dill pickle, chips, fresh lemonade, and Myrtle's meringue-topped lemon pie—the special of the day."

His mother laughed and began to gratefully dig in to her lunch. They fell quiet for a few minutes while they ate.

Jack watched his mother with pleasure when she wasn't look-ing. Althea Teague was an energetic, friendly, capable woman, and Jack had always admired her as a businesswoman, as well as loving her as a mother. Tall and attractive, with a short crop of snow-white hair now, she still exhibited the same big, warm smile he remembered from childhood. Jack glanced over at the photograph of his father, Verlin Teague, sitting on her desk. He'd been a tall, handsome man in his day, too, and Jack knew his own good looks came from the two of them. Jack still missed his father, even after six years.

Althea caught his glance. "Your father loved Myrtle's lemon pie just like you."

"Yeah, I remember." Jack looked away, not wanting to stay on this subject. "How did the doctor's visit go on Thursday?"

"Fine." She waved off any discussion on that topic, returning their conversation to business as she began to eat her pie. "How many sales did you write this morning?"

"One this morning and two yesterday." He flashed her a smile and leaned back in his chair to finish off his lemonade. "I'm a happy man."

"Hmmmph." Althea took a bite of pie and then looked at Jack with a frown. "I'm glad to hear that, but you almost lost us another important sale on Thursday. Fortunately, I salvaged it yesterday afternoon and wrote out the contract. Your client insisted I get the commission and not you."

Jack gave his mother a questioning look. "What are you talking about, Ma?"

"I salvaged the Oakley sale, Son, no thanks to you."

Jack's eyebrows shot up in surprise then. "The widow bought the house?"

Althea shook her head. "Yes, surprisingly she did. Although you'd think after what she witnessed with that little trollop Ashleigh Anne Layton that she wouldn't have wanted to do business with us, even if we were the only realty company in America."

Jack dropped his eyes. "Did she tell you about that?"

"No, I heard Ashleigh Anne bragging about it to one of her friends on the telephone when I let myself in the office late Thursday. I do admit I stood out of sight and eavesdropped on her conversation. It sounded quite graphic, Jack."

He ran a hand through his hair. "Ashleigh probably exaggerated things, Ma."

Althea leveled a steely look at him. "I doubt that, Jack. What I'm angry about is that you brought that girl in here to temp again after I distinctly told you not to. And that you acted as base as you did in plain view on the Oakley's front porch, right next door to our church, with a potential client standing right inside the doorway. Honestly, Jack."

"I didn't know the client was still in the house, Ma." He felt his irritation rise. "I saw no car out front, and Ashleigh insinuated the woman had already left. As for the rest, well, you know how Ashleigh is."

"All too well. But I'd like to think I raised you with better sense. You're fifty years old, Jack, and that girl isn't even twenty-one yet."

He shrugged. "I've always thought age somewhat relative. . . ."

Althea interrupted. "I'm not interested in a debate here, Jack. What you did was wrong, ethically and professionally. Ethically, because your actions were trashy, and professionally because you were working and on the payroll. And so was Miss Layton."

Jack rubbed a hand across his neck. "Ashleigh can drive any man a little crazy, Ma. You don't know how she can be. She doesn't give a man much chance to think logically."

"So, you're telling me it was perfectly normal that you acted at the complete mercy of your testosterone levels in broad daylight, on the job, and with one of our temporary employees?"

Jack got up restlessly to toss his sandwich papers in the trash. "You're making too much out of this, Ma."

"I don't think so, Jack. And to be quite frank, I think there might be even more to this story."

Jack colored and snapped back defensively. "What did Mrs. Conley tell you?"

"Nothing, Jack." His mother watched him steadily. "But it seems clear to me from what Grace Conley *didn't* say that you acted rudely toward her and offended her in some way. Perhaps she might have spoken more candidly with me if she hadn't realized I was your mother. I have to admit that was a strike against me at first."

"Yeah, well, things didn't start out well with her on Thursday. I ran late for the appointment, and then the Ashleigh thing happened. I tried to work past it, but Mrs. Conley got pretty prickly."

"I can hardly blame her." His mother pulled out a check and passed it over to Jack. "Here's her deposit check and a down payment she insisted on giving me that is larger than what I quoted to her."

Jack looked at the check. "Whew!"

"We just might have lost this sale, Jack. Grace Conley told me she'd decided looking at the bed-and-breakfast was a mistake on Thursday after meeting with you, but that several other factors occurred causing her to change her mind."

"Did she say what they were?"

"No, she was quite discreet." Althea tossed her lunch bag into the bin beside her desk and leaned back to relax. "But I can tell you this. I personally found Grace Conley absolutely charming. I think she is going to be a natural to run the Oakley. She's obviously well educated and is a real lady. She told me quite a bit about her background and experiences, and I found myself very impressed."

"Did she tell you she's never worked?" Jack sneered. "Plus, she's hardly a young woman anymore, Ma."

"Be careful, Jack. I'm much older than Mrs. Conley, and I don't think I experience any problems functioning in the daily work world. Do you? Nor do I think you should discredit the experiences and responsibilities Mrs. Conley carried raising four children successfully and supporting her husband in a large family business concern."

Jack popped his knuckles restlessly. "She's been a pretty, showpiece "kept woman" all her life, Ma. You know the type. I hate to think of her moving over here and falling flat on her face. She's never run any type of business before."

Althea lifted her brows. "You know, I think Grace Conley may surprise you, Jack. I sensed a mix of competence, graciousness, and determination in her that I liked very much."

"Well, I hope you're right." Jack paced over to the side table by the door to flip through the pile of mail there.

Althea caught his glance when he turned back around and smiled at him like the cat that swallowed the canary. "I told Mrs. Conley if she ever wanted to do a little temp work, that we sometimes needed extra help here at the office. I also mentioned that good help was hard to find. She seemed to find that amusing."

"I'll bet she did," Jack grumbled, grabbing up his mail and heading back to his office.

Jack found himself in a bad mood for the rest of the day. Who would have thought that Conley widow would really buy the Oakley Bed-and-Breakfast? Plus, Jack hated it that his mother had learned about that little incident with Ashleigh Anne.

Feeling restless, Jack drove out to the Shady Grove later in the afternoon. He rarely drank, but today seemed like a good day to down a beer and talk to some of the locals down at the Grove. As he headed toward the front door of the little bar and grill, he heard Ashleigh Anne's shrill laugh ring out. Obviously, she was working the bar this afternoon and tonight. Jack paused, shook his head, and then turned around to walk back to his vehicle.

"No way, Jose. The last thing I need is another encounter with that little skirt today." Jack kicked at a clump of gravel by his sporty, red Jeep Commander and decided to head for home.

On the way to his house, Jack stopped at the Oakley Bed-and-Breakfast to tack a "Sold" banner over the Teague Realty sign by the highway. Naturally, Jack felt glad the house had sold. Mavis Oakley was a good woman, and he'd be pleased to call her and tell her the place had finally turned over. She'd be happy to learn the new owner expected to keep running the place as a bed-and-breakfast. Mavis and Carl had put a lot of work and years into the old inn and had hoped someone would continue the business.

Jack drove down the long driveway and parked close to the old inn. While here, he'd make sure everything was okay and then secure the locks. He didn't want any more problems this near a closing.

After checking the house, Jack walked around to the gazebo, bringing a hammer and a couple of nails from the back of his Jeep. He planned to fix that loose step once and for all.

He searched for the offending nail. "Well, here's that loose nail you pointed out to me so clearly, Mrs. Grace Conley." Jack hammered the nail down with a vengeance and then added several more nails to secure the step firmly to the foundation underneath.

He sat down on the mended step then, remembering his little episode with Grace a few days ago. Admittedly, he'd experienced trouble ever since getting that woman off his mind. Because of that, he wasn't sure he liked the idea of her living here full time, too near his home across the river and too near his office only a block or two away. He usually walked through the

Oakley's yard every day going and coming home when he didn't drive. The swinging bridge offered a good shortcut to the path that wound up the hill to his house above the river.

Jack scowled. "Maybe I can just avoid her when she moves in here." That seemed like a good plan. He knew Grace was the hearth-and-home type of woman he tried consciously to avoid anyway whenever possible. He'd been married once, and that was quite enough for him. Thank you very much. He never wanted to go there again.

Jack's eyes shifted over to the grassy spot where he and Grace Conley had tumbled when she fell. Noticing something glittering there, he reached down and picked up a butterscotch candy wrapped in a shiny gold wrapper.

Remembering the taste of butterscotch on Grace's lips, Jack groaned. "Oh, yeah, Grace Conley. I'm going to avoid you for quite a while until that taste leaves my memory for good."

Jack walked back around to his Jeep, opened the door—and then saw a playing card lying on the driver's seat. "What's this?"

He picked up the card curiously. A queen of diamonds with the words "Be Careful" scrawled across the front in black letters. Jack knew that card had definitely not been there when he'd parked his Jeep earlier.

He blew out a breath.

"Well, I see Crazy Man's out and about tonight," Jack said out loud with annoyance. Cautious now, he reached under the seat to get a tire iron and walked the property around the house once more, but found no sign of the man.

Jack shook his head. They'd had episodes with this man around the area for over a year now. He left notes and warnings. Sometimes he spied on people and stalked them. And he seemed to know, all too well, people's business that shouldn't be his business. People had sighted the man once or twice at a far distance, draped in an oversized coat with a hat pulled down over his face. But no one felt absolutely positive this was the man they sought at all, because he always disappeared so quickly.

Pulling out his cell phone, Jack made a call to Townsend's sheriff, Swofford Walker. "Hey, Swofford; it's Jack Teague here. I just got one of Crazy Man's nutty messages on my front seat when I came back to get in my Jeep."

"See any sign of the man, Jack?"

"No. And I looked around."

"I wish you'd called me first before you checked. We still don't know if the man might be dangerous if someone gets too close." Jack could almost picture Swofford's full face knotting in irritation.

"Yeah, I should have done that. Sorry."

"So, where are you?"

"I'm over at the Oakley Bed-and-Breakfast. I was putting up a "Sold" sign before I went home."

"Can you stay there for fifteen or twenty minutes until I can get there, Jack?"

Jack sighed. "Sure."

Later, after Swofford had arrived and written up his report, the two of them went through the bed-and-breakfast and walked around the Oakley's grounds again. Naturally, the sheriff kept the face card Jack had found on the seat of his car.

"Got any idea what this means, Jack—'Be Careful'?" Swofford asked, scratching his head at the card after he secured it in plastic to check for fingerprints later. He reached down to pull up his belt, too, which invariably slipped down below his full belly.

"No. Not a clue," Jack said.

But he was lying.

He knew instinctively the queen of diamonds had to be Grace Conley. Crazy Man must have witnessed the little episode with her in the backyard at the gazebo. The man sure liked to sit in the seat of judgment and warning.

Waving the sheriff off at last, Jack climbed into his Jeep to head for home.

"Well, don't you worry, Crazy Man," Jack said out loud as he made the turn into his home driveway a short time later. "I'm going to be very, very careful around Grace Conley, you can be sure. Very careful indeed."

Still, it troubled Jack that a strange man watched and listened so often around the River Road area where he lived. And left his little warning notes around so frequently. There was obviously something "not quite right" about that man. Perhaps it boded well someone had bought the Oakley at last. Maybe Crazy Man had been hanging out at the Oakley with the place vacant so long.

Walking up the steps to his house now, Jack could smell tantalizing wafts of the pot roast Aunt Bebe must have cooked that day. He quickened his steps, hungry now and eager to be home.

CHAPTER 5

Grace walked around in the large dining room in her home in Nashville, checking to see if she had the table completely ready for the family dinner that night. She always liked to set up the dining room ahead of time to lighten her workload when her guests arrived.

The fine family china and silver were on the table tonight, and everything sparkled in the late afternoon sun filtering through the dining room windows. Grace smiled as she walked around the table, looking at the homemade nameplates she'd painted the year she took ceramic classes. Charles's nameplate still sat at the head of the table. Grace hadn't been able to persuade Mike, her eldest, to assume his father's place there yet. Charles's place continued to be set up—empty—in respect to the family head, lost unexpectedly nearly three years ago to a sudden, massive heart attack.

She touched her fingers to Charles's nameplate. "Well, Charles, all the children and the grandchildren will be here tonight. I guess you remember it's Margaret's twenty-first birthday. How about that? Our baby is twenty-one. It just doesn't seem possible."

Grace and Charles had raised four children together: Mike, now thirty, Ken, twenty-eight, Elaine, twenty-six, and Margaret, twenty-one today. Mike and Ken, born less than two years apart, had played happily from their earliest years and had always been close. Now they both worked in top management positions with the Conley Carpet Enterprise their father had left them. Mike's wife, Barbara—whom Mike had met at a business conference—also worked with Conley in sales and public relations, while Ken's wife, Louise, taught school.

Charles had given the boys the lake property when they joined the business, and both had now built houses there on Old Hickory Lake. Mike's boy Chuck, now five, and Ken's four-year-old son, Ethan, had bonded like Mike and Ken, while Mike's little girl, Lauren, at three, looked forward to getting together with her three-year-old cousin, Ava, when they had family gatherings. Ava was Elaine's oldest, and Sophie, Elaine's youngest—at eighteen months—was the baby among the five grandchildren.

Grace continued talking to Charles as she walked around the table. "I'm glad the boys liked the carpet business, because our girls certainly didn't. The way Elaine doctored everything as a little girl, I wasn't surprised at her decision to study to be a pharmacist. It's a good fit for her. She was always so calm, practical, and orderly. And I'm happy she found Frank Duncan. He's a good match for her quieter nature."

She frowned. "Although I wish Frank would quit pressuring me to move into one of those villas in that retirement community he manages. Oh, I know it's nice there, Charlie. But most of the people there are older than I am. I married you at only eighteen, if you recall, and had our first three children before turning twenty-four. Even our late child, Margaret, arrived before I hit twenty-eight. I'm only forty-nine now, Charles, while most of the people in Greenwood are in their seventies or older."

On the sideboard nearby lay the latest set of brochures Frank had given Grace before she went to pick up Margaret at college. The literature detailed all the benefits of living in the Greenwood Retirement Community and contained pictures of available properties Frank had inserted. Frank's own mother, also widowed, was already well settled and happy in one of the villas in Greenwood, and Frank didn't understand why Grace wasn't eager to join her there. Frank never seemed to really listen to

Grace when she tried to express her reservations about moving to Greenwood. You had to give Frank credit, all right—he was personally sold on the retirement community he managed.

Grace shook her head. "Not a chance, Frank," she said, shoving the brochures into the top drawer of the sideboard, out of sight.

Walking on around the table, Grace stopped to put her hand on Margaret's chair. "Margaret has only one more year of school, Charles. I assume she'll get another scholarship to go on to get her masters in music—and that she'll begin performing in some way as well. Jane hopes she'll become a concert pianist as Jane was, but Margaret will have to make her own decision about that. And I'm sure she will."

Grace smiled. If one constant character trait dominated about Margaret it was her stubborn determination to go her own way. With her Grandmother Jane constantly goading her since childhood, Margaret had probably needed to develop a healthy backbone just to keep her own identity intact.

Back at Charles's chair at the head of the table again, Grace paused. "I hope you understand, Charles, that it's time for me to make a change. I don't want to stay on here in this huge house, rambling around by myself. Not without you. And you know part of the reason Frank has been encouraging me to move to Greenwood is because he and Elaine want to buy this place. Frank has that inheritance from his dad now, and Greenwood is not too far from the house here in Belle Meade. Also, Frank thinks someone should stay in the family home—and it seems that Elaine is the only one who really wants it. The boys are established and content up at the lake. Neither of them wants to move here. And Margaret has other ideas. She has no particular interest in the homeplace."

Grace put dinner napkins around on all the plates, including at the children's places in the eat-in kitchen around the corner. "Things might get interesting tonight, Charlie. I'll be looking to you for support. You will probably be the only one who will understand the decision I've made."

She smiled wistfully. "You always used to tell me that some day there would be time for me to pursue some dream of my own. I guess it's now or never, Charlie."

It was much later that evening by the time the Conley family sat down to dinner. Oh, different ones trickled in earlier to visit and hang out, but dinner didn't formally start until seven for the adults. The children needed to be fed first, and then settled in with a Disney movie in the living room next door to the dining area. The baby, Sophie, had to be rocked and put down for the night in her port-a-crib.

Grace's two corgis, Sadie and Dooley, were so excited to see everyone they could hardly stand it. They greeted everyone at the door as they arrived and then played outside uproariously in the backyard with the children. Now, they lay curled up on the living room sofa napping while the grandkids watched their movie.

Dinner for the adults was a happy affair as everyone visited and caught up. Grace served a succulent prime-rib roast, dilled potatoes, julienne green beans, several salads and sides, home-made yeast rolls, and Southern iced tea with mint. She'd made Margaret's favorite red velvet cake for dessert, since it was her birthday, and the children had joined in to watch Margaret blow out her candles and open her gifts.

Now, all the adults were settled around the dining room table, mellowed out, finishing their cake and drinking after-dinner coffee. The children had returned to their movie, happily carrying their birthday bags filled with toys and games Grace had purchased for them.

"Mother, thanks for making the party bags for the children," said Elaine. "You always remember those little touches that make such a difference."

Grace smiled her thanks at her oldest daughter, reaching across to squeeze her hand. She had always been close to Elaine.

"And thanks for the great meal, too." Mike looked down the table and caught her eye. "Everything was wonderful, Mom."

Ken cleared his throat loudly, a familiar ploy to catch everyone's attention. "You know, Mom, we've all been chattering away the whole evening telling you about all our news, but you haven't told us anything about what you did while you were away. I know Margaret said you went to her recital, and I think she said you went up to Gatlinburg and toured around Townsend. What else did you do?"

It was exactly the opening Grace had been waiting for. She took a deep breath, smiled, and answered. "Well, I bought a bed-and-breakfast while I was in Townsend—a wonderful, old, historic inn on the Little River."

The room grew suddenly quiet.

Grace smiled at her children. "The place has been beautifully kept and profitably run by the previous owners. It's called the Oakley Bed-and-Breakfast now, after the past owners, but I think I'm going to rename it the Mimosa Inn."

You could have heard a pin drop for a few moments in the room before Mike replied in a quiet voice. "Did you say you *bought* a bed and breakfast, Mom?"

"Yes." She looked at the stunned faces of her family.

Margaret regained her wits the quickest. "Are you crazy, Mother? Whatever possessed you to do such an impulsive, out-rageous thing? Plus you never even breathed a word about this to me the whole weekend—not even when we were packing up the cars at the dorm. When did you even find time to see a bed-and-breakfast and make a decision about one, anyway? And why would you do something stupid like this? Honestly, Mother; this just isn't like you at all."

A murmur of shocked and outraged voices filled the air now.

"Maybe the sale's not final," Frank put in, always the practical administrator. "I'll contact my attorney the first thing to-morrow and ask him to start some proceedings so Grace can back out of this. I'm sure Mother Grace can still do that. She might lose her deposit, but I don't think they can hold her to the sales contract."

"Yeah, we probably can still stop this." Mike leaned toward Frank in agreement. "I'll call our Conley attorney, too, as soon as I get to the office. I'm sure he can find a way to get Mom off the hook. Some sort of loophole. Maybe he can bring in the widow-still-in-grief aspect or something. That should help."

Ken looked at Grace in bewilderment. "Mom, whatever were you thinking to do something like this? And without asking any of us? What do you know about running a bed-and-breakfast, for goodness sakes? You're not a businesswoman. You're a mom. You cook and do crafts and go to civic meetings and stuff. You've never even worked or anything. And what education have you gotten to even prepare you for this?"

Grace sat up straighter. "Running a bed-and-breakfast is not much different than running a big household like I've done all these years, Ken. And if you'll remember, I do have a college degree."

"Pah! A degree in home economics that is practically useless today." Margaret rolled her eyes in disgust. "There isn't even a degree in home economics anymore, Mother. Like Grandmother Jane said, you found a way to get a degree in something becoming obsolete. The whole college even has some different name for that field of study now."

"I'll have you know the skills and learning from that degree are still valid." Grace felt her face flame. Everyone had always teased her about her degree. "In fact, I learned just the sort of skills that will be useful in running a bed-and-breakfast in the field of home economics, Margaret Jane."

"Look," put in Ken, trying to restore balance like a typical middle child. "We didn't mean to put down your degree, Mom. That's not the point. But classes in things like cooking, nutrition, sewing, and table arrangement don't begin to prepare you for all the aspects of budgeting, accounting, business planning, and marketing that are a part of running an actual bed-and-breakfast."

Grace reined in her annoyance. How little regard these children had for her abilities! "Kenneth, if you will think back for a minute, perhaps you'll remember that I have handled the household budget, planned countless events for Conley Carpets and area civic groups, and been a part of marketing and public-relations efforts for many worthwhile concerns over all these years."

Ken shook his head, frowning. "It's not the same, Mom."

"And what about our family home here?" Margaret swept her hand around in a dramatic gesture. "We've all lived here since we were little kids. This is where we celebrate Christmas, Thanksgiving, birthdays, and every other kind of event. Doesn't this place mean *anything* to you?"

"Now, Margaret, don't get overly dramatic." Grace made an effort to keep her voice calm. "You know you have all suggested to me that I need to downsize and give up the house here. So I have been thinking about that for quite some time now. Plus you know Frank and Elaine want to buy this house. Their lease is up soon on their rental, so the timing is perfect. The house isn't going to strangers; it will still be in the family for holiday occasions. And, in addition, you'll all be able to come and stay with me at the Mimosa in Townsend. It will be like a vacation away from home."

A frown creased Margaret's pretty face. "No, it won't. It will be awful! Townsend is a poky little mountain town. It's nothing like metropolitan Nashville. No theaters, no symphony, no nice restaurants, no malls. I'm not even sure there's a post office!"

"Of course there's a post office, Margaret Jane." Grace frowned in irritation. "And Townsend is a lovely, scenic town in the foothills of the Great Smoky Mountains with more metro-politan cities nearby for the asking. It isn't as remote as you're trying to paint it. Also, it is the ideal kind of place for a prof-itable bed-and-breakfast—right on the highway into the Smok-ies with the scenic Little River at its back. There's even a swinging bridge across the river behind the inn."

Frank cleared his throat as Grace paused for breath. "Well, of course, I'm sure it's quite nice there, Grace." He offered Grace an indulgent smile. "But I thought you were going to buy one of the villas over at Greenwood—one like my mother has. That's what we all had in mind when we encouraged you to downsize. You've raised your family and done a fine job of it.

Now, it's time for you to settle back and carry less responsibility, not more. Enjoy your autumn years."

His tone was as kindly patronizing as usual. As was his smile.

Annoyed, Grace tried for a tactful reply. "Now, Frank, I know your mother enjoys her retirement home at Greenwood. But you must remember she is much older than I am, and her health is not as strong as mine. You were a late child, and she's almost seventy, while I'm not even fifty yet."

"The years go by very swiftly, Grace," said Frank.

Grace rolled her eyes. "Well, then all the more reason for me to make a few of my own dreams come true while there is still time."

Elaine, usually quiet during family skirmishes, finally leaned forward to speak. "Mother, you're not doing this just so Frank and I can have the house, are you? I would feel awful if you're sacrificing the home you love and moving away so you won't have to see someone else living here."

Margaret, ever the drama queen, put her hands on her hips in irritation. "See what you and Frank have done, Elaine—pushing and pressuring Mother to get out of her home so you can have it? You're making her move away from us all. And I don't blame her for not wanting to move over to Greenwood. Grandmother Jane said she wouldn't want to live over there with all those old people who sit around and reminisce about the past and talk about their aches and pains. She said it would drive her crazy."

Grace suppressed a giggle. That did sound like Jane. She was eighty-six now, and no one had dared to suggest to her that she move into a retirement community. She lived in an uptown townhouse she'd bought after Charles's father had died, and she'd made it clear to all of them several times she had no intention of leaving it. Pearly Mae, the help Jane had employed since her early married years, still lived with her and looked after her needs.

"Margaret, I'm not moving because Frank and Elaine would like the house. However, I am very pleased they want it. You know it's too large for me. It needs a family. And I'm glad it's going to stay in our family."

She paused. "However, I do have one exception I want to make in the sale."

Frank sat forward, looking nervous now.

"I want to retain the garage apartment for myself so I can have a place to stay whenever I want to come see the family. It has a nice little kitchen, a good-sized living area, a big bedroom, and a bath. It will do very nicely for me when I want to close the Mimosa for a week now and then and come to visit with my family. And I won't feel like I'm imposing on anyone if I have my own little place."

"Oh, we'd be pleased for you to keep the apartment, Mother." Elaine reached across the table to take her hand. "And I would want you to come back any time you like—and to stay as long as you want. Ava and Sophie love you so much. They will both miss you."

Barbara, Mike's wife, leaned forward then. "That's the part that is hard for me to understand, Mother Grace. All of your family lives here in Nashville, including five grandchildren who love you. Why do you want to leave us? Have we done something to upset you?"

"Absolutely not, Barbara. And I will miss being close to everyone. But Nashville is not so far from Townsend. I can come home often—and you can come to see me as often as you'd like."

Grace heard Margaret mutter. "Not bloody likely."

Ken's wife, Louise, tapped her fingers on her water glass restlessly. "Well, there are some other problems with your moving that you haven't seemed to consider."

Her voice sounded snippy, and she looked annoyed. "You often keep the grandchildren for us when we have to travel, you know—or when we go on vacation. This summer, you've already committed to keep our Ethan for several weeks—and to keep Mike and Barbara's two, Chuck and Lauren—while we all go on that Alaskan cruise and when we have our week at Hilton Head, and for the Friday nights when we all go to the symphony. Also in the fall there are the ballgames. You always keep all the children when we go to the Vanderbilt games. You always have. It's like a tradition. The children look forward to it. Traditions are important to children, Mother Grace. And, as you know, children thrive better when they have stable family lives."

Louise smiled her nicest schoolteacher smile at Grace. "I really don't think you've been giving enough thought to your grandchildren. You know, you can't go back and recapture these years. And children grow up all too soon."

Grace looked around the table at the adults who had once been her own little children and knew this to be all too true. She listened to the murmur of their voices as they began to chart up all the free babysitting services they were going to be deprived of if she moved. She felt a little ashamed of her children for bringing these commitments up. They were thinking of themselves now, and of what was convenient for them, more than thinking of her—or their children's—happiness.

Mike looked toward the head of the table where Charles used to sit. "What would Dad have thought about your doing this, Mom? Have you considered that?"

Grace bristled at Mike's words—particularly at his tone of voice. "Actually, I think your father would have been more respectful of my decision to make this move than any of you."

"I seriously doubt that," Margaret put in sarcastically. "Ken's right. You have no background preparing you to run a business. And Dad would have known that."

"Your father and I visited bed-and-breakfasts together in all our travels around the U.S. and in our trips abroad. It was a special pleasure of ours. You should remember I kept scrapbooks of our visits. And your father and I often talked about possibly buying our own bed-and-breakfast someday."

"Pipe-dreaming and putting together scrapbooks of visits to inns does not prepare you to run one, Mom." Mike scowled at her. "And Dad's not here anymore to help you run a business. I'm sure he wouldn't approve of your doing this on your own. As the head of the family now, I have to express that for him."

Grace was growing tired of this discussion. "Look. Although

this may seem like an impulsive decision to all of you, it is— after all—*my* decision. I am an adult woman, not a child who needs guidance. And Charles made sure I would have my own income. You all know that. You may not have much confidence in my ability to run a bed-and-breakfast successfully, but I may very well surprise you. It is often difficult for children to imagine their mother in a career capacity—especially when she's been at home at their beck and call for so many years. And, obviously, none of you seem to be aware of the work I did and responsibilities I carried in all the nonprofit endeavors I was involved in all these years."

Margaret rolled her eyes dramatically when Grace paused.

"The point is, I *have* bought this bed-and-breakfast. I do not intend to change my mind about that decision, even though you are obviously not supportive of my plans. And I have every intention of moving to Townsend as soon as I can make arrangements here. Mrs. Oakley, the former owner, says I still have time to get in touch with many of her former clients who come in June and July—and that I also have time to advertise and attract new clients for the late summer and for the fall. Many people visit the Smokies then to see the colors."

Only a set of scowling faces met hers. "You might want to remember I also have family in East Tennessee. My parents, my sister and her family, and my brother and his family live nearby in South Knoxville—about twenty minutes from the inn. In a sense, I am going back to my family as well as leaving family here. My own roots are in the East Tennessee area, children. And I want to do something useful with the rest of my life. I've been so busy with family and home that I haven't had time to try my own wings like most of you. I think it is my time to do that. I feel really happy about this decision. I wish you could feel happy with me."

No encouraging words came back—just continuing frowns.

"What about all your beautiful furniture?" Louise looked around with sorrow. "It won't be the same here when the place is all cleaned out."

Grace smiled. "Much of the bed-and-breakfast is furnished. So I plan to leave most of the formal furnishings here with Frank and Elaine, if they would like to have them. They both like antiques. And I plan to talk with each of you privately about things in the house you might want for your own homes."

Barbara wrinkled her nose and sent a warning look to Mike. Both the boys had very modern tastes in their lake homes. It would be unlikely either of them would want much from the house here.

"Some of the furnishings I'll take with me, of course, Louise. I'll also take some of the furniture over to the garage apartment to fix up my little place there."

Margaret laughed and sent a telling look around the table to her siblings. "That will be a challenge! What do you plan to do with all those piles of craft items, some not even half finished, and all the boxes of craft supplies that have filled up that apartment to the gills for ages? I hope you'll finally trash that stuff."

A snigger ran around the table. This was an old joke.

Grace had done crafts of one kind or another since she had first married. Well, actually, she'd even done crafts before that. She possessed a creative streak and liked to make things with her hands. Over the years, she'd taken a multitude of different kinds of arts and craft classes around the Nashville area. Charles and the kids had viewed Grace's crafting as a curse that kept one household area or the other constantly covered with assorted messy projects on old newspapers. As the children grew up and left home, Grace had taken over the garage apartment as her work and storage area. Okay, to be truthful— mostly as her storage area. She'd meant to clean out the place for years now. But had never gotten around to it.

Mike spoke up. "News flash, Mom. I am *not* going to help clean out and carry off all that craft stuff. So don't even think about asking me."

Ken echoed Mike's sentiments.

Grace's mouth tightened. "I haven't asked anyone to help me. I'll take care of it by myself."

Margaret giggled. "You may have to rent an entire moving van just to carry off all that junk."

Again, Grace felt annoyed with her children. They'd never valued the crafts she had made or the skills she'd learned in doing them. Charles hadn't been much better.

Her anger flared. "I'll have you know there is some very nice work packed away in that garage. It's not junk."

Barbara gave her a kind but patronizing look. "Yes, but people don't decorate with craft items in their houses anymore, Mother Grace. Things have changed."

Grace thought about the décor of the Oakley then—colorful, old-fashioned, full of bric-a-brac and handcrafted items. She decided not to tell her children what the Oakley looked like just yet.

Sighing, Grace braced herself for another barrage of criticisms. She could hear the family tuning up to talk about the waste of their father's hard-earned money on a hair-brained scheme like this. This was all going much worse than she'd even imagined.

Actually, the arguing might have continued into the night if the grandchildren hadn't started to tire. Then everyone began to leave to take the children home to bed. It had grown late. All but Grace worked the next day, as well—even Margaret. She was doing a short teaching internship in the music department at a nearby college.

The good-byes were tense and strained as Grace saw her family off.

Just as Grace thought she could begin to let down, Charles's mother Jane showed up. She'd been to a concert pianist performance, but had stopped by on her way home to wish Margaret a happy birthday. Of course, Margaret immediately told her about Grace's buying the bed-and-breakfast, and then Jane lit in on Grace in full force.

"I can't believe you've made such a foolish decision, Grace. I always told Charles that marrying a girl with small town roots and from so little money was a mistake. But you did well, being a good wife to Charles, all in all, and you kept a nice home. I can't say you ever disgraced us until now—although there were times I'd like to have seen you have more polish. And I always wished you'd become accomplished at something along the way, rather than flitting about in all those silly crafting classes over the years. I used to dread the holidays—wondering what new homemade item I'd have to unwrap and pretend to like."

Grace winced. It was no secret that Charles's mother had never liked her. Jane had been internationally famous, after all, as a concert pianist before she married. It was hard for Grace to match that. Jane hadn't even married until thirty-three, and then she'd only had the one child: Charles. Her expectations for him, naturally, had been high. It hadn't taken Grace long to realize she didn't exactly measure up with Jane.

Jane hobbled over on her cane to put an arm around Margaret. Jane was a blond, like Grace and Margaret. But she was a bottle blond now with a pencil-thin body and a hard, tight face. There had always been an arrogance and outspokenness about Jane that intimated Grace. Grace liked peace. She was no match for Jane's sharp words and biting criticisms.

Jane gave Grace a critical look down her nose. "So now you're going to sell your home right out from under your own child, here, before she's even grown and gone. How do you think that makes Margaret feel, Grace? She came to the door crying. I saw it, even though she tried to hide it."

Margaret was obviously more upset than Grace had expected her to be.

"You know I'll make a place for Margaret at the bed-and-breakfast, Jane." Grace had never been able to call Charles's mother by a more intimate term. "It's not as though she won't have a home anymore. And the inn is quite large."

"It will hardly be the same, though, will it?" Jane's tone was condescending. She patted Margaret on the cheek and spoke to her fondly. "Your dear father would turn over in his grave if he knew what your mother had done."

Jane turned a hard glance on Grace. "It's thoughtless and selfish of you—going off and leaving all your family here. I have often been disappointed in you, but this time definitely takes the top prize."

Grace sighed. Jane would certainly miss bossing her around in the future—that was for sure.

As if reading her thoughts, Jane narrowed her eyes and gave Grace a hard stare. "I'm sure Margaret can stay on here with Elaine and Frank in her own home." She patted Margaret's arm affectionately. "I'll talk with Elaine. There is no reason you should be forced to leave your family home until you're ready to have one of your own."

As Margaret wept then, Jane gave Grace a glowing look of triumph. Jane had been trying to turn Margaret against Grace ever since the girl had shown the first spark of musical talent. This was simply another little victory for Jane.

Nevertheless, it hurt Grace to have her entire family angry with her. And as the weeks of preparation and packing went by, Margaret decided she would not move with Grace. Jane Conley had talked to Elaine and Frank, and they'd offered to let Margaret stay on with them over the summer until it was time for her senior year at college. Grace felt a little surprised Margaret agreed to this decision, since she and Elaine had never gotten along very well. Furthermore, Margaret didn't get along with Frank well, either. He was too outspoken to suit her, while Elaine was too quiet and practical to complement Margaret's artistic temperament. Plus Margaret got tired of Ava and Sophie quickly, both still so small and demanding. With some amusement, Grace had watched Margaret make a concentrated effort to entrench herself in Elaine's affections these last weeks—determined to stay behind with her and to not move away with Grace.

When moving day finally came, few in Grace's family were there to see her off. In fact, most of them had avoided her as much as possible after Margaret's birthday dinner in early May. When they did call or come by, they tried again to talk her out of moving. Their overall sentiment was that she was sure to fail in trying to run a bed-and-breakfast and that she would come crawling back to them all in Nashville then, repentant and embarrassed. It angered Grace and made her more determined than ever to succeed.

By the time she moved, Grace found herself quite ready to tell her children—and even the town of Nashville—good-bye. The last weeks had been stressful. Still, she cried half the way to Townsend, grieved that none of her family could be happy for her. And hurt, too, that they sent her off with so little love and affection.

CHAPTER 6

True to his resolve, Jack had successfully avoided any contact with Grace Conley after she moved into the Oakley Bed-and-Breakfast in June. Not that it was even called the Oakley anymore. Grace had erected a striking professional sign on the highway announcing the new name of the bed-and-breakfast as the Mimosa Inn. Now that the mimosa trees on the property were coming into full bloom, the name seemed especially appropriate.

Even Jack grudgingly admitted that the new sign, now swinging invitingly from a high, wrought-iron pole, was stunning—and that the changes going on at the bed-and-breakfast seemed to indicate Grace Conley did actually know how to work hard after all. The inn was newly painted, the yard neatly landscaped, and fresh sweeps of flowers now colorfully accented the property. Grace had quickly networked to discover local workers eager for extra money. They'd power-washed the walks and patio, cleared out brush on the property, carried off useless items from the Oakley's attics, storage closets, and outbuildings—and literally made the property sparkle.

Jack found himself a little proud of Grace Conley's moxie. As his mother had said, Grace had surprised him. Furthermore, everyone around the River Road liked her. She always had fresh coffee or iced tea, and a warm smile, ready for anyone who stopped by to visit her. Plus her home-baked goods were already becoming legendary. Jack knew the young minister of the

Creekside Church, Vincent Westbrooke, stopped over every morning to have coffee and fresh muffins with Grace. If she had paying guests, Vince often joined them for a full breakfast.

Jack sat outside on the back patio of the realty office reviewing these thoughts one morning in late June. Jack's cousin, Roger Butler, was comfortably settled on the patio with him, drinking coffee and poring over the blueprints of a log cabin he was building for a new client. Jack looked at his cousin affectionately. He wore an aged, wrinkled, corduroy jacket he favored over a checked shirt, and his glasses drooped down his nose as he leaned over his work. Unlike Jack, Roger was round-faced and comfortable looking, his looks coming from his father's people, the Butlers, more than the Teagues.

Seeing that Roger was preoccupied, Jack let his gaze drift over the bank's parking lot next door and then across Creekside Lane into the front yard of the Mimosa Inn. Grace Conley was out walking in the yard. Every so often she leaned over, as if weeding or picking flowers or something. It was too far to see exactly. She wore a long pink skirt that exactly matched the color of the mimosa blossoms blooming all over the yard. Jack frowned. Did the woman plan that sort of thing?

Roger's voice interrupted Jack's thoughts. "You know, Jack, you can't continue to avoid Grace Conley forever." Roger grinned at him, pushing his glasses up with one finger. "Besides, it's not like you to avoid an attractive woman anyway."

Jack frowned. "Things didn't start off well with Grace Conley and myself. I've kept my distance for a reason, Roger."

"Yeah, but it's starting to become too obvious." Roger leveled him with a considering glance. "Word's gotten around about the little Ashleigh Layton episode. And now people are starting to say you're too embarrassed to confront Grace Conley again. Everybody's noticed that you never drop by the inn, when you always used to do so when Carl and Mavis lived there. Plus, you seldom walk to work anymore and cut through the Mimosa property. You've even avoided church since Grace started attending there. It's starting to amuse people that you seem to be downright scared of Grace Conley—especially since she's so nice."

"That's ridiculous!" Jack jerked upright to glare at Roger and slopped his coffee on his slacks. "Who's saying that, anyway?"

Roger shrugged. "Oh, I've heard a few comments here and there."

"Well, there's nothing to them." Jack slumped back into his chair, still glaring, and studied Roger's deadpan expression. He and his cousin had been best friends since childhood. Few people knew him as Roger did.

"Do you think I'm being cowardly not going over to see Grace Conley?"

Roger scratched his chin. "Well, I can't help but wonder why you're avoiding her, Jack. It is odd, even knowing about the Ashleigh incident."

Roger's gaze followed Jack's to where Grace was still walking in the yard. "The other thing that makes this even more peculiar is how much your girls love Grace Conley, Jack. Samantha says they are over there almost every day on one excuse or another. Grace feeds them and has them doing odd jobs for her around the house. She's organizing a Junior Scout troop for girls their age. Even my Daisy is thrilled about that. You know none of the mothers wanted the responsibility of having a troop. It's a dang lot of work. Yet, here Grace Conley has taken it on when she doesn't even have a child that age herself. It's making a big impression around here, that kind of thing. And it makes you seem even more churlish for avoiding her when she's been so good to your twins."

Jack kicked a post on the deck. "Yeah, Meredith and Morgan talk about her all the time. It's 'Grace this' and 'Grace that'; it's enough to make me gag."

Roger laughed. "Listen, Jack . . . why don't you let me in on why you're really avoiding the widow Conley?"

Frowning, Jack hedged the question. "We had a little misunderstanding, Miz Conley and I. She made it clear to my mother that she didn't even want me to get the commission on the sale of the Oakley. That seemed to imply to me that she wouldn't be eager to see me coming around."

"Do you want to explain that little misunderstanding in more detail? It must have been a lulu to have caused her to cut you out of the commission on the Oakley."

"It was just something silly." Jack crossed his arms defensively. He didn't want to admit, even to Roger, that he'd kissed Grace Conley out by the gazebo. Or that she'd slapped his face for it. He at least owed her that secret. She'd obviously told no one about it herself.

Roger studied him. "I see. Meaning you're not going to confide in me, right? So be it, Jack. But you still need to be a big boy and walk over to the inn and make nice with Grace Conley. If only because your girls spend so much of their time there—if for no other reason."

Jack scowled thinking about it.

"You can use the excuse of telling her about Crazy Man." Roger straightened his blueprints out on the patio table to study them more closely. "The last time there was an incident with him, it was at the bed-and-breakfast. You can go over there and warn her to be careful. Look real chivalrous."

"Yeah, maybe I'll do that some time."

"How about now?" Roger pushed. "She's out walking in the yard. You don't have an appointment until later. This is an opportune time, Jack. Remember your dad always said not to put off until tomorrow what you can well take care of today."

Jack blew out a breath. "Okay, okay. I'll walk over and see if I can make nice."

Roger reached over to clap him on the back. "It's not like going to the guillotine, Cousin. The times I've seen Grace Conley over at our place visiting Samantha, I remember noting she's a right fine-looking woman.'

"I didn't know Grace Conley had been to your place visiting Samantha." Jack looked up at Roger in surprise.

Roger shook his head. "Shoot, man, where have you been? Those two women have become as thick as thieves. Sam's been hungry for a woman friend, and she and Grace seem to get along like they've always known each other. Plus our girls, Daisy and Ruby, are about as crazy about Grace as your girls. The woman's a natural with children. And she seems to have a gift for getting along with everyone around here except for you."

"Well, that's just great." Annoyed, Jack banged his coffee cup down on the table in irritation, the coffee sloshing out over the side of the cup again.

"Hey, watch it, Jack. Those are my blueprints you're splashing your coffee over." Roger picked up a napkin to wipe off the corner of his blueprints and then rolled them up to put them back in the carrier tube, out of harm's way.

He stood up and looked at Jack pointedly. "Man, you need to work this out. It's causing you to act *real* out of character. And it's causing people to talk."

Roger started toward the back door to the realty office, but turned to give Jack a considering look. "Frankly, Jack, you don't really need much more negative talk circulating about you. There's been enough already of late, and it's bad for business."

Jack winced as Roger let himself in the back door. Roger had every right to care about the business. He was a partner, after all. His specialty was architecture, but he held a real estate license, too. Like Jack, he'd worked in the family business since he was a kid—sweeping up, putting out or taking down signs, running errands, and, eventually, selling property. When they were younger, Jack and Roger had been a bit of a handful. Even into their young adult years. But then Roger met Samantha, when she'd moved here to teach kindergarten at the elementary school in Townsend. And Jack had watched Roger change.

Those years afterward had been bittersweet ones. Jack had thought he and Roger would always be bachelors together, both nearly in their forties when Roger fell for Samantha. Jack tried, at first, not to like Sam because she'd broken up their bond. But he couldn't hold out for long against Samantha Morrow's comfortable goodness. Over time, as he watched Roger and Samantha marry and find happiness, he began to think he might like to find the same. Instead, he'd gotten involved with Celine Rosen.

It was probably because he'd subconsciously wanted to fall in love and settle down that he'd been so taken in by Celine. Jack shook his head. Marriage was never a place he wanted to go again. It was entirely too painful.

He stood up then, resolved to action. It was time to pay his respects to Grace Conley. He might have played the field hard and fast in the years since Celine had left, but he knew how to behave himself when he needed to. He could handle the widow Conley.

His mind made up, Jack strode across the parking lot, crossed the road to cut between two big maples on the inn's property line, and started across the driveway toward Grace. The sound of his footsteps on the drive caused her to turn and watch him walk toward her across the yard.

God, she was so beautiful, thought Jack. She still impacted him like a punch in the breadbasket. She was incredible. The skirt she wore was a soft fuchsia pink, floating around her calves. She had on a simple white T-shirt with it and some sort of white slip-on sandals. Her legs were bare today, her toenails painted a glittery shell pink to match her lipstick. Jack studied her mouth as he came closer, her lips full and lush. Inviting. Jack well remembered how they tasted and how Grace's body had felt on top of his. He shook his head a little to try to clear his thoughts.

"I thought I saw you out in the yard," he said, trying to sound casual.

"I was deadheading the flowers." She opened her hand to reveal the dead flowers she'd clipped from a clump of coral and white periwinkles.

Jack looked around. "The place looks nice."

"Thank you."

She wasn't making this easier. "Look, I thought I should stop by for a few minutes to talk since my girls are spending so much time over here."

"Of course." She smiled graciously. "Would you like to come up on the porch and have a cup of coffee? I can run in and get some. It seems too nice a day not to be outside while it's so pleasant."

"Yeah, that would be good."

Jack followed her up the steps, trying not to focus on the sway of her full hips underneath her skirt as she walked. He wondered if she knew what an incredibly sexual appeal she put out. Perhaps her husband had been smart to keep her close to home.

"I'll be right back," she told him, letting herself in the front door.

Jack had time to regain his composure and settle himself into one of the newly upholstered wicker chairs before she returned. She carried a wooden tray, and Jack stood up immediately to help her with the door as she negotiated her way onto the porch with it. The tray held a cruet of coffee, two colorful mugs, and a plate of small muffins. Hustling around her feet wiggled two small corgis who made a dash for the yard as Jack shut the door.

Grace, catching a glimpse of them out of the corner of her eye, set the tray down and clapped her hands twice. "Sadie and Dooley, you two get back up here right this minute."

The two small dogs turned and obediently came up the porch steps.

She gave them a stern look. "Did you ask me if you could go out in the yard?"

They hung their heads like chastised children.

"Well, then, you'll have to wait for a while before you can go out in the yard again. Besides, you know I don't like you to be in the front yard, anyway. The highway is too near."

She seemed to remember Jack was there then.

"We have a guest," she told the dogs. "Go and say hello and then go lie down."

The dogs dutifully came over to sit in front of Jack and offer him a paw.

Grace looked at Jack pointedly. "They want to shake hands with you if it's all right. That's how they greet guests."

"Oh. Sure." Jack shook each paw in turn and marveled to see

the small dogs then go over to lie down on the porch right where Grace had indicated.

Jack watched them, impressed. "They're very well-behaved little dogs."

"They *were* better behaved. It's been a challenge teaching them so many new rules in a new setting since we moved here. We're still working on it." She leaned over to scratch the dogs' ears affectionately and gave each a small treat from out of her skirt pocket.

Then she poured out two cups of hot coffee. "I'll let you fix your coffee the way you like it." She gestured to packets of sugar and a small pot of cream on the tray.

Jack fixed his coffee and then watched her stir cream and a half packet of sweetener into her own cup. He noticed she still wore her wedding ring, along with a milky opal on her second finger beside it. There was a bluish opal on her other hand and a ring circled with diamonds on her ring finger. Jack remembered her opals from before. He saw two more tucked into her pierced ears.

"Born in October?" he asked, making an effort at conversation.

She looked surprised at his question and then smiled as she saw his eyes studying her hands.

He sent an easy smile back at her and propped his feet up on a stool. "I remembered that opals are the birthstone for October."

She took a sip of her coffee. "Yes, and I'm fond of them. And you are right about my birthday being in October; it's October the sixth. Although I think I won't mention the year I was born or what age I'll be this fall." A touch of a dimple winked in her cheek.

"You have dimples." He tapped his cheek as he spoke.

"Not like yours and the girls'." She seemed to study him then before she took a bite from one of the muffins. "Your girls are so charming, Jack. You've done a beautiful job in raising them."

Jack was taken aback at her comment. Most women didn't even want to talk about his children. In fact, they usually avoided the subject.

Grace crossed her legs gracefully, flipping her foot up and down rhythmically as she talked. Jack tried hard not to let his eyes follow the movement. Her bare foot and leg were tantalizing.

"Meredith and Morgan have both been so gracious to me since I moved in. They come and help me with chores nearly every day. And they're lovely to my guests. Actually, I'm so glad you've stopped by. I've wanted to ask you if it would be all right if I pay them a little something for their work here at the inn— or if I buy them a gift. Of course, I could have asked Aunt Bebe. But it seemed more appropriate to ask you. You are their father."

She looked up at him with those silvery blue-green eyes, and Jack found himself speechless—like a love-struck adolescent. Not the norm for him.

Not seeming to notice, she put a couple of muffins onto a small plate and passed them over to him. "These are blueberry. I made them this morning. I didn't have guests today at the inn, but Vincent so looks forward to my muffins."

She lifted a shoulder. "And the girls like to spread them with honey for an afternoon snack."

Jack bit into a muffin and realized they were homemade and still hot. The taste of warm blueberries and sweet muffin filled his mouth. No wonder Vincent Westbrooke wandered by every morning.

Grace pushed her hair back behind her ear with one hand, and Jack found himself wishing he could have done it. She was a true blond, and her hair had a soft, silky quality to it. It fell just below her shoulders, and Jack could tell a professional had cut it to layer softly around her face.

Leaning over to pour more coffee, he caught the floral notes of Grace's scent again. Without thinking, he asked, "What's the name of that cologne you're wearing?"

"It's perfume, not cologne. Called Pleasures. It was always Charles's favorite." Her expression darkened then, and she sighed.

"Was Charles your husband?"

She smiled. "Yes. We were married for almost thirty years. I still have wistful moments now and then, of course—when memories come back." She looked at Jack. "Perhaps you do, too. The girls told me they lost their mother when they were only babies."

Jack scowled. "I have no wistful moments about the girls' mother, Miz Conley." His voice sounded overly harsh, even to him. "She walked out on me when the girls were infants. Left me a Dear John note to find in the morning. She discovered the reality of motherhood and being a wife unappealing."

He looked out into the mimosas, remembering for a minute the pain of that day. The shock and the hurt of rejection.

A hand reached over to wrap itself softly around his. "I'm sorry, Jack. That must have been very hard."

He looked up to find her watching him.

She traced a finger idly over his hand. He doubted she was even aware she did it. "Being hurt like that might make some men angry at women."

Not comfortable with her probing, he grinned roguishly and changed the focus of their discussion. "Well, as you know, Grace Conley, I'm quite fond of women."

She flushed and withdrew her hand carefully from his. "Maybe. And maybe not, Jack Teague."

A quiet silence fell, and Jack could hear the bees humming around the morning glories still in bloom beside the porch.

"Listen. About the girls." He spoke at last. "You don't need to pay them to be helpful. It's good for the character to do things without always expecting a reward."

"You have a point." She smiled. "But would a gift of thanks be all right?"

"Perhaps." Jack considered the idea. "However, I think the fact that you're taking on the girls' Scout troop is gift enough. You didn't have to do that, you know."

"I know. I wanted to. No one twisted my arm, if that's what you're worried about."

Jack ate the last of the little muffins, trying to resist licking his fingers, and drank another sip of his coffee. It felt nice sitting out here on the porch with Grace Conley. He wondered now why he had put off coming over here for so long.

The little tan and white dogs slept quietly under Grace's feet, snoring softly. They hadn't even begged for the muffins Grace had brought out.

"There's another thing I needed to mention to you." Jack turned to look at Grace. "We have a troubled man around the area who likes to spy on people and leave messages about."

"A Peeping Tom?"

"Maybe. We're not really sure. Our sheriff here in Townsend, Swofford Walker, has only documented two potential sightings of the man. And neither were conclusive."

"How long has this been going on?"

"About a year now." Jack stretched out one of his legs on the porch. The movement woke the dogs.

Jack leaned over to pat them before he continued. "What the man usually does is leave odd little signs, like warnings or judgments. His notes say things like: *I saw you. . . .* or *. . . Be careful.* The longest one I remember hearing about said: *Surely your sins will find you out.*"

"What does he write these messages on?"

"Note cards. Tear outs from magazines. Postcards. Even on playing cards."

She sat forward thoughtfully. "Ahhh. I might have gotten one."

"What?" Jack sat up straight to look at Grace directly then. His sharp voice unsettled the dogs, who looked up at him anxiously.

Grace stood up. "Come in the house, and I'll show you. I put it in the drawer in the entry table. I had no idea what it was. I almost threw it away."

The small dogs followed them in and headed for the kitchen.

At the entry table, Grace opened a narrow drawer and pulled out a playing card—much like the one Jack had found on the seat of his Jeep.

She laid the jack of hearts card in Jack's hand. "It says *Watch*

Out on it." She pointed to the words, scrawled across the card in black ink.

Jack took a deep breath. "When did you find this, Grace?"

"I found it right after I first moved in last month. It was in the mailbox, mixed in with the day's mail. I thought it might have been a prank by one of the children in the area." She frowned. "I don't like to remember some of the pranks my own children perpetrated. Especially the boys."

"You'll need to tell the sheriff about this, Grace. Even though it happened several weeks ago. Swofford is trying to keep a record of all the messages. Hoping to find a thread in them that will help him learn who's doing this."

She looked at Jack in some alarm. "Do you think this man is dangerous?"

He took her hand, enjoying having an excuse to touch her. "I don't know. Right now his stunts are mostly bizarre. I wouldn't let it worry you. But I would lock my doors at night. And tell the sheriff if you see or hear anything suspicious."

Grace bit her lip. "Have you or the girls had messages from this man?"

"I have—twice. Usually, like yours, the messages don't make much sense."

"Oh, I think I know the meaning of my message." She pulled her hand free of his and looked directly into his eyes. "At first I thought you sent it to me, Jack—as a little joke—telling me to watch out for you."

Jack felt a rush of anger and frowned at her. "I may have flaws, Grace Conley, but I would never play a prank like that. If I had something to say to you, I'd come over here and say it face-to-face. I wouldn't send crazy messages."

She gave him a steady look as if assessing the truthfulness of his statement. "Is this who the girls are talking about when they speak of Crazy Man?"

He nodded. "It's a tag he's picked up. It seems to best describe the odd things he does. The fact that he may be mentally unstable is what worries everyone around here the most. With a person like that, you never know when his spying and annoying messages might turn into something more dangerous."

"I'll be watchful." Grace tucked the card back into the drawer. "And I'll call the sheriff. Do you know his number?"

"I'll write it down for you." He pulled a business card from his shirt pocket and jotted down the number on the back with a pen he found on Grace's entry table.

Jack glanced at his watch then. "I can't stay until Swofford gets here. I have an appointment."

Grace gave him a teasing smile. "It's good to be on time for your appointments, Jack Teague. All sorts of trouble can happen when you're not."

Jack's heartbeat quickened. She was flirting with him. He plucked up a butterscotch candy from the dish on the entry table, unwrapped it, and placed it slowly in his mouth. Jack watched Grace's lips as he did so.

She licked her lips nervously, and Jack knew she remembered as vividly as he that day they'd met. "Some things are worth the trouble, Grace Conley."

He turned to go. "You take care, now. It was good to see you again."

Jack slipped out the door, kind of pleased he'd had the last word this time. As he tasted the burst of butterscotch from the candy on his tongue, he decided he wouldn't wait so long before he came back to visit the next time, either. This situation with Grace Conley was proving to be more interesting than he'd expected.

CHAPTER 7

Grace had known that eventually she would see Jack Teague again. Like a silly schoolgirl, she had thought about it often enough. Wondered how she would act, how Jack would act. Wondered if there would be any attraction again.

As the weeks went by, her days so busy with the inn, she thought she would think of Jack less. But being with his girls most every day kept him close in mind. She'd seen his dimples flash in the twins' cheeks and recognized the sparkle of his chocolate eyes in theirs. As she grew closer to the girls, it became harder to hold a grudge against their father for the way they had met that first day. But that didn't mean she didn't still remember every detail of it.

Walking across the yard at last, Jack flashed her a smile, and Grace worked hard not to suck in her breath at its physical impact on her. Jack Teague was a devilishly handsome man. He made Grace have girlish feelings and yearnings she hadn't felt for many years. Charlie was the last man who had impacted her like this, still able to give her goose bumps after almost thirty years of marriage. With Charlie gone now, she was hardly eager to start a relationship with a man at this time in her life. Especially a man like Jack Teague. He was a heartbreaker if she ever saw one. Plus Grace didn't want her name linked with local names like Ashleigh Anne Layton, and a few others she had heard about, whom Jack had diddled with. No, she would have to be careful about Jack Teague.

Jack cocked an eyebrow at Grace as he stopped a few feet from her, giving her an easy greeting. He wore tan slacks that fitted his long legs neatly and a deep-brown dress shirt matching the rich brown of his eyes. He looked nice. Too nice. And he walked and moved, as she remembered, with a smooth, swaying gait. Confident. Easy. Sexy.

Grace shook herself for her thoughts while she told him, with a calm voice revealing none of her feelings, that she'd been deadheading the flowers. They chatted, and Grace invited him up on the porch for coffee.

She'd expected that eventually Jack would come to talk about the time his girls were spending with her. She hadn't known Meredith and Morgan were his daughters the first day she met them in May. When she learned their last name later, and that Jack was their father, it had been a surprise. A shock actually. Somehow, she hadn't pictured Jack as a father type. It caught her up. Made her realize she shouldn't completely judge someone from only one meeting.

As she'd spent time with the girls, gotten to know them—and Samantha Butler, married to Jack's cousin Roger—she'd learned many good things about Jack. But she had heard a few snippets around the Townsend area, too, that let her know Jack was a man to be careful with, as well. He did have a reputation as a ladies' man.

"Jack can't help it that he's so charming," Samantha told her one day. "Roger told me ever since they were kids, Jack has attracted too much attention from women." She laughed then. "Roger always calls it unfair how nature gave Jack this irresistible combination of chemicals that draws women to him like bees to honey."

Grace wasn't sure how to respond. "I suppose some men possess a sort of sexual charisma—even men who are not always handsome in a traditional sense."

"Yes, and Jack has the charisma plus the looks. God help him. Sometimes I think it's more a curse than a blessing." Samantha stopped to pick a stitch out of the hem she was mending on one of Daisy's skirts. "You know, Althea said Jack's father, Verlin, had the same charisma with women. And like Jack, he was a fine-looking man. Bebe—that's my husband Roger's mother and Verlin's sister—said Verlin was a lot like Jack when he was younger. But after he fell in love with Althea, Bebe said Verlin Teague never looked at another woman. He was a reformed rake from then on."

Grace thought back on that conversation as she fixed coffee for Jack in the kitchen. When she returned to the porch, the dogs slipped out with her. Grace noticed they didn't bark at Jack. A point in his favor. They were usually very protective of her with strangers.

When Jack and Grace settled down to drink their coffee, Jack began to flirt with her. What else could you call it? He noticed her jewelry, her dimples, and asked about her perfume. It wasn't the normal sort of conversation to share with a man you hardly knew. Vincent Westbrooke came by every morning for coffee, and he'd never asked what kind of perfume she wore.

Grace couldn't help thinking of Charlie as she told Jack the name of her perfume. It was Charles who'd picked the fragrance, Pleasures, for her many years ago, saying it perfectly suited her. He'd also kissed her behind the ear and whispered to her that she would always be his greatest pleasure. Grace sighed. There were still unexpected moments like this, when memories of Charlie washed over her and made her sad.

When Jack asked her about him, Grace answered candidly, admitting she often thought of Charlie at odd moments. She assumed he might think of the girls' mother fondly, too. She was wrong. His bitter words echoed in her mind: *I have no wistful moments about the girls' mother, Miz Conley. She walked out on me when the girls were infants. Left me a Dear John note to find in the morning. She discovered the reality of motherhood and being a wife unappealing*

His voice took on a different tone as he bit out the words, and Grace saw pain etched across his face when he paused and looked out toward the yard.

She hadn't known until that moment that his wife had left him. From what the girls said, she'd assumed their mother had died. Perhaps he'd told them that. She needed to ask Samantha later.

Moved by Jack's obvious hurt, Grace reached out instinctively to wrap a hand over his where it literally clenched the arm of his chair. She realized then she might have gained an understanding as to why Jack seemed to hold so little regard for women.

A memory played back in her mind of how indifferent Jack had seemed to Ashleigh's attentions. She traced a finger idly over Jack's hand as she considered it. Being hurt made some men angry at women, distorted their trust toward them. When she probed the idea, Jack pulled back, letting Grace know she might have hit a nerve.

He artfully changed the subject then, dismissing the idea of any personal problems by reminding her, with a roguish grin, that he was actually quite fond of women, as she should know from experience.

The little devil, she thought—even as she felt a heated flush run up her neck. She had wondered how long it would be before he made mention of their first meeting.

However, despite Jack's denial, Grace still wondered if an anger toward women didn't simmer deep inside Jack due to the way Jack's wife had left him. Charlie had known a man like that once. Grace remembered him; he used women indiscriminately in revenge for being hurt.

They sat silently for a few minutes. Grace could smell the scent of flowers on the air mixed with the good aroma of their coffee and muffins. Despite their past, she felt a few moments of odd contentment sitting here with Jack Teague on her front porch.

Lost in reverie, she almost missed his next comments about the girls and some local Peeping Tom who watched people and left messages and warnings about. A prickle of unease touched her as he described the warnings, and Grace took Jack into the house to show him the card message she'd received, watched the concern on his face.

Jack Teague wasn't, perhaps, as much a bad boy through and

through as she had originally thought. Grace had always been insightful about people. Charles had often said so. He'd frequently asked for her take on people.

Jack was fussing now about her need to call the sheriff, hardly the behavior of a totally selfish and self-absorbed man. He checked his watch, too, worrying that he couldn't stay until the sheriff arrived.

A small memory surfaced, and without thinking she said, "It's good to be on time for your appointments, Jack Teague." Grace sent him a small smile. "All sorts of trouble can happen when you're not."

She'd surprised him by teasing him. She could tell by his expression. Perhaps she shouldn't have done that. He turned to study her thoughtfully, and his assessing look began to make Grace uncomfortable. What was he thinking, she wondered?

Jack leaned an arm casually against the wall and reached into the candy dish on the entry table to take out a butterscotch candy. He took his time unwrapping it and slowly put it in his mouth, watching Grace closely the whole time. Studying Grace's mouth, with a touch of a smile, as he savored the candy.

Wretched man. He was reminding her of that day when she'd been eating a butterscotch candy before he kissed her. She licked her lips nervously in remembrance, and his dark eyes caught and held hers. Grace felt a sensuous shiver slide up her spine.

"Some things are worth the trouble, Grace Conley," he said in a slow voice.

Mercy, she should have resisted the temptation to tease Jack Teague. It was like playing with fire trying to go up against him in the area of flirtation. Whatever had she been thinking? And she a widow, a mother, and—hopefully—a respectable innkeeper.

He turned to leave then, knowing full well he had the upper hand and that he'd flustered and embarrassed her. And then he was gone. Grace could hear him whistling as he walked down the sidewalk. She felt like throwing something after him. He'd certainly had the last word today.

She turned back into the house with a sigh. Well, maybe she wouldn't see much more of Jack after this. He'd avoided her for weeks before coming to have his little talk with her about the girls. Perhaps he'd find himself another young girl to chase now. From what she'd heard, Jack preferred younger women to women nearer his own age as Grace was.

Grace started down the hallway and then stopped at the long mirror on the wall to look at her flushed face. "If you're not careful, Grace Conley, you'll make an old fool of yourself over that playboy. Just because he gives you a zing doesn't mean you have to lose your good sense."

She studied her figure appraisingly in the glass. "You look pretty good for forty-nine, Grace. But you *are* forty-nine. You remember that. Jack Teague is used to having those sweet young things to kiss and hold. A young, tight body like that is long in the past for you. So I wouldn't get any foolish ideas and start acting like a silly widow who doesn't know her limitations."

Grace had been a beauty in her youth, sought after in her own time, much like Jack still was. But it was different for women. With time they just became women-of-a-certain-age, even if still attractive. Grace had come to terms with that many years ago—but suddenly she wished foolishly that Jack could have seen her when she was eighteen or twenty. When she could have met his handsome looks with some of her own.

She wandered into her bedroom and saw Charles's picture on her dresser and felt even worse. Charles had always thought that she was beautiful. And he had always been proud of her— and of any of her small accomplishments.

"I miss you, Charlie." She went over to put a hand on his picture. "Obviously, I could use your stable good sense right now, too. I'm doing fine with the inn. I'm really proud of all I've been able to accomplish, of how easily I seem to fit into this work role. It's perfect for me. And I've found I'm really happy again. I haven't been happy for a long time, Charlie, and the change feels good."

The bedroom furniture in the master bedroom was the set she and Charles had shared in the Nashville house in Belle Meade. Grace had bought a new sky-blue bedspread to coordinate with the color scheme here, had reupholstered two side chairs, and had changed small things—but the furniture was the same. She thought wistfully of Charles as she sat down on the bed.

"This is the first man who's made me experience any strong emotions since you passed away, Charlie. I feel silly having these emotions at my age. And I feel guilty toward your memory when I do, too. It doesn't seem right."

She kicked off her sandals and lay back on the bed. "I know we always said that, if anything happened to one of us, we'd want the other to move on. To love again, if possible. To continue to have joy."

Grace picked up a cushion on the bed to hug it against her. "I just wish my body and heart had more sense than to wake up emotionally to a man like Jack Teague."

She reached over to put a hand on her Bible on the bedside table and offered up a small prayer. "Lord, you know I've always tried to be a good and righteous woman. You really need to help me here when I'm being tempted by someone like Jack. He may be single, a father, and a respected man in his profession. But he has a dangerous reputation. I don't want to lose what I've been building here by being foolish. So I ask You to help me. Give me a strong dose of wisdom, good sense, and prudence in being around Jack. I admit I am attracted to him. But I know it's not a wise attraction."

Grace found her thoughts moving oddly to her mother then. And to her sister Myra. Wishing she had one of them to talk to. She'd gone over to see the family when she got back. Shared her decision to buy the bed-and-breakfast. Told them she hoped to see them all more now. But there had been a bit of reserve.

I've been gone a long time, Grace realized. And they have all been here together, moving on and growing closer through the years. I'm the only one who left. And, admittedly, I haven't come back as often as I should have.

Her parents still lived in the same Cape Cod, stone house in rural South Knoxville. Grace felt a rush of sweet childhood memories every time she visited there. Her father and mother, Mel and Dottie Richey, still worked every day in their business, Richey's Formal Wear, out on Chapman Highway. Grace had grown up in and out of the shop. She, her older sister Myra, and her younger brother Leonard, had played hide-and-seek in and out of and underneath the wedding gowns, bridesmaids' dresses, and tuxedos in the shop. Grace had learned to sew there with Mrs. Petree, who did all the alterations. Grace supposed she'd developed her love of fashion in the store.

But she'd gone away to college in Nashville at Vanderbilt on scholarship, while Myra had stayed home to commute to the University of Tennessee in Knoxville and marry her high school sweetheart, Philip Kline. Actually, Myra had married Philip before Grace even left home, being four years older than Grace. And Leonard had just turned twelve when Grace went away to college. Now, Leonard was married, too, and he and Myra both worked in the business. Only Grace had left.

"I want to get close to my family again, Lord. Over the years, Charles and I were so busy with our own lives in Nashville. I know I didn't get home often enough. And Charles's mother Jane never had any real use for my family. That made it hard whenever they came to Nashville to visit. She always came over and acted rude to them."

Grace paused and sighed. "Plus there was so much difference in the way we lived." Grace had married into a wealthy, prominent Nashville family. Her own family, although wonderful, good people, lived more simply, and they all worked hard. After Grace had married, she'd stopped working and stayed home, and that had made her even more different from her mother and Myra. She knew they hadn't always respected her lifestyle and how she lived. It rankled sometimes.

Grace had friends in Nashville who were close to their sisters, and she had always envied that, wishing she and Myra were closer. However, Grace had known, even by late middle school, that Myra didn't like her much. She'd never understood why. She thought that would change when they became adults, when the age difference between them wasn't so significant. But it had never happened.

She looked over toward Charlie's picture again. "There's still that reserve between Myra and me, Charlie. When I was over at the house with everyone, I still sensed it. You always said I was discerning, but I've never been able to discern why Myra doesn't like me. I'd like to figure that out."

Grace sat up with resolve then and tossed the pillow back onto the bed. "Enough negative thinking and moodiness. I have a wonderful new business, new friends, and new interests. And I *am* going to find a way to form a bond with my family again. I also *am* going to get sensible about Jack Teague and stop acting like a teenager over him every time he comes around. And I *am* going to breach this big rift with my own children in Nashville about this move I've made, in due time. Show them that I'm successful and happy and that I did the right thing."

With that, Grace set off to the kitchen to start planning dinner. She had guests coming in tonight. And she had work to do.

CHAPTER 8

Jack made sure that word got around Townsend that he'd been by to see Grace Conley. He started walking back and forth to work again many days, purposely walking across the swinging bridge and cutting across the backyard of the Mimosa Inn. Taking the well-worn path that led through Grace's property to Creekside Lane. He went back to church on Sunday and sat with his girls and his mother in their regular pew. As Roger had suggested, it was important to put to rest any negative rumors that he had personal problems he couldn't resolve with the widow Conley.

However, the fact that Jack thought about Grace Conley more than he should was his own business. And his own dilemma to wrestle with. Grace had turned out to be a bigger problem than Jack had expected. She stayed on his mind and in his thoughts. He watched for sights of her walking out in the yard of the Mimosa or down along the River Road. She took long walks most every day. Jack had started noticing things like that, fought himself not to go and walk along with her. She took strolls down the River Road, took the loop trail over the two swinging bridges that spanned the Little River, and ambled across the highway and up to Tiger Drive to get library books and to attend the Townsend book group that met there. She biked, too. Often with his girls—down the River Road or out to the highway to get ice cream. He was envious when his girls talked about it. Jack liked to hear their impressions of Grace, but he often thought too much about their stories later on.

"Guess what we're doing today?" Morgan told him at the breakfast table one morning.

"What?" Jack smiled at her while he salted his eggs.

"Ms. Grace is taking us into town to get Scout uniforms. We ordered them, and they've come in at J.C. Penney's." She poured a glass of orange juice from a pitcher on the table. "Aunt Bebe said it was all right for us to go with Ms. Grace today, but that we needed to ask you for some money. We're getting our Scout books, too."

Bebe, or Beatrice Butler—Jack's aunt and Roger's mother—came into the room carrying a plate of hot pancakes then. "Grace Conley offered to take the girls with her when she went into town today. I thought it would be all right."

Jack nodded.

Meredith smiled at Jack. "We're going to have our very first Junior Scout meeting next week, Daddy, and we're going to start working on our first badges soon."

Morgan forked two hot pancakes onto her plate. "Ms. Grace says we all have to do our bridging activities first. That's how you move from Brownies to Scouts. Then we'll have an official ceremony and be real Scouts and everything."

"That sounds good." Jack helped himself to several pancakes and slathered them with syrup. "Did Ms. Grace tell you how much money you'll need?"

Aunt Bebe answered that. "I have the order information and the total. We ordered everything a week or so ago from a catalog Grace had. It isn't much, Jack. The girls are going to wear their own white shirts and khaki shorts—or slacks when it's cooler—with their Girl Scout vests. And the badge and Scout books were very inexpensive."

Jack nodded, working on his breakfast while it was still hot. It was a pleasure to enjoy Bebe's cooking in the mornings. During the school year, Jack fixed breakfast for himself and the girls and then dropped them off at the nearby elementary school on his way to the realty office. After school they rode the bus to stay at Aunt Bebe's house until he could pick them up. But in the summers when school was out, Bebe came over early in the morning to stay with the girls most days. Other days Jack dropped them at her house.

"Great breakfast, Aunt Bebe," Jack said. He truly meant it. "It reminds me of the big breakfasts you used to fix for Roger and me when we were kids out of school for our summer vacations."

Bebe grinned. "Those were good days. You two boys sure could eat."

The girls chattered on to Bebe, talking about the Scout troop and the things they already were planning to do. Jack tuned out, thinking back to his own younger years.

When he was five, Bebe had come back home to Townsend— widowed by a war tragedy. She'd moved back into the old Teague farmhouse with Jack's grandfather, Duncan Teague. Bebe's older brother, Verlin, had been married and working with his father in the family realty business by then. Grandfather Duncan was a recent widower, and he had been glad to have his girl come back home to cook and clean house for him. Plus he loved her four-year-old boy Roger, just as Duncan was crazy about Jack.

Jack and Roger bonded immediately, and since Jack's mother, Althea, worked in the realty business with Duncan and Verlin, Bebe took on Jack's care—along with taking care of Roger. Jack had known a series of sitters before that, and Bebe brought him a new stability and sense of family. Roger became like a brother to Jack, and Aunt Bebe became a second mother figure.

Nine years ago, when Celine had walked out on Jack and left him with two babies still in diapers, Bebe had stepped in to mother his girls. Jack would be eternally grateful to her for that. With Bebe's and Althea's care and love, the girls had suffered less from being deserted than they might have if Jack had been on his own.

Jack got up to get another cup of coffee, and gave Bebe a hug

and a kiss on the cheek. She was white-headed now, wore bifo-
cal glasses, and was more full-figured—but she was still beautiful to Jack. "You're an amazing woman, Bebe. I hope I
remember to thank you often enough for all you do. And for all
you've always done for me and the girls."

"Pooh. Now what brought on this sentimental moment,
Jack?" She hugged him back fondly. "You know you're just my
other boy—and that these are my precious grandchildren as
much as Daisy and Ruby are."

Daisy and Ruby were his cousin Roger's children. When
Roger and Samantha had started their family, Samantha had
given up her teaching job for a few years to stay home with the
girls. Two years ago, when her old job had opened back up at
Townsend Elementary, Samantha had gone back to teach
kindergarten. Bebe kept four-year-old Ruby during the school
year, and kept ten-year-old Daisy along with Meredith and
Morgan after school.

Bebe patted Jack's shoulder now as she came to sit down at
the table. "You know, I've often thought how good God has
been to me—giving me a family of boys to raise when I was
young and then a sweet family of little girls to raise when I grew
older."

Jack grinned at her. "Are you saying Roger and I weren't
sweet?"

"There were moments when you two boys *were* sweet." She
laughed. "Like when you were both asleep."

The girls giggled over that.

"Were Roger and Daddy bad?" Meredith asked, cocking her
head to one side.

"Sometimes," Bebe answered. "Between the two of them
they kept my days lively and full, I can tell you that."

Morgan's eyes brightened. "Tell us a story about Daddy and
Uncle Roger when they were bad, Aunt Bebe."

Bebe smiled at her indulgently. "Well, let's see . . . I remember
one time those boys nearly scared two lives out of me getting
themselves lost in Tuckaleechee Caverns."

Jack saw Morgan's and Meredith's eyes grow wide with fascination, and he chuckled. He remembered this story well, too. "You want to tell it, Jack?"

He nodded. "Back in the sixties when Roger and I were growing up, the cave didn't get as many visitors as it does today. Sometimes the owners got a little lax back then about policing the entrance real well. Roger and I found an opportunity to slip into the cave unobserved and then followed along with a tour group. We had us a fine time learning all about the history of the cave, how the Cherokees discovered it long ago, and how the giant stalagmites and stalactites formed. When the group got ready to leave, we lagged behind, not wanting the man at the entrance gate to catch too close a look at us."

Jack paused and took a drink of his coffee. "The problem was, the owners were getting ready to shut down the cave for the day. We didn't know that. While we dawdled around, the owners, the Vanadas, locked up and then turned off the lights. And there Roger and I were, locked into a pitch-dark cave."

Morgan gasped. "Were you scared?"

"Scared to death." Jack grinned and shook his head. "You haven't seen dark until you experience dark in an underground cave."

"Like when they turn off the lights now during the tour of Tuckaleechee," Meredith said. "I was really scared then, even when you held my hand."

"The lucky thing for us was that Roger had one of those little penlight flashlights in his pocket. By using that we finally found our way back up toward the entrance. But when we got there, everything was locked up tight. We hollered and hollered, but nobody came to let us out."

"What did you do?" Morgan asked, leaning forward and biting her lip.

"Sat down against the door and waited. We didn't know what else to do."

Bebe shook her head in remembrance. "In the meantime,

Althea, Verlin, and I were searching all over the place trying to find Roger and Jack. We knew they'd gone across the highway, up the Tuckaleechee Road, and down Old Cades Cove Road to their friend Danny Miller's place. The boys shouldn't have gone that far, of course, but we learned they'd both been seen there when we started searching. Danny's dog had just delivered new pups, and we found out the boys had sneaked over there on their bikes to see them."

She gave Jack an admonishing look. "Jack told me they were going down to the store on the highway to get colas and penny candy."

Jack laughed. "We did do that, Aunt Bebe. We simply extended our trip a little."

She tut-tutted. "It was the bikes that saved those poor boys from spending a long, dark night in the cave. Some of the men on the search team found the bikes propped against the fence near the parking lot at the caves."

Bebe shook her head. "Land-a-mercy, I remember Bill Vanada and Harry Myers were sure mad when we roused them out of a good sleep to come open up their cave to see if you two boys were in there."

"They weren't as mad as my daddy was." Jack wrinkled his nose in remembrance. "I don't think Roger or I sat down without wincing for two days after that."

Meredith blinked, her mouth forming a big O. "Did you get a spanking?"

"We did, and we deserved it. What we did was wrong and dangerous." Fathering had taught Jack to put the right endings on his stories.

"Wow, that's a cool story." Morgan grinned. "I'm going to tell it to Ms. Grace today. I wonder if she's ever been to Tuckaleechee Caverns."

Jack smiled. "Well, maybe your Girl Scout group can work on a rock or geology badge and go there as a troop. You could get a group rate for everyone. It would be fun."

"That's a swell idea, Daddy." Morgan's eyes lit up.

"We visited the cave so long ago I've forgotten almost every-thing now," Meredith put in. "I'd like to go again. Maybe you could come, too, Daddy?"

Meredith was sweet like that, always thinking of others.

"I'd like that, peanut." He tweaked her cheek.

Bebe eyed the clock in the kitchen. "You'd better get on to the realty office, Jack. You said you had a nine thirty appoint-ment."

"So I do," he said, getting up to leave and buzzing both the girls and Aunt Bebe on the cheek before he left.

Jack felt happy and blessed to have his girls in his life, and he thought about them often through his day. He also thought about Grace Conley. It was good of her to take his girls to get their Scout uniforms. Maybe he should get her a little gift for being so nice to Meredith and Morgan. It would give him a chance to stop by to see her again to present it to her. He'd like that. He wanted to see if she still stirred him up. Jack found women attractive, but he also found that he tired of most of them quickly. The electricity kicked in for a while, and then the initial attraction faded. He'd be glad when his attraction to Grace faded. It was disruptive. Kept him antsy and unfocused. Distracted. Even irritable. He wasn't used to that.

It was Friday night now. Since Meredith and Morgan were spending the night at Stacy Clark's for a birthday sleepover, Jack had a free night to go out. There was a party over at Rookie Beezer's place. A group of the singles from around the area was going to be there. Jack dropped by about eight and hung around for an hour or so. He laughed, had a few beers, flirted with some girls, danced, and listened to jokes and stories. And was bored. Utterly. As the evening wore on, the group got rowdier and louder. Couples broke off and found quiet, dark places to neck. With many of the guys drinking too much, the noise level rose. The stories and jokes got raunchier, too. Feeling restless, Jack slipped out onto the deck behind Rookie's place. He leaned his arms on the deck rail and looked off down the mountain, savoring the quiet. After a few moments, Wyleen Deadrick let herself out the screen door to join him.

"You seem a little blue tonight, Jack." She came up to stand beside him and put a friendly arm around his waist.

Wyleen knew Jack well enough for that, but he made no response in return.

"What's wrong, Jack? You haven't seemed like yourself tonight." Her fingers began to comfortably find their way around his back and under the belt of his pants. She looked up at him with suggestive gray eyes. Pretty eyes. Wyleen was still a fine-looking woman, even after having been married twice now.

"I heard you took your name back again after your divorce from Grady."

"Yeah." A faint smile played over her lips. "I didn't like the name Millhouse much. And Grady's mother was real glad to see me go back to being Wyleen Deadrick. She wasn't very fond of me, you know."

Considering that Wyleen had cheated on Grady the whole three years they'd been married, Jack could hardly blame Grady's mother. And Jack liked Grady Millhouse.

He edged away subtly from Wyleen and looked at his watch. "I gotta go get my girls, Wyleen." Jack didn't usually lie, but he suddenly wanted to leave Rookie Beezer's place and this whole scene.

Wyleen put her hands on Jack's chest and leaned up to kiss him. She tasted like beer and cigarettes, and Jack felt suddenly revolted.

Kindly, he backed off and patted Wyleen's cheek. "You be good now, you hear?" It was a standard line of Jack's, and it brought the low chuckle he expected.

"You should know that I'm always good, Jack." She raised her eyebrows and gave him a suggestive look. "And you know where I live if you want to come by one night. We could make a few more good memories."

Jack knew he could drop by tonight, but he had no desire to. He and Wyleen had a little past together, but there was nothing more to it than that. And tonight, he felt no attraction to her at all. Jack shrugged. Actually, there was no one here he felt any attraction to. He didn't even know why he wasn't having a good time. It was Friday. He was free and single; he should be having a great time. He had a lot of longtime friends here at Rookie's. But the truth was he felt discontented with them tonight. He even felt discontented with himself.

He drove home, let himself in the house, and then wished his girls were there for company. The house seemed entirely too quiet, and Jack's discontent increased. Maybe he was having some kind of midlife crisis or something. He'd read some articles about that somewhere, sitting in the dentist's office or at the barber shop. He couldn't remember now where he'd read about it. He wished he could.

Not liking the fuzzy feeling in his head from the beers he'd drunk at Rookie's, Jack made a pot of coffee. It would probably keep him up late. But, heck, it didn't seem like he was likely to fall into a good sleep right away anyway, the way this night was going.

Jack took his cup of coffee outside on the screened porch. Feeling restless there, too, he walked down the path that wound down the hillside from his house until he came to the rock patio that looked down on the river. He slipped into one of the old metal chairs there and propped his feet up on the rock wall.

It was a nice night. A full moon and the light from it played down on the Little River that flowed through Townsend. He had a nice view here—high on the hillside where he'd built his house a few years after Celine had left him. As soon as he could, he'd sold the cabin they'd lived in up on Rich Mountain, and he'd moved back home near his family by the river. Roger had designed his house here—a weathered, gray-gabled home tucked high above the river in the woods. It was a private place; you had to be looking for it to find it. Jack had been happy here raising his girls—except for those occasional times when he'd heard from Celine and when she wanted money.

She'd given up her custody rights to the girls after she left and they divorced. But she had contacted Jack for a handout every now and then in the early years. Now that she was a star and famous in the soaps, he didn't hear from her anymore. He hoped he never did again. Jack knew now that she'd only married him because she'd found herself pregnant.

"Did you ever love me?" he had asked Celine once.

She'd shrugged carelessly. "You were the area playboy when we met, Jack. I didn't think that sort of thing concerned you. We were good for a while in the way it mattered. You know. Then I found out I was pregnant. I thought for a bit marriage and a family might be fun."

Celine had studied her nails before looking up at Jack candidly. "I was wrong. I wasn't cut out for the marriage and family thing." Celine had paced around the room restlessly then. "This is not where I belong, Jack. I need to get back to Hollywood. I have my looks again now after the babies. This is my time. If I wait much longer, I'll miss my chance."

He shouldn't have been surprised to find her gone not many weeks later. The foolish thing was that Jack had fallen in love with her. She was a good actress, all right. And she'd taken him in. She had been a stunning redhead with cat-green eyes. The fact that she was in Townsend doing a movie had fascinated Jack. He'd never met anyone like Celine Rosen before. Admittedly, he'd felt smug back then to squire her around, even smugger to have her fall for him. She seemed a lot like him—reckless, free, and uninhibited. But he had been wrong about her being right for him. She was selfish and only able to love herself.

Across the river, Jack saw the back porch lights switch on at the Mimosa Inn and watched Grace come out into the light of the porch. She let herself out the back door and started down toward the river. The dogs ran with pleasure around the yard.

Jack smiled. "So, you're restless tonight, too, Grace Conley."

He watched her stroll down to the river and stop to look up toward the hill where his house stood. She couldn't see him sitting on the rock patio behind the wall. But he could see her.

Jack felt a tightening in his gut. "Are you thinking about me, Grace? Looking up here toward my home? I'd like to know."

He realized suddenly that Grace was the reason he hadn't had a good time at Rookie's party tonight. She had gotten to him. He hoped he got over it soon. For Grace wouldn't be like Wyleen Deadrick and invite him over for a night to enjoy a good time. She was a different kind of woman. And Jack had no business being attracted to her.

Grace walked out onto the swinging bridge, and Jack's heartbeat quickened. He didn't know how he'd handle it if she came climbing up the hill to him. Probably not well. His thoughts were not gentlemanly ones tonight.

Sensual passion slid up Jack's spine as he watched Grace stand on the swinging bridge looking down the river. He wanted her—that was for sure.

"You better go home, Miz Grace Conley," he said. "The big bad wolf's out tonight. It would be dangerous for you if you ran into him right now."

The corgis whined at the entrance to the bridge, obviously afraid to walk out on it. Jack heard Grace's laugh float up to him as she shook her head in amusement at them. Her laugh tickled through Jack's senses, pumping his blood.

Grace turned then and walked slowly back across the bridge, her hips swaying softly in the loose fabric pants she wore. Jack gripped the arms of his chair to keep from calling out to her.

"You're driving me crazy, Grace Conley." His words were soft and raspy. "I sometimes think it would have been better if you hadn't bought the Oakley back in May. If you'd stayed angry at me and just gone back to Nashville. We wouldn't be in this fix if you had. And I'll be danged if I know what we're going to do about it."

Jack's eyes followed Grace as she walked through the yard and let herself back in the Mimosa Inn. Then he sat quietly and watched as the lights winked out on the porch and eventually in the rest of the house. It was a long time before he made his way back up from the rock patio to his own house. He had spent a lot of time thinking. But he couldn't say he'd found any good answers.

Well, time would sort things out. He told himself this as he locked up the doors before starting back to his bedroom to call it a night. When he settled into the big king-size bed in his room, sleep was slow to find him. He fleetingly thought of getting up and going to Wyleen's, but he knew that wasn't the answer right now.

Instead, he found a good mystery in the cabinet by his bed and proceeded to read himself to sleep.

CHAPTER 9

The early weeks of summer slipped quickly by. Grace was surprisingly busy at the Mimosa. The reopening invitations she'd sent out in May to Mavis Oakley's old customer list had brought many repeat clients back to the inn. In addition, a few choice magazine ads, word-of-mouth, and drive-by traffic through Townsend had brought in even more. A steady stream of guests came to the inn each week now, and Grace's balance sheets were looking very impressive.

Here on Tuesday, on a weekday, when Grace had no guests, she'd finally gotten back to work on the woodcraft shop Carl Oakley had left behind. The shop, about the length of a double garage, had two parts. The back held a workshop, and the front a sales area with built-in display shelves, counters, and tables. Between the workshop and sales area the wall was partially open so anyone in the back—working on a project—could see anyone who came into the front door of the shop. Likewise, customers could look through to watch the crafter at work while they browsed.

Of course, it had taken days for Grace to clean out the place—and to discover that there were a half-bath and a storage room in the far back of the shop. Now, most of the boxes of supplies sat piled in the shop's storage room or, temporarily, in the next-door garage. Grace had repainted inside and out. Since the front of the shop had a small porch across it and two windows, Grace had added green shutters to the windows and painted the old wood furniture pieces on the porch to match—so the shop would coordinate with the inn.

She was hanging a pair of begonia plants from the porch rafters when she saw her mother, Dottie Richey, come up the driveway.

"Hi, Grace," her mother called. "I went to the front door of the inn and saw your note saying you were here in the shop."

Grace stepped down from the porch to give her mother a hug. "What a surprise, Mother. I'm so pleased to see you."

"Well, I've owed you a visit. And it's hard to get away from the business." She smiled at Grace. "You know how that is now that you're running the bed-and-breakfast, don't you?"

"I do." Grace blew back the stray hairs from her face. "And I'm afraid you caught me in a mess." She looked down at herself, attired in old work clothes sprinkled with paint and dust. "A mess in more ways than one."

Grace's mother walked up the steps to peek into the door of the shop. "Is this a storage building?"

"No. The former owner, Carl Oakley, was a woodworker. He had a shop here." Grace pointed toward the back. "He worked in the back of the store and out here in the front he sold the walking sticks, birdhouses, picture frames, and other woodcrafts he made. After he died, his wife just left everything here the way it was."

Grace's mother walked inside to check out the interior of the store, while Grace gave her this short explanation. Dottie turned around to look at Grace. "It looks nice since you've painted it. What are you going to do here, Gracie?"

Grace's heart warmed at the old childhood nickname. "I thought I might have a little craft shop here—open it at whatever hours I could manage around my business at the inn." She dropped her eyes. "Probably not much will come of it. But it might be fun."

"Stop selling yourself short." Her mother's eyes flashed. "You're very gifted, and I've long wondered why you haven't done more with your abilities."

Grace could feel her brows lift in surprise.

"Not used to compliments, are you?" Dottie's voice was touched with sarcasm. "I'm not surprised."

She smiled at Grace then. "Let's go sit down on that nice little porch out front. I've been over in Maryville seeing about an upcoming wedding we're doing all the formal wear for, and it would be good to get off my feet."

"Oh, sure," said Grace. "Do you want a cola? I have some in a cooler in the back."

Her mother nodded.

Grace got two cans of diet soda and brought them back out on the porch. She found her mother in one of the newly painted rockers.

"This is such a nice place, Grace." She took the cola Grace offered and took a long drink. "I'm proud of you for starting a new life for yourself, for getting busy and using your talents."

Smiling, Grace took a sip of her soda, too. She studied her mother then. Dottie was silver-haired now. Her dark hair had turned white early, as had Myra's. Myra looked very much like Dottie; both had the same short hair and hazel eyes, and both were shorter and more full-busted than Grace. Their father, Mel, was white-haired, too, and it looked like Leonard would follow suit in time. All the Richeys had been dark-haired except for Grace.

Grace noticed her mother was watching her, too. "You look more and more like your Grandmother Martha Steen as time goes by—a true, tall, blond Norwegian. I'm going to bring you my portrait of her to hang in your inn. The resemblance is striking."

"I always looked different than everyone else in the family." Grace dropped her eyes again. "And *was* different, too. All of you stayed in the formal wear business, stayed right in South Knoxville. Stayed close."

Grace's mother reached across to pat Grace's hand. "We each have to be who we are, Gracie. And celebrate that—different or not. You're still our family, even if you walked to a different beat."

"Did I always? Walk to a different beat?"

Her mother laughed. "How can you ask that? Surely you can

remember what a wonderful and unique girl you were. Always busy. Always organizing and creating. Full of ideas and plans. Bright and always so beautiful. That was a gift, too."

"I'm not so beautiful now." Grace blew out a long sigh.

"Nonsense. You are stunning. Haven't you looked in the mirror lately? And you still have that beautiful ease and charm about you when you move. Almost sensual. Your father had to beat the boys off with a stick from the time you were young. But you always kept your head there. You knew what you wanted from a young age."

"Did I?" Grace looked at her mother in surprise.

Dottie shook her head. "Gracious, child. Just because you married young and then had your family quickly, surely you haven't forgotten your early dreams."

"I remember I modeled while in school. I loved that. And I was majoring in design."

"You were gifted in design. You just couldn't decide then if you wanted to design houses or clothes. I remember you told your grandmother, rather saucily one day, that you were going to design and run something special one day." Grace's mother looked around. "It looks like you've done it, Gracie. If not sooner, then later."

"Well, I can't claim credit for designing the Mimosa, Mother. And my children are certainly not happy about my being here. Neither is Jane."

"Aggravating woman, Jane Conley. She never had a good thing to say about you, either. It used to make me so mad I wanted to spit nails." She reached over to pat Grace's hand again. "And your children will come around. You give them time."

"I hope so." Grace frowned.

"You told me all about their reactions when you visited over at the house. I just think they are finding it hard to envision you as anything but their mother. That's all you were for so very long, you know."

"Was that wrong?" Grace looked at her mother questioningly. "I did so love being home and raising all of them, being there for Charlie, helping him with the business by entertaining clients and friends. It wasn't like I was ever idle. There were so many civic responsibilities. So much to do and so many expectations."

"Ahhh." Her mother caught her eyes. "Much of what you did was from your heart, Grace. But much of it was because of the expectations of others, as well. You married into wealth, and there were expectations about what Charles Conley's wife should be like. You worked hard to fulfill those expectations. And you did a good job of it."

"But?"

Dottie smiled kindly, patting Grace's hand again. "But you lost a little of yourself along the way. You were so busy being what you should be that you forgot a little of who you really were and what you might be in yourself."

Grace frowned, feeling a little piqued at the criticism. "Charles was happy with me, Mother. If he hadn't died, things would have been okay."

Her mother was silent.

Grace's mother's silences had always spoken more than words.

"You've been disappointed in me, haven't you?"

"Sometimes. I have to be honest." She gave Grace a candid glance.

"In what ways?" Grace really wanted to know.

"In how you let Jane push you around. In how you let Charles dictate to you. In how overly eager you always were to please Charles, Jane, and so many others." Dottie paused and frowned slightly. "Also in the way you were so busy living up to an image that you forgot to please yourself. I thought you lost yourself somewhat over the years."

"Ouch." Grace winced.

Dottie Richey caught her daughter's eyes. "I would never have said this, Gracie, if I hadn't seen you take life in your hands again. If I hadn't watched you snatch back your life against opposition and begin to live your own dreams. It hasn't been easy for you, and I wanted you to know that your father and I applaud you. And we were all thrilled to see what you're creating here when we came to your open house last month. We're truly proud of you, Gracie."

Grace looked at her mother in surprise. "I think that's the first time I've heard you say that in a long time."

Her mother snorted. "I'd say it's the first time you've heard anybody say it in a long time."

"That's not really fair, Mother." The criticisms were prickling. "Charlie loved me and was always proud of me. He said so often."

"He was proud when you were the lovely hostess, the beautiful wife, the devoted mother, the gracious Mrs. Conley." She gave Grace a direct look. "But how often was he proud of you when you branched out doing something on your own—like going back to college, taking those crafts classes, winning those arts and crafts awards, or making your own dress that time for Michael's wedding? If I remember, Charles made you go out and buy an expensive one instead from a Nashville boutique. One that wasn't handmade. Like it would have been an insult—wearing a dress you had made yourself."

Grace looked down at her hands.

Her mother's voice softened. "You mustn't misunderstand, Grace. The difference was that I celebrated all those things. You do beautiful work. I have your lovely craft items all over my house. I cherish them. You made this purse for me, remember?" She held up a richly embroidered purse.

"You still have that?" Grace marveled. "I made that five years ago."

"It's my favorite purse." Dottie smiled. "I hope the fact that you're cleaning out this woodwork shop means you'll definitely open a little shop of your own here where you can sell your own beautiful things, too."

"I'd thought of it," Grace admitted. "But I'm usually so discouraged about my crafting work that I was afraid to admit the idea to anyone."

"Well, it's a wonderful idea." Dottie's eyes lit up. "Come show me what you have in mind."

And so it was that Grace spent the next hour getting to know her mother in a new way as they talked about the craft shop Grace planned to create.

As Grace tucked her mother in the car several hours later, after they had also toured the house thoroughly again, Grace couldn't resist asking her mother one final question that was in her heart. "Mother, why doesn't Myra like me?"

"And what makes you ask that, Gracie?"

Grace twisted her hands. "Well, I know we haven't been close. And it isn't hard to see that there's something there between us. Some rift or divide."

Dottie looked up at Grace. "First, Myra is four years older than you are, Grace. I had my three children rather spread out. Sisters that far apart in age are not often close like sisters who are only a year or two apart."

"It's more than that, Mother, and you know it." Grace sent her mother a pointed look.

Getting back out of the car to lean on the hood, Dottie asked, "Why do you think there is a divide, as you put it, between you and Myra, Gracie? I guess we need to talk about this."

Grace hesitated. "I really don't know. But I first felt it back in late middle school."

"Well, let's look back to that time." Dottie's voice was matter-of-fact. "Myra was seventeen, tall, thin, awkward, and wearing braces. She was introverted and shy with anyone she didn't know well. She often wished for more friends and wished for a boy to notice her. You were only thirteen then—but already blond, beautiful, extroverted, and talented. You had a score of girlfriends and already had boys mooning around the house over you and calling you on the phone. You got invited to the eighth-grade dance that year; Myra didn't even get invited to the junior prom."

Dottie shifted so that she could look more directly at Grace. "Honey, it was hard for Myra to see life come so easily to you when it was so difficult, and often painful, for her. Myra stayed and worked in the store because she was comfortable there. She felt safe and loved there; she could be herself there. She was fearful to branch out too far. Unlike you—who made plans to go before any of us were ready to consider it."

"I never realized. . . ."

Grace's mother nodded. "No. You never realized. That's one of the reasons there is a divide, as you put it. You never even saw Myra in any realistic sense as a person and not simply a big sister. Then after you married, you never saw Myra's limitations and how you might have become a friend to her."

"Now, wait a minute, Mother." Grace's temper flared. "That's not fair. I never did anything to hurt Myra."

"No. And you never did anything to reach out to Myra, either."

"But she was the oldest. She should have reached out to me." Grace felt confused by what her mother was telling her.

"Did you not hear what I just said about how you were different?" Dottie shook her head. "You were the one who had the social skills to reach out, Grace. And think about all the times you came over for a visit after you married—and told us all about your family's week at the beach house, your cruise in the Bahamas, your latest trip to Europe. Did you ever consider that, if you'd really wanted to be close to Myra, that you might have invited her and Phillip to go on one of these trips with you just one time—and paid their way? You and Charles could easily have afforded to take them. Friendships are built with sharing and generosity, Grace."

Dottie paused, looking out toward the mimosas in the front yard. "In case you haven't noticed, Grace, life has not been easy for Myra. Phillip has his little insurance business, but he never made much money with it. Myra has always worked with us, has always needed to work, but our business is only small and comfortable. You married very well, Grace—to coin an old phrase. And yet you never shared."

Grace stood speechless for a moment. "I never even thought. . . ."

"Perhaps that's the divide." Her mother interrupted her protest. "That you never thought."

"I didn't mean to be inconsiderate, Mother. But getting the two families together wasn't easy. And there were problems." Grace shook her head, trying to look back at why she had done things the way she had. "Jane was always so hostile and unpleasant about my family. Charles sort of drifted along with her, I guess. I don't think he would have wanted my family to go along on trips."

"Yes, and, if I remember correctly, Jane went on most all of your family vacations with you. Her husband, Hixon, did, too, before he died. The Conleys were always first with you after you married, Grace. We all felt it, but Myra resented it. Sometimes she expressed anger about it for your father's and my sake. She's very protective of us."

Grace leaned against the car, feeling stunned. "Mother, I'm so sorry. I never realized. I never even thought that you would want to go on a vacation with us. Especially with Jane along." She frowned.

Dottie laughed. "Well, I wouldn't have wanted to go on even a long day trip with Jane Conley, and that's a fact. But your father and I wouldn't have minded more time with you. You, Charles, and the children didn't visit often."

"Well, you had such a small place, and there were six of us."

Dottie shook her head. "We could have made do. It's you and Charlie who wouldn't have found things up to your standards. That's the rub, Grace. We all always knew why you visited so seldom. You came to view us as a notch below you on the social ladder. We accepted it—to a degree—but as I said, Myra resented it."

"That's not true!" Grace felt her face flush. "We never thought we were better than others because we had a lot financially."

"Is that so? Yet, you only socialized and vacationed with your own kind." Dottie said the words kindly, but there was a wistful look in her eyes as she said them.

Grace was quiet for a minute. "This is a lot to think about, Mother."

"I know," Dottie said, getting into the car again after giving

Grace a kiss on the cheek. "If I hadn't seen, for the first time recently, that you wanted to be close to your family again, I wouldn't have said anything at all. But I could see your heart wanting to come home again, Grace. And I felt that only honesty would help you see why there's been a division for so long."

"I'm really sorry, Mother." Grace knew her face showed her anguish. She felt simply stunned with all these revelations from her mother.

"Today is always a new day, Gracie." Dottie smiled. "And home is always a place you can come back to—and be welcomed into with love and open arms. But friendship takes a little more time and work. Myra loves you, Grace. And I think you could have her friendship if you wanted it. She's a very good person and has wonderful attributes. And interests and gifts of her own that you know little about."

"Like what?" Grace asked.

Dottie laughed and started the car. "I think I'll leave that for you to find out on your own, Grace—since you don't seem to know."

Grace stood looking down the driveway after her mother for a long time, thinking. She had wanted answers about her family, but these certainly weren't the answers she had been expecting.

"How come you're just standing in the driveway, Ms. Grace?" Grace heard Morgan's voice behind her.

She turned around to see the twins then, dressed today in blue jean shorts and halter tops.

"Are you okay, Ms. Grace?" Meredith looked concerned. "You look sad. And you're too nice to be sad."

Grace ruffled Meredith's hair. "I may not be as nice as you think, Miss Meredith."

Seeing the door of the woodworking shop open, Morgan turned in that direction. "Have you been working in the shop again, Ms. Grace? Do you need us to help you some more?"

Grace smiled. "I think that would be great, Morgan. You and Meredith were good to help me paint. Maybe you'd like to help me start moving boxes back into the shop from the garage now."

Morgan started toward the garage in response. "Cool. Are you going to do woodworking like Mr. Carl?"

"No. I'm going to open a crafts shop."

Meredith's face brightened. "And call it the Mimosa Crafts Shop?"

"Absolutely. That's a perfect name. And I'm going to sell my crafts there—and maybe some crafts from other people on consignment. A lot of the boxes we're going to unpack have my crafts and craft supplies in them."

"Oh, boy." Morgan quickened her pace. "Maybe you'll teach Mer and me how to make some craft stuff, too. We always wanted Mr. Carl to teach us, but he wouldn't let us back in his workshop. And he didn't want us to even touch his tools."

Grace grinned. The girls' enthusiasm was lifting her spirits again already.

"Maybe we could do a crafting badge with Scouts." Meredith's bright eyes looked in Grace's direction. "Is there one?"

"Actually there are several; I'll show them to you in the Scout book later." Grace smiled at Meredith, purposed to be in a good mood versus a negative one. If she had some family troubles to worry over, they were not the girls' troubles to bear.

Besides, on the plus side, one good thing had come out of the day: a new surety about giving the craft shop a real try. Her mother had encouraged her there. Although the other revelations had been painful, Grace was glad for her mother's honest answers to her questions. How could Grace fix what she didn't know was broken? Hadn't she just been praying about that? It grieved Grace to know she'd hurt and neglected her family—in their eyes, at least. But she could work on changing those perceptions. And she could work on developing a friendship with Myra. Already, Grace and her mother were growing closer again.

The July day grew hot, and by afternoon, Grace and the girls were all sticky and sweaty—as well as dirty—from working in the shop.

Morgan stopped to fan herself with a piece of cardboard.

"Whew, it's hot. You know, we've got on our bathing suits under our shorts. Let's go down to the river and take a swim and cool off."

"Can we, Ms. Grace?" Meredith jumped up and down with excitement. "And will you swim with us? There are nice steps going down from your patio. It's easy to get down into the creek there. You won't fall or anything. And we can run across the creek to the house and get our tubes and an extra for you. It's fun to sit in them and let the stream take you for a ride."

Morgan joined in. "Please, Ms. Grace?"

"Okay." Grace gave in with little argument. It was hot. "I'll go put my suit on and join you at the creek. You go get your tubes. And you let your Aunt Bebe know that we're going to swim. Be sure it's all right with her."

"It will be okay if we have an adult with us. That's the rule." Morgan added this as the girls streaked out the door.

Realizing that a swim sounded wonderful after working in the shop, Grace headed into the Mimosa to find a bathing suit. After greeting the dogs and taking Sadie and Dooley outside for a short walk, Grace picked out an old beige swimsuit she hadn't worn for a while and slipped into it. Then she scooped her hair up into a ponytail, found a towel, put a few cokes into a cooler, grabbed a box of cheese crackers for a snack later, and headed for the stream.

A short time later, Grace was whooping and hollering almost as much as the girls as they played on the big tubes down in the river. As a rapid caught her tube, Grace flipped off and into the water. She came up totally drenched and laughing and then looked up to see Jack Teague standing on the patio watching her.

He was smiling, but his eyes were sultry. Grace could feel his gaze slipping over her wet body—and she suddenly felt oddly embarrassed, even though she knew she was well-covered in the beige one-piece suit.

Jack had on shorts today with a golf shirt neatly tucked into them. He wore socks and running shoes. If he had been working at the office, he obviously hadn't dressed up much. Grace found herself noticing the light dusting of dark hairs on his legs.

"Daddy!" called Morgan. "Come and join us! The water is perfect!"

To Grace's shock, Jack grinned and started pulling off his socks and shoes to comply. He took off his watch and unloaded his wallet and keys from his pocket, placing them on a patio table, and then he pulled off his shirt. And he smiled devilishly at Grace the whole time he stripped, those dimples of his flashing. What was that man up to now?

CHAPTER 10

Earlier that day there were less appointments on Jack's calendar. He could relax on slower work days like these, take some time off. Go casual. This morning he'd caught up on tasks around the house and then walked over to the office to check his mail.

Althea hung up the phone as Jack walked into the office and looked up at him with a strained face. "There was another incident with Crazy Man last night."

Jack stiffened. "Did it involve Grace?"

His mother looked at him oddly. "No, Son. It involved Roger and Samantha's little Ruby."

"Ruby? What do you mean Ruby? She's only a little kid! What happened, Ma?" Jack, shocked at the idea, snapped out the questions. Ruby wasn't even five years old yet—a charming, gamine-faced little girl with an adventurous spirit. She was Roger and Samantha's younger daughter, and they were all foolish about her.

The worry on Althea's face was obvious. "Roger and Sam found a note in their mailbox. A clip-out from an old newspaper, about a child being molested and raped, was taped to the top of the paper. Below it were the words: *Be careful about your child so she will stay safe.*"

Jack allowed an expletive to slip out before he could help himself, meriting a frown from his mother. "When did this happen, Ma? Have Roger and Sam called the sheriff to report this?"

"Yes to calling the sheriff, and as to when, Roger and Sam only found the note this morning. Evidently, someone tucked it into the mailbox after the mail ran. Bonnie Bratcher, the mail carrier on Roger's and Sam's route, said there was nothing in the box when she passed by earlier at eleven."

"So the man put the message into the box in broad daylight this time." Jack ran his hand through his hair in exasperation. "This is getting serious, Ma. This man is really demented. Do you think he might hurt Ruby or another child around here? My Lord, Ruby is only four years old. She's just starting kindergarten this fall. What kind of sick person would think about hurting a little girl like Ruby?"

"We don't know that the man means he might hurt Ruby." Althea tapped her pencil on the desk restlessly. "What we do know is that Ruby decided to skinny-dip in the river yesterday. Samantha had a phone call and went in the house for a short while to answer it. She left Ruby playing in the backyard. When she came out, she couldn't find her. You know how Ruby is about getting into things and wandering off. She's so different from Daisy, who is so sensible."

Jack couldn't help but grin. "Ruby got the Teague blood."

Althea rolled her eyes. "Well, anyway . . . Sam went searching frantically all over the yard and house, and then started down the street behind their house, looking and calling. She happened to look down to the stream below, and there was Ruby wading around in the river by the bank and trying to catch water flies on the water—without a stitch of clothes on."

Jack's eyebrows jerked up.

Althea smiled despite herself. "The child had simply pulled off her sun-suit and underwear and decided to wade right into the water. Her reasoning when Samantha scolded her was that she didn't want to get her clothes wet and get in trouble. She didn't seem to see any problem with walking out of the yard and across the street and down to the river without telling Samantha—or with being buck naked."

"But that was dangerous." Jack held back his own grin. "The

current in the river can be swift. She could have fallen in and even drowned."

Althea grimaced. "Believe me, Roger and Sam are both aware of that. And Sam feels awful that she took her eye off the child long enough for Ruby to get into that situation. But Ruby is nearly five now and should be more responsible. Sam and Roger both had a serious talk with her, of course. But what was done was done."

Jack looked thoughtful. "And our resident man of judgment must have seen Ruby in the river."

Althea nodded. "The sheriff believes Crazy Man was giving a warning to Sam and Roger about keeping Ruby safer—not threatening that he might hurt her."

She paused, and Jack jumped in. "But Swofford's not sure about that, is he? What do we know about this man, anyway, Ma?" Jack dropped into the chair in front of Althea's desk. "Very little. We don't really know what he might or might not do."

Althea fidgeted nervously with her pencil again. "No. But so far all his notes have only been warnings. He hasn't ever hurt anyone or tried to hurt anyone—and this has been going on for a year now."

Jack twisted in the chair restlessly. "This man has got to be found and stopped, Ma. I don't like it when he starts targeting his messages at children. And I don't like the idea that he was watching Ruby wading around in the creek naked. If he had goodness in him, he would have persuaded her to get out of the water and not left her there in danger, only watching her."

"It does sound abnormal," Althea agreed. "And I think you'd better talk to the girls, Jack. Let them know what's happened. Not to scare them, but to make them be more careful and watchful. They run around here with a lot of freedom."

Jack scowled. "Yeah, I know. And they think of Crazy Man as a kind of joke. They don't see him as potentially dangerous."

Althea got up to get a cup of coffee. "I hate to alarm the girls or hurt their sense of trust, but they do need to be careful until this man is found."

"I'll go talk to them right now. I think Bebe said they'd gone over to help Ms. Grace in cleaning out Carl's old shop. They're either there or they've gone on back up to the house."

"Well, go sign those papers on your desk before you go," his mother said. "And answer your phone messages. There's one from the Abernathys; they want to drive down to look at that vacation rental again, on the back side of the river. I think they might be ready to buy."

Jack flicked a look down the hallway that led to his and Roger's offices as he got up. He could only imagine how upset Roger must be about this incident with Ruby. "Where's Roger, Ma? Is he in his office?"

"No. He's working over at the house today. He didn't want to leave Samantha and the girls alone." She heaved a sigh. "Bless his heart. You can understand how he feels."

Jack nodded. "I'll walk over to see him after I talk to the M & M's." This was Jack's nickname for Meredith and Morgan.

Althea grinned, Jack's bit of humor cheering her up as he'd hoped it would.

Leaving the office a little later, Jack phoned Bebe to see if the twins were back at the house yet.

"They're still with Ms. Grace," Bebe told him. "They came back to get their tubes, and they're playing down in the river now. Ms. Grace is watching them." There was a pause. "Jack, if you're on your way home, I'd like to go down to Roger and Sam's place now. They've had a rough time of it. And I'm sure their girls are upset. I've made a casserole, some sides, a salad, and some fresh cookies. I want to take food down so Sam won't have to worry about making dinner tonight."

"Sure, Bebe. That's nice. I know Sam and Roger will appreciate it. And don't feel you need to come back and cook for us afterward. I'll rustle up something for the girls and myself tonight."

"Thank you, dear. But I've made enough food for all of us. You bring the girls on down about six. Althea's coming, too. This is a time for a family to be together."

Jack rang off and then cut across Creekside Lane to the Mimosa Inn. He walked up the driveway and then started down the path to the river. He could hear girlish shrieks and laughter even before he got close to the stream's edge.

As he drew closer and sprinted up the patio steps, Jack heard a woman's whoop and laugh mixed in with the girls' voices. Looking down to the river, he saw Grace Conley surface from under the water and struggle to her feet against the stream's swift current, laughing and pushing her wet hair back from her face. She'd obviously tumbled from the big tube beside her.

Jack caught his breath. The bright sun was glistening on her skin and glinting off the water streaking down her arms and legs. Mercy. Was she naked? Jack blinked and gulped before realizing Grace simply wore a beige, skin-toned bathing suit. The color of it was so similar to that of her lightly tanned skin that it looked, at first glance, like she wasn't wearing anything at all. The thought was tantalizing.

In fact, Jack thought, Grace was tantalizing. Her wet suit snuggly hugged her lush curves, giving Jack a view of her body he hadn't had the opportunity to see before. Rooted to the spot, he let his eyes drift lazily over her from top to bottom, liking everything he saw. Wishing he could put his hands on her. She was incredible. He wondered if she had any idea how beautiful she was. Or how her body called out to a man like a siren.

Jack's blood surged as Grace looked up at him with those silvery blue-green eyes of hers. Water dripped down her beautiful, flushed face and slid down her slicked-back blond hair. Her lips were lush and full. A warm laugh still crinkled the corners of her mouth and danced in her eyes. Lord. A woman like this could drive a man insane.

"Daddy!" Morgan called, spotting him. "Come and join us. The water is perfect."

Jack didn't hesitate a minute. He wanted in that water and nearer Grace Conley.

He pulled off his socks and shoes, unloaded his pockets onto the patio table, and then pulled his shirt lazily up over his head. Jack saw Grace's eyes following his movements, and he smiled at her as he stripped. That little flush he saw creeping up her neck gave away all her feelings, despite what she hoped she could conceal from him. She was a cool one and not a woman to let her emotions be easily read, but Jack could sense her attraction to him sizzling in the air. A man would have to be a fool not to feel the undercurrents that flowed between them. She pulled at him like an undertow.

Laughing and jesting with the girls, Jack walked down the patio steps and into the current of the Little River. He was impulsive by nature, and it didn't matter that he was still wearing his shorts and boxers instead of swim trunks.

Meredith and Morgan shrieked and paddled over so that he could catch them up and toss them out into the water. It was a game they loved to play with him.

"Toss Ms. Grace! Toss Ms. Grace!" called Morgan as she came up laughing from the water.

Jack raised his eyebrows at Grace and started toward her.

"Don't you even think about it, Jack Teague." She gave him a warning look and stepped backward.

He grinned at her playfully and ignored her, wading over to catch her up in his arms before she could back away farther.

The girls giggled and whooped.

Jack enjoyed the feel of Grace's bare skin against his, relished the feel of his hands under her soft bottom. He jostled her, as though he had tripped over a slick river rock, so she would put her arms around him to catch herself from falling.

The feeling of her arms wrapped around his neck, her breasts up against his chest was heaven. His face was close to hers now, and he found his gaze focusing on her lips.

Grace caught her breath and hissed at him softly. "We have young girls here, Jack Teague. Your *own* girls, if you'll remember. You need to put me down right now. These girls have eyes."

"So they do." He smiled at her, and then tossed her right out into the river.

She came up spluttering while the girls shrieked in pleasure.

At Morgan's and Meredith's urging, Jack started playing shark-in-the-water with them next, plunging down under the water to sneak up on them and playfully attack them. He soon had Morgan up on his shoulders, and at Meredith's urging,

Grace let her climb up onto her back so they could have a proper water fight. All of it just gave Jack more opportunities to touch Grace again, to watch her body shift and move, to thrill at how her wet suit clung to all her curves when she slid under the surface and stood up fully soaked.

She was a thrilling, fascinating woman, and he wondered when he would tire of her. So far, it seemed that every time he saw her, his feelings and attraction for her just intensified. Of course, he wasn't able to get his fill of her, and that was probably escalating his hunger. Nice girls had a way of driving a man mad that way. It was one of the reasons Jack had always avoided them.

"Enough for me," Grace said at last, climbing up the stone steps from the water to the flagstone patio. She dropped into a chair and draped a towel over her.

Jack played a few minutes more with the girls and then climbed out to join her.

"What's in your cooler?" he asked her, snagging the box of crackers to dig out a handful to eat.

"Colas. Help yourself. I brought several."

Jack picked out a cola and popped the top.

"Daddy!" called Morgan. "We're going to paddle upstream to the other bridge and then float back down in our tubes. Is that all right? You'll be able to see us as we come down if you shift your chair."

Jack nodded and moved his chair around so that he could look back up the river to keep an eye on his girls.

He wiped some of the water out of his hair with Meredith's towel and then settled back to enjoy the warm July sun, propping his feet up beside Grace's on a wrought-iron bench.

His eyes traveled with appreciation up the long expanse of Grace's legs. "You're a beautiful woman, Grace Conley. It's been a real pleasure seeing so much more of you today."

"And you're an insufferable flirt, Jack Teague. Didn't your mother teach you how to act with more manners and restraint around women?"

"She tried." Jack grinned. "But I've always had such a deep

and sincere appreciation for women, Grace. A man can't deny his nature."

"No, but he can *temper* his nature." She pursed her lips. "Which is obviously something you've had little practice with."

Jack shrugged casually and leaned his leg up against Grace's. "It's more fun to follow your instincts."

Grace shook her head, moving her leg away from his. "And that's what makes you dangerous." She looked out toward the stream and frowned. "I'm not a woman who's looking for an affair, Jack."

He smiled at her. "Is that your way of telling me you're not going to follow up on your attraction to me?"

Her eyes flashed. "I can't deny there's some attraction. I wish it weren't there, but it is. Like it or not. But I won't act on it, Jack."

"You want to." His voice had softened, and he trailed his fingers up her arm.

She pulled her arm away. "I often want to do a lot of things that are wrong for me, or simply wrong in general, but that doesn't mean I have to do them. I have a very strong will, Jack, and very strong ethics. Obviously something you don't seem to have or to worry about."

"Oh, I'm strong willed, too. I just believe more in following my feelings and not denying them."

She turned to send him a pointed look. "I don't mean to sound preachy, Jack, but how can you sit in church every Sunday, have two little girls to raise and a good family here in the area, and not worry more about your reputation?"

He shrugged. "I've never had much reputation in that way. Never cared about it, either. I figure God created attraction between a man and a woman. If some women like to enjoy that attraction, who am I to deny them?"

Grace dropped her feet to the patio with a stomp. "That's an insufferable, arrogant attitude, Jack—and shows a shameful disrespect to women and a flagrant disregard of all the women who really love and care about you."

He let his eyes slide over her. "I'll bet you've had men looking at you and wanting you for a long time, Grace Conley. Didn't you ever want to just let loose and see what came of it?"

She glared at him. "Watching movies, I've often wondered what it would be like to be an artful thief or to poison someone I disliked, but that doesn't mean I'd ever try out those behaviors to see what it felt like. Ways on the dark side have their enticing draw, Jack. They always have. But you don't have to yield to that draw."

Jack raised his brows in admiration. "A very diplomatic answer, Grace. Touché. And one that managed to answer and yet not answer my question."

She turned and locked her eyes on his. "You could be a good and fine man if you wanted to, Jack. You are so admirable and well-respected in so many other ways."

He winced. "Change isn't so easy, Grace, even if a person had a mind to change."

"I've changed," she challenged him. "I've made some very big changes in my life coming here. Walked against what everyone thought I could and should do. And made a lot of people angry."

"Samantha and Roger told me you almost alienated your children coming here." He caught her eyes. "What did they want of you, Grace?"

"They wanted me to move into a nice, prestigious retirement center. Into a lovely condo by a shady park, a small lake, and a fine walking trail. To put up my feet and take it easy."

She snipped out the last words distastefully. Jack laughed. "And, obviously, you had no interest in retiring and taking it easy."

"Do I seem that old to you that I should want that?" Her voice had a pained tone to it, and she turned anguished eyes to him. "How could my children see me as used up and over the hill? Not fit for anything but lounging around for the rest of my life, cooking for them for holidays, and babysitting their kids? I'm only forty-nine years old, Jack, not eighty-nine. How could they see me as finished up just because they've grown up and started their adult years now?"

Tears had slipped into the edges of her eyes. Jack hated seeing that. He stood up impulsively, leaned over her chair, and kissed her soundly, bringing his hands up to gently caress her face. He surprised her with the gesture. She let out a soft little moan and let him deepen the kiss and run his hands up under her damp hair before she pushed him back.

"Is that supposed to help me feel better, Jack?" Her eyes snapped up at him.

He grinned down lazily at her and ran his fingers over her lips. "Yeah, it is. It should let you know, of a surety, that you're very much alive and vibrant, Grace Conley. And certainly not finished up."

She frowned at him. "Sit down, Jack, before your girls come into sight and see you putting the make on their new friend and Scout leader."

Jack looked up the river for the girls. He could just see them coming around an outcropping of rocks, their backs turned as the current rolled their tubes in the swift water of the stream. He sat down, feeling censored by Grace's continuing frown. Didn't she feel the passion simmering under the surface between them? How was she able to push it aside so easily?

Her eyes narrowed. "You said passion should let me know I'm alive and vibrant. Not finished up. Is that what it does for you, Jack—hitting on all the young girls like Ashleigh Layton and Twyla Treece? Does getting excited physically with them make you feel young again?"

"That's a little bit insulting, Grace. And personal." He scowled at her.

"Maybe. And maybe it's the reason you keep acting on your emotions without restraint—to try to keep feeling young."

Jack grinned and tossed back a sarcastic reply. "You'd have to try it to know if it works, wouldn't you, Grace?"

She flipped her towel at him. "Oh, that's a typical comment I would expect from you, Jack. Can't you be introspective and think about why you respond to so many things with sexual overtures?"

"I'm not big into getting overly analytical about things."

"Well, that's obvious." She practically snorted.

Jack looked up the river to see the girls moving closer. "Look, Grace. I know we're very different people. I didn't ask to be attracted to you. I didn't come seeking it. It just happened. And I'm having a real awkward time trying to figure out what to do with what I feel about you. Is that analytical enough to suit you?"

He paused to study her. "You can't deny you're attracted to me, Grace, and have physical feelings toward me—even if you don't want to admit them easily. I'm not sure why all this has kicked up between us. You haven't wanted it. And neither have I. But it's there." He grabbed her wrist. "And getting nasty and insulting toward me will hardly make your feelings go away, Grace."

She winced. "Well spoken, Jack. And I deserved that. I have been a little tactless in the way I've talked to you. You have a right to live your life as you wish, after all. My view about it isn't that important."

He stood up to wave to the girls as they drew closer to the patio of the Mimosa. "You're wrong there, Grace Conley." He looked down into her silvery eyes. "I've come to care rather too much about your view of me. And it's a real new experience for me, I can tell you."

Jack saw her eyes widen in surprise before he walked down the steps to haul his girls out of the river. They joined him and Grace chattering happily then, unaware of the stirred-up emotions still swirling around in the air.

As Jack listened to their young voices, he saw a shadow move in the trees at the edge of Grace's property. He tensed immediately. But it was only a squirrel when he looked closer.

The moment reminded him of why he'd come looking for his girls originally. Seeing Grace coming up out of the water like a sultry mermaid had wiped all thought of Crazy Man and the morning's problems right out of Jack's mind.

He shook his head to clear his thoughts. "There's been another incident with Crazy Man," he told them, finding a break in the girls' chatter. "And I need to talk to you about it."

Jack told them then about Ruby's going skinny-dipping, and

about Crazy Man's obviously seeing her and then leaving Sam and Roger a warning about the incident this morning. Jack saw the anxious panic in Grace's eyes, which she was wise enough not to express. He talked candidly to the girls about how they needed to be more careful until the man was found.

Meredith looked thoughtful then. "Daddy, do you think this man is bad and that he might try to hurt Ruby?"

Jack saw the edge of fear in her eyes and sought to soothe. "The sheriff doesn't think so, Mer. But when someone's mind is disordered, they often do things they wouldn't do ordinarily. I think Crazy Man was simply worried about Ruby."

Morgan wrinkled her nose in thought. "Maybe he was worried some bad person would do something to hurt Ruby, and he wanted to warn Uncle Roger and Aunt Samantha about that."

"That's most likely it, Morgan." Jack reached across to pat her knee. "But you can see that we still need to be careful until this man is found, can't you?"

"Yeah, we'll watch more," Morgan said.

Jack was glad to hear this, as Morgan had always been the more levelheaded of the two twins.

Meredith looked around dreamily, her thoughts already drifting from the subject at hand. "You should have a party here, Ms. Grace. It's such a pretty place. Everyone who lives on the River Road, Creekside, and right across the river could come and bring things. And we could cook on your big barbeque grill and play games in the yard. It would be nice."

"That's a cool idea, Mer!" Morgan's eyes lit up, her thoughts shifting quickly from fears about Crazy Man, too. "And Daddy can do good barbequing."

"Is that right?" Grace asked, with a teasing glance in her eyes as she looked Jack's way and lifted her eyebrows.

Jack realized she was glad to see the children shift their thoughts away from the harsh thoughts of Crazy Man trying to hurt little girls.

"Well, I am good at the grill, if I do say so myself." He grinned at her. "Burgers, ribs, chicken, you name it."

"I want hamburgers," Morgan piped in.

"And homemade ice cream." Meredith added that. "Uncle Roger has a freezer, and we have one. We could make two kinds!"

Grace smiled at the girls' enthusiasm and cocked an eye at Jack. "Do you think everyone would like to come?"

"Sure." Jack assured her. "We haven't held a gathering around here in a long time. Not since your big open house in early June."

"Will you call and invite people if I provide the place?" Grace asked.

"Will do." Jack felt pleased to see their relationship slip back into a more congenial mode. "I'll come around and talk to you about it later when I get in touch with everyone. Will this Friday night be too soon? It seems like if you plan too far ahead, there are always problems."

"Friday will be good. I don't have any guests coming to the inn until Saturday night. So that will be a great time for me."

Jack tossed towels over the girls and started them on across the bridge to change their clothes. He picked up his own clothes, wallet, and watch, and stopped to slip his shoes back on his feet.

He glanced across at Grace. "I hope the girls didn't talk you into hosting a gathering you weren't up for, Miz Conley."

She turned to smile at him as she gathered her own things. "No, I'm pleased to host a get-together here. And I think it will be good for Roger and Samantha and their girls to get out and have a good time after their bad experiences this week. You will invite them, won't you?"

"I'm going over there to see them later. Bebe made supper for us all. It's a good time for a family to pull together when there's been a problem like this."

She sent him a thoughtful look. "That's just the kind of thing I like so much about you, Jack. How you think of others so often before yourself."

His eyes flicked over her with appreciation before he turned to leave. He had a desire to touch her again, but quelled it so he could leave her on a positive note. Halfway across the swinging bridge, he looked back to see her watching him.

She waved casually and then started toward the house. He let his eyes drift after her as she walked in that swaying, seductive way of hers up through the yard toward the inn, and then he followed his girls up the hill to their own place. Mercy times ten. Just watching her walk through the yard had stirred him all up again.

CHAPTER 11

Grace spent the rest of the afternoon getting Carl's old shop set up for business under the Mimosa name. The dogs kept her company, sleeping in a cool corner where they could keep an eye on her. They had grown comfortable in their new home, and Grace's guests at the Mimosa found them to be charming.

Finding a blank wood sign Carl Oakley had left behind in the storage room, Grace painted decorative pink mimosa blooms and the name of the shop on it and hammered it into the ground in front of the store. Then she started putting out and pricing her crafts. She planned to have her first open hours on Thursday from eleven to four.

Hearing footsteps on the porch, she looked up to see Samantha Butler at the door.

"Hi. Could you use some company, Grace? Bebe has the girls, and I felt like I needed a break." Sam pushed back a stray wisp of hair that had escaped from the loose bun at the back of her neck. Her gray eyes looked up anxiously from a full face. "I guess you heard what happened."

"I did." Grace went over to give her new friend a hug. "You and Roger must have been terrified."

Samantha nodded, reaching to shake hands in greeting with Sadie and Dooley who had come out to meet her. "It's been a hard day. But I think we've both convinced ourselves, as the sheriff says, that Crazy Man was only sending us a warning to be more careful—versus a threat that he might try to hurt Ruby. Swofford brought over a record of all the notes and warnings people have received from the man in the last year, and there's a similarity between them all. Swofford believes the man sees himself as some sort of vigilante or watchdog around our area. He believes Crazy Man is more like a busybody or a Peeping Tom than a real danger."

Grace perched on a wooden stool that Carl Oakley had built and watched her new friend. Samantha Butler was a round-faced, dark brunette with a softly full figure and, usually, a happy, optimistic countenance and manner. Although Samantha had young children, she was in her early forties—not many years younger than Grace. Samantha and Roger had married late, and Sam didn't have their first child, Daisy, until she was thirty-two.

"You know, I didn't think I would ever marry," Samantha had told Grace once. "I was already thirty when Roger and I met, and he was nearly forty. But love bit us as hard as if we'd been teenagers—except that we were old enough to truly recognize a good thing when it hit us this time."

She'd laughed with pleasure and then added a comment Grace still remembered with fondness. "I knew the day I met you that we would be friends, too, Grace."

Over the summer months, the two women's friendship had deepened, even though Grace's children were grown and Samantha's still young.

Pacing around restlessly, Samantha continued to fill Grace in on the events of the day. Suddenly, she stopped to look around, momentarily distracted. "Why, Grace, you almost have the shop set up. It looks wonderful! I'd been so preoccupied I hardly noticed."

She walked closer to a shelf Grace had just filled from an empty box on the floor. "Did you really make all these beautiful things yourself?"

Grace nodded, laughing.

"So tell me about them. I'd like to get my thoughts on something else for a little while." Sam leaned over to pick up a nest of decorative boxes from a shelf.

Grace knew Sam needed to focus on another subject and happily obliged. She walked over to join Sam near the display shelves.

"That section in front of you, Sam, evolved from my découpage and stenciling phase of crafting." Grace chuckled as she gestured to the shelves loaded down with découpaged and stenciled boxes, plaques, and trays. "Over there to your left are all the craft projects I made in my quilting, smocking, and sewing stage." Purses, quilts, aprons, and an array of other items filled the shelves and hung on display racks.

Samantha walked over to admire a row of small children's clothes, bonnets, and bibs. "What beautiful smocking! Didn't your children want these for their own little ones?"

Grace smiled. "Believe me, Sam, I made an abundance. I think they all got more items than they knew what to do with. When I get on a crafting roll, I kind of get obsessed." She looked around and shook her head. "That's why there's so much here."

Sam walked over to a row of shelves filled with unfinished wood items. "These are Carl's items here, aren't they?"

"Yes. I thought some people seeing my advertisements might come expecting to see some of his work. They're nice—especially the carved canes and the log-cabin birdhouses he made."

Grace followed Samantha as she wandered around to the different sections of the small shop. There was a pottery and ceramics section, a section of jewelry—from the year Grace learned to make her own beads—and a section filled with tole-painted items, and a few framed acrylics.

"You paint, too?" Sam turned to look at Grace with surprise. "These are wonderful." She walked around examining the paintings Grace had hung on the wall and propped up against the shelves. "I love this painting of the rooster. Will you save it for me for my kitchen? I collect roosters, if you haven't noticed . . . and chickens and roosters decorate my kitchen. I think I have just the spot in mind for this little painting."

"Sold." Grace smiled at Sam. "But you have to buy it if you want it. My mother convinced me that I shouldn't continue to simply give away my work. She was really quite sweet about encouraging me when she visited."

Sam leaned against a counter. "I can't believe your family in Nashville never valued your arts and crafts work. It is truly good, Grace."

"Even the ceramics?" Grace grinned and pointed to a shelf overflowing with painted and fired ceramics.

"Yes, even the ceramics. Because you didn't make the usual tacky items so many people create. You made unique and useful pieces. And added your own decorative touches. I especially love the piggy banks; every one of them is painted and decorated differently."

Grace looked wistful. "I made each of my children a bank with his or her name on it for Christmas one year when I was learning ceramics. The children were small then and really loved their banks." She shook her head. "I don't know why I made so many after that, though. I found thirty-four of them when I unpacked my ceramics boxes."

She scratched her head. "I think I made them for a civic group bazaar or something. But they didn't all sell."

"Well, never mind." Sam gave her a hug. "They'll sell here. This mountain area is a great place to sell crafts. People come here expecting to find handmade items to buy and take home. They'll love your things. You wait and see."

Grace looked around in pleasure. "Seeing them all again, I'm glad I didn't simply haul them off and chuck them like the children suggested. They almost convinced me that crafts had gone out of style."

"Pooh. Crafts will never go out of style."

Sam picked up a bib apron to examine it. "Which of these crafts do you still do, Grace?"

Grace shrugged. "I guess I could do any of them. I still have the patterns, the tools, a lot of leftover materials." She smiled. "Charles even indulged me and bought me my own kiln when I did so many ceramics. I brought it with me, and I have kept all my molds. Everything is in the back of the shop and in the storage closets."

"Well, get ready to craft again, Grace. It will be nice that you can make more of the things that people like and buy the most." She gave Grace a little punch. "And maybe you'll get creative and make some new things you haven't tried before."

Looking around the little shop, Grace wondered if Samantha and her mother were right—if anyone would actually buy all these things she'd made.

Remembering Samantha's problems, Grace directed their discussion back to Ruby again. "How is Ruby handling your family's receiving this note from Crazy Man? She's only four. Does she even understand it?"

Sam actually laughed then—a good sound to hear. "I think she's all right, Grace. After pouting from being scolded, she started to enjoy all the attention she's gotten. I think she's begun to feel like a local celebrity. She tells everyone who stops by now that Crazy Man wrote a note about her."

Grace giggled. "Leave it to Ruby."

"Actually, Daisy has been more upset by all of this than Ruby. We've had to have several talks about sexual issues I probably wouldn't have talked to her about until she was older if this hadn't happened. Daisy is only ten. But she's asked honest questions, and I felt I should answer them. Do you think I did the right thing?"

Grace nodded. "Yes. Talk to your girls while they're young. When they get older they begin to think they know it all. It's harder then sometimes."

Samantha sent Grace a knowing look. "You miss Margaret, don't you?"

"I do. I miss all my children, but especially Margaret, since she was still living at home. I felt terrible she wouldn't come with me—that she stayed at the house in Nashville with Elaine and Elaine's family." Grace sighed. "Despite Margaret's high-strung temperament and out-spoken ways, she and I have always been close until now. She was my last child—and much younger than the others. I do miss her."

"I'm sorry." Sam patted Grace's arm. "Maybe when she comes back over here for college you'll see her more often and get close again."

"That's a long time away, though." It wasn't even mid July yet.

Sam looked at her watch. "I guess I'd better get back. I need to help Bebe with dinner. Good luck with the store opening Thursday. And thanks for hosting our get-together on Friday night. We decided on six as the start time. Will that be all right? I know you're having the grand opening of the shop from eleven to four Thursday, Friday, and Saturday. Should we have made the time later?"

Grace shook her head in the negative.

Samantha acknowledged that and continued on. "All right, then. I think Roger and Jack were making a few calls and working on the guest list when I left. We'll let you know when we have a count. But everyone will bring things. You won't have to do much more than provide the place. We'll get tables and chairs from the church and haul them over to the yard to set up. It will be fun. Don't you think so?"

"I do. I'm looking forward to it."

She walked Samantha out and let the dogs nose around in the shrubbery before she went back to work in the shop.

Later than evening, Grace was sitting in the library at the front of the house making up a list of things she wanted to do before Friday, when she heard a knock on the front door. The dogs pricked up their ears and jumped off the couch, where they'd been curled up beside Grace napping. They woofed softly—obviously wishing they could bark more aggressively.

Grace eyed them in warning. "Don't even think about it, you two," she said to them firmly. She had trained them since they were small not to bark every time someone came to the door or to jump on people when they came into the house, either.

Grace stood up, knowing she needed to answer the door. Remembering the stories about Crazy Man, she looked over at the clock on the desk cautiously. It was seven at night and starting to get late. Who would come to the house this late?

A familiar voice rang out. "It's Jack, Grace."

Grace walked into the front entry and opened the door with relief, glad to see Jack's familiar face.

As she opened the door, he reached down to take the proffered paws of the corgis in greeting, talking to them both affectionately.

Grace smiled at him, letting her glance run over him while he petted the dogs. Her heartbeat escalated like it always did whenever Jack was around.

He looked up to catch her assessing glance before she could hide it. "Well, it's nice to note you're so glad to see me," he said lazily, giving her a smug grin.

She bristled. "I was just pleased it was someone I knew. After all that talk about Crazy Man, I got a little spooked when I heard someone at the door so late." She turned and started back toward the library. "Come on in. I'm in the library. Have you eaten, Jack?"

He grinned. "Entirely too much. Bebe believes making a feast soothes everyone whenever there is a family crisis. Tonight was no exception."

Grace looked past him out the door. "Where are the girls?"

"They're spending the night with Daisy and Ruby. Samantha thought it would be good for all the girls to have a little fun tonight—to take their minds off things. They had settled in to watch some fairy princess movie when I left." He chuckled. "Chick stuff."

With a wave of prickly apprehension, Grace wondered what Jack Teague was doing at her house so late—with his girls safely settled at the Butlers to spend the night. It made her nervous to realize she was alone in the house with him.

She led him into the library off the entry hall—somewhat cautiously now—gesturing him to an easy chair while she settled back down on the small sofa nearby. She purposefully left the front door of the house open, too, except for the screen, to let Jack know, subtly, that she assumed he wouldn't be staying long.

He settled back in the chair and stretched his legs out. "I've always liked this room with its wall of books and cozy chairs. Makes you want to settle down to read a good book."

The dogs came over to curl up happily beside Jack's chair, getting a few more scratches in the process. They obviously had no apprehensions about Jack at all.

"What do you like to read, Jack?" Grace tried to make polite small talk and not let her eyes drift over him. He wore tan shorts and a brown golf shirt that exactly matched the chocolate color of his eyes.

"Mysteries. Thrillers. Maybe an occasional Western. What about you?" He reached down to casually scratch the dogs behind their ears again.

"I like mysteries, too. And historical romances. It's interesting to visit other eras and places in a book." She smiled and then shifted with discomfort, picking at a speck of lint on the sofa arm to occupy her hands and try to distract her thoughts.

Like a silly teenager, she found herself wondering if Jack might try to kiss her again. Was he still attracted to her? Her eyes shifted to his face with her thoughts.

Jack caught her eyes with his, studying her.

Grace twisted her hands in her lap nervously now.

"It's getting me all excited, Grace, watching you fidget and worry about what I might do while I'm visiting you here." He gave Grace one of those devilish smiles that lit up his dimples and crinkled his eyes.

Annoyed, Grace sat up straighter, trying to regain her composure. She felt a slight flush rise up her neck as she did. "Perhaps the direct approach is better with you, Jack. What are you doing here, anyway?"

He leaned back and grinned at her. "Now, that's not a very neighborly way to act, Grace. I brought the guest list over to you."

Jack pulled a folded sheet of paper from his back pocket and handed it across to her. "There will be seventeen coming on Friday night, Grace. The Teagues—including the girls and I, Ma, and Bebe—from across the river. From the River Road and Creekside there will be Vincent Westbrooke and the Butlers: Roger, Sam, Daisy, and Ruby. From the next house down, Sally and Berke Carson plan to come, but not Berke's mother Jo. I think Sally said she had a cold. Then from the last house on the River Road there will be the Clark clan: Gavin and Freda and their four kids, Kyleen, Dean, Stacy, and Julie. That's it—our small neighborhood in a nutshell. You'll sort them out Friday if you don't know them all already."

He ran his hands through his hair as an ending. Grace followed the motion, fighting the thought that she wished her own hands were there.

Mentally she scolded herself for the direction of her thinking and tried to relax. She put on a plastic smile. "It sounds like a good group. I think I've met almost everyone, although I know some better than others."

His eyes assessed her lazily. "If you'll look on the list, Grace, you'll see what food everyone has volunteered to bring. It's a lot. Roger, Berke, Carson, and I are in charge of the grilling, and we're buying the hamburger meat and buns. We'll also come early and bring over the tables and chairs we'll need from the church. Vince and Gavin Clark are helping with that, too. All the families are bringing fixings, sides, desserts, coolers full of drinks and ice, paper plates, utensils, and cups."

Jack angled in his seat and stretched his legs to prop them on the footstool in front of the little sofa where Grace sat. She tried not to focus on his legs so near hers.

Mentally she chided herself. *He's only here being a good neighbor, telling you about this gathering coming up on Friday. Why are you so conscious of him? Of every move he makes. You're acting like a silly schoolgirl! Stop it, Grace.*

Jack's voice floated over her thoughts. "Samantha told me to tell you to make a couple of pitchers of that great fruit tea of yours, if you would. She knows you're opening your shop Thursday and Friday for the first days of business. She doesn't want you doing anything more, although she said you probably would anyway."

Grace listened politely, trying to concentrate on what Jack was saying. Whatever was wrong with her? You'd think she'd never been alone with a man at night before!

A small silence descended before Grace realized Jack had stopped talking. She looked up and saw him watching her.

He dropped his feet off the stool and stood up then. In a quieter voice he said, "I'm going home now while I can, Grace Conley. If I stay in this sizzling tension any longer I'm going to pick you up and carry you back to the bedroom and work off some of this agony."

She knew her eyes had grown wide and her posture rigid.

Jack smiled lazily. "Don't you think you should walk me to the door, Miz Conley?"

Grace stood to her feet, her legs feeling wobbly and rubbery. She unconsciously smoothed her hands down the front of her shirt, trying to straighten it.

Jack's eyes followed her hands as they passed over her breasts. "That did it," he said. In two seconds, he had taken the few steps separating them, grabbed her by the arms, and leaned down to kiss her with a kiss that could never be termed polite.

Grace grasped the front of his shirt to hold herself up. An explosive passion seemed to wash over Grace's senses. She heard some gasping little breath escape her before Jack crushed her closer against him, his mouth devouring hers and his hands roving up under her hair and then down her back and lower. When he pulled her more tightly to him, his hands cupped under her hips, Grace felt herself grow dizzy with sensation.

Jack pulled back from her for a moment to look down into her eyes with a searing gaze. Their eyes locked tightly, and both of them were breathing heavily.

Just as he leaned back toward her with a seductive, satisfying smile, a voice behind them said sarcastically, "Well, well, isn't this an interesting situation to find my mother in."

A cold bucket of water tossed over her wouldn't have more

quickly arrested Grace's passion. Jack backed away with a regretful shrug and turned around.

"Margaret." Grace tried to greet her daughter in a bright and normal voice—but knew her voice sounded strained. "I had no idea you were coming, dear."

Margaret rolled her eyes. "That's certainly obvious, Mother."

Forgetting their normal manners, Sadie and Dooley barked a greeting and clicked across the hardwood floor to weave around Margaret's legs in pleasure.

"No barking," Margaret reminded them. But Margaret leaned down to greet them both affectionately.

Struggling to recover her equilibrium and her manners now, Grace started her introductions, trying to steady her voice. "Jack, this is my daughter Margaret Jane. Margaret, this is my neighbor who lives across the river, Jack Teague."

Jack lazily and calmly reached out a hand to take Margaret's. "I'm delighted, Margaret. I can see you inherited your mother's beauty. I am charmed to meet you."

Grace felt nettled. Nothing seemed to rattle this man. She still felt shaky and weak-kneed, and he seemed calm and unruffled.

"I am so pleased you decided to come see me." Grace went over to give Margaret a hug now. "How long will you stay with me?"

"I'm not sure." Margaret shrugged casually and smoothed a loose strand of hair behind her ear. Her blond hair was pulled back in a smooth ponytail, and she wore white shorts and a black T-shirt that said: Beethoven Rocks.

Grace smiled. "Well, you can stay as long as you like. Why didn't you call?"

"I left impulsively. Elaine and I had a fight." Margaret wrinkled her nose. "Elaine got all bent out of shape about something that happened. We had a few words, and then Frank got into it." Her voice had grown expressive and dramatic now.

She waved her arms. "You know how Frank is. So pompous and self-righteous. I don't know how Elaine stands to live with that man. He goes on and on."

Margaret leaned against the side of a wing chair and made a

face. "I finally got tired of it and possibly said a few things I shouldn't have." She shrugged.

Grace smiled. *Possibly said a few things* was hardly the right way to describe what Margaret had probably let loose at Frank. She tended to get wound up.

"What brought on all this little hoopla?" Jack asked.

Margaret looked toward Jack in surprise, seeming to remember then that he was still there.

She flicked her eyes up and down him, sizing him up—Grace knew that look—before she continued. "Well, I was watching the girls after lunch while Elaine ran out to the store. The girls were playing with some blocks and stuff, busy and happy, and I was practicing the piano."

Margaret paused. "It was a Tchaikovsky piece, and I got caught up in the movements and got absorbed." She lifted her eyebrows expressively. "And then the next thing I knew Elaine was rushing in the room shrieking and freaking out. Evidently, Ava and Sophie had gone out into the backyard. I guess I didn't hear them. And they were playing in the fountain with their clothes on when Elaine drove back up."

Margaret flopped into the wing chair she had been leaning against, the dogs settling on the floor close to her feet. Grace and Jack, following her signal, sat down again, too.

Margaret continued her story. "It was really no big deal. That fountain isn't even two feet deep at the edges. You'd think I purposely took them out onto the freeway and left them there from the way Elaine was overreacting."

"Were they all right?" Grace asked anxiously.

"Of course." Margaret gave her an annoyed glance. "That's the whole point. They were just playing around in the water. Of course, they shouldn't have been. Ava knew better and she knew they weren't supposed to even go outside alone without me. Or climb into the fountain with their shoes and clothes on. But that didn't stop them. Oh, no, the little brats. And Elaine wasn't even mad at them at all. Only at me. Frank was even worse. He came home from work to jump on me. So after twenty minutes of his ranting and raving, I just went up to my room and packed some stuff and took off."

And came to me, Grace thought with pleasure.

Jack laughed, enjoying the story. "How old were these little girls?"

Grace answered that. "Ava is three and Sophie is eighteen months. The water in the fountain is not very deep to adults, but it would be waist deep to little Sophie."

"I know. *And they both might have drowned!*" Margaret parroted Elaine's voice, complete with shrieks and hand gestures. "I've heard it all. And I'm certainly sorry they slipped outside while I was playing piano. But what was I supposed to do about it after the fact? Wear sackcloth and ashes and wail and flail myself with switches?"

Grace watched Jack's mouth twitch. He was getting a good look at Margaret's dramatic take on life.

Margaret blew out an exasperated breath. "I must have said I was sorry a hundred times. But it wasn't enough. They had to launch into a reiteration of all the ways I was so often irresponsible. Honestly, Mother, I was totally over it."

"Well, you can stay here with me as long as you like." Grace leaned over to pat Margaret's knee. "There is plenty of room. And I've already fixed up the top suite in the inn; you can use it just like your own little apartment. I think you'll like it."

Margaret looked around then as if seeing the bed-and-breakfast for the first time. "Good grief. This place is colorful and cluttered enough, isn't it? I don't remember you mentioning that it looked like the inside of a children's picture book or a Mary Engelbreit calendar."

Jack took this moment to walk toward the door, obviously suppressing another grin. "I think I'll head on home and let you girls catch up on all the home gossip."

The dogs lifted up their heads and thumped their tails to sleepily acknowledge that Jack was leaving, but didn't get up this time. However, Grace stood to walk him to the door.

Margaret waved a hand at Jack. "I'd say it was nice to meet

you, Mr. Teague, but I'm not sure of your intentions toward my mother yet. So I'll reserve judgment."

She gave Jack and Grace a pointed look. "Perhaps it's good I came when I did. Daddy always said it was dangerous for girls to live on their own. I guess he might have been right." She smirked and raised an eyebrow.

Jack snickered. "He might have had a point. And it's particularly dangerous for beautiful women like you and your mother. You lock your doors after I'm gone. Okay?"

"We will." Margaret gave him a saucy smile. "Perhaps Mother should have locked her doors much earlier."

"Perhaps." Jack said this lightly and then turned to give Grace a long look. He smiled that rascal of a smile at her then, his dimples winking in his cheeks.

"And then perhaps not," he added quietly, his voice dropping to a husky tone meant only for Grace's ears.

He blew them a kiss on two fingers before he left, shutting the door behind him.

"Holy kamoly!" Margaret let out the expletive after they heard Jack's footsteps recede into the distance. "Where did you find *him*, Mother? He seems like all the kinds of men you used to warn Elaine and me about all wrapped up in one package."

Grace could feel herself blush.

She saw Margaret studying her. "You're blushing. And it looked to me like Jack Teague was getting ready to kiss you when I came in. Was he?"

Grateful that Margaret had apparently not seen the episode before, Grace angled to change the subject. "I'm so glad you're here, Margaret. Where are your bags, dear?"

"In the car."

"Come. I'll help you bring them in."

Grace opened the door and then stopped in her tracks and gasped, her hand flying to her heart, as she saw a shadowed man's form coming up the darkened porch. Margaret plowed straight into Grace's back when she stopped, almost knocking Grace down.

The shadow moved into the porch light. It was only Vincent. He was dressed in a beautifully cut black suit, crisp white shirt, and black tie. A neat triangle of white handkerchief stuck out of his lapel pocket. He looked incredible. Grace heard Margaret's soft "wow" in her ear.

"Did I startle you, Grace?" His smooth, resonant voice rolled over them.

"A little." Grace hated to say how much or why. Recovering herself, she smiled at Vincent, opening the screen door and starting outside. "I was going out to help bring in my daughter's bags. She's just arrived from Nashville." Grace gestured behind her. "Vincent Westbrooke, this is my daughter, Margaret Jane Conley. Margaret, this is Vincent, one of my neighbors."

Margaret stepped forward as Vincent reached out his hand. He took her hand, and then Grace watched Margaret's eyes jump to Vincent's face in surprise. And then back to his hand.

Grace had a feeling she knew what was happening.

Vincent smiled and reached out to take Margaret's other hand in his. He held both hands up to study them and then looked at Margaret steadily.

"Margaret Jane Conley," he said at last in a silky voice. "I am so very pleased to meet you."

Margaret, never one at a loss for words, actually fumbled with a reply. "I'm very pleased to meet you, too," she said at last.

She looked down to where Vincent still held both her hands in his and frowned slightly. "I don't mean to be rude, Mr. Westbrooke, but did you notice that your hands have become very warm. In fact hot. Are you quite all right?"

"I am fine, Margaret. Just fine." His words seemed like a caress, and he looked down into Margaret's eyes with a deep intensity. "It's simply a small irregularity that happens with me sometimes. Don't let it trouble you." He released Margaret's hands and smiled at her, a soft, gradual, assessing smile. Grace saw that it was a very different smile than the one Vincent usually gave to her.

The two young people stood staring at each other as several

minutes ticked by. Grace felt awkward. She finally cleared her throat and started to make a comment about Vincent's hands and what the heat meant. But then she saw him caution her with a slight shake of his head.

"What brought you by this late, Vincent?" she asked instead. "Is anything wrong?"

He smiled easily. "No. Nothing is wrong, Grace. I was out at a lecture and felt I should stop by to thank you for hosting the get-together for everyone who lives around the River Road this Friday. I'm looking forward to coming."

Grace patted his arm affectionately. "Well, I'm looking forward to having everyone over."

Vincent seemed to recover his poise then and to remember Grace's earlier comments. "Let me help bring Margaret's bags in for you before I walk back home."

"That would be nice." Grace smiled at him.

Margaret led Vincent out to the car to get her luggage. Grace followed to carry in some of Margaret's other boxes and totes. She knew, from experience, that Margaret never traveled light. It took all three of them two trips to bring everything in.

After greeting the dogs, Vince insisted on helping them carry everything upstairs to Margaret's new third-floor apartment. Since the upstairs rooms had been emptied out by Mavis Oakley, Grace had put pieces of furniture from the Nashville house there that she knew Margaret would like and be comfortable with. It pleased Grace to see Margaret's delight in finding the old familiar pieces in the sitting room and bedroom. The subdued Magnolia theme and muted color scheme suited Margaret, too.

Seeing that Margaret was starting to unpack and settle in, Grace walked Vincent back downstairs to see him out.

"Thanks for the help, Vincent." Grace smiled at him as she opened the front door. "You came at the perfect time, just as Margaret arrived."

"Yes. I did." He looked thoughtful. "Thank you for not telling her about my hands yet."

"Does it embarrass you?"

"No. Not at all." Vincent looked surprised. "It's only that

there were extra sensations with Margaret. More than the heat. And it didn't seem to be the right time to discuss it yet."

He paused and studied his hands as if considering this thought before looking up at Grace with a candid stare. "Margaret is the reason I was brought to Tennessee, Grace. I got that witness very strongly. Margaret is the woman I am supposed to spend my life with."

"Wha . . . what?" Grace knew she sounded shocked, but couldn't help it. "How can you possibly know that?"

"I know. The witness was very clear, and the heat strong." Vincent looked at Grace calmly and smiled. "I hope you don't mind, Grace."

"Well, uh . . . no. But, Vincent, you really don't know Margaret very well yet. She can be somewhat temperamental. And she's a little high-strung. She's a musician, a gifted pianist."

"I felt the creativity."

Grace rolled her eyes. "Margaret has very decided plans and goals, Vincent. Marriage is not one of them right now. She plans to continue her studies, possibly do concert work or teach."

"Goals are important."

"There's another problem." Grace felt she needed to be candid. "Margaret is not in a very strong place in her faith. In fact, of all my children, she has resisted religion the most. There were many times Charles had to threaten to discipline Margaret to get her to go to church."

"And?"

"And you're a minister."

Vincent seemed undeterred by her comments. "She's attracted to me, Grace. I could feel it." He smiled. "And I certainly am to her."

"Well, yes, and that's very nice." Grace knew she sounded patronizing, but, really, this conversation was somewhat ridiculous. "But Margaret does not know yet that you are a minister, Vincent. That could be another problem."

Vincent reached out and patted Grace's cheek. "Don't worry. God will work everything out in His right time."

"Yes, but God has never had to deal with Margaret." Grace knew that sounded silly even as she said it.

Vincent laughed. "Well, it will be fun to see how God handles it all, Grace. Won't it?"

He turned to leave, and then turned back toward Grace as an afterthought. "I'll see you in the morning for coffee and muffins. Sleep well."

Grace shut the door and muttered to herself as she made her way up the two flights of stairs to Margaret's rooms. "I admit I hoped life wouldn't be boring if I moved here, but I never counted on it being quite this eventful."

CHAPTER 12

Jack stood on the stone patio behind his house and looked down across the Little River to the Mimosa Inn. He'd come home to eat lunch with Bebe and the girls before heading back over to the office. It was Friday, and it had been a hectic morning. He'd shown several properties and could have shown more this afternoon, but he'd left his hours after lunch open to help Grace set up her backyard for the neighborhood gathering tonight. The weather was perfect—sunny with blue skies and a soft breeze. Jack looked forward to the evening. He was a social animal.

He whistled as he started down the hill. Grace's little shop was open today; he could pop in and visit with her for a short time if she wasn't busy. See what she wanted him to do to help her set up.

As Jack started up the porch of the new Mimosa Crafts Shop, a cluster of tourists came babbling out of the store, carrying mimosa pink shopping bags. Inside, two women were browsing around and talking. He saw no sign of Grace, but as Jack looked around, he saw Margaret come out from the back of the store.

She nodded at Jack in greeting and then held up a handmade, quilted purse to show one of the women. "Believe it or not Mrs. Hensley, I actually found a handbag in the back of the store with the black background you asked me to look for."

The woman snatched it with excitement. "Oh, it's exactly what I wanted, dear! Thank you so much for going back there to look for me. I'll take it and all these nice things, too."

She piled a stack of crafts items onto the check out counter and then turned to her friend. "Are you ready to go, Trudy?'

"Yes. But I want to buy that ceramic Christmas tree in the corner there." She pointed. "I've always wanted one of those. My sister has one that she made, but I'm all thumbs when it comes to making crafts. I am so tickled to find one already made up that I can just buy and take right home." She frowned. "Dear, do you have a box you could pack it in? I wouldn't want it to get broken."

Margaret looked across at Jack, lounging against the wall. "Make yourself useful, Jack Teague, and go in the back of the store and get one of those empty boxes piled up outside the storage room. There's one by the door that Mrs. Gentry's tree should fit neatly inside of. And get some of those newspapers, too, so I can wrap them around the tree."

Jack retrieved the box and helped Margaret pack up the ceramic Christmas tree. She'd rung up both the sales while he was gone. At Margaret's directive, he carried the boxed tree out to Mrs. Gentry's car.

Coming back into the shop, he found Margaret draped over a chair, her feet propped on a tole-painted toy chest. She wore cropped pants, strappy sandals, and a colorful, geometric tunic. She had her hair pulled back into a neat bun, and she looked smart and chic.

"Thank goodness this place is finally quiet for a few minutes." Margaret blew out a long breath. "I haven't had a minute to sit down for the last two hours. There have been people in here all day! And yesterday was even worse."

"You sound rather surprised at the shop's success." Jack perched on a stool and gave her a smug smile.

"Oh, don't you start, too, Jack Teague. I've had various neighbors and friends of my mother's making comments like that to me all day." She frowned. "Who would have ever thought people would actually like and buy all this stuff? It's unbelievable. Did you see that woman going on and on about that ceramic tree? I remember the year Mother made those. She gave one to my grandmother Jane for Christmas, and Jane gave it to her maid—said it was the tackiest thing she had ever seen."

Margaret glanced over to the corner where another Christmas tree sat on the shelf. "It lights up you know. You plug in the cord, and all the little colored lights on the tree limbs light up— so it looks like a real tree."

"You wanna buy the last one?" Jack cocked an eye at her. "Your mom might give you a discount."

Margaret shook her head. "Not hardly. Go look at the price on that tree. It's simply unbelievable someone would pay that for a ceramic Christmas tree."

Jack walked over to look at the green tree—all covered in tiny lights with a star at the top. "I kind of like it. My Aunt Bebe has one sort of like this. It wouldn't be Christmas at our place if Bebe didn't set it up in the front window. Aunt Bebe used to always put a few little gifts for my cousin Roger and I under the little tree, too. We got in trouble one year for unwrapping them early and trying to wrap them back up again so she wouldn't know."

Margaret laughed. "Sounds like you were a rascal even when only a boy." She looked at Jack thoughtfully then. "I guess you're looking for my mother."

"I was. Is she at the house?"

"Yeah, but I wouldn't go up there if I were you. She's having a big fight with my Aunt Myra."

Jack was intrigued. "Grace is having a fight?"

"You got her up on a pedestal, don't you?" Margaret laughed.

"No. I've seen her mad a time or two. I just have a hard time imagining her scrapping with another woman."

Margaret guzzled some water out of a bottle. "It's more of a word fight than a physical one, Jack."

She paused. "Aunt Myra came over from Knoxville to check

out the grand opening of the shop. Mom had invited her and my grandmother Richey, but only Myra could get away today. I was in the back and missed what set Myra off in the beginning, but when I came out into the shop she was all red-faced and practically hollering about how Mother never understood her or something. She was getting real dramatic and waving her arms all around and everything."

Shrugging in annoyance, Margaret drank some more of her water. "Mother, being ever the artful diplomat, suggested they go up to the house to talk. There were a few customers in the shop, and they were getting an earful." She glanced toward the house. "Knowing Mother, she's calmed Myra down by now and has her drinking tea, nibbling cookies, and having a heart-to-heart sister catch-up."

Jack grinned at Margaret. "So that's how you ended up in charge of the store all by yourself."

Margaret bristled. "You act like I can't manage it. I'll have you know I'm doing fine. Mother said she'd have been overwhelmed handling everything herself if I hadn't been here yesterday and today. She never had any idea the shop would be this busy."

"Calm down, Miss Conley. I think you could handle just about anything that came along if you needed to. You're a sharp girl." Jack reached into the candy dish on the check out counter and picked out a peppermint.

"Why, thank you, Jack Teague. I think that was actually a compliment."

"You want more compliments?" He gave her an appraising look. "You don't seem like the type to fish for compliments. Surely you get plenty with those classic blond looks of yours. I'd say the boys fill your ears with compliments all the time."

He paused as he studied her eyes, silvery blue green like her mother's. She was a beauty. Her hair was a deeper blond than Grace's, her lips less full. Margaret was a little shorter than Grace, her figure slimmer. But there was a remarkable resemblance.

She sent him a snippy retort. "Women like compliments on things other than their looks, Jack."

Jack ignored her. "Did your mother look like you when she was younger?"

She crossed her legs on the trunk and leaned back in her chair. "I don't remember. She was just a mom to me. But Dad had her painted. The portrait is in the back hallway beside her bedroom at the Mimosa. She's really gorgeous in it. Check it out sometime. She has on a long, sleek, blue velvet dress."

Margaret gave him a cocky grin. "You've got a crush on my mom, don't you?"

"Is that what you think?" Jack raised an eyebrow.

"No, actually I think you have *rather more* in mind regarding my mother. But not the honorable ring-on-the-finger kind of agenda." She gave Jack an appraising glance of her own. "Frankly, I've been surprised that there's any attraction at all between you and my mother. Especially of my mother toward you."

Jack felt piqued. "Why? You think I've got something lacking?"

"Besides morals? No, not really. It's only that you're not what I would think of as my mother's type. In fact, you're the sort of man Mother always warned Elaine and I to stay far, far away from."

Jack winced at Margaret's honesty. "And what kind of man is that?"

"Good-looking, charming, oozing pheromones, and dangerous."

"Well, thanks!" Jack grinned.

"*And* with a bad reputation." Margaret interrupted him before he could say more. "Don't thank me too soon; I wasn't finished."

She stood up to walk over and lean toward Jack. "You're very pretty, Jack Teague, but I don't want you hurting my mother. She just lost my dad a couple of years ago and then moved over here against all the family's counsel—all on her own. She stubbornly defied us all. Yet, surprisingly, from what I've seen, she's actually doing okay here. The bed-and-breakfast seems to be doing well, and it sort of suits Mother somehow. She's made friends and actually seems happy." Margaret stopped. "She's different here. Sort of confident. More comfortable with herself. It's been kind of nice to see."

Margaret paused as if thinking this out.

"And?" Jack prompted.

She frowned at him. "*And* I don't want her becoming another bullet on your cowboy belt. It would hurt her and cause her to lose respect around here."

"And you think I would do that?" Jack snarled his answer.

She reached up and stretched. "I don't know what you might do, Jack Teague. I just know what I hear."

"You been asking questions about me?" He met her gaze.

She gave him a stubborn look. "I have a right. She's my mother, after all."

Jack bit back an angry reply. He eyed Margaret silently. "Seems to me you're not in much of a position to preach to me. You've done your share of hurting your mother lately. You and your siblings. All stomping around and throwing a fit when Grace wanted to pursue her own life. And follow her own dream. You even tried to make her move into some old folks' retirement center."

"I wasn't the one pushing her to move there." Margaret put her hands on her hips, eyes flashing. "That was more Frank and the others—not me."

Jack grinned, glad to be turning the tables on Margaret. "I didn't exactly hear any tales of how *you* encouraged your mother to follow her heart and her dreams—championed her in wanting to live her own life. Seems like I heard you were right in there calling her stupid and foolish—even bowing up your back and refusing to move over here with her."

Margaret crossed her arms in annoyance, her face flushing. "You don't understand. We felt afraid for her. We didn't think she could do anything like this."

"And you were wrong?" Jack knew his words would nettle her.

"Maybe." She stuck her chin up stubbornly.

"I see. Then *maybe* you might be wrong about me, too."

"It's possible," she agreed reluctantly as a group of new customers let themselves in the door. "We'll see."

Jack took that opportunity to retreat. Taking Margaret's advice, he avoided going up to the house, assuming Myra was still there. Instead, he waited until the evening to see Grace. He found his eyes seeking her out throughout the gathering that night. Watching her. Admiring her poise and ease. She was a consummate entertainer. Circulating around among all the people—gracious, charming, seeing that everyone was taken care of. Spending just the right amount of time with each person before moving on to the next.

"Pretty woman," Roger said at one point, catching Jack's eyes on her.

"Yes, she is," he acknowledged.

"Be careful, buddy." Roger chuckled. "Once you slide down that slippery creek bank, it's hard to get back out."

Jack didn't answer.

"You in over your head already?"

"I don't know, Rog. But she's messing with my mind and my sleep."

"Been with anybody else lately?"

"No." Jack snapped out his reply.

Roger patted him on the back, wisely not making a comment back. "I think I'll go get Samantha to play a game of badminton with Vincent and Margaret. It looks like they're trying to find some partners. Can you keep an eye on Ruby?" He gestured to Ruby who had fallen asleep in the hammock on the patio.

Jack smiled at the sight of Ruby curled up in the middle of the big hammock. "Sure. I'll sit here on the patio and keep a watch over her."

He went over to one of the ice chests and found a wine cooler to drink. It was the closest thing to an adult beverage Grace would allow with children sharing the evening. Several of the men had argued with her about it, but Grace had put her foot down. Jack smiled remembering it.

"Having nice thoughts?" a quiet voice asked.

Jack turned his head toward the sound to see Grace coming across the patio. She wore some sort of floaty culotte skirt with a matching blouse, both in a rich plum shade. Pretty enough to be dressy, casual enough to play games in. Her outfit was simple, yet striking, setting off her figure perfectly. The rich color complimented the shiny, lighter tone of lipstick and nail polish she wore. Even the slides she wore on her feet were dark plum in color. Jack had always been a man to notice details about women—what they wore, how they acted, how they smelled. And Grace was always beautifully put together.

He patted the seat beside him. "Come keep me company. I'm watching Ruby so Roger and Samantha can play badminton."

Jack saw Grace glance toward the hammock with a tender expression.

"Precious child," she said. She picked up a sweater tossed over a nearby chair and draped it across Ruby's legs before she sat down.

Jack caught the soft floral scent of her as she settled into the old metal lawn chair. She slipped off her slides and propped her bare feet up on the chair across from them.

Jack's eyes slid down her legs and across her feet. Agony. He yearned to take her feet into his lap. To run his hands up her legs and under the folds of her plum skirt.

"It's been a nice gathering, hasn't it?" she asked, oblivious to his thoughts.

He nodded. "You've been a good hostess."

"Thanks, and I appreciate your coming early to help set up the games and tables." She pointed out into the yard. "Look what a good time the girls are having playing croquet."

Jack looked out to see Morgan and Meredith laughing and playing with the other children who lived around the River Road.

"The girls were so excited we found that old croquet set in the garage storage room. Plus the badminton racquets and birdies, and the horseshoes." She looked around the property. "This is a wonderful yard for games—so flat and spacious."

Jack agreed. "Where are the dogs?"

"On the back screened porch where they can watch everyone." She laughed. "They were disappointed not to be out here, but with so many people, I couldn't properly keep an eye on them if I'd let them join us."

"It's wonderful how well you've got them trained. I can see a similar gift of management in operation when you gather the girls together for their Scout meetings." He shook his head. "I used to pick them up from their Brownie meetings and always found a noisy chaos. Mrs. Waters is nice, but she had no gift for leadership. You, on the other hand, do."

"Why thank you, Jack. That's a very nice compliment."

"And well deserved. Kyleen told me you'd agreed to take on the fifth-grade Junior Scouts along with your fourth-grade girls because they didn't have a leader either."

"Yes, and Kyleen is going to help me with the combined troop. She is fifteen and has always been a Scout. She would be a Cadette right now if there was an active troop, so I told her she could work on her Cadette credentials as my assistant leader. The girls love having an older teenager helping us out."

"How many girls do you have now?"

"Sixteen. I had eight fourth-grade girls, and now I've added eight fifth-grade girls." She sighed. "There's been more interest since the word has gotten out, but I'm not sure I can manage more. Even with Kyleen."

"Samantha told me you even have all the girls showing up for Scout meetings in their uniforms. How'd you manage that? Daisy said hardly any of their group would wear their uniforms to their Scout meetings last year."

Grace frowned and lifted her chin. "I wear a uniform to every meeting. And I told the girls if they wanted to be in my troop they would have to wear a uniform every week as well. Any girl who does not come in uniform cannot carry leadership roles or have snacks."

Jack chuckled. "I'd say that last one did it."

"It does tend to be influential." She giggled. "I make nice snacks. Or we all make them together when the girls arrive."

Jack propped his feet up beside hers on the chair, wanting to make physical contact with her. Leaning his bare calf against hers, he felt a sensual thrill.

She grew quiet for a moment, and Jack knew she felt the heat building between them. He trailed a finger along her arm on the chair.

His voice turned almost husky as he continued their conversation, trying to remain casual. "Freda Clark and Sally Carson told me you collected donations from the businesses around the area to buy uniforms, Scout pins, and books for many of the girls in the troop who couldn't afford them."

"Some of the families around here are not very well-to-do." She pulled her arm away from his tracing finger. "There are some single mothers and some girls who don't have much. I wanted all the girls to have uniforms without pressure on the families."

His voice was soft. "You're a good person, Grace Conley. I'll bet you were a good mother, too."

"She was an excellent mother," said a voice behind them. Margaret came up, gave her mother a kiss on the cheek, and flounced into one of the chairs across from them.

"Are you behaving yourself, Jack?" She eyed his leg leaning up against her mother's with a raised eyebrow.

"Absolutely." He made no effort to move his leg. "How was your badminton game?"

"Vincent and I beat Roger and Samantha by ten points. Samantha took it gracefully, but Roger is still grousing over it." She got up to go rummage in one of the coolers to find a cola.

Jack laughed. "Sounds like Roger. He always was a sore loser."

Margaret sat down again and propped her pretty bare legs up on the side of her mother's chair. Jack saw Grace pat Margaret's leg affectionately.

"Seems like I saw Vincent Westbrooke trailing around after

you most of the evening." Jack couldn't resist teasing Margaret. He always got such sparks when he did. "It seems like you've captured our young preacher's attention."

Margaret's eyes flared. "That's one of the reasons I came over here to hide out with the two of you. I was finally able to make my escape while Vincent got tied up talking to Berke and Sally Carson."

"You're not attracted to Vincent?" Jack grinned at her. "A lot of young girls in the valley come to church on Sunday just to get a look at him. But it's seldom that one of them ever attracts an eye from him. Most would say you're lucky."

"Well, I don't feel lucky!" Margaret snapped her answer.

"Margaret, mind your manners," her mother chided. "Vincent is a fine young man. There's no reason to speak derogatorily about him."

Margaret heaved an exaggerated sigh. "Mother, Vincent Westbrooke is a *preacher*. And a preacher in a poky little town. Nothing personal, Jack—but this is just *not* my kind of place. And I am absolutely *not* cut out to be linked up with a preacher."

Jack grinned. "You've got morality issues?"

"No, that's you, Jack!" Margaret sent him an impish smile. "I just have ambitions, and I see no sense in letting Vincent Westbrooke think I have any interest in him whatsoever."

Jack caught her gaze. "You're lying to yourself, Margaret, if you think you have no interest in him. I've watched you around him. You're attracted to him all right."

She glared at Jack. "Well, so what if I am? That doesn't mean I'm going to *do* anything about it. I was attracted to the cute UPS man who came to the shop door this morning, too, but I'm not going to encourage him either."

"Why, you're a snob, Margaret Conley!" Jack loved goading her.

"No, I just know you need to be careful who you get involved with. Some people may be pretty and attractive, but they're the wrong people for you."

A memory flashed in Jack's mind. His voice quieted. "I know what you mean about that."

Grace reached over to put a hand on his while Margaret was preoccupied in drinking her cola. She smiled at him softly.

Dang woman. She'd gotten to where she could read his mind. She knew he was remembering Celine. How did she do that?

Margaret's voice interrupted his thoughts. "Your little twins are flirting with those boys over there, Jack Teague."

"What?" He sat up and looked around to where the girls were still playing croquet. "What are you talking about? They're only playing croquet. They're not even ten years old."

Margaret blew a stray hair back off her face. "Ten or not, they're flirting with that cute little Dean Clark and the friend he brought with him. What was the other boy's name, Mother?"

"Neal Hancock. He lives farther down the River Road. Dean asked if he could bring a friend so he wouldn't be the only boy."

"Well, your girls are flirting with Dean Clark and Neal Hancock." She gave Jack a smug, Cheshire-cat grin. "Must take after their father."

Jack found his heart pounding. "Do you really think so? Maybe I should do something. Those boys are thirteen. Morgan and Meredith are not even ten yet. They don't know anything about boys."

Grace's soothing voice spoke out. "Settle down, Jack. This is only innocent childhood flirting. It's normal." Grace's calm hand came to rest on his again.

She directed a critical glance at Margaret. "And quit teasing Jack about his girls. It's bad enough the two of you spar with each other all the time, but don't bring Morgan and Meredith into it."

"Oh, all right." Margaret flounced back in her chair.

Jack continued to watch the girls, still uncomfortable with Margaret's observation. "Do girls really start thinking about boys this early?"

Margaret rolled her eyes. "Honestly, Jack. Didn't *you* start thinking about girls that early? Get real. Girls and boys start trying to get the attention of the opposite sex in preschool now."

Still seeming to sense his discomfort, Grace patted his hand once more. "I'll talk to them about some things if you'd like, Jack. It's probably time they had some personal talks. Especially after what happened with Ruby." Jack saw Grace glance toward the small figure huddled sleeping in the hammock.

Margaret looked toward Ruby, too. "You know, a couple of times I thought I felt someone watching me around here."

Jack heard Grace gasp in reaction. "Where were you when this happened?"

"Taking a walk down the street once. Out in the backyard another time. Wading my feet down at the river the last time. It really creeped me out." She wrinkled her nose.

"Do you think it was just your imagination, since you've heard so many stories about Crazy Man?" Grace studied her daughter.

"No." Margaret looked thoughtful. "Twice I thought I actually saw someone. You know, like a shadow or a movement behind a tree or a shrub."

Jack caught Grace's eye questioningly.

She looked at Jack with a worried frown. "Margaret doesn't make things up like this, Jack, even though she tends to be dramatic at times."

Jack sat up to lean toward Margaret. This worried him. "You should have told us about this before, Margaret. We're trying very hard to catch this man. We really don't know if he might be dangerous or not. If you see or sense anything again, you come straight to me and tell me. You hear?"

"I'll tell *my mother* if I see anyone again." She gave him a deliberate look. "You're not my father, Jack Teague. So don't give me orders."

She jumped up and flounced off toward the yard. "I think I'm going to go play croquet with the kids."

"Did I say something wrong?" Jack asked as soon as Margaret was out of earshot.

"No." Grace patted his hand again. "What you said sounded

like something Charlie would have said to her. It just made her remember."

Jack scowled. "Well, since she's made it clear she won't come to me, will you let me know if she hears or sees anything again?"

"I will. And let's don't talk about it anymore. Here come Samantha and Roger. They're having such a happy evening tonight. Let's not spoil it by having any more conversations about that demented man."

CHAPTER 13

A week slipped by, and Grace had guests at the inn. They sat gathered in the dining room helping themselves to the Sunday buffet breakfast Grace always served. Grace and Margaret sat in the kitchen with plates of their own.

"Good morning," Vincent said, letting himself in the back kitchen door. "I see there are several cars outside. You must be busy today."

Margaret mumbled something about how their being busy didn't seem to stop some people from making themselves at home. Grace hid a smile as she went to pour Vincent a cup of coffee.

Vincent was dressed to preach in a tailored, navy, pin-striped suit, and he looked like a million dollars. He even smelled good—wearing some sort of musky scent. Grace watched Margaret assess him covertly. A woman would have to be dead not to notice Vincent Westbrooke, yet Margaret did her best to act cool and disinterested whenever he came around.

Grace put Vincent's cup of coffee on the kitchen table. "Go in the dining room and fix yourself a plate." She smiled at him. It felt like having Mike or Kenneth back at home for Vincent to drop in every morning. "And introduce yourself while you're there. The Quinn family is leaving for Ohio this morning, but the McAllisters and the Bridges are staying over another night. They might like to visit the church service this morning. You could ask them."

"I will." He ran his fingers lightly across Margaret's shoulder as he passed her chair. "I hear you are visiting the church this morning, too. You'll enjoy hearing Mrs. Carson play the piano. She has a gift."

"So I've heard." Margaret's tone was sarcastic.

Grace shook her head at Margaret as Vincent went into the dining room. "There's no need to be rude."

Margaret rolled her eyes and countered in a derisive tone. "Well, it's doubtful I will be impressed with the performance of dear, old Mrs. Carson, playing piano in the Creekside Independent Presbyterian Church in Townsend, Tennessee."

"There's no need to be smug and arrogant, either." Grace gave Margaret a critical glance. "Although Mrs. Carson is almost eighty, she's a beautiful, gracious woman. And you may be surprised at how well she plays."

"Right. I'm sure I will." Margaret offered her mother a contrived smile.

She got up to get herself another cup of coffee. "Don't worry, Mother. I'll be nice. I promised you I'd visit, and I will. But I'm only doing this to help your business and your image here in the valley. I want the inn to continue to be successful—and the shop, too. So I'm doing everything I can to cooperate. I hope you appreciate that."

"I do appreciate it." Grace leaned over to kiss Margaret on the cheek as she sat back down. Margaret had come around about the changes in Grace's life more than Grace had expected her to, and Grace was grateful. "I also appreciate the good reports you've given to Elaine and the boys. I actually think they're all planning to come over when it's time for your school to begin."

Margaret grinned. "I talked them into packing up the rest of my stuff and bringing it over Labor Day weekend so you and I don't have to drive over to get it. I think Frank was eager *not* to have me come back to Nashville. He was *very* cooperative."

She took a bite of the egg and sausage casserole on her plate. "I also selfishly wanted them to come to my opening concert at the college. The music department is presenting a concert that holiday weekend so visiting parents can come. It makes the college look good to show off the school's talent. The school is hosting an art show and some sporting events, too."

"Well, I'm excited." Grace peeked into the dining room to check that everyone was comfortable. "It will be the first time all of my children have visited me here."

"Well, they may not be crazy about everything. Don't expect too many compliments." Margaret was always so candid. "But they will love the river and the yard. This place is remote, but the property is pretty. And the mountains are nearby."

Vincent came back into the room carrying a loaded plate of egg and sausage casserole, biscuits, and fruit, and then sat down at the kitchen table with them to begin to eat. Margaret all but ignored him, applying herself to her food and reading the Sunday paper.

Grace noticed that Margaret's actions never fazed Vincent, no matter how often she snubbed him. He always treated her with cordial warmth and charm no matter how she acted or what she said.

"Here's the blueberry jam you like." Grace put a jar on the table in front of Vincent's plate.

"Thanks." He smiled at Grace—not a rascally smile like Jack's, but a pleasant smile. It crinkled his eyes and brought out the cleft in his chin.

She smiled back at him. "You're welcome."

Vincent spread jam lavishly on a biscuit and then dug into his breakfast with relish for a few minutes. He caught Margaret's eyes when she glanced over at him and gave her a knowing smile that made Margaret's cheeks heat up.

Vincent pushed back his plate then and started on his coffee. "You both might be interested in knowing we're having a special speaker at the church next Sunday. He's an old colleague of mine from Montreat. I've known him since I was a boy."

"What's Montreat?" Margaret asked, looking up from her perusal of the Sunday newspaper.

"It's a four-thousand-acre religious conference center in the mountains of North Carolina, not far from Asheville." Vince focused those intense blue eyes on her. "My family lives in Montreat, and I grew up there. Before I came here to Creekside I worked as the conference director with Montreat's youth and young adult ministry program."

"You mean you grew up right in the middle of a religious center?" Margaret wrinkled her nose.

Vince smiled. "I did. There were always ongoing conferences for churches and organizations, musical events and meetings of artists' groups, educational association gatherings, and special retreats going on. It was never dull. And the area is beautiful there. Montreat sits amid twenty-five-hundred acres of wilderness."

"Well, that explains a lot," Margaret mumbled. "Growing up in some religious center in the boonies of the mountains *has* to have its effects."

Covering for Margaret's rudeness, Grace asked with interest, "What do your parents do there?"

Vincent took a sip of his coffee. "My father is in marketing and development. My mother works in several organizational capacities and is usually a greeter and hostess when new groups come in."

"That sounds interesting. Do you have any brothers or sisters?"

"I have one younger sister, Laura. She always loved the outdoors—dragged me along collecting mushrooms and biological species from an early age. She went into plant pathology, is working on her PhD at North Carolina State."

Margaret looked up with interest. "Looks like she's going somewhere with her life." She studied him. "With a smart family like yours, how did you end up in the ministry and in a poky little church in Townsend, Tennessee? Couldn't you have done more with yourself?"

"Margaret!" Grace was shocked.

Vincent, unruffled by Margaret's remarks, reached across the table and put a hand on hers. "I came here for a reason, Margaret. And because I was called. You know, there is a great deal you don't know about me." He said the latter in a softer, silkier voice.

"Well, there's a lot you don't know about me, too." Margaret lifted her chin, but then her eyes went back to where Vincent still held her hand. She tried to pull it away, but he held on to it for a minute.

"I may know more about you than you think. I know you cherish a dream in your heart to write music—but you've never told anyone about it. You didn't think it fit in with the program. I know you wrote a song when you were young, but that someone laughed at you over it and it hurt you."

Margaret flushed and jerked her hand free from Vincent's. "Did Mother tell you that?" She flashed an angry look at Grace.

Grace shook her head. "I didn't even know that. Is it true, Margaret?"

Margaret stood up, her face flushed. "I don't like people probing into my private life, Mr. Westbrooke. Even pastors."

"Not even God?" he asked pleasantly, standing up also.

She flashed back a quick answer. "I don't believe in that sort of thing."

"Perhaps not now," he answered her. "See you in church, Margaret."

He started for the door. "And thank you for the breakfast, Grace."

"You know you're always welcome." She smiled at him.

Margaret flounced out of the room when he left. "That man infuriates me. Nosy. Intrusive. Always hanging around here. Never taking the hint that I'm not interested in him. He's insufferable."

Margaret was stormy throughout the early part of the church service an hour later. Grace felt pleased Margaret had still been willing to come. Margaret was volatile sometimes, and even now, in church, Grace found herself a little worried about what Margaret might do. However, as the service moved on, Grace noticed that Margaret's mood seemed to change.

Watching her, Grace saw Margaret's eyes focused on Jo Carson at the piano in front of the church. The congregation was standing and singing at this point in the worship service. It was the practice of the church to frequently slip from bits of one hymn or song to another, as though the tunes were linked together in a medley. The congregation used their hymnals at certain points, while at other times they followed the words of the songs projected on a screen behind the narthex.

Vincent led the congregational singing himself, in a fine tenor voice. He and Jo Carson seemed to have a special kind of communion about what direction the songs should go in each Sunday. The choir followed along flexibly with whatever pattern they set. Several in the choir had gifted voices and often sang solos.

The services at Creekside were quite different from what Grace had been used to in the big Presbyterian church in Nashville. Vincent's messages were more like teachings and very Bible-based. He included informal times in which the congregation could offer prayer requests or praises. Sometimes he let members give short testimonies about what God had done in their lives. The informality took some getting used to, but Grace liked the differences now.

She had also learned to take her Bible to church every Sunday. Vincent always had the congregation turning to passages while he preached. Grace had felt odd the first Sunday when she realized everyone was participating in the service in this way while she didn't even have a Bible with her.

The service had moved on to the offertory now, and Jo Carson played the piano while the Sunday offering was being taken up. She moved through a medley that included parts of several old hymns that had always been favorites of Grace's.

Margaret leaned over toward Grace to whisper. "She's hardly even looking at her music. Once I even saw her playing with her eyes closed."

"She's very good." Grace whispered this comment back and smiled, glad Margaret seemed to be enjoying the service. Grace hadn't been able to persuade her to even go to church for several years.

Leaning in again, Margaret added, "There were some times earlier when I don't think she was sure what she was going to play. She'd stop and look toward Vincent; he'd start to sing something, and she'd pick up and follow him. It was odd. Sometimes she seemed to move into a new chorus after a completed one, and he would follow her. It's as though they were tuned in to each other."

The offertory ended, and Vincent moved into his Scripture lesson and message. He preached on finding your true calling and vocation in the Lord. It made Margaret squirm. Grace wasn't sure if that was because something in the message made Margaret uncomfortable or if Vincent's compelling voice and intense blue eyes made her uncomfortable. He was a very charismatic speaker.

As the service ended, Margaret surprised Grace by pulling her back from starting out of the church. "I want to go talk to the pianist," she said.

Jo still sat at the piano bench talking to another parishioner.

Grace spoke to her as they walked up. "I'm Grace Conley, in case you've forgotten my name, Mrs. Carson. I own the Mimosa Inn next door to the church."

"Yes. And I missed your lovely gathering last week because I had a cold." Jo smiled and nodded toward Grace cordially.

"This is my daughter Margaret. She's a music major at Maryville—and a pianist. She wanted to meet you."

"I'm pleased to meet a fellow pianist." Jo reached out a hand toward Margaret, and Margaret slipped her hand into Jo's for a moment in greeting.

Margaret moved closer to the piano. "I'd be interested in seeing the music you're playing from. You did such diverse medleys, and I liked the way the songs flowed from one to the other so smoothly. Is that a technique you learned in music school?"

Jo Carson chuckled softly. "No, child. I never had the opportunity to go to music school or college."

"Well, who did you study under individually?" Margaret was curious.

"I never had formal lessons, child. We had the old piano in our home that had belonged to my grandmother, and I picked up playing by ear. Started early, I was told. My father said I just had the gift for it. Later an aunt spent some time teaching me to read music and gave me a hymnal to practice from. Lord, I remember being so excited to get that hymnbook. Over the years, I learned every single hymn in that old book."

Grace saw that Margaret's mouth had dropped open.

"You never took formal lessons?" Margaret's voice sounded disbelieving. "But how did you play all those songs in the service without music? How did you follow? And sometimes I thought for sure you were hearing a song you already knew and then moved into playing it."

"Oh, honey, I was playing by the Spirit then. A church service belongs to the Lord, and sometimes He just gives me the song He wants to have sung. I hear it within, and then I give a nod to Vincent and I play it. Sometimes he is hearing the same thing within. And sometimes he hears the instructions first, and he nods to me and I follow. It's nice how God orchestrates it. So if it seemed to go well, He deserves the credit."

Even Grace had trouble following that explanation, and Margaret, for once, was speechless.

Jo Carson smiled. "I started playing for this church as a young girl of about sixteen, and I've been playing here ever since. It's a kindness that God has continued to let me serve Him in this way for so long."

Jo Carson's son Berke and his wife Sally came up to join them then. They all lived a short distance down the street on the River Road. Grace knew Berke and Sally had come back home to move into the old Carson homeplace with Jo after Berke's father died. Berke and Sally's two children were grown, and Berke and Sally had wanted to leave the northern winters. Berke worked for a computer repair company in the area and Sally as the secretary for the Creekside Church.

"Are you ready to go, Mother?" Berke asked. "If so, I'll help you up and out to the car."

"It was nice to meet you, Margaret." Jo said as her son linked her arm in his and helped her walk down the steps from the piano.

"Yes, it was nice to meet you, too." Margaret said these words quietly, staring after Jo Carson.

Sally watched them start up the aisle. "Her eyesight is getting worse. She has macular degeneration, you know. It isn't safe for her to try to get down these steps on her own anymore."

"But how does she see to play?" Margaret was incredulous.

Sally smiled. "She knows the keyboard in her heart. At home, she might play for hours. She can still play about any song she listens to often enough. We've gotten her tapes of the classics, and she plays many of those by ear. But hymns are still her favorites. It's a wonderful gift she has."

Sally talked then about what a nice time she and Berke had at the gathering at the Mimosa the week before. Grace noticed Margaret simply continued staring quietly after Jo Carson.

At the door of the church, Vincent stood talking to his congregants as they left the service. He took Margaret's hand, and Grace knew from the way Margaret acted that she was affected by his touch.

He smiled at her. "I'm glad you talked to Jo Carson. She said she'd like you to come and visit her one day. She'd like to hear you play."

"I'll try to do that." Margaret offered a forced smile.

"I enjoyed your message," Grace added.

She and Margaret walked down the church steps and started down the street toward the Mimosa. As they reached the door to the screened porch, Grace looked over to see tears streaming down Margaret's face.

"Why, Margaret, what's the matter?"

"She plays totally by ear." Margaret sobbed. "She's never taken a formal lesson, and she can play like that. So well. So freely. It seems so unfair. After all the hours and hours and hours of lessons and practice I've had. That someone could just play like that. Without any of the work and the agony and the criticisms and the struggle."

Grace reached over to hug her child. "She practiced and practiced, too, Margaret. Didn't you hear her say so? And Sally said
she still does. It hasn't come without work and labor on her
part, either."

"But she didn't have to endure all the lessons!" Margaret
sniffed, the tears rolling freely down her cheeks now.

"Maybe you're looking at it wrong. You had the *opportunity*
to have lessons. I don't think Jo Carson ever did. If I remember,
Sally told me Berke's mother grew up with very little. Her family lived up in the mountains, and there were nine children. I
doubt there was money for lessons. Wasn't it good that God
gave her a way to use her gift? Without that, she wouldn't have
been able to do anything with her talent. There would have been
no opportunity."

Margaret frowned as she followed Grace from the porch into
the kitchen. "Well, that's a pretty story, Mother. But it's hard
not to feel resentful when you've worked as hard as I have—and
then to meet someone who can sit down and play like that without having had to study at all."

Grace dropped her purse and Bible on the kitchen table. "I
don't think you need to feel jealous of Jo Carson, Margaret. You
possess a beautiful gift of your own—well developed and well
exercised. There's hardly a comparison between the two of you."

Margaret sat down moodily in a kitchen chair. "I didn't
know Vincent could sing and lead music. You didn't mention
that to me."

"I didn't think to." Grace sat down at the table to join Margaret.

"He must have musical training to be able to do that. But he's
never mentioned it to me." She scowled.

Grace chuckled. "It's not as though you strike up many conversations with Vincent Westbrooke, Margaret. There may be a
great deal about Vincent you don't know."

"You sound just like him!" Margaret glared at her mother.
"That's what he said this morning."

"I'm sorry." Grace shrugged. "I forgot he said that. But you
can hardly blame Vincent that you know so little about him."

Margaret fidgeted with the strap on her shoulder bag. "It's really amazing how he and Jo can tune in to each other to perform the music the way they do. She said they hear the music within. How do they do that?"

Grace thought for a minute. "In the same way God talks to you in your heart when you pray and ask for answers. Or in the same way you get a leading from God about what you should do sometimes, I think. Only they get it about the music to use in the service."

Margaret caught Grace's eyes then. "This isn't the kind of church we've always belonged to, Mother. It's different."

"You don't like it?"

"I don't know." Margaret looked thoughtful and sighed.

Grace looked at the clock. "I have homemade chicken salad left over from yesterday. Would that be all right for lunch? We could eat fruit and biscuits with it. I have some of both from the buffet this morning."

"That would be fine." Margaret stood up. "But let's go change first."

She started down the hall, and then turned to look back at Grace.

"I feel different here, Mother. It's as though all the rules I've lived by don't seem to apply. It's sort of unsettling."

Grace smiled. "To me it's been freeing, Margaret. I felt very restricted and bound in my life in Nashville, in many ways, but I never realized it until I came here."

"You do seem different here. And happier." Margaret grinned. "I doubt you miss Jane climbing up your back all the time."

Grace winced. "No." She raised her eyes to Margaret's. "I don't mean to be disrespectful to Charles's mother and your grandmother, but it was hard always knowing that she disliked me."

"She always tried to make me hate you."

"That's rather harsh, Margaret." Grace caught her breath.

"No, it's the truth. And I always felt torn between the two of you. Never knowing who I should try to please or emulate."

"Well, it seems like deciding who to emulate should have

been easy. Jane was a concert pianist. She'd experienced the success you dream of. I know you admired her."

"I admired her talent." Margaret paused. "But she has a cruel streak. I didn't admire that. Sometimes she was cruel to me."

Grace looked at Margaret in surprise. "Was she? I never knew that. I thought she doted on you."

"As long as I did what she wanted. Thought what she wanted me to think. Acted like she wanted me to act. She was very controlling, Mother."

"She was with me, too. But I never realized she acted that way with you."

Margaret shook her head. "Honestly, Mother. Jane was controlling with all of us. With Daddy, with the boys, with Elaine, with me—and with you. Everyone bowed and scraped to her. I was always torn between whether I loved and admired her or whether I hated her."

"Margaret!" Grace exclaimed. "This is your grandmother you're talking about."

Margaret put her hands on her hips. "Oh, please. Will you deny that one of the reasons you wanted to move here was to get away from Grandmother Jane? She was horrid to you for as long as I can remember. I used to wonder how you could stand it. As I got older, I got angry at you for how you let Jane treat you. For how you let her insult you and get away with it."

"I had no idea you felt like that." Grace twisted her hands. "She was Charles's mother. I had grown accustomed to her ways. I tried to get along with her for your father's sake. He always asked me to overlook her ways when she acted unpleasant or rude. He said it was simply the way she was. He wanted there to be peace."

"Yeah, I hated that, too, about Daddy. He never stood up for you when Jane went after you. He just let her verbally abuse you. We all did. It was an awful feeling sometimes, Mother."

Grace felt shocked at these revelations. Tears started in her eyes. She couldn't help it. She hated to think her children had felt these things without her knowing it. How they must have disrespected her!

Margaret gave her a small smile. "In a funny way, I was proud of you when you stood up to us all and said you were moving over here regardless of what we thought. I mean, we were all mad because it wasn't like you. But even while I was mad, I was sort of proud of you."

She came back to give Grace a hug. "And since I've been living over here with you, I'm more proud of you. If I haven't said so, I want to now. You're running a business and doing it well. You've opened a shop and are selling those crafts we all thought you were crazy to make. It's kind of cool, Mom. You're becoming your own person here. It's sort of neat."

"Well, thanks, Margaret. Those are nice compliments." Grace wiped some tears away, still a little overcome. "And I'm sorry I disappointed you before. It wasn't an easy situation with Jane. I always tried to make peace. It seemed like the only solution given how your father felt."

Margaret looked thoughtful. "It wasn't only you. I've let her push me around, too. Dictate to me too much. Hurt me and humiliate me without fighting back. I haven't handled her much better. Except that most of the time she liked me more."

"Because she thought you were exactly like her."

"But I'm not!" Margaret's face grew stormy. "I don't want to be like her! She has a dark heart. I want to have a good heart."

Grace put a hand out to touch Margaret's cheek. "You do have a good heart, Margaret."

"Maybe. I don't know. I feel all disquieted lately. Like there is something I want that I don't understand. Like there is something pulling at me."

"Do you want to talk about it? We can if you'd like."

Grace waited quietly while Margaret thought about this.

"If you were feeling all confused and stuff, what would you do, Mom?"

Grace's eyes moved automatically to the Bible she had left on the kitchen table.

"Don't even say it," Margaret warned, following her eyes. "You'll sound like Vincent. He told me out of the blue one morning—when you'd gone out of the kitchen—that all the an-

swers I needed were in the Lord. Just like that, without my saying anything that would lead him to say anything like that. I
swear, Mother, his kind of religion gives me the creeps sometimes."

"He's probably right about the Bible being where the answers
are, Margaret."

"Maybe for some people. But I'm not sure I'm cut out to be
the religious type." She lifted one shoulder and then started
down the hall again to go change her clothes.

"I think I'll be glad when school starts again," Margaret said
as she started up the stairway, almost talking to herself. "That's
probably why I'm feeling restless."

Grace looked after her daughter thoughtfully. There seemed
to be a lot of changes working in Margaret right now. And for
Grace, every day seemed to bring new revelations about what
people had been thinking about her that she'd never known before.

CHAPTER 14

As Jack crossed the swinging bridge on his way to work the next day, he saw Vince sitting on a bench by the river with his head down and his hands dropped between his legs. Either he was dejected or praying. It was hard to tell. If dejected, Jack figured it was over Margaret Conley. He certainly didn't envy any guy who tried to take Margaret on.

Feeling sympathetic, Jack walked the half block down Creekside Lane to where Vincent sat. Vince's dog, Joel, greeted Jack with doggy enthusiasm, weaving around Jack's legs joyously, his tail wagging like a happy flag. Jack reached down to scratch the dog's ears.

"Morning, Jack." Vincent looked up with a smile. The boy wore old shorts and a T-shirt this morning, but still managed to look polished. Scooting over on the bench, Vince made a place for Jack to sit down.

"Couldn't decide if you were praying or crying over a woman when I looked down from the bridge and saw you." Jack dropped down beside Vincent and gazed out over the Little River. The sun sparkled over the water, making a pretty sight.

Vincent turned amused eyes toward Jack. "And what woman do you think I might be crying over?"

Jack directed a pointed look down the road toward the Mimosa. "Those Conley women could drive a man to prayer or tears. I should know."

Vincent grinned. "I'm not concerned about Margaret. If she's the One, the Lord will work things out in due time."

"Sounds like the kind of thing a preacher would say. Well-spoken. But there's a man under those preacher's robes, too. I'd say he's experiencing a little frustration."

"Is that what you're experiencing, Jack? A little frustration? Or is it more?"

Jack frowned at him. "You're got a gift for redirecting conversations, Preacher. Did you learn that in theology school?"

"Maybe I learned it from the Lord. And maybe you could use getting a little closer to Him yourself."

"Now you're making me wish I hadn't stopped by to say hello."

Vincent picked up a rock and skimmed it across the water. "Were you ever close to God, Jack? Maybe as a kid?"

"What makes you think I'm not now?" Jack felt annoyed.

Vince skimmed a few more rocks across the water, not answering.

Jack scowled. "Okay. I got converted as a kid, if that's what you're asking. But I drifted off in my teens, I guess. Girls chased after me, and I enjoyed them. I always got cast in the Bad Boy role, no matter what really happened. I guess I settled in to the pattern, justified or not sometimes. What was the point in fighting it?"

"But you married. I heard you were a good husband. And I know you're a good father."

Jack's voice grew bitter. "Yeah, and what good did that do me? Celine took off and left me. Wanted better things than me, the girls, or Townsend, Tennessee. Flitted back off to Hollywood. And the fast life there."

"You mad at God about that?"

"Sometimes." Jack surprised himself with his honesty. "And sometimes I'm mad that a lot of good Christian folks suggested I must have cheated on Celine or she wouldn't have run off on me. Seems like I also recall some other good Christian people told me I drove my daddy to an early grave, too. I guess I've come to think rather poorly of Christians and their ways of judgment and caring. I haven't been overly eager to be counted in their ranks."

"But you come to church. You bring the girls."

Jack was quiet.

"You're a smarter man than you pretend to be, Jack. You've been hurt in the past and been angry, and you've taken on a role to protect yourself. You've equated Christianity—and God—with the flaws of Christian people. And forgotten that all people have flaws . . ."

"That all have sinned and come short of the glory of God?" Jack interrupted to quote the Scripture sarcastically.

Vincent shrugged.

"And so what's your answer, Preacher? You think you or I can fix all those people? You think you can fix the church?"

"No." Vincent looked at Jack with those intense blue eyes of his. "I can only fix myself and my relationship with God. Even as a minister, that is all I am totally responsible for. And that's all you're responsible for."

"It's a little late for an old dog like me to change, Vincent. I have a reputation around here that people are not going to let me escape from easily, even if I wanted to change."

"You don't really believe that," Vincent said. His cell phone rang, interrupting their talk. Vincent pulled it out to take the call.

He hung up and turned to Jack, putting a hand on Jack's arm. "Your mother just had a heart attack, Jack. She's been taken into Blount Hospital. Bebe is with her. They tried to call you first. We'll need to head over there right now. It's serious."

The next hours were a nightmare. The agony of the time seven years ago when Jack's father had died haunted him. He didn't want to lose his mother, too.

He paced the floor of the hospital waiting area. Vincent sat with his head in his hands. This time Jack knew he was praying. Jack saw Bebe's lips moving several times, too. She was praying, also. He knew Roger and Samantha were praying quietly, holding hands tensely, worried about Althea. But Jack couldn't even find words to pray. He didn't feel worthy to ask favors of God. Vince was right. He'd blamed God for the misguided ways of people, blamed God for every time things didn't work out fairly for him, and blamed God for Celine's leaving him. He'd even faulted God for taking his father early. Jack was in no place to ask favors of God.

Samantha made a call on her cell phone. She looked toward Jack when she hung up. "Grace is going to pick up the girls at Bible School. You know they've been going every day this week. Grace has Ruby, now, and she said she'd pick up Daisy and the twins as soon as the program lets out. She'll talk to them. She said to tell you not to worry." Sam looked down, tears starting in her eyes. "Grace said to tell you she would be praying, too."

Jack felt like kicking the wall. Here was another good person praying. What was the matter with him? Here his own mother lay battling death, and he couldn't even find words to pray for her.

By the time the morning slipped away, Jack felt haggard. Althea had made it through surgery and was in recovery. The doctor had been out and told them she was holding her own, but only barely. He couldn't be sure if she would pull through.

Then he came out a second time. The report was better. He now thought Althea would make it. That she was going to recover. Samantha burst into tears and hugged Roger. Jack hugged his Aunt Bebe, his tears falling, too.

Jack was able to go in to see his mother a little later—at about two. She looked pale, full of tubes and still unconscious. It frightened Jack to look at her. To think she might die. That he might still lose her.

"It may be several hours before she regains full consciousness," the doctor told him when Jack went back out to join the family. "But I think she's going to make it. She's strong."

"Praise God," Bebe said, sitting down with the emotion of the day's events overcoming her. She put her face in her hands and wept.

Vincent went to sit with her and comfort her. He had the

words to say she needed to hear. He was only a kid and he had the words to say. It shamed Jack. He should have been able to offer her some comfort.

"I'm going outside for a while," he mumbled to Roger. "I need some air. I'll be back a little later."

He got in his car and drove. Aimlessly at first. Heading back toward Townsend from Maryville, just wanting to get away from the guilt and pressure he felt.

Vincent was right. Jack had been mad at God. He'd blamed God for things that weren't His fault. He'd lived the devil of a life these years. And let his mother down. He knew she felt disappointed in him. And, now, maybe he'd never have a chance to tell her he was sorry. Maybe never have a chance to even try to change.

His car turned off on a familiar side road, and he pulled up in front of the Shady Grove. He wanted a drink. Just one or two to steady him. To get him through this awful moment. Then he'd drive back to the hospital.

In the bar he found Ashleigh Anne. She'd heard about Althea. She was sweet, and she felt sorry for him. He needed that. Needed someone to feel sorry for him.

He drank too much. He didn't remember how much. Just remembered that he started to feel better. To feel numb. To not hurt. He thought he remembered Ashleigh leading him out of the bar. But everything was fuzzy. And then he stopped remembering anything at all.

A long time later, Jack thought he heard banging on a door. And then voices. Women arguing. He tried to shake himself awake. To open his eyes. Lord, his head hurt. He scrunched his eyes open to look up, and he saw Grace.

Grace? What was she doing here? And where was he?

He tried to pull himself up, and then saw Ashleigh Anne standing in the doorway. He looked around in confusion and saw that he was in her bed, the sheets and covers a tangle around him. And Ashleigh wearing some little scrap of a nightgown.

Mercy! What had he done? How had he gotten here?

He tried to sit up and felt his head would split wide open.

Grace looked down at him with disgust. "Your mother needs you and is asking for you. I told Roger I'd try to find you. Bebe came home and took the girls to her house earlier, so I was free to come and look for you."

Jack shook his head, trying to clear it. He made another effort to sit up, and found that he was only wearing his boxer shorts. He looked to Ashleigh for answers, and she only shrugged.

Grace ignored everything and handed him his pants from off a chair. "Get dressed, Jack. And go wash your face and brush your teeth. Puke if you need to. But then we're going to get to the hospital to see your mother. Roger says she's getting anxious calling for you. And she doesn't need to get upset right now."

Jack's head pounded as he attempted to pull on his pants. It was even worse when he leaned over to put on his socks.

He glanced up at Grace. She was expressionless.

"You want some coffee?" Ashleigh asked from the doorway. "I got some instant. I can make you a Styrofoam cup to go."

He nodded at her. And she turned and headed toward her kitchen.

Jack looked at Grace again as he buttoned his shirt. "How did you know where to find me?"

"I went looking for your car. Roger told me some places to look. I found your red Jeep at the Shady Grove, and the bartender told me where to find you." She knelt down on the floor and helped him tie his shoes. The gesture made him want to weep. Could this day get any worse? He hadn't imagined it could until now.

Jack moved shakily into the bathroom next door to Ashleigh's bedroom. He took a whiz and brushed his teeth with Ashleigh's toothbrush. He borrowed her comb to try to tidy up his hair. He looked awful. Finding some seasonal eyedrops that were supposed to reduce redness and irritation of the eyes, Jack dosed his eyes liberally with the liquid. It stung like the dickens, but he hoped it would erase some of the redness there.

He tucked in his shirt and made his way back out to the bedroom. He felt somewhat better now, although twelve hours of sleep would certainly help things more. God, he was tired. And hungover. He knew the symptoms.

"What time is it?" he asked, looking for his watch, rings, and billfold on the side table by the bed.

"Eight o'clock at night." Grace's answer was direct.

"I left the hospital at two. That was six hours ago." Shock and disgust hit him like a brick then. "Is Ma all right?"

"She's going to make it. Roger said you knew she would be all right when you left."

"No. I wasn't sure. She looked so bad. Like my dad. So pale and full of tubes."

"And so you thought going on a bender would help her?" Grace's voice was like ice.

Jack felt his anger flare. "Where's my car?"

"Your Jeep's still at the Shady Grove. You're in no shape to drive. I'll take you to the hospital."

"Here's your coffee, Jack." Ashleigh came back into the room, carrying a large Styrofoam cup with a wisp of steam still rising off the top.

Jack grabbed it greedily, nodding his thanks to Ashleigh.

"We need to go." Grace started toward the door.

Ashleigh waved a couple of fingers at them as they went out the front doorway.

Lord, what a nightmare, Jack thought, as he climbed into Grace's town car. He couldn't imagine a more humiliating scenario, and he'd been in some doozies in his lifetime.

Grace got in the car and started the motor without saying a word. Soon they were on their way back down the highway heading for Maryville and the hospital. Jack nursed his coffee. There was little else he could do. And he couldn't think of anything to say that wouldn't make the situation worse.

"How are the girls?" he asked at last.

"They were scared at first. But they are better now. Of course, we got the word from Samantha at around two that Althea made it through the surgery and was relatively stable. That helped." She looked over toward Jack. "I promised the twins you would take them over to see their grandmother tomorrow at the hospital if she felt well enough to have visitors."

He nodded. "Thanks for picking them up. That was good of you. We all appreciate it."

She didn't answer and only drove.

When they turned in to the hospital, Jack said, "Come in with me, Grace. I know Ma would like to see you."

"It's not necessary." Her tone sounded stiff.

He looked at her then. "I'd like you to come, Grace. I'm not deserving, but Ma is. It would please her to see you."

As they started up the hospital elevator a short time later, Jack turned toward Grace. "What did you tell Roger, Bebe, and Samantha?"

"Should I have lied to them?" She gave him a daggered look.

"No." He winced. "I just need to know what I'm in for."

"Then keep your mouth shut." Her voice was tight. "I told them you had a few too many drinks and that someone drove you back to your house. Given the situation, even Ashleigh agreed it would be kinder to everyone for them to think you simply didn't handle Althea's illness well and downed a few too many drinks on an empty stomach."

"I forgot I didn't have lunch. Even breakfast. I had planned to get something when I got to the office this morning." He hit his head. "It was stupid of me to drink anything at all on an empty stomach."

Jack reached a hand across toward Grace's, but wasn't surprised when she pulled hers back. "Thanks, Grace. For coming to look for me. For covering for me with the family."

"I didn't do it for you." Her voice was tight and tense. "I did it for Bebe and Roger and Samantha. And even your mother. It seemed bad enough that you took off like that with your mother just out of surgery."

She looked at Jack with anguished eyes. "Whatever were you thinking, Jack? To take off that way? To go to a bar when your mother just had a heart attack and almost died."

Jack turned honest eyes to Grace. "I was scared, Grace.

Scared she was going to die like my father did. And I felt help-
less because I didn't know what to do to make it better for her.
Or for anyone. I couldn't even pray. I couldn't even comfort
anyone. I didn't even feel I could approach God for my own
mother. I didn't know if I would ever be able to share with Ma
my regrets about so many things. Or be able to tell her I was
sorry. Or that I loved her."

"I see." Grace fell silent then.

"I didn't handle things well."

"No. No, you didn't."

"Vincent said I needed a Greater Source to lean on in hard
times than myself. He said just a person's self was too small to
see you through the tough times. That it would fail you."

The elevator stopped. She gave him a look of mixed anger and
compassion. "Well, that's something to think about, isn't it?"

Feeling like a royal idiot, Jack got out of the elevator to face
his family. It wasn't as though they hadn't all been disappointed
in him enough times before. He knew that well enough. It was
simply that this time he felt repentant for it down to the core of
his bones. Lord, he wanted to be different.

A little later, Jack sat in his mother's room holding her hand,
glad to see the mask of death had lifted off her face. She looked
pale, but had smiled tentatively at him when he came into the
room.

She squeezed his fingers. "I'm going to be all right, Jack."

Tears pooled in Jack's eyes.

"You know, from the time you were just a little boy, you always ran off and hid when something really scared you. It used
to worry me. I always thought you'd grow out of it."

"Guess I didn't." Jack saw no reason to lie.

"Was it Ashleigh who took you home from the bar, Jack?"

Jack had already told his mother his story and repented. Told
her how sorry he was for all the miseries he'd caused her. Told
her how much he loved her.

"Yes, ma'am."

"Did you sleep with her?"

"Ma, I don't even know. I don't remember. I remember leaving the bar with her, and the next thing I remember is waking up with Grace standing over me—and Ashleigh standing in the doorway with a nightie on."

Althea shook her head. "She's a good woman, Grace Conley. After watching you with her this summer, I thought maybe you might be falling in love with her. And she with you."

"Well, I'd say I've blown any chance of that possibility with her now."

"Do you love her?"

"I don't know. I'm so hardened, I don't know if I'd recognize love if it bit me, Ma. But I do know I care a lot for Grace."

"Well, I guess she knows the worst of you now."

"Yeah, I'd say so."

"It's hard for a woman to forget and forgive a man for going to another woman when she loves him."

"I doubt Grace loves me."

"Hmmmmm." Althea muttered. "I don't know. There's a feeling when the two of you are around each other that seems awful strong."

"I've sure felt that."

"Jack, if you're really purposed to turn your life around, like you told me, there might be a place in it for you and Grace."

"I don't know, Ma. She's a fine, good woman. And I might not be able to get past this with her. Even to see where things would go with her."

"Well, I like her. I can tell you that."

Jack got up to walk across the room. "Ma, why didn't you tell me the doctor said you had heart problems? He told me he'd talked to you about it at your last exam. Said you needed to take care. To take some medication, modify your lifestyle. You didn't even tell me. You changed the subject when I asked you about your visit to the doctor."

"I don't like illness. I didn't want to think about it."

"And you thought if you did that, it would just go away?" Jack turned to shake his head at her. "Obviously, it didn't."

"Well, it might have," she persisted stubbornly. "Health conditions do sometimes. And you know I've never liked doctors and such much. Half the time, I don't think they know what they're talking about."

Jack shook his head. "Maybe I got some of those 'run away from your troubles' genes from you, Ma."

She grinned up at him. "Could be."

"Will you try to take better care of yourself now that you've gotten a second chance here, Ma? Do what the doctors suggest? Try to stick around for a while?"

"I'll work on it." She reached out a hand to take his. "I want to hang around and see how you make all these changes you promised me you're going to try to make in your life."

"I meant all that, Ma."

"I know you did, Son. And I'm proud that you want to turn over a new leaf. It's never too late to start over in life. Or to make changes."

"Well, I guess we'll see," Jack said. "We'll see."

$\mathscr{C}$HAPTER 15

Earlier the same day, Grace sat in the kitchen of the Mimosa—talking with Vincent over a cup of coffee and letting down after a hectic weekend. He'd dropped by that morning, as he often did, hoping to find Margaret in the kitchen. She'd gone over to the college to attend a planning meeting about the music concert to be held next month when the students returned.

"You had an eventful weekend," Vincent commented as he dug into scrambled eggs left over from the breakfast Grace had made for the McAllisters and Bridges before they checked out.

She cut some slices of fresh banana bread and put them on a plate beside him. This was a favorite treat of Margaret's, and Grace knew she'd skipped breakfast before heading out to her early meeting. She'd be back soon—hungry and full of news. Grace looked forward to it. She liked having a house full of life and sharing.

"Yes, Vincent, my weekend was almost *too* busy." Grace sat down to eat breakfast with Vincent. "I had three families at the inn over the weekend. We enjoyed the nice neighborhood gathering, and I opened the shop."

"I saw a lot of cars parked near the shop and down the street behind the church on all three days." Vincent looked up to smile at Grace. "And through the grapevine I heard the opening was a big success."

"You know, I'd never, in a million years, have expected that little crafts shop to be so overrun with customers." She propped her chin on one hand remembering it. "It was very gratifying."

"It turned out to be a blessing Margaret came when she did, too. I heard she helped out a lot in the shop."

"She did. And that surprised me. She's acted differently since she's been here."

Grace looked over to see a small smile on Vincent's face.

"Does that smile mean anything I should know about, Vince? I saw you walking with Margaret last night."

His answer was evasive. "She got upset about Jo Carson. It was a hard thing for her to understand Jo's gift. I don't think Margaret has been around deep spirituality much in her life." He sent an apologetic look Grace's way. "I don't mean to offend you in saying that, Grace."

"No. You're right." Grace poured Vince another glass of orange juice. Like her boys, he always drank two glasses of juice with his breakfast. "I suppose that's my fault for not encouraging my children to seek deeper things. I was introduced to a more meaningful spiritual walk as a girl. My family prayed together. We had family study times with the Bible and other spiritual books. A strong faith was a part of my upbringing."

Grace paused, thoughtfully. "The Conleys had a more formal faith. I often thought churchgoing for them was more like a civic responsibility. It looked good. And they went to one of the larger, more prestigious churches in the community. Charles even said once that it was good for business to attend church regularly."

"And you were happy there?"

Vincent's question caused Grace a moment of honest assessment. "I thought so at the time. It was a beautiful church. There were some kind people. I was active in the work of the church."

"But, looking back now, you think there was something missing."

Grace frowned. "Perhaps. I see, particularly, that none of my children got, in their church upbringing, a depth of faith like I experienced in that church."

"Or in their home?"

Vincent's intense eyes searched Grace's, making her uncomfortable. "Charles didn't believe in having family prayer or Bible times at home. He felt religion belonged in church."

"I see."

Grace blew out a breath.

"You think I didn't provide enough spiritual background for my children, don't you?"

"I didn't say that. But what I do know is that Margaret has never given her heart to the Lord. She's what a professor of mine in theology school termed a 'church-attending Christian.' She's gone to church and thought that enough."

Grace felt offended at that. "Margaret and all my children went to communicant's class and joined the church when they were young. They learned in the class about becoming a Christian and what it means. I saw to it that they all went, Vincent."

"But Margaret went through the motions there. She didn't make a decision to give her heart to God then, just a decision to join the church. There's a difference, Grace."

"Well, I know that. But I always assumed . . ." Her words dropped off.

She found Vincent watching her carefully. "You made your decision as a girl when you joined the church, didn't you?"

Grace felt a flush rise up her face. "I did."

"So you assumed that when your children went through the class at church and joined the church you and Charles attended, that they would each make a decision, too."

Grace dropped her eyes. "I guess I did."

"Did you ever tell them how you came to know the Lord?"

"You mean give them my testimony, like I hear some people share in your church sometimes?" she asked.

He nodded.

Grace searched her memory. "Maybe not in that particular way, but I thought I shared my faith with my children." She frowned. "Although it was hard. Charles never had as deep and personal a faith as I did. And Charles's mother, Jane, was very disdainful of overly intense faith and of religious people. In fact, she was often scornful of me when I talked about praying over matters of concern. She made fun of me for the time I spent going to Bible studies and Christian fellowship groups."

"And Margaret spent a great deal of time with Jane."

Grace winced. "She did. Do you really think Margaret is not right with God?"

"Grace, I think you know the answer to that. People do not resist the Lord and criticize things of real faith unless their hearts are not right."

Grace felt crestfallen. "What should I do, Vincent? Confront her with it?"

"No. Find a right time to share your own testimony with her. Perhaps let her know how much faith means to you if you get a leading to do so. If the Spirit leads you further, let her know you hold regrets that faith wasn't cherished more by the Conleys."

"I can do that." Grace looked at Vincent candidly. "And I think you have many deeper experiences in faith than I do. You talk about a relationship with all three members of the Trinity— like you have intimacy with all of Them, in some separate way as well as in a corporate way."

"A relationship with the Trinity is available to all for the seeking, Grace. God is no respecter of persons. Growth in God is a journey, but God doesn't make people take the journey. He simply invites them."

"I'd like to move into a deeper faith walk. Being here, I've realized that. I think I even suppressed my faith in my married years, to fit in and go along with my husband's family's beliefs. To be an accommodating and respectful wife."

Vincent smiled. "It is never too late to grow in God. I have some books you might like to read on the subject. I've always believed the best people to listen to, when you want to find a new direction, are people who have already found that direction. People who haven't, and are comfortable in staying where they are, will discourage your seeking."

"I think that's true with almost anything, Vincent. People

who have experienced something are always the ones who can best tell you about it. The others just know what they've heard others say. And that's not always reliable."

"You're right." He got up, preparing to leave.

"I think I'll go sit down by the river and pray." He smiled at her. "Give you some quiet time here this morning to do some of that yourself."

Grace watched Vincent walk down the path from her back porch. He was dressed in shorts, a T-shirt, and boat shoes with no socks, like when she'd first met him. He looked so young to have such a deep faith already.

Returning to the kitchen, Grace offered up the beginnings of her own prayers. "Lord, thanks for bringing that young man into my life. And help me to find the way into a deeper spiritual walk with You."

She sat back down at the kitchen table to open her Bible for some quiet time. "God, please help me find a way to share with Margaret, too." Grace knew this would be no easy task. Margaret often got up and stomped out of the room when Grace even talked about things of faith or opened her Bible to study.

Grace sighed. Vincent was right. Margaret showed all the signs of someone who had no relationship with God at all. She was, as Vincent said, just a "churchgoing Christian" and even the churchgoing aspect had become a sporadic thing since Margaret started college. To be frank, Grace wasn't sure how close any of her other children were to God either. It hurt her heart to admit it. She'd read them Bible stories and taken them to church when they were growing up, but she couldn't remember whether she ever had a deep conversation about conversion with any of them. She prayed for forgiveness for that.

"Lord, I wonder how many people sit in church every Sunday without having any kind of real relationship with You? Without having ever given their hearts and lives to You? And without ever hearing a message in their church urging them to get right with God or even telling them how to become a true Christian?"

Grace began a new kind of quiet time that morning, praying over these issues. Praying for her children. Reading her Bible and searching for answers as to how she could grow her own faith. She was drawn to the fervent faith she saw in Vincent. The depth of his relationship with God showed in his eyes, his actions, and his words. And it was inspirational. Maybe it would impact Margaret, too.

As this thought settled in her mind, Grace heard the front door open and heard Margaret's steps coming down the hallway toward the kitchen. Grace looked up to greet her with pleasure and saw an angry, flushed face.

"I am *so* mad." Margaret threw her books and notebook down on the kitchen table and paced around the room with agitation.

"Whatever is the matter, Margaret? Have they canceled the concert? Did someone upset you at the school?"

"*This* is the matter." She tossed a flier onto the table in front of Grace. "Just look at this!"

Grace studied the flier. To her surprise, a large picture of Vincent was in the right hand corner.

Margaret came over to hang over her shoulder. "Listen to this." She started to read from the brochure. "The well-known and beloved inspirational writer Reverend Vincent Westbrooke will be at the campus again for another lecture on his best-selling biblical series *Faith 101*." She stabbed her finger at the words.

Pointing down farther on the page, she read more. "At only twenty-five, Westbrooke has become a renowned authority on the Bible, with his ongoing spiritual series that invites the reader into a deeper study of the books of the Bible. In this campus lecture, Vincent Westbrooke will discuss his newest book, being released this month, entitled *Isaiah,* which is Westbrooke's fourteenth book in his acclaimed Bible study series."

Margaret flounced over to sit down in a chair across from Grace now. Tears hugged the edges of her eyes. "There were people standing in line to get tickets to this lecture, Mother. The lecture is free, but, according to one of the people at the college, the auditorium is often packed for Reverend Westbrooke's lectures. So tickets often go fast."

Grace poured Margaret a glass of juice and cut her a piece of banana bread and pushed it toward her. Margaret drank and ate without seeming to notice what she was doing. "This woman told me she owned every one of Vincent's books. She said it was a wonderful blessing he lived in this area and was willing to give his lectures at the college so frequently."

She pulled out a paperback book and tossed it down in front of Grace. "I went to the bookstore to see if they had any of Vincent's books. They were sold out of the new one that's just come out. I bought the first one on Genesis so you could see it."

Margaret got up to pour herself a cup of coffee then, noticing Vincent's breakfast dishes in the sink. "If that man had still been here when I came back, I'd have really given him a piece of my mind!"

"Why are you so angry, Margaret?"

She sat back down and burst into tears. "I didn't know any of this about him. It's just more of those secrets he's kept from me!"

Grace smiled. "Margaret, again I need to remind you that you have hardly encouraged Vincent to confide in you. You do your best to ignore him."

"Well, that was because I thought he was only a little nobody preacher in a poky mountain town!"

Grace eyed Margaret thoughtfully. "And so you feel differently about Vincent now that you know he is a well-known writer as well as a preacher?"

Margaret stirred her coffee savagely. "He knew I didn't respect his being only a preacher. I made that clear often enough. And he never corrected me. Never told me he was a writer, too. Or that he was a best-selling author."

She reached a hand across to poke her finger again at the book she'd laid in front of Grace. "Do you know the publisher is starting to reprint these little books in other languages? Read on the back side of the book! The series is being called 'one of the most insightful and understandable Bible study series of the century.' Can you believe that? I could simply kill Vincent! I can't believe I had to learn about this by finding a flier about him at the campus."

"Why should Vincent have told you about this?" Grace found it hard to follow Margaret's logic.

"Honestly, Mother. You know he's attracted to me. Why wouldn't he have told me this if he wanted me to like him?"

Grace shook her head and gave Margaret an indulgent smile. "Maybe Vincent wanted you to like him for what he was and not for his accomplishments."

"They're the same thing."

"No, Margaret, they're not. Character is who we are. Accomplishments are just the icing and the way we use and express our gifts."

"Oh, pooh. That sounds like something Vincent would say."

"Are you trying to say you would have found Vincent more attractive if you had known he was an accomplished writer?"

"Well, of course. You can't allow yourself to be attracted to simply anyone. Jane always told me I needed to be careful to guard my heart so that I could marry well. She said it was one of the most important things a person with a gift could do. Or any woman, for that matter."

Grace winced. "And you believed that?"

"Why shouldn't I? She said you married up in status and married well when you married Daddy. She said I could at least do as well."

Grace blew out a breath. "Margaret, I married your father because I loved him. The fact that his family was wealthy didn't factor into my decision." She chose her words carefully now. "There were times when I thought the finances and the emphasis on them in the Conley family more a curse than a blessing. They seemed to judge everyone too critically as to whether they were monied or whether they were not. That often worried me."

"You mean you wouldn't care if I didn't marry well? Jane said money would help pave my way to becoming famous, that contacts would help me get on the right concert tours and into the right schools. She said talent alone isn't enough."

Grace felt disappointed at her daughter's words. Quietly, she said, "Talent was evidently enough for Vincent. He didn't come from an affluent family. Many people's gifts find a way to prominence without them having a lot of financial means."

Margaret indulged in another spate of tears. "I keep getting confused here. I always seem to be torn between all the different things people say I should do."

"Margaret, you need to learn to listen to your own heart more."

"That's the typical kind of response you always give!" Margaret's eyes narrowed. "Jane always said you were too sentimental and not practical."

"And you believe that's true?"

"I don't know what to believe anymore!" Margaret's reply was a wail, followed by another sweep of tears.

It wasn't the best of times, but Grace told Margaret then about how she had come to know the Lord as a young girl and how it had helped her through life to make the best decisions and to know the right way to go. "It didn't always mean I knew the right answers. But it meant I had a more reliable source to turn to than just myself."

Grace reached across to take Margaret's hand. "I'm not sure I know the right answers for your life, Margaret. And I certainly doubt that Jane does. But I believe with all my heart that God does. And I certainly think He would like you to be happier than you are now."

Margaret's gaze hardened. "I don't know about that. Just leaving everything to faith sounds like a cop-out way to handle things, Mother."

She got up and gathered up her things.

"I'm going to go practice the piano," she said. "I think better when I practice. And I need to vent some of these emotions."

A few minutes later, the house filled with the sounds of Margaret's playing. Grace looked through Vincent's book while she listened and finished her last cup of coffee. From what she could see, Vincent had presented a guide and help for understanding and thinking about the Scriptures in his little book. But the discussion wasn't theological; it was just practical and easy for anyone to understand. In addition, from what Grace could see, it was faith-established. While many books seemed to confuse one's thoughts about the Scriptures, often questioning the Bible's accuracy and meaning, Vincent's seemed to strengthen and affirm the Biblical account.

Grace was reading with rapt interest when the phone rang to interrupt her thoughts. She picked it up and immediately heard Samantha's anguished voice. "Althea Teague has had a heart attack, Grace. I wanted to know if we could bring Ruby over to stay with you so that Roger, Bebe, and I can go straight to the hospital."

"Bring her over anytime. I'm so sorry, Sam." Grace's answer was immediate.

The rest of the morning was tense as Grace waited to get word about Althea's condition. She knew Jack had gone to the hospital and that Vincent was there, too. Grace had told Sam earlier she would pick up Daisy, and also Jack's twins, at Bible School when the girls got out later in the day. Grace wanted to do something to help. She also sent word to Jack, through Sam, that she would be praying for Althea. And she did.

To Grace's surprise, Margaret and Ruby Butler seemed to make a quick connection. Margaret sat on the floor playing board games with Ruby now. Before that, they had colored pictures together. Naturally, Ruby had been told her great-aunt was sick and in the hospital. But Margaret's special attention to the child made the day go easier for Ruby. Margaret showed similar affection for Daisy and the twins after Grace went to pick them up from Bible School.

At dinner time, Bebe came to pick up all the girls to take them home with her to spend the night. Althea was stable now, and Bebe felt she could leave the hospital to rest. Roger and Samantha were staying longer. Bebe mentioned that Jack had left for a while, but grew close-mouthed about where he was.

"I'm sure he'll be back right away," she said. "Jack has never been good with tense situations like this. Even as a boy, he often took off for a while until things changed for the better. It's just his way of coping."

A short time later, Roger called to talk to Grace.

"Has Bebe picked up the girls?" he asked.

"Yes. Is there anything else I can do, Roger?"

Roger cleared his throat. "Um, yeah . . . if you would. Althea's been asking for Jack. I thought you might be willing to go look for him. He might be at the house and not answering the phone. Jack's like that sometimes when he's upset. You could drive up and see if his car is there."

"I'll be glad to do that, Roger."

"Uh . . . and there's something else." He cleared his throat again, obviously uncomfortable. "You might need to look a couple of other places if you don't find Jack at the house. I hate to ask you to drive around and look for him. But sometimes Jack loses track of time. And Althea is worried about him. She doesn't need that right now. We need to get Jack up here so she'll calm down and rest."

Grace blew out a breath. "I'll go look for Jack, Roger. Just tell me the places to look. And give me your cell phone number in case I need to call you and ask anything. I know my way around pretty well now, but it will be getting dark soon."

It took checking Jack's house, his office, and several friends' houses before Grace found Jack's car at the Shady Grove and learned whom he'd left with. She got directions from the bartender to Ashleigh Anne Layton's house and cried all the way there.

The pain Grace felt in learning that Jack was with Ashleigh awakened her to the fact that she'd been foolish enough to fall in love with the man.

"Dang you, Jack Teague," she said out loud as she turned down the road to Ashleigh's small cottage. "I knew better than to get involved with you. And drat it if I didn't let you get to me anyway. Here I should be weeping for Althea—and worried about her recovery—and I'm weeping for myself like a lovesick teenager."

She stopped her tears by the time she knocked on Ashleigh's door. And then she had to have a volatile argument with the girl to get inside. Finally, Grace managed to push past the girl. Seeing Ashleigh wearing a frilly nightgown that barely covered her body gave Grace a pretty good idea where she would find Jack.

Sure enough, Grace found Jack in Ashleigh's bedroom, sprawled across her bed with the covers partially thrown over his body. He wore only a pair of boxer shorts. Grace wasn't sure if he was drunk or just asleep, but when he tried to pry his eyes open to look at her, she knew he'd been on a pretty good bender.

She looked down at him in disgust. What was he thinking to be in a situation like this when his own mother was lying up in the hospital, still not out of the woods from a heart attack? Grace blew out a breath of disappointment.

With little alternative, Grace told Jack the situation with his mother and waited while he dressed so she could drive him back to the hospital. He was obviously in no shape to drive there himself. While he dressed, Ashleigh went to the kitchen to make him a cup of coffee.

When Jack finally groped his way into the bathroom, Grace sat down on a chair to wait and then looked up to see Ashleigh watching her from the doorway.

"Seems like we've been in this situation before." She grinned.

Grace scowled at her. "You know Althea is in the hospital. This is hardly a time for jokes. To be frank, I'd like to tell people you took Jack to his house after you hauled him out of the bar, if you don't mind. It would spare the family some sorrow right now. The bartender actually gave me the idea. He said you might have driven Jack home, but if not, he told me how to find you."

Ashleigh considered this. "I can do that," she said at last. "Is Althea all right?'

"She will be. Right now she's worried about Jack."

"Perhaps you were, too. You've been seeing a lot of Jack." It was an observation more than a question.

"His girls spend a lot of time at my house, Ashleigh. He lives across the river from me. But we're not dating, if that's what you mean." Grace felt like saying that the girl was welcome to him, from what she'd seen of Jack tonight—but she held her tongue.

Ashleigh seemed to pick up on Grace's expression. "Don't be too hard on Jack. He didn't have that much to drink. But it went to his head quick. I think I got out of him that he hadn't eaten all day. I don't think he meant to get crocked."

Ashleigh twiddled with the strap of her nightgown. "I like Jack. I don't mind to admit it. He knows how to make a woman feel good."

She sent Grace an honest glance. "But nothing happened. He was too drunk to get his Johnson up. And he kept talking about you. It kind of took away from the mood, if you know what I mean."

Grace looked up at Ashleigh in surprise.

She shrugged. "Yeah, I thought you'd like to hear that. You're sweet on him whether you want to admit it or not."

She smiled at Grace. "Although I like Jack, I wouldn't mind seeing him hooked up with someone nice. That Celine Rosen did a real number on him in the past. I was only a kid then, but I heard about it. It wouldn't hurt Jack to have a little happiness. So don't be too hard on him about this. He was scared. Thought his mother was going to die on him like his father did."

Ashleigh looked toward the bathroom. "He came into the bar to have a drink to calm himself down. I didn't help things. I pushed more on him. Commiserated with him. It wasn't nice of me, but I was thinking about myself. Figured if I could get a few drinks down Jack that maybe . . ." She shrugged. "Like I said, I like Jack."

Grace made no comment, but she nodded at Ashleigh.

"I won't tell anyone Jack was here. I'll even tell Cody at the bar that I took Jack home. You can let everyone think you found him over at his own house."

"Thank you." Grace managed to say. She did mean that.

Jack came out of the bathroom then. He was dressed, had washed his face, combed his hair, and brushed his teeth. She could smell the toothpaste. His shirt was tucked in, and he looked better—but, to any close observer, his eyes were still a dead giveaway that he'd had more than a few drinks. And he was still hungover.

The trip back to the hospital was a tense one.

Grace expected a spate of apologies from Jack, but none were forthcoming. Yes, Jack had shown interest in her in the past, kissed her, and talked sweet to her a few times, but evidently it meant nothing in Jack's eyes. And as Grace had told Ashleigh, she and Jack weren't dating or anything. Even if Jack had called her name out when he was drunk, that didn't really mean anything. In truth, Grace had been a fool to let herself fall for Jack Teague. She knew very well who he was and what he was.

Before they got to the hospital Jack finally talked out some of his feelings to Grace, his worry over his mother, what he'd done and why. The regrets he had. She felt little sympathy. But when Jack got off the hospital elevator and confronted Roger and Samantha, Grace reiterated her story of picking Jack up at his home, lying through her teeth.

Roger gave Grace a pained look when he learned it was Ashleigh who'd hauled Jack out of the bar and had taken him home. "Thank you, Grace," he told her later when Grace had finished her brief visit with Althea, leaving Jack with her in the hospital room. "If I'd known you'd run into as much trouble with Jack as you did, I'd have searched for him myself. I'm sure you didn't have a pleasant time of it."

"I raised two boys through their teens and young adult years." She gave Roger a matter-of-fact look. "It isn't the first time I've had to deal with a man who is a little inebriated."

Roger winced. "Yeah, but all this couldn't have done any good for the relationship you and Jack were building."

Grace gave Roger a steely look. "Jack and I have no relationship, Roger."

She tried saying those words over and over to herself on the drive back home, but she knew in her heart that the words were a lie. For better or worse, she had gotten her heart wrapped up with Jack Teague. To be truthful, she doubted anything would come of it. But that didn't make the pain of realizing how much she cared about Jack any easier. She wished she could hate Jack after what she'd witnessed tonight. But it simply wasn't that easy. When you loved, even foolishly, you tended to love despite all.

CHAPTER 16

The rest of the week was difficult for Jack. Not that he expected it would be easy.

He drove back and forth to the hospital for most of the week, seeing to Althea. It was good to see his mother's color gradually begin to come back and to see the tubes removed from her little by little.

Roger asked Margaret to fill in at the real estate office until Althea could come back to work, and to Jack's surprise, Margaret said yes.

"It's not because I like you," Margaret told him candidly. "But because Roger and Samantha asked me to do it. I like them. And having some extra money before school starts will be nice, too."

Actually, Jack found Margaret's candor and honesty refreshing. Everyone else seemed to be tiptoeing diplomatically around what they really thought of him and how he'd acted when his mother was in the hospital. Even though people didn't know he'd stayed with Ashleigh Anne Layton that afternoon, they knew he'd been at the Shady Grove drinking, that he'd gotten snookered, and that Ashleigh had driven him home. He'd always be grateful to Ashleigh and Grace for keeping that extra episode to themselves about what really happened that evening. But it weighed on his conscience.

It didn't help that he'd gotten another note from Crazy Man either. Written on a napkin from the Shady Grove bar, it said: *I know what you did.* Jack wasn't sure if this was simply another chiding from the resident vigilante about his getting drunk that night or if the man really knew more. It made him nervous, thinking about it sometimes. However, now that he'd confessed all to his mother that night in the hospital, it wouldn't really matter too much if the rest eventually got out. Like most small scandals, it would blow over in time.

The note from Crazy Man had arrived in Jack's home mailbox this time. That vexed him, too. His girls might have been the ones to find it. He was glad he'd picked up the mail that day. He didn't like the idea that the man knew where he lived and had come up his private drive into the woods to bring the note. Jack also didn't like thinking about Crazy Man's being that close to his home and family. Still, Jack didn't call and tell the sheriff about this note. He put it in a Ziploc bag and locked it up with his private papers. Swofford might have started asking too many questions down at the Grove if he'd gotten Crazy Man's note written on one of the bar's napkins.

Climbing out of his car at the realty office now, Jack saw that one of Jerrell Webb's boys, Cecil, was mowing the yard. Jack waved at him as he headed up the walkway to the office. He'd need to write out a check for Cecil to pick up when he left.

Margaret looked up from the computer as Jack let himself in the door. "Some guy said he was supposed to mow the grass today. I hope it was okay."

"Yeah. It's Cecil Webb, one of Jerrell Webb's boys. The Webbs mow all the properties around here. They do good work."

She wrinkled her nose. "Well, he's silly-acting. Came in here wanting to hang around and be chatty and tell jokes."

Jack laughed. "Cecil's just outgoing and friendly—and perhaps a little simple-minded. But he's harmless."

Jack picked up the mail to flip through it. "His brother, Beecher, is exactly the opposite. He's a broody, moody man and hardly has a word to say."

Margaret snorted. "Typical of the people around here."

"There are peculiar people everywhere, Margaret." Jack sat

down in the chair opposite Margaret's desk. "Besides, it might surprise you to hear how talented all the Webb family is in the musical field. They have a bluegrass band called the Webb Creek Band. They're rather well-known in the area."

Margaret looked up in surprise. "I think I've heard them. They came to Maryville a couple of years ago as a part of a fall bluegrass festival. Three men and a pretty blond singer?"

Jack frowned. "The pretty blond singer was Ira Nelle, Beecher's wife. She got killed about a year or so ago. Tragic thing. She had a beautiful voice. And she left two little boys behind. The loss has been hard on the family."

"I imagine." Margaret looked thoughtful. "It's hard to lose a parent."

Jack studied her covertly then. He was sure she was thinking about her father, and he knew how that loss felt, too.

"How's Althea?" Margaret asked.

"Getting cantankerous and anxious to get out of the hospital." Jack grinned. "It's a good sign. I think they're going to let her come home on Friday, if all goes well."

"That's tomorrow." Margaret looked at the calendar. "That seems soon. She only went in on Monday."

"The hospitals don't keep people long today." Jack propped his feet up on the chair across from him. "But we'll have some nursing care at home. And, of course, Bebe will be there."

Margaret nodded, finishing up what she was working on at the computer and then starting to print her document. She lifted it out of the printer tray, added it to a stack of other letters, and handed them all over to Jack.

"Here's the last of those letters you asked me to type. If you'll sign them, I can get them posted this afternoon."

Jack looked over the letters. "You're doing a good job here, Margaret. If I haven't said thank you for filling in, I want to say so now. It's often hard to get good temporary office help here in Townsend."

"So I've heard," she said sarcastically.

Jack winced. "If you want to knife me again, I could turn around and let you have a go at my back."

She shrugged, unrepentant. "No need. There are plenty of others enjoying a go at your back. I'll stay with the direct approach. It's more honest."

"Actually, I've rather appreciated that direct approach this week." Jack got up to pour himself a cup of coffee.

"What? My stabbing at you all week with my candid comments?"

Jack grinned and sat back down. "No. Your honesty about it. You didn't admire my actions, and you haven't been too timid to say so."

Margaret shook her head. "What got into you that day, Jack? That was a really dumb thing to do."

"I don't owe you an explanation." Jack's words were sharp in reply. He got up in annoyance to pace over to the window to look outside, turning his back on Margaret.

Margaret, in wisdom, didn't say anything for once.

He turned back to look at her. "The whole scene made me think too much of the time when my father died. I panicked and didn't handle the situation well."

Margaret put a hand under her chin thoughtfully. "No, you didn't. And it hurt my mother. I told you I didn't want that to happen."

Jack slumped back into his chair. "I'd give anything if it hadn't been your mother who came and found me."

"Mother's dealt with drunks before. It was the fact that you'd been drinking with that ditzy little Ashleigh Layton that hurt her. Plus the fact that it was Ashleigh who was the one who took you home." She gave Jack a long look. "There were some pretty strong implications in that to think about."

"Yeah, I know." Jack didn't offer anything more.

Margaret shook her head. "I haven't wanted to like you, Jack Teague. But, admittedly, I've developed a grudging fondness for you this week. It's surprised me."

Jack quirked a small smile toward her.

"Now, don't get overly excited about that observation. But I've seen some good attributes in you this week while I've worked with you that sort of counterbalance the bad."

"And?"

"And maybe you have possibilities."

"To link up with your mother?" He raised a brow in question to her.

Margaret wrinkled her nose. "I wouldn't go that far. Although I'll admit Mother has mooned and brooded about you all week and not been herself. I was thinking more in terms of the possibility that you could become a more decent person."

Margaret's words rankled. "And what about you, Miss Less-Than-Perfect? Don't you think you could use a little changing for the good?"

"We weren't talking about me." Her answer was clipped and prim.

Jack grinned. "Perhaps we should. You haven't been very nice to your mother in the past, either. And recently, you haven't been very nice to our resident good-looking preacher. In fact, you seem rather snippy with him. Almost bit his head off the other day when he stopped by here."

Margaret tapped her nails on the desk and shifted restlessly in her seat. "I'll admit I'm annoyed with Reverend Westbrooke." Her tone grew brittle.

"How come?" Jack propped his feet up again, glad to have Margaret in the hot seat now instead of himself.

"Did you know he was a best-selling writer?" She gave Jack a challenging look.

"Sure." Jack scratched his neck casually. "Most everyone around here does. Writes some sort of devotional books or something. His books are pretty well-known in their field, I hear."

"That's an understatement." Margaret's voice was snappish. "His books stay practically sold out in the bookstore. They're being printed internationally now, and he can get a huge fee to speak almost anywhere in the U.S."

"So why is that a problem?" Jack often found it difficult to figure Margaret out.

"He didn't tell me about it, that's why." Margaret flounced up out of her seat to go over to the small office refrigerator to get herself a cold drink—some sort of fancy bottle Jack didn't recognize.

"What's that?" he asked, eyeing her drink.

"Green tea. It's good for you."

"Got another?" He raised his brows in interest.

"Sure. And there's half a sandwich in there I couldn't eat from lunch. You can have that, too, if you want it."

"Thanks." Jack went over to dig out the sandwich and a bottle of the green tea from the refrigerator.

He sat back down and propped his feet up again. "What's really the problem with Vincent's having written some books and being well-known for them? I should think—since you're so snobby about reputation and money—you would be impressed with that."

Jack saw Margaret squirm.

He laughed then. "That's it, isn't it? You feel guilty that you've given Vincent the cold shoulder all these weeks—thinking he was only a small-town preacher—and now you feel angry at yourself, knowing you might have misjudged his worth."

"You have a smart mouth, Jack Teague."

"Too close to the mark?" He gave her a teasing look.

"He should have confided in me." She stuck her chin up.

"When? While you were turning your back on him and ignoring him? While you were pretending you weren't attracted to him when you were? Or maybe while you were hiding out from him all the times he was looking for you?"

"You're ticking me off, Jack." She gave him a mutinous look.

"So, are you ready to admit you might like the preacher more now that you know he's a little more successful materialistically than you first thought?" He took a long drink from his tea. "It seems to me you have some worldly ways about you that are almost as objectionable as mine. No one respects a little gold digger."

She stood up in anger.

"That's not true, Jack Teague. You take that back."

"Are you going to deny you're more interested in Vincent Westbrooke now that you know he's more successful than you thought he was?"

To Jack's surprise, Margaret burst into tears. "I really hate you, Jack Teague."

"No, you don't. We just shoot straight with each other, you and I."

He laid down his sandwich and went around the desk to hand her a tissue. "Don't be so hard on yourself, Margaret. And don't be so quick to think Vincent doesn't understand your feelings. Why don't you talk to him about it?"

"I have." Her reply was snippy.

Jack chuckled. "To rail and snap at him, no doubt."

Margaret looked up defensively. "Well, I was upset."

Jack patted her on the shoulder. "You need to analyze what you're *really* upset about, Margaret. You need to think about what you really feel about Vincent Westbrooke—beyond what he does for a living, preaching or writing or whatever."

"I've been trying to avoid that kind of thinking." Margaret looked up at him with eyes still wet. But her words were honest.

"Hard to hide from your thoughts," Jack commented.

The door interrupted their conversation as Cecil Webb came in to tell them he was finished with the yard. Jack went back to write him a check, leaving Cecil to attempt to entertain Margaret again with another of his jokes. He seemed oblivious to any of the emotions stirring in the air.

Jack thought of his conversation with Margaret again on Sunday as he worked his way into the crowded pew to sit beside her. His girls had wanted to sit with the Butlers, which put Jack and the twins squeezed between Roger, Samantha, Daisy, and Ruby on one side and Margaret and her mother on the other. Jack could only be grateful he hadn't been jockeyed into a seat beside Grace. Sitting with his leg up against hers throughout the service would have been an agony right now. He'd only seen Grace in passing this week, and their interactions had all been brief and strained. What could he say to her after what happened anyway?

There was a guest minister at the church today: Reverend Grady Hartwell. Vincent introduced him as he started the service. Hartwell worked at Montreat and traveled as an evangelist. Jack knew Hartwell was a friend of Vincent's family and had known Vince since he was only a boy.

Reverend Hartwell was a fine-looking man, with rich brown hair and warm gray eyes. He had a solid ministry career and a strong family life now, but his past had been dark. He told about it with candor in his message, sharing how far he had sunk into a disreputable lifestyle in graphic detail.

"My personal gods were alcohol, drugs, myself, and a good time," he told them, shaking his head. "And I believed, some of the time, that I was happy. I thought religion was for weak people, and I couldn't see anything in it that I thought I needed. I couldn't even see much in religious people I wanted to emulate."

Jack squirmed in his seat at that.

Hartwell walked away from the pulpit, carrying a hand mike. "It wasn't religion I really needed anyway. It was faith. And it was Jesus. But I had to sink to a really low point before I came to terms with my need."

Margaret seemed to be restless beside Jack, moving about in her seat, fiddling with her purse. Nothing like a powerful testimony of a changed life to stir people up.

Grady Hartwell leaned forward to speak to them with passion. "I had to walk down a lot of dark, harsh, and lonely roads before I finally found the Roman's Road. The day I found that road really changed my life."

He walked back to the pulpit to pick up his Bible. "I encourage each of you to open your own Bibles and follow me through these passages in Romans, starting at Romans chapter 3:23: 'For all have sinned, and come short of the glory of God.' "

He flipped the pages of his Bible. "The good news to follow is at Romans 5:8: 'But God commendeth His love toward us, in that, while we were yet sinners, Christ died for us.' "

Jack knew these Scriptures. He'd heard them since he was a boy, but they burned in his heart today in a new way.

"Romans 6:23 says: 'For the wages of sin is death; but the gift of God is eternal life through Jesus Christ our Lord.' "

Jack noticed, with surprise, that Margaret had a Bible with her today. She was looking up the Scriptures and following the message along with everyone else.

"You know," Reverend Hartwell was saying, "all my life, people tried to make finding faith sound like a hard thing. But it's the easiest thing there is. Look over a few chapters further to Romans 10. Right there—God's way into the secret garden of grace is made real plain. You realize your own way isn't going to cut it. That you can't establish your own righteousness, that you need to repent of your selfish life and your selfish ways and submit your life to God. A repentance and a readiness to change come first. Then the next step is easy."

He walked out from behind the pulpit again, carrying his open Bible in his hand. "In Romans 10:9-13, the Word tells you that all you have to do then—in order to come into the Kingdom of God—is confess with your mouth that Jesus is Lord and believe in your heart that God raised Him from the dead. That's it. Repent, want to change, believe, and confess your belief to others."

He stopped to look out at them and shook his head. "I fought doing this for about half my life, wanting to do everything my own way. Not wanting to submit or yield myself to anyone, even God. How stupid I was."

Reverend Hartwell smiled then, a radiant smile. "But I didn't stay stupid. I changed. And God did the rest. And He has been working his miracle-working changes in me ever since. I am, like the Bible says in second Corinthians 5:17, 'a new creature now. Old things are passed away and, behold, all things are new.' Grady Hartwell is a different man now—and all due to one decision made in a church meeting, pretty much like this one, on another warm summer morning thirty years ago."

He closed his Bible and looked out at them. "I want you to know that I had a totally different message prepared to give today. This is a Presbyterian church, and a salvation-based, testimonial message didn't seem appropriate to prepare." He grinned. "But God had something else in mind. And after being a stubborn, mulish, and unregenerated old fool—following in my own ways—for so long, I've finally learned better now. When God nudges me to do something His way these days, I tend to listen better."

He chuckled. "Now here's the thing. God's encouraging me to have an old-fashioned altar call today. I know the history of this old church, and, in times past, there were altar calls here. Sinners who needed to be saved came right up here to the altar to give their lives to the Lord, and old reprobates who had drifted away from God came up here to rededicate their ways to the Lord once again. Folks playing church, but without a true, deep personal faith came up here to make a change."

Reverend Hartwell looked out over the congregation. "There are some of you in each of those categories here today who need to come up front and set things right. I know it isn't what you usually do here, but it's what needs to be done today."

He walked down the steps to the front of the narthex. "Coming forward in a church service is an old-time, brave way of saying before God and everyone: I am changing my life today. God honors that bravery and 'stepping out in faith' by meeting you, often with dramatic power and might."

Jack squirmed in his seat again. He wished for a moment that he'd stayed home with Althea this morning and let Bebe bring the girls to church.

"If God is drawing you to come down and set things right with Him this morning, you know it as I'm speaking it now. There are several of you who have drifted from God here today and some who have never come to know God intimately and who want to." He paused. "There also are a few here who simply haven't realized until recently that there was a life of faith and greater happiness even possible. This morning is orchestrated just for these whom God is calling. The Lord wants you to come into His family today. Friends, it is a beautiful thing to come to know the Lord and to be welcomed into the Kingdom and Family of God."

He held out a hand. "So, as Jo plays the piano, I want those of you whom God is nudging and touching to come down front here to take my hand and to pray with me. And I ask those still in your seats to remain quietly and to pray until the Lord is finished with all He has to do here."

Jo began playing the old hymn "Just as I Am," and Jack's brow broke out in a sweat. He knew the pull of God on his own heart and he knew God was dealing with him. It was just a matter of whether or not he was ready to yield to that pull.

He sat and thought of the promises he'd made to his mother and of the desires he had to see if change could really work for him, and made his decision. He stood up.

As he started to move to his left in front of Margaret's knees, he looked down to see her weeping and clenching her hands in her lap. He leaned down and spoke to her. "I dare you to go down front with me, Margaret. You know God is dealing with you."

Her eyes jerked up to his in anguish.

Jack felt a wrench on his heartstrings at the look on her face, and he reached down his hand to hers. She grasped it like a lifeline, and he pulled her to her feet. Together, they moved out into the aisle and started down front to see if God could really change their lives as they hoped.

CHAPTER 17

Grace decided she would remember this week of her life, in amazement, for years to come. She'd never been to a revival in her entire church life, but she certainly had witnessed one on Sunday morning. Furthermore, it was her daughter who'd been one of the ones to give her life to the Lord that morning. Even more incredible, she'd watched Margaret walk down front to the altar, weeping with emotion, and holding Jack Teague's arm.

She'd heard what Jack had hissed at Margaret before he started out of the pew. Grace had been so caught up in the pastor's message she hadn't even noticed Margaret was upset and crying. She now knew the term was "under conviction." Unlike Jack, Grace probably wouldn't have realized what Margaret needed to do at the moment or why she was so upset. She owed Jack for that, she guessed.

The back door opened, and Vincent came into the kitchen.

"Hi, stranger," she greeted him. "When did you get back?"

"Late last night. I flew back to Montreat with Grady on Sunday and spoke at several meetings going on at the assembly grounds." Vincent grinned. "It was Grady's payback for his coming down here to preach. I also enjoyed some time with my family."

Grace looked up at Vincent with a question in her eyes. "Did you know what Reverend Hartwell was going to preach here?"

Vince shook his head. "No. I just wanted him to come down

and see my little church, meet some of my congregation. Grady is my dad's cousin. Maybe you didn't know that."

"No, I don't think you mentioned it."

Vincent got a cup of coffee, helped himself to an apple muffin from the warmer, and sat down at the kitchen table with Grace. He looked around. "Is Margaret here?"

"No. Margaret has already left for the office. She's still working over at the realty while Althea is recovering."

Vincent spread apple butter over his muffin and took a bite. Then he grinned at Grace. "How's Margaret doing?"

Grace shook her head. "She's been different, if that's what you mean."

"Different how?" Vince stirred cream and sugar into his coffee.

"Charged, excited, animated. Like she gets when she has a new enthusiasm." Grace gave Vincent a direct look then. "You'd better not tell her what I said, you hear?"

"Scout's honor," he promised. "I hated it that I had to leave after what happened Sunday. I've missed all the fun."

"I suppose it has been fun." Grace considered that. "It's a joy to hear Margaret excited about Christianity . . . see her reading her Bible, hunting for religious programs on television to watch, studying spiritual books, talking about faith. It's hard to believe she's the same girl who used to balk at going to church at all and who literally made fun of me for going to church groups and Bible studies."

Vincent smiled widely, the dimple in his chin deepening. "Isn't God something? He's just a constant amazement to me."

Grace frowned. "It seems like more happened to Margaret in that prayer with Reverend Hartwell than simply deciding to become a Christian."

"More did, Grace. God has a call on Margaret's life, and He's starting His work on her."

Grace's eyes widened. "How do you know that?"

"I heard Grady's prayer with her, for one thing. The rest I saw. It was powerful what happened to Margaret on Sunday." He spread more apple butter over his muffin. "There will be more change to come."

"I assume it will all be good." Grace frowned at the thought.
"How can you ask?" Vincent looked up at her in surprise.

"I don't know. It just seems sort of overwhelming, seeing
Margaret go through such a transformation. I don't remember
an experience like that when I got converted."

Vincent smiled and reached across to pat Grace's hand.
"Don't worry, Grace. Margaret's coming to know God more
closely will only strengthen the love and bond between you two.
She won't grow away from you; she'll grow closer to you."

Grace smiled back at him. "You always seem to know what
my worries are before I express them, Vincent."

"How about Jack? Has there been a lot of change in him this
week, too?"

"Margaret says she and Jack are talking about the Bible and
about faith some at the office. That's about all that I know." She
looked down at the open newspaper on the table then to avoid
Vincent's gaze.

"You and Jack still haven't sorted out that problem from
when Althea had her heart attack, have you?"

Feeling prickly over that comment, Grace got up to carry her
coffee cup to the sink. "That isn't your concern to worry over,
Vincent."

"I know, but I'm fond of Jack."

"Everyone is fond of Jack." Grace knew the words sounded
sarcastic as soon as they were out of her mouth.

Vincent shook his head, got up, and followed Grace across
the kitchen. He turned her face to look at him. "God has made
changes in Jack, too, Grace. Be as ready to forgive and to give
Jack a second chance as God has."

Tears smarted in Grace's eyes. "This is a personal issue, Vincent."

"I know," he said, going over to sit back down at the table. "I
should keep my oar out of this. But I'd like to see things work
out between you and Jack. I think there's something special between the two of you."

Grace didn't reply to that. She wasn't sure if the statement was even true. She'd thought so once, but now she didn't know what to think anymore.

Vincent looked at his watch. "Did Margaret eat much before she went to work?"

"No. She took off without eating at all. I wish she hadn't. It isn't healthy."

A smile lit Vince's face. "If it's okay, I'll take her over a few of these muffins. I'd like to see her, and it would give me an excuse to stop over at the office."

Grace smiled in spite of herself. "You do that, dear. I'll wrap them up for you. And I'll send her some juice, too."

She let Vincent out the back door and then sat down at the kitchen table to consider some of the things he'd said. Thinking about Jack, in particular, was painful. She'd grown accustomed to seeing him, to spending time with him, and she missed his company. It was silly, when she'd only known him since May. But it was true.

Trying to divert her mind, Grace went over to her desk to get some materials to work on and brought them back to the table. She was hosting the Townsend book club for lunch next week at the inn, and she needed to plan the menu and think about how to decorate the tables. It was Friday now, also, and she had guests coming in to the inn for the weekend. She needed to bake and to get the rooms ready. This afternoon, she also needed to help Kyleen Clark open the craft shop. With the shop growing busier than Grace had expected, Kyleen had started helping Grace part-time. This arrangement had worked out well for both of them. With the inn so busy, Grace really didn't have time to be in two places at once as her guests started to arrive.

Grace was looking through her recipe box for the directions for a coffee cake she wanted to bake for breakfast in the morning, when she heard a soft little knock at the back door. She looked up to see Morgan peering through the glass door.

"Come in." Grace waved at her. She hadn't locked the door after Vincent left.

Morgan came in and wandered over to the table.

"What are you doing, Ms. Grace?"

"Hunting for a recipe I want to make for my bed-and-breakfast guests who are coming in tonight." She smiled at Morgan. "There are still a few apple muffins in the warmer on the counter if you want one."

"Okay." Morgan headed for the counter. "Can I get a glass of juice, too?"

"Sure. Where's Meredith?"

Morgan's reply was snippy. "We don't always do everything together, Meredith and I. She's down at Stacy Clark's house visiting."

It wasn't like Morgan to be cross and out of sorts.

"Is anything wrong, Morgan?"

"No." She bit out her reply as she slumped into a seat at the table across from Grace. "I can go if you don't want me to visit."

Grace smiled to herself. Morgan was so much like Jack, irritable and out-of-sorts when she had something on her mind.

"You know I'm always happy for you to visit." Grace reached over to pat Morgan on the hand.

"Morgan, while you're eating your muffin, maybe you could look over this list of outdoor badges and tell me which ones you think the girls would most like to work on." Grace pushed the list and her Scout book across the table to Morgan and then went back to her search in the recipe box. The child would talk when she was ready.

Morgan ate her muffin and looked through the Scout book at the badges Grace had listed and flagged. "I think everyone would like to do the camping badge." She pointed at the page. "And we've all been talking about wanting to do a badge about rocks—so we can visit Tuckaleechee Caverns as a troop." She showed Grace that page also.

"Those are good ones to consider, Morgan. I think I'll put those two badges, and a few others, on my list and then let everyone vote for the badges we'll work on this fall."

"That would be good." Morgan continued to fiddle through the book, but Grace could tell her mind was on something else now.

"Grace?" she asked at last. "Do you think my mom is dead?"

Grace took a deep breath. "Why do you ask that, Morgan?" She wasn't sure how she was going to handle this conversation.

"Well, I know Daddy has always said she's dead. But I think he just said that so we wouldn't be hurt, knowing she left Mer and me."

"What makes you think that, Morgan?"

"An old memory," she admitted. "Once when I was little, I was snooping in Dad's office and saw this letter lying open from Celine somebody. I sort of looked at it. I could only read a little bit then. And because I didn't know who Celine was, I didn't pay much attention to it. Then, I guess, I sort of forgot it."

She hung her head. "Now I know from something Aunt Samantha said that my mother's name was Celine. Dead people don't write letters, Ms. Grace. I got to remembering that letter and got to wondering."

"Those are pretty heavy things to think about, Morgan."

"Yeah. That's why I didn't bring Mer with me. She doesn't know. And she's kind of sensitive and gets upset easily about stuff. I wanted to talk with you by myself about this first."

"I think this is really something you should talk about with your father, Morgan. I didn't even live here when you children were small."

Morgan looked up in alarm. "You won't tell Daddy I came over here to ask you about my mother, will you, Ms. Grace?"

"No. But I think you should talk to your father about this. If he was trying to be protective with you and Meredith, he'll tell you that now. He knows you're older. I think you can trust him to tell you the truth, whatever it is."

"You don't think he'll get mad?" Morgan bit on a nail nervously.

"No, honey, he loves you. He won't get mad." Grace smiled at Morgan.

Morgan fiddled restlessly with the Scout book. "Thanks for saying you wouldn't tell him, Ms. Grace."

"I might not always promise that, Morgan. I would never keep anything from your father that he would really need to know to keep you safe or to help you." She caught Morgan's eye. "And I will expect you to talk to your father soon about this, or I might feel I should tell him after all. You shouldn't carry a worry and concern like this around with you for long, Morgan."

Morgan nodded. "It's funny to think we might have a mother living somewhere." Morgan chewed on her lip. "I'd like to know her if she's still alive. Even if she left us. Does that sound stupid?"

"No, that sounds normal. Every child wonders about his or her parents and what they might be like if they haven't known them."

"Dad won't think it means I don't love him that I'm wondering about our mother?" She looked up at Grace with worried eyes.

"No, not at all. He'll understand."

Morgan blew out a breath of relief. "I guess I'll talk to him tonight." She looked up at Grace with a grin then. "Thanks, Ms. Grace."

Grace smiled at her.

Morgan hopped up from her chair then. "I think I'll go up to Stacy's house now and see what she and Mer are doing."

"I'll walk out with you. I need to take Sadie and Dooley outside, anyway."

Grace saw Morgan and the dogs outside. Sadie and Dooley took off madly chasing each other down the backyard, and Grace laughed to watch them. Morgan played with them, laughing, for a few moments before she took off skipping down Creekside Lane—obviously in a lighter mood now.

As Grace sat on the back steps in the sunshine, watching the dogs play, she naturally thought about Jack. She wondered how he would handle his talk with Morgan later—wondered if telling his daughter about Celine would hurt him. Getting up from the steps, she strolled down the back drive toward the mailbox. The mail had run, and she needed to check the box before she called the dogs and took them back in. As she passed the shop, she saw an envelope taped to the front door.

Grace walked up the steps to retrieve it, opened it up—and

then dropped it in alarm as she realized what it was. Another message from Crazy Man—and a truly frightening one. Her heart beat madly as she bent down to pick the envelope back up. Grace called the dogs and took them quickly into the house. In the kitchen, she paced back and forth, thinking about the message she'd received. Then she went to the phone and called Jack's cell. She needed his help to know what to do.

"Jack here," he said, answering the phone congenially.

"It's Grace." Her words tumbled out in a rush. "I've had another note from Crazy Man. I'm afraid, Jack. Can you come over?"

"I'm ten minutes up the highway from you, Grace. Lock the doors until I get there."

Grace did, and when she heard Jack's car and then his knock a little later, she opened the front door to him with tears in her eyes and flung herself into his arms. He held her close and said soothing things to her, and it felt like coming home. Grace leaned fully into him and let her senses take in the male scent of him and the musky undertones of the familiar cologne he always wore. A side of her knew she was staying in his arms a little longer than she needed to, but she really didn't care at the moment.

He pulled back from her at last, reaching out to wipe off a few stray tears from her face with his thumb. Jack's eyes were tender as he looked down into her face. But the smile he gave her was as devilishly handsome and irresistible as she remembered.

"Remind me to thank Crazy Man later for this," he said, grinning.

"Oh, you!" Grace pulled away and glared at him. "This is serious, Jack."

"I know it is, or you wouldn't have called me. Tell me about the note."

"It's in the kitchen." She turned and started down the hall. "Come back and I'll show it to you."

He followed her into the kitchen, where she picked up the

note from the kitchen table. She read Jack the words with a shaky voice. *"Protect your girl. There are wicked men around here."*

The words were written in the usual black marker, but were plastered across a collage of cutouts from area newspapers telling of rapes and murders of young girls. Grace handed the note to Jack to look at, her hands still shaking.

"Confound it." Jack studied the note with an angry frown. "That man's crossed the line with this one."

Jack reached out a hand to steady Grace's and urged her into one of the kitchen chairs. "Where did you find this, Grace?"

She told him.

"I'm going to call the sheriff," he said. "And we'll need to talk to Margaret."

"Oh, do we have to, Jack? I don't want her upset and frightened!"

"She needs to be on the alert, Grace. We can't know what this message means. And we both know Margaret has had more sightings of Crazy Man than anyone. She told me the other day she'd felt someone was following her when she walked down to visit Jo Carson. And last week she said she got 'creeped out,' as she put it, while she and Vince sat out on the stone bench by the creek talking. She suddenly felt like someone was watching them."

"I hate that this has happened right now." Grace dropped her head into her hands. "This has been such a happy week for Margaret. I hate to spoil it."

Jack reached out a hand to take one of Grace's in his. "Margaret's a big girl, Grace. And she has a Higher Power to lean on now when there is trouble. She'll be all right."

The next hour or so was eventful. The sheriff came, the story was told again, and the house and property of the Mimosa were searched. Then the sheriff, Jack, and Grace went over to the realty office to talk to Margaret. Margaret took it all in stride, more than Grace would have thought.

"Maybe it's like the situation with Ruby." Margaret tapped

her nails thoughtfully on her desk. "Maybe it's only a warning to me to be more careful. Maybe this man knows there's some danger, and he's trying to alert me."

"Maybe." Sheriff Walker scratched his head, pushing back his cap. "Or maybe the man's getting more aggressive. We can't know. But I don't like cutouts from the newspapers about rapes and murder pasted on warning notes like this. It ain't natural to try scaring folks in this way. And I don't like it one little bit."

He tucked the note into a plastic bag. "I'm gonna have this analyzed real good for prints. And I'm going to get a couple of deputies, and we're going to start going out through the community to see what we can learn about this man—see if anybody knows anything about him. Somebody's gotta know something. And this kind of stuff has got to be stopped."

Swofford stood and hitched up his pants. "You women keep your doors locked, and you call me if anything at all unusual happens, you hear?"

Jack walked Grace back over to the inn after the sheriff left.

She felt suddenly awkward with Jack then, walking along beside him and knowing he had held her not so long ago.

As they came to her doorstep, she turned to him, searching for some sort of conversational note to fill up the moment. "Morgan came to talk to me this morning about something that was troubling her, Jack."

The sensual tension that had been building before was broken quickly as Jack took this statement in. "What's bothering Morgan?" His voice was alarmed.

Grace smiled. "Just something she needs to talk to you about, Jack. I encouraged her to come to you with it, and she promised me she would tonight. I thought it would help if you knew—so you'd be open to talk with and to listen to her."

A small frown touched his forehead. "I always listen to my girls, Grace."

"I know you do," she soothed. "But you know how Morgan is—so much like you sometimes. Irritable when she has something important to say that is difficult. Reluctant to talk about it. I simply wanted you to be ready to listen."

He looked down at her quietly for a moment, and then sighed. "You know me rather too well, don't you, Grace Conley?"

Unsure of Jack's meaning, Grace didn't answer, dropping her eyes.

He leaned over then and gave her a soft kiss on the forehead. "You remember to lock your doors tonight, Grace. And I'll see that I'm attentive to whatever it is that Morgan needs to talk to me about."

Grace looked up then to find Jack studying her with a deep gaze. They stood like that for a moment, just looking at each other, and then Jack nodded a good-bye and turned to start back toward the realty company—leaving Grace weak-kneed and confused.

CHAPTER 18

Jack watched Morgan fidget through dinner that evening. He felt grateful that Grace had alerted him to the fact that Morgan had something on her mind. It was obvious she was worrying over it. Oblivious to Morgan's unrest, Meredith happily shared her day's events with them, chatting away with excitement about the visit the Scouts planned to make to the Little River Railroad Museum soon.

"It's part of our walking tour for the My Community badge we're working on." She reached for one of the brownies Bebe had left for their dessert. "Ms. Grace said it's good to learn more about your community and what you can do to make it better. We're going to do a cleanup project down at the park by the river, too. Maybe even paint the picnic tables if we can get permission. And plant some bulbs to come up in the spring."

Meredith glanced at her watch. "It's time for our TV show, Morgan."

"You go watch it, Mer. I'll help Daddy clean up, and then I'll be there later. I've seen this episode, anyway."

"Okay." Meredith grabbed another brownie and headed out of the kitchen. They soon heard her footsteps as she galloped up the stairs to the den.

Jack watched Morgan moodily help clean up the kitchen table and load the dishes into the dishwasher. He finally felt sorry for her.

"There's a full moon out tonight, Morgan." He looked out the kitchen window. "You want to go down to the patio and look at it? We could sit there for a little while and watch it shine down on the river. Maybe see some stars."

"Yeah, that would be good." Morgan's voice almost sounded relieved.

Jack took a cup of after-dinner coffee with him and led the way down to the patio. He sat down in his favorite chair and propped his feet up on the rock wall. The moon above shone like a glowing, white ball in the dark sky.

"Daddy," Morgan said after a while. "I need to talk to you about something, and I don't want you to get mad."

"Did you break something valuable in the house or black some kid's eye?"

She giggled. "No."

Jack waited.

"Daddy." She paused. "Is our mother really dead?"

Jack caught his breath. This was not what he'd expected. "What makes you ask that, Morgan?"

"I put a few things together recently and got to wondering." She told him about the letter she'd found and about hearing Samantha mention their mother's name.

"Have you and Meredith talked about this?"

Morgan shook her head. "No, I haven't told Mer. You know how she can get kind of emotional and stuff. I thought I needed to ask you about it first."

Jack noticed she didn't mention that she had talked to Grace earlier in the day. "That's a pretty big and serious question, Morgan."

"Yeah, I know."

"I think if we're going to talk about this that Meredith needs to be here, too. Why don't you go and get her? This is a good place to talk with the moon looking down on us."

Morgan looked up. "Yeah, it's real pretty. I'll go get Mer."

Jack listened to her footsteps recede toward the house. The break gave him a few minutes to catch his breath and think about what he wanted to say. He'd known this time would probably come some day; he'd just thought it would be later when the girls were much older.

When Meredith came back with Morgan, grumbling about having to miss her television show, Jack started in. "Morgan has asked me if your mother is really dead or not, Meredith. I thought, if we were going to talk about this question, that you should be here, too."

"You mean she isn't?" Meredith's incredulous voice came out in a squeak.

Jack grinned, in spite of himself. "No, actually she isn't dead. She's alive. She just doesn't keep in touch with us anymore. She was never interested in being a wife or a mother, and she left us when you girls were only small babies."

The girls were silent for a minute, and then Morgan asked, "Did you tell us she was dead so we wouldn't be hurt that she left us, Daddy?"

"That's pretty much it, Morgan. It was a hard thing, and I didn't want you girls to be hurt by it. I always thought I'd tell you when you got older—when I thought you could understand it better."

"Why did she do that, just leave us?" Meredith's voice was quiet and pained.

Jack winced. "She left a note saying she didn't think she felt cut out to be a wife or a mother. She wanted to go back to Hollywood and get into acting again."

"You mean she's an actress?" Meredith's voice was incredulous. "Is she somebody famous?"

Morgan kicked at the rock wall. "Pooh. I haven't ever heard of any famous actress named Celine Teague." She frowned.

Jack worked hard to keep his voice calm in reply. "Your mother is a soap opera actress, and she uses her maiden name, Celine Rosen. She took her own name back after the divorce. She's pretty well-known in her field, I guess."

"Are the soaps like the daytime stories that Aunt Bebe watches sometimes when she's ironing?" Meredith asked. "She says they're not very virtuous, and she always turns them off when Morgan and I come in."

Morgan giggled. "Yeah, she likes one called *As The Years Go By,* but she doesn't like to admit that she likes it."

"Is that the one our mother is in?" Meredith looked at Jack questioningly.

"No. It's another one. Some medical show. I can't even remember the name of it, Meredith. But your mother is a pretty big star in it."

"Wow. Our mother is a movie star." Meredith sat forward in her chair in excitement. "Can we tell people?"

"No, silly." Morgan glared at her. "Then we'd have to tell everybody she cared more about doing movies and getting famous than about taking care of us and Daddy. It's kind of a crummy thing to have to tell people."

Meredith's face dropped. "Does anyone else know?" She turned her brown eyes up toward Jack in question.

"Some people know." He reached over to pat her head. "Your grandmother and Bebe know, and some of our other relatives and friends who lived here a long time ago also know what happened. But a lot of people don't know. We don't talk about it much."

"Because it was a mean thing to do, and you don't like to tell it." Morgan spit the words out. "It's selfish and mean to go off and leave your husband and your little babies because you want to become a movie star."

Meredith sighed. "But maybe it was her great dream. Maybe it was her one chance, and she had to make the sacrifice."

Jack snorted. "There's no sense in over-romanticizing the facts, Meredith. Although I'm sure it makes you feel better to do so."

Meredith frowned. "I was only trying to put myself in her place and to think why she would do it."

They were silent for a few minutes.

"Do you have any pictures of her?" Meredith asked. "Is she beautiful?"

"She is a very fine-looking woman—red-headed with cat-green eyes and ivory skin. She could catch a man's eye. But I got angry when she left, and I burned her pictures and everything else she left behind."

"I bet we could find her picture on the Internet." Morgan offered this.

"No doubt." Jack wanted to insist the girls not do that, but he tempered his response. If he sounded too oppositional to their learning about their mother, they would probably feel more compelled to covertly seek out information about her.

"Does she ever write to us?" Meredith asked this.

"No, I'm sorry, pumpkin, she doesn't. I haven't heard from Celine for over four or five years now. In the first few years after she left, I occasionally got a letter from her—when she needed money. I guess it was one of those last letters that Morgan saw."

Jack looked over to see tears dribbling down Meredith's cheeks. "It sort of hurts to know she didn't love us or want us, Daddy. Mothers are supposed to love their babies and little children."

Morgan looked mutinous. "I bet Ms. Grace would never have walked out on her babies. How come you didn't marry someone nice like Ms. Grace, Daddy?"

"You can be sure I've asked myself questions like that a hundred times or more, Morgan. But I want you both to know I did love your mother when I married her, and I loved having both of you. I have never regretted being your father."

Meredith came over to sling herself into his arms. "I love you, Daddy. And I'm sorry you got hurt by our mother."

Jack felt close to tears himself by that point. "Let's have a tri-hug," he said, opening up his arms to take Morgan in, too. "We're a team, the three of us. Two M & M's and a Jack. We've been okay all these years, and we're going to be okay in the future. You hear?"

They nodded. In a few minutes, Morgan went back to her chair, and Meredith curled up on Jack's lap to look up at the moon with him.

"Daddy?" Meredith asked. "How come you haven't ever dated Ms. Grace? She's real nice. And I think you like her."

"Daddy likes stupid, young bimbos like that dumb Ashleigh Anne Layton and that silly Twyla Treece," Morgan's voice snapped back.

"Morgan, you're talking disrespectfully." Jack gave her a warning glance.

"Sorry." Morgan hung her head. "But it embarrasses me and Meredith what people say about you and *girls,* Daddy. We like Ms. Grace, and we sort of got to hoping you might like her, too. You look at her like you do sometimes."

"And what do you know about that?" Jack frowned at her.

She gave him a prim look. "We're not babies anymore, Daddy. We know about stuff now. And we listen a lot."

"Maybe since Daddy had his change at church on Sunday, he'll be changed in not running after girls anymore. I heard my Sunday school teacher say she hoped that would be so." Meredith smiled up at him.

Jack shifted in discomfort. Sometimes living in a small town was like living in a goldfish bowl. Everybody knew your business, and no one hesitated to comment on it.

"Do you like Ms. Grace, Daddy?" Morgan pressed.

"Of course, I like Ms. Grace." Jack knew his voice sounded irritable, but he was beginning to feel a little crowded here.

Morgan leaned back in her chair to look at the moon. "Then you should ask Ms. Grace out," she advised. "Women know that you like them when you ask them out. How is Ms. Grace going to know you like her if you don't ask her out or anything?"

"I guess you have a point." Jack grinned to himself. "I'll give some thought to it, Morgan. But don't you girls be cooking up romantic notions for me. Grace and I are not fresh, young kids anymore. A lot of that courting, cooing, getting married and everything is for the young kids."

"Like Vincent and Margaret." Meredith announced this matter-of-factly.

"What about Vincent and Margaret?" Jack looked down at his daughter.

She giggled. "Me and Morgan saw Vincent kiss her down by the river earlier today."

"Meredith! You weren't supposed to tell that!" Morgan reached over to punch her arm.

"I forgot!" Meredith wailed.

"You shouldn't spy on people." Jack gave them both an admonishing glare.

"We didn't mean to. It was an accident." Morgan spread her hands.

Jack gave them both a cautionary look. "Well, don't tell anybody else about it. That sort of thing is private."

"Okay." Meredith got off Jack's lap then. "Can we go back and watch TV now, Daddy?"

Jack looked at his watch. "No. You need to get your baths, and then it will be nearly bedtime."

"Will you read to us?" Meredith asked. "I want you to finish the Harry Potter book we started. It's getting to a good part."

Jack nodded. Even he liked the Harry Potter books.

An hour or so later, Jack came back down to the patio to sit in the dark and look up at the moon. All in all, the talk with the girls had gone pretty well. They'd been upset, but it hadn't been as bad as he had imagined it would be.

He frowned into the dark, remembering those early months after Celine had walked out on him, remembering how humiliated, hurt, and angry he'd been. He'd given a lot of that hurt up on Sunday—in a meaningful prayer with that minister. He'd felt lighter since. Better. Off the wrong path in some ways, more back on the right one.

Jack smiled thinking about Margaret and Vince. Jack and Margaret talked every day at the office—they had gotten pretty close—but she hadn't told him about that kiss. However, the knowledge didn't surprise Jack much. He'd watched the attraction simmer between those two since the beginning. It kind of tickled him to think of the preacher finally making his move. Who knew what would come of that?

As those thoughts passed through his mind, Jack looked down toward the Mimosa Inn across the river, thinking of

Grace. He was grateful to her for warning him Morgan had something on her mind. And he respected the fact that she'd been discreet with the confidences of his daughter. Hadn't even told him—but had urged Morgan to talk with him. She was a wise woman. And a kind one.

The back door of the inn's porch opened as Jack thought about Grace, and he watched her come out with the dogs. He'd learned Grace's routine . . . and often sat here to watch her walk in the yard with the dogs at about this time every evening before she turned out the lights to go to bed. She had on one of her Capri sets—this one in lavender like the color of the morning glories that bloomed by the front porch of the inn. The color looked pretty on her. Jack watched her walk down through the yard to the patio by the river, saw her glance up toward his house.

Jack's thoughts grew hungry and sensual as he watched her swaying walk as she started back toward the inn. No woman had ever stirred him as Grace had or kept him as intrigued—and as antsy and lovesick—as Grace Conley. He'd expected the intensity of his feelings for her to die out as time passed, but it hadn't. His feelings had only increased. He entertained rich fantasies about Grace Conley now on a regular basis. She had gotten deeply under his skin.

He stood up to get a better look at her as she let the dogs into the back door of the porch. And, then, as if sensing him watching her, she turned and saw him, standing on the patio. The full moon made him visible on the hill. She hesitated for a moment, looking toward him, and then she waved and started down into the yard again.

Jack sucked in his breath. She was coming to him. Jack wasn't sure if that was a good thing. His thoughts were wolfish, and his body was hungry for her. What was she thinking—coming to him like this? He stayed on the patio, trying to calm himself as he watched her walk down through the yard, across the swinging bridge over the river, and then out of sight for a few minutes as she climbed the hillside path.

She emerged at the side of the patio and smiled at him shyly.

"I saw you and decided to come up and see if you'd talked to Morgan."

"Sit down," he offered. He gestured to a chair, not moving closer to her—afraid to get too close to her.

She sat down easily, crossing one leg over the other, beginning to kick her foot up and down lightly. Her feet were bare in her slides. He tried not to look at them or at her.

Jack cleared his throat. "It was good of you to warn me that Morgan had something on her mind. It was a weighty topic. We needed to talk about it. She told you what it was, didn't she?"

Grace nodded. "I've been thinking about it all evening. Wondering if she talked to you—and how it went."

"It went okay. Better than I might have imagined." He frowned. "But the girls were hurt. I knew they would be. Morgan was angry, and Meredith cried."

He heard Grace sigh deeply. "Those poor girls. It was a hard thing to learn."

"Yes." Jack's voice felt tight.

Seeming to pick up on the pain in his voice, she came over and knelt beside his chair. "And how about you, Jack? Are you all right? I've been worried. I knew it would be hard for you to tell your girls that story of when Celine left."

He put out a hand to touch her face. His voice in reply was ragged and husky with emotion. "You should know better than to come and offer your sympathy and kindness to a man who is hurting—especially in the dark under a full moon. And especially to a man like me."

She looked up into his eyes.

"You're a good man. I'm not afraid of you, Jack Teague."

"You should be." He rasped the words out before he leaned over to slip his arms around her and bury his lips in hers. It was heaven, and the little moan that escaped her only escalated his emotions. He teased at her lips with his tongue until she let him in. Their passion flamed then, and Jack lifted Grace up from her knees to pull her across his lap. The feel of her against his body was glorious. She wriggled on him as she settled herself into his arms, driving him crazy. He buried his hands in her silky hair and his mouth into her soft neck, tasting her skin, enjoying the floral scent of her that filled his senses.

"Oh, Jack," she murmured in her deep, throaty voice as his mouth skimmed under her ear. He recognized the arousal in her voice, and it stirred him even more. He moved his lips back to take hers hungrily once again.

As his hands played over her back and as he drew her more tightly against him, Jack remembered her earlier words, said to him in such trust: *You're a good man. I'm not afraid of you.* He grinned to himself. Walking down front Sunday had resurrected his conscience, he guessed. He hadn't heard from it in a long time.

He pulled back from his kiss and took Grace's face in his hands. "You have no idea what you do to me, Grace Conley." His voice was soft, and he traced his fingers over her lips tenderly. "Everything about you calls to me like a siren. I hope you know what an incredibly beautiful, sensual, and desirable woman you are. Everything in me wants to make love to you, Grace, to see you naked in my bed, to feel your body under mine, to take you to the peaks and to hear you cry out my name in rapture. Since I can't do what I yearn to do with you, I have to at least tell you what I want to do."

Her eyes grew dark with arousal and pleasure. Jack groaned.

"Come here and let me kiss you again. At least I can have that pleasure. And I'm going to touch you some, until I have to stop myself."

Jack gloried in her then for a little while, until his desire had his breathing heated and his body throbbing. He lifted Grace off him then and pulled her to her feet as he stood. He missed the warmth of her as soon as she pulled away from him, so he gathered her against him again—body to body, head to toe, loving the way she felt against him as they stood together. He let his hands rove down her back and to her full hips. Tempting himself, he pulled her against himself once again.

He looked down into her eyes—silvery green and swimming with emotion. Saw her passion and desire. And saw more. Deeper feelings that she had been trying to hide, the kind of feelings that only slipped out of people when their bodies were stirred and their defenses were down.

"I don't deserve your caring, Grace Conley, but I treasure it. My feelings toward you are strong—stronger than I've ever felt for a woman before. I want you to know that." He traced a finger over her full lips again—moist and lush from where he'd kissed them.

She smiled at him with her heart in her eyes, melting him.

"Listen, Grace. I want you to know how sorry I am about that day with Ashleigh. I was drunk. I wasn't myself. It's not an excuse, but I regret it." He looked down into Grace's eyes and wanted to be honest with this woman above all things. "I hadn't been with a woman before that afternoon with Ashleigh since I met you, Grace. You had consumed my thoughts. And I haven't been with anyone since that time. I don't know if hearing that makes any difference to you, but I wanted you to know. I'm sorry I was with Ashleigh that day. I don't even remember what happened."

Grace smiled a small smile. "According to Ashleigh, nothing much did. As she put it, you were in no shape to perform; you'd had so much to drink."

He leaned back his head to shake it. "Mercy. Women tell each other everything. A man has no secrets—even from his shames."

She dropped her eyes.

Jack studied her. "Just knowing I couldn't . . . uh, perform . . . doesn't redeem me much. You still found me in the woman's bed sheets in my boxers."

She traced her finger across his mouth, stirring him again. "Well, it did help a little when she told me you kept calling out my name. She said it sort of killed the mood."

Jack laughed. He couldn't help himself.

Grace giggled a little, too.

"You see, Grace Conley, even drunk and with another woman, I was thinking of you. You've gotten a real hold on me."

She gave him a considering look then. "I'm not a woman

who will share, Jack. You should know that about me. If we became more serious, I would never tolerate indiscretion. You need to know that. I know some women are very tolerant in that area, but I am not."

"I hear you." He met her gaze with a thoughtful one of his own. "I'll be honest enough to admit I couldn't bear to think of another man's even touching you. I don't know what that says about our relationship, but we're both on the same page there."

She smiled at him coyly then. "Do we have a relationship?"

He laughed. "According to Morgan, no. She says a man has to take a woman out on dates to show her he likes her. You think you might be game to start dating an old reprobate like me, Grace Conley? I'm working a lot on changing lately, but I might still be a poor risk."

Grace gave him a pleased smile. "I think some dating might be just the thing. We have gotten the cart before the horse somewhat in our relationship."

He winked at her. "Makes you wonder what it might turn into when we do all the wooing and courting before the end of the evening, doesn't it? I don't know if I can stand much more sensual tension with you, woman. You already drive me crazy."

She pushed at him and laughed. "Honestly, Jack. You embarrass me."

"Too late for that." He smiled down at her and traced his finger over her mouth and then leaned to kiss her with warmth again. She went limp and soft in his arms, and he reveled in the power he had to arouse her.

"I need to go back," she said at last, pulling away and looking thoroughly well-kissed.

Jack smiled at her. "When can we go out, Miz Conley? Tomorrow night?"

"I think we could do that." She smoothed her hands over her hair, making an effort to straighten it. "I have guests at the inn for the weekend, but Margaret will be there in case they need anything for tomorrow evening. Where would you like to go?"

"I think we'll go over to Pigeon Forge to one of the dinner

theaters. There's a first-rate show at one of them I'm familiar with—and I've heard the menu is good. It will be fun. And it will make a nice memory for our first official date."

"Well, then." She looked pleased. "I guess I'll see you tomorrow."

"I won't walk down with you, Grace, because I might be tempted to try to come in with you." He enjoyed seeing her blush at that. "So I'll just watch from here as you walk home, see that you get safely there."

Jack watched Grace trace her way back down the hillside, across the swinging bridge, and up through the yard to her back porch. An odd joy filled his heart as he watched her. This was proving to be a time of new beginnings for him. Who knew what would come of this? He was certainly in new waters.

CHAPTER 19

Grace walked through the damp yard of the Mimosa Inn, keeping an eye on the dogs—who were nosing through the side brush along the edge of the property. It was a lovely July morning, the day already warming up rapidly.

She and the dogs had taken a walk around the house, past the morning glories in full bloom beside the front porch and past the mimosas now at their peak, the trees rich with color. As they worked their way by the gazebo, Grace noticed an old magazine on the bench. She walked into the gazebo to retrieve it. Flipping it over, she saw that it was a flashy movie star magazine. A page was turned down in the now soggy publication, and Grace opened it to see a picture of a vibrant redhead on the arm of a handsome man in a tuxedo, coming out of some Hollywood event. She saw the words Celine Rosen below the picture and frowned.

This must be a magazine one of Jack's girls left behind. Jack had told Grace, when they went out to dinner the other night, that the girls had only asked a few questions about their mother since their talk. Obviously, from this magazine, they were still interested in learning more about her. Grace stood for a moment, wondering what to do about this information. Then she laid the wet publication back down on the bench and left it there. The girls might come back looking for it. Grace decided to stay distanced from this one. After all, it was normal the girls would be curious. Samantha had said she'd caught them watching the soap opera Celine starred in one day over at her house last week. She'd turned off the show and told them the content was too adult for young girls to watch. Samantha hadn't mentioned the episode to Jack, thinking it would upset him.

Grace made her way across the yard to the back door of the Mimosa Inn. As she let the dogs and herself in, she could hear Margaret playing the piano. Grace walked down the hall and into the parlor. Margaret sat at the piano in shorts and a T-shirt, her fingers moving skillfully along the keys.

"It's a little early to be practicing." Grace leaned over the grand piano to plant a kiss on Margaret's cheek.

Margaret continued playing a few minutes more and then stopped to write some notes on a musical score she had propped on the piano stand. "I dreamed a song," she said. "And I wanted to come down and see if I could pick out the melody and get the notes down before I forgot it."

"It sounded lovely." Grace looked at the musical notes Margaret had penciled in over several sheets. "Play it all for me."

Margaret did, while Grace sat on the sofa to listen.

"I heard words, too." Margaret paused, and then started to sing as she played.

The words were spiritual ones, and the message a sweet one of God's love and grace toward His people. Grace was touched.

"I didn't know you were writing music, Margaret," she said, as Margaret finished and stopped to make some corrections on her score sheets.

"The songs have just been coming to me lately." She looked at her mother and smiled shyly. "Jo says it's because I have more of the spirit now—and can hear more clearly from God." She gave her mother a zealous look. "There is so much more to faith than I ever dreamed before. It's like a journey that just keeps taking me deeper and deeper."

Margaret had always been passionately consumed by any new interest she became involved in. Reading every single Nancy Drew book one year when she was young, making those notebooks of all the famous composers, collecting stickers, or becoming a fervent fan of some rock group. It seemed odd to Grace that now it was faith Margaret had become so obsessive about.

Margaret looked up at Grace with bright eyes. "Did you know Fanny Crosby heard all the hymns she wrote, too? She said the words and the music rose up through her spirit and into her mind—sometimes a little at a time, and sometimes whole hymns all at once."

Margaret picked out one of Fanny Crosby's hymns on the piano. "This is one of her hymns." Grace heard the familiar melody of "Blessed Assurance, Jesus is Mine" float across the room.

Pausing, Margaret added, "Did you know she wrote over eight thousand hymns in her lifetime? And, of course, the most miraculous thing is that she was totally blind when she did it. Isn't that incredible?"

"I seem to remember reading about her life once long ago. How did you learn so much about Fanny Crosby, Margaret?"

Margaret smiled. "Jo has a book about her life. I read it. It was simply fascinating. It made me start praying to hear music—to be used like that."

Grace caught her breath. "All these changes in you are a little hard for me to keep up with, Margaret."

"Yeah, isn't it something?" Margaret giggled. "I look in the mirror and can't believe all the changes God has made." She looked over at her mother. "It seems like I ought to look different on the outside since so much has happened on the inside."

Studying her, Grace decided there were differences. "You smile more. Your eyes are clearer and happier. I haven't seen that temper you're so famous for in quite some time." She smiled. "I thought it might be because you were seeing more of Vincent."

"Hmmmmm. That's one I haven't worked out yet." Margaret stretched. "Have you eaten breakfast? I'm hungry."

"Let's go make something together." The two walked down to the kitchen and began to work on getting out eggs and fruit to make breakfast.

Grace pulled a skillet from the cabinet. "I'll scramble the eggs if you'll cut the grapefruit and slice off a couple of pieces of that wheat bread on the counter."

Margaret sighed. "I didn't realize how much I loved your cooking, Mother, until you moved away. Elaine just doesn't have your touch."

"Elaine is a busy working woman and has two small children."

Margaret carried two grapefruit halves and the loaf of wheat bread over to the table. "That's true. But cooking is a gift, too. Neither Elaine nor I inherited the cooking talent you have."

This backhanded compliment pleased Grace.

"That's one of the reasons your inn is so successful, Mother. All your domestic skills are a perfect fit for running a bed-and-breakfast."

Grace brought their eggs over to the table, and they sat down to eat.

Margaret pinned Grace with a thoughtful look. "You're dating Jack now. If things get serious, will you give up the bed-and-breakfast? It would seem sort of a shame to do so."

Grace found herself instantly annoyed. "Just because I'm spending time with Jack Teague doesn't mean my life is getting ready to change, Margaret. I like the Mimosa. I don't need to think about giving it up—like I might have had to do when I was younger."

"See, that's what worries me." Margaret scowled. "If I allow myself to get serious about Vincent, I might need to make some big decisions I'm not ready to make."

Grace raised her eyebrows at her.

"You know. I'd have to be a minister's wife. Vincent would want to have children. There would be housework and socks to fold and ironing to do." She wrinkled her nose. "I'm not very interested in those things."

"Have you talked about marriage with Vincent?"

"No!" Margaret's answer was emphatic. "And I don't think I

want to. I mean I *like* him. A lot." She considered that. "Maybe more than a lot. But other things are important, too. Like the piano. And my music. Those are my priorities."

"And you feel you'd have to give those up to be married?"

"Jane said you couldn't have a serious musical career and be married." Margaret sectioned her grapefruit with ferocity. "That's why she waited to marry until she was ready to come off the stage."

Grace shook her head. "And even after she did come off the stage, we *all* heard a million times what a sacrifice it was for her."

"She *was* very good, Mother." Margaret's answer was defensive.

"Of course she was. I know that. But your life and Jane's are not the same. You have to find your own way that is right for you, just as Jane found hers."

Margaret blew out a breath. "Yeah, I know. That's the problem. I'm not totally sure just what I want anymore."

"And what does Vincent say about all this?"

"Oh, you know Vincent." Margaret rolled her eyes. "He never worries about anything. As he says, he just 'lays everything up into the hands of the Lord.' I'm afraid I'm not quite there yet." Her tone was snappy.

Grace laughed. "Neither am I. And I know that I worry too much."

Margaret took a big bite of toasted wheat bread spread with mountain honey. "Will you teach me how to make this bread sometime?" She gestured to the loaf of homemade wheat bread on the table.

"Sure. It isn't hard."

Margaret got up to get herself another glass of juice.

"What are you going to do today, Mother?"

"I'm going to sew and make some more of those quilted purses. I've sold almost all the ones I had in the shop." Grace finished up her last bite of egg. "And then I have the Scout meeting this afternoon. We're going down the street to tour the Little River Railroad and Lumber Company Museum on our community walking tour. The girls are looking forward to it. What about you?"

"I'm going to go do some shopping. I'm going up the highway to Boyce Hart's gallery. I think Boyce's wife Jenna is working today. I like her. We talk about New York. She still has an apartment there, you know. She said I could go stay there if I ever wanted to check out music schools in the city." Margaret finished off her toast. "I think I'll get one of Boyce's Smoky Mountain paintings for Vincent for his birthday while I'm there. There's one of this old historic church in Cades Cove that he really loves. I can afford a small signed and numbered print, and Jenna said they'd give me a special on the framing."

"When is Vincent's birthday?"

"Next week on Wednesday. I sort of hinted that we might invite him for dinner that night—have a special supper and a cake or something. I thought I'd ask Jack, too." She grinned at Grace mischievously, more like the Margaret who Grace knew so well.

Grace cocked an eye at her. "And can I assume that I'm cooking this birthday dinner?"

Margaret grinned. "I was hoping you would. Vincent loves your roast beef and mashed potatoes. Maybe we could have that? I'll help. And I can make the cake."

"That sounds like a good deal. I can do Wednesday."

Later that day, Grace wandered through the Little River Railroad and Lumber Company Museum on the River Road with the Scouts. She'd walked by the train engine and the museum hundreds of times, but she'd never taken the time before today to actually walk through the museum or to explore the museum gift shop. The historic museum proved to be interesting—and the little gift shop charming.

Grace and the girls were reading about Colonel W. B. Townsend's life and the early days of the Townsend community, when Grace's cell phone rang. Grace fished it out of her shoulder bag to answer it.

"Mother!" Margaret's voice rang out, frightened and strained. "That man is following me—you know, Crazy Man. I *know* it's him. I sort of recognize him from the times I thought I saw him watching me. He has on that same hat—like a cowboy hat. I thought I saw him sitting in an old black truck when I came out of the Hart Gallery, but I wasn't sure. But now he's following me."

"Good heavens, Margaret! Where are you?" Grace asked, pulling away from the talk of the girls to hear Margaret better.

"Well, I was driving down the main highway through Townsend heading back toward the inn, but when I saw that man following me in my rearview mirror, I turned off on the Wears Valley Road—trying to lose him. I didn't think he would turn and follow me, but he did. He's staying a good distance behind me, but I swear, I really think he's following me, Mother."

"Oh, Margaret." Grace paced anxiously. "Look for some business or place where you can pull over along the road and run inside."

"There really isn't much along here. It's rural, and the road is narrow and winding. Listen, you call the sheriff, okay? Maybe he can come follow us and catch this man—if it's him. Describe the truck to him and tell him where I am. I'm going to keep driving down the highway. Give the sheriff some time to get here. After a while, I'll find a place to pull off. Or I might speed up and try to lose him. Maybe go to that waterfall place Vince took me to . . ." Her voice crackled out. "I'm losing my phone signal now. Call the sheriff, okay? . . ." And then Margaret's voice faded out.

Panicked, Grace called into her cell phone. "Margaret? Margaret? Are you still there? Are you all right?"

Morgan came over to stand close to Grace. "Are you okay, Ms. Grace?"

Grace saw that most of the girls were watching her with concerned faces. She patted Morgan's shoulder. "No, dear. I'm afraid I'm not okay. There's some trouble with Margaret. I need to go home."

She looked around in panic for Kyleen and then quickly explained the situation to her. "Can you watch the girls and walk them back to the house? I need to make several calls in the gift shop quickly and then run down to the house in case Margaret tries to call me on the land line there."

Her heart pounding, Grace raced over to the depot gift shop to look up the sheriff's number. After reaching him—and then phoning Jack—she headed out of the shop to start back toward the Mimosa. Kyleen and the girls rushed out to follow her.

"The girls want to go back with you." Kyleen looked apologetic. "They heard us talking and they're all worried about Margaret. They're also scared about Crazy Man and what he might do."

Back at the Mimosa, the girls called their mothers one by one to come pick them up. Grace tried her best to put up a valiant front, not wanting to make the girls any more fearful than they were. Word got out quickly in the community. Jack came over to stay with Grace as the last of the girls were being picked up. Meredith was in tears by now, worrying about Margaret—and Morgan, as usual, was angry, talking about what people should do to someone who scared people like Crazy Man did.

"It isn't right!" she exclaimed.

Vincent came barging in the back door at that moment. "I just heard. Have you had another call from Margaret? Is she all right?"

Grace noticed this time Vincent wasn't as calm as he usually was in crisis situations. If she hadn't been so worried herself, she would have smiled.

Vincent kept pacing the floor and running his hands through his hair while Grace and Jack tried to tell him what had happened.

"I was in Maryville doing a book talk," he said. "And when I got home, I got Jack's message on the machine. . . ." His voice trailed off.

The phone rang then. Jack grabbed it before Grace could.

"It's the sheriff," he mouthed to them. Jack listened, relaying the information from Swofford Walker as he heard it. "They lost the truck. They saw it in the distance, but it turned off and they lost it." He shook his head in exasperation.

Grace stepped forward. "What about Margaret? Is she all right?"

Swofford obviously heard her question. "Swofford said they've driven down the road looking for Margaret, but they can't find her car." Jack paused, listening. "He says she must have turned off somewhere. A man working out in the field said he saw her car speeding down the highway. He noticed it because she was going way too fast. He also noticed the truck come along later. It's the only sighting the police have of her."

Jack pushed his hair back from his forehead restlessly. "They don't think the truck was following her when it turned off. They think the man saw the police cars and turned off on a road he knew to lose them."

Jack talked for a few more minutes and then hung up. "They don't know where Margaret is." He paced across the room restlessly. "Grace, what did she tell you again about where she might go?"

Grace tried to remember. "Something about a waterfall."

Jack slumped into a chair and then looked at Vincent. "Margaret had this crazy idea, Vince, that she'd lead the guy along for a while so the sheriff could get there. Then she said she'd speed up and lose him if she couldn't pull off somewhere."

Grace tried to think. "She said something about going someplace where you and she had been, Vincent . . . to a waterfall or something."

Vincent's face lightened, and then he smiled in relief. "Thank God. I know where she's gone. I'll go see if I can find her. She must be frightened."

"I'll go with you." Jack stood up.

"So will I." Grace reached for her purse and phone.

"No." Vincent shook his head and held up a hand. "Let me go. Please. I want to go alone. I feel that I'm supposed to. I don't think there is any danger of Crazy Man's having followed her there. Margaret will just be hiding out—afraid and worried. Wondering when it might be safe to try to come back. Also, if she's not at the falls, the two of you may need to go find her somewhere else when there is a lead."

Vincent looked at Grace. "Will you trust me to go? I know right where Slippery Rock Falls is. That must be the waterfall she's talking about. It's up Piney Road off Highway 321 on a narrow, rural, ridgetop lane behind the Buckeye Knob Camp. I took her there not long ago. I know right where the path is that leads to the falls."

Grace looked into Vincent's passionate blue eyes. How could she say no?

She nodded, leaning to Jack instinctively for support.

"Vince could be right." Jack agreed. "Swofford might get a lead on where Margaret has gone or find her himself. Then we might be needed. We don't know if she really was able to get off the main highway and find her way to these falls, anyway. You were cut off, after all. She might have had several plans running through her mind. "

"I promise I'll call you if I find her." Vince was already starting out the door. "I'll call as soon as I know something."

Grace sighed as Vincent shut the door behind him. "Do you think we're doing the right thing to let him go alone?"

Jack nodded. "Yeah. Margaret might not have been able to turn off the highway and try to get to those falls. Vince said she'd only been there once. The sheriff may find her car up the road soon. She might have pulled off somewhere, like you suggested to her, and gone into a business or store."

"Then why hasn't she called?" Grace's voice shook at the question.

"I don't know." Jack put his arm around Grace in comfort.

"Where are your girls?" She looked around.

Jack grinned at her. "I guess you were so upset you didn't notice that Samantha took them home with her when she picked up Daisy."

Grace shook her head.

Jack led her toward the kitchen. "Let's go make something to eat and then sit down to wait."

"I couldn't eat anything, Jack. I'm too upset."

"Well, I can." He flashed her a smile. "Stress always makes me want to eat. You can help me find something to eat even if you don't want anything yourself."

Jack started toward the kitchen.

Grace looked after him anxiously. "You'll stay here and wait with me until we hear?"

Jack turned back to kiss her lightly. "Where else would I be, Grace?" His voice was gentle. "Of course I'll stay. I'm not running out on this one."

True to his word, Jack stayed with Grace for the next tense hour or two, answering the phones for her, fending off the concerned—or simply nosy—calls that came in. It was Jack who took the call from Vincent saying he'd found Margaret and that she was all right.

"They're on their way home," he told Grace. "Vince wanted Margaret to leave her car, but she insisted on driving herself back."

Grace smiled in relief. "That shows more than anything that Margaret is all right. Praise God."

"Yeah." Jack smiled and then gave Grace a thoughtful look. "You know this is the first time I ever prayed with a woman about anything?"

"Really?" She looked over at Jack, remembering that the two of them had prayed for Margaret's safety earlier before Vincent came. And then had prayed again when Vincent left that he or the sheriff would find Margaret and bring her back safe and sound.

Jack flexed his fingers and studied them. "Did you used to pray with your husband, Charles?"

Grace saw his gaze lift to her eyes. "No. Charles would have been uncomfortable doing that. So, I guess this is the first time I've prayed with a man about anything, either—except for praying with a minister or with my father when I was little."

A smile stretched across Jack's face. "Well, that's something, isn't it?"

"Yes. And you were a great comfort to me in this trial, Jack. I'm grateful."

He shrugged, but she could tell he was pleased. "I'm glad I could do it right this time. It felt good."

Before she could comment on that, Margaret called to talk to Grace herself. And soon, in a flurry of hugs and excitement, she and Vince were back. Margaret sat in the living room telling them everything that had happened in her wonderfully dramatic way.

"I am *so* disappointed they didn't catch him." Her mouth tightened. "I *know* it was him following me. I got a feeling—and goose bumps—when I saw him, and then he followed me when I turned off the Townsend highway."

Jack, ever practical, said, "It could have been a coincidence, Margaret."

"No." She gave him a steely look. "I recognized that hat pulled down over his eyes. A cowboy hat. Not many people wear cowboy hats here, Jack. And there was something creepy about the way he watched me from his truck in the parking lot, a kind of glazed-over look." She shivered.

Vincent took her hand in his. "They'll find him now. They have more of a description than ever before—plus a description of the truck he was driving."

"It had a front headlight out. I told the sheriff that." Margaret leaned back into the sofa, settling into Vince's arm comfortably.

He looked down at her, and there was something different in the way they looked at each other. Grace felt almost uncomfortable watching Vincent gaze intently down into her daughter's eyes and seeing Margaret look back up into his face to smile softly.

She shifted her eyes to Jack's and saw him raise an eyebrow and grin. He'd noticed it, too. Something was different with Margaret and Vincent.

Margaret turned then to smile at her mother and Jack broadly. "Vincent and I are going to get married, Mother."

Grace sucked in a breath in surprise.

Margaret looked up at Vincent again with that worshipful

gaze Grace had never seen on her daughter's face before. "Vincent was the first thing I thought about when I was afraid and when I was hiding out at the falls, Mother. And when he walked into the clearing beside the falls, I knew. Just like that, I knew. We're supposed to be together, Vincent and I. He knows, too."

Margaret smiled radiantly at Vincent once more. He hugged her closer under his arm before lifting his eyebrows and passing a smug and knowing look across at Grace. She knew he was remembering that first night he met Margaret—right here at the Mimosa Inn not so long ago—and what he had told Grace that night.

Jack grinned. "Guess you had a right witness, Vince, to go find Margaret on your own and be the hero. Look what it got you? Congratulations, Preacher!"

Margaret threw a sofa cushion at Jack. "You be nice, Jack Teague. This is a special occasion."

Late that night, Margaret came padding into Grace's bedroom in her nightgown to curl up on the bed with her. Margaret had always loved to lie in bed at night and talk to Grace when she was smaller.

"Are you happy, Margaret?" Grace asked.

"Yes. And *very* sure I've made the right decision, if that's what you're wondering."

"You weren't so sure this morning. Are you positive it wasn't just the emotions of the day that played into this sudden pronouncement?"

"No. I was thinking of it before he came to find me. Even knowing, somehow, that it would be Vincent who would come to find me. I guess that sounds silly."

"No. Not silly."

"He told me he loved me when he came, Mother. It was the first time. And I couldn't keep the words back from telling him the same."

Grace patted Margaret's hand. "Those are special memories to cherish."

Margaret hugged a pillow to herself and then turned to give

her mother a shy smile. "You know how passionate Vincent is when he's preaching? Well, it's no comparison to what he's like when he's feeling romantic! Whew! Who would have thought?"

Grace found it hard to comment. This was her little girl, after all.

Margaret grinned at her mother. "I guess that's too much information, huh?"

Grace laughed and reached over to squeeze Margaret's hand. "Just as long as you're happy, darling."

"I am. I really am, Mother."

"What about those concerns you had when we were talking earlier this morning? Have you forgotten about those?"

"No." Margaret hugged the pillow to her. "We talked about everything, Mother. Vincent said that, wherever I wanted to go to school after I graduate next summer, he would go with me. He has his books, you know. He doesn't really need his pastor's income. He said he could always find places to preach or give lectures on his books in whatever place I get the best offer to study. He's willing to go wherever I need to go."

"That's very generous."

"He is *so* supportive of my dreams and goals, Mother. He also really believes I have a gift for writing music. He said, laughing, that maybe we'd just end up back in Montreat someday, living near the conference center where he grew up, writing books and writing music—him doing lectures and events and me playing for praise and worship services. That was a sweet idea, wasn't it?"

Grace kept her comments to herself about this. She had a feeling that none of Vincent's words were ever idle words. She sighed. At least Montreat was only about two and a half hours away.

"Did you talk about a date when you might get married?" Grace asked.

"Probably not until I graduate." Margaret giggled. "If we can wait until then."

Margaret turned to look at Grace. "Do you think I could live with you and commute to Maryville this year, Mother? That way I would be closer to Vincent. We could see each other more."

"Of course." Grace squeezed Margaret's hand. "It would delight me to have you live here with me instead of in the dorm."

As Grace drifted to sleep later, she thought how nice it was that the daughter she had thought she'd lost would be so close to her now. On a last thought, before sleep claimed her, Grace wondered what Jane Conley would have to say about all this. She was pretty sure it wouldn't be "congratulations."

CHAPTER 20

The atmosphere was tense around the River Road community over the next week. It made Jack nervous that Crazy Man had appeared so openly. He knew he'd been cross and overprotective with the girls because of it—causing Morgan and Meredith to flash out in anger at him several times.

"You can't lock us up in a cage because some crazy goon is leaving notes and was maybe following Margaret around!" Morgan had shouted at him defiantly with both hands on her hips several days ago.

Jack had just told the girls he wasn't going to let them go over to Kinzel Springs to a spend-the-night party one of the Scouts was having for her birthday.

"It's *only* to spend the night at Mary Jean Watkins's house." Meredith gave him a wounded, puppy-dog look. "There will be a mommy and a daddy there."

Jack snapped his answer back. "Well, I don't know the Watkins very well."

Actually, Jack knew Joe and Elizabeth Watkins quite well. They were wealthy, and the socialite types in this rural community and Jack wasn't sure how conscientious they would be in minding a large group of fourth and fifth-grade girls at their big home in the mountains. The whole idea made Jack nervous.

"You're being mean, Daddy. Everyone else is going. It's not fair!" Morgan stomped out of the kitchen and ran up the stairs to her bedroom.

Meredith drifted out after her, dribbling tears and giving Jack accusing stares.

He and the girls engaged in another zinger of a fight two days later. Morgan and Meredith went tubing without having an adult with them. Jack couldn't find them at the house, and he overreacted—losing his temper and saying a few words he regretted now.

Morgan had yelled at him in retaliation. "I'll bet our mother wouldn't talk to us like that and say bad words!"

That accusation had led to yet another fight. The atmosphere between Jack and his girls had been mutinous now all week.

Things seemed testy at Grace's, too. Jack could feel her strain every time he stopped by. The sheriff had suggested Margaret not go out alone—and that she should try to have someone with her at all times. Vincent had stepped up to take the protective role of staying close to Margaret. Not a tough job, in Jack's eyes, considering how smitten Vincent was with Margaret. But Grace still felt nervous that the sheriff and his staff had not found Crazy Man.

In all honesty, Jack's mood had not been helped by finding another note from the man in his car last week—right after the incident with Margaret. It had been scrawled on one of Jack's business cards, left on the front seat of his Jeep. It read: *I saw you with her.*

Jack had no idea whether this note referred again to the man's seeing him with Ashleigh Anne that day when Althea was hospitalized or to some new incident since—like seeing him with Grace out in the moonlight. Both issues were highly confidential, and Jack balked at sharing the notes. Covertly—and somewhat guiltily—Jack tucked the new note away with the other one he'd found earlier and didn't give it to the sheriff. His conscience smarted him over this indiscretion—and it made him crosser carrying his guilt around about it.

It was Friday now, and Jack was heading over to Bebe's to pick up the girls. It had been a hectic day for him, showing property all morning and through his lunch hour to a set of demanding clients. Grace had called at about noon and suggested he and the girls come over to the Mimosa for dinner, and Jack had welcomed the idea. The quick hamburger he'd grabbed at a drive-through hadn't been very satisfying.

Grace's voice rolled over Jack's phone, throaty and mellow. Even the sound of her voice turned him on these days. "Margaret and Vince are going into Maryville to dinner and a movie, Jack. So I thought maybe you and the girls might like to come here for dinner. I'll make the girls my lasagna; they love that. And I got a movie at the video store we can all watch together."

Jack felt grateful for the offer. He hoped it would help heal the breach with the twins. He hated it when they were angry at him.

He found Bebe sitting on the porch cutting up some late okra into a pan.

"Where are the girls?" he asked after buzzing her on the cheek.

She looked up in confusion. "They didn't come over here today, Jack. They told me you were going to drop them off at Grace's for the day instead."

Jack muttered an expletive. He doubted they were at Grace's. He'd just talked to her earlier, and she hadn't mentioned anything about the girls' being there when she offered her invitation to supper.

"Dang girls. I wonder where they've taken off to!" He paced the porch, trying to think. "I let them talk me into allowing them to walk over here this morning, Bebe—rather than me dropping them off. It's only a short distance on our own private drive. I never thought to check to see if they got here. They walk over here all the time."

Bebe offered him a sympathetic look. "Well, it never dawned on me that they were telling me a fib when they called me either, Jack. Don't be too hard on yourself. They probably just wanted to sneak off and do something they knew neither of us would approve of. It's not like you and Roger didn't pull the same sort of tricks yourselves when you were that age."

She put her pan of okra down and stood up to brush off her apron. "We'll start calling everyone we know. Those girls will turn up. You can cut a piece of fresh apple pie while you are phoning. I just took it out of the oven."

Jack grinned. Bebe always offered food in a crisis.

Thirty minutes later, Jack and Bebe stood comparing notes, trying to see if they could think of anyone else to phone. No one had seen the girls.

A curl of fear crawled up Jack's spine. "That loony man's still on the loose, Aunt Bebe."

Bebe tried not to look panicked at the thought, but Jack saw the alarm pass over her face. "Let's not jump to conclusions, Jack."

However, they were both upset enough to call the sheriff now. And to begin making other calls around the community—in case anyone had seen anything suspicious.

Finally, Jack called Grace. He hadn't wanted to upset her until he simply had to.

She acted amazingly calm. "Have you been up to the house to check the girls' rooms for clues? When my children pulled tricks like this, I usually found clues in their rooms about what prank they had gotten up to."

"I didn't think of that."

"Well, why don't you head to your house to look? I'll walk up the hill to meet you and help you out."

A short time later, Jack and Grace had finished a search of the kitchen at Jack's house—where Jack had last seen the girls—and started to look in the girls' bedrooms. The two cheery bedrooms, decorated in sunny yellows and blues, connected with a small sitting area between them where the girls each had a desk to do their schoolwork.

"Where do Meredith and Morgan keep personal stuff they don't want anyone to see?" Grace asked.

Jack scratched his head in thought. "They have what they call a 'treasure box.' It's actually an old pink jewelry box with one of those old snap clasps. It was Bebe's when she was a girl, and she gave it to them. They usually put things in there they consider valuable." He laughed. "Like an old dime-store ring they found when we were out hiking one time."

"Well, you look for that. I'll check both their desks."

Jack soon found the treasure box under Morgan's bed. It was locked, but Jack located the key in Morgan's bedside table.

Grace sat down on Morgan's bed to look through the box with Jack.

"Good heavens, Jack! Look at this." She held out a movie magazine picture of Celine Rosen to Jack. Familiar black words were scrawled across it in bold pen. The message, blazoned across the picture, read: *He ran your mama off.*

Jack felt sweat break out across his brow.

"That wicked man!" Tears filled Grace's eyes, and she shook the picture as if wishing it was Crazy Man. "Whatever possessed him to send two little girls something like this! Especially at their age and when they've only just learned who their mother is!"

Jack sat stunned for a moment. Why would anyone do this? Who would hate him this much to upset his little girls this way? To revive old valley gossip from long ago. "Do you think the girls believed this, Grace?"

Grace shook her head and blew out an exasperated breath. "I don't know, Jack. Children are very impressionable."

Taking the jewelry box from Jack to dig further into it, Grace pulled out an old school note, which she read and then discarded, and then a folded computer printout.

She scanned over it and looked up at him with panicked eyes. "Oh, Jack, this is a printout of an e-mail from Celine, dated last week. She invited the girls to come out to see her in California. She was evidently responding to an e-mail they had sent her earlier. She even offered to arrange airline tickets for them."

Jack snatched the e-mail from Grace to read it himself, his heart pounding.

"I'll bet that's where they have gone, Jack." Grace jumped up from the bed and started across the room, looking around. "Do the girls have suitcases? Where do they keep them? We need to look."

Jack felt stunned. "They're not even ten. They can't travel by themselves." He couldn't seem to take all this in. "How could they get to the airport? Surely they wouldn't just take off like this. California is all the way across the country."

Grace was already digging through Morgan's closet. She turned back to look at Jack where he still sat on the bed, trying to think. "Jack, you're not helping me here. Those girls might have flown out to California to see their mother."

She paced back across the room to pick up the magazine picture again. It had water stains on it and looked weatherworn. "This is the picture from that movie magazine I found out in the gazebo—just before all that mess happened with Margaret. I figured it might belong to the girls, but I left it there for them to come back and get later on. My guess is that Crazy Man was listening to them talk about their mother out there in the gazebo. He could easily have been hiding in all that brush behind it. He must have taken this magazine later on and decided to write this note to the girls."

Grace put her hand over her heart. "But why would he do such a thing? Why would he frighten and upset two little girls?" She paced across the room. "I'd like to get my hands on that man, I can tell you. I'm mad enough right now to take him on all by myself!" She punched a fist into her hand.

Jack fingered through the trinkets of the girls' treasure box to see if there might be any other clues. He found a folded slip of notebook paper under a four-leaf clover one of the girls had taped between two pieces of waxed paper. Scribbled on the note paper in Meredith's childish scrawl—with daisies replacing all the dots over the i's—was Celine's name, and a street address in Hollywood. Or at least Jack assumed that's what it was.

He held it up to Grace. "Where do you think the girls got this? Even I don't have Celine's most recent address."

Grace studied it. "You can get anything off the Internet today. Especially about movie stars. And you know Celine Rosen has become quite a star in her own right. Celine might have given it to them, too."

Jack shook his head. "Grace, do you really think Morgan and Meredith might have flown out to California to Celine's? They're not even ten! How would they know what to do—how to get to the airport? Or how to get their tickets?" He knew he was repeating words he'd said earlier, but he couldn't seem to help it.

"Those are smart girls, Jack." Grace picked up the printout of the e-mail from Celine to study it again. "Plus it certainly looks like Celine was a party to their travel plans. She tells them here she'd be delighted for them to come to see her before school starts. My guess is that she called and talked to them and then made their travel arrangements."

"Why wouldn't they have told me about this?" Jack shook his head.

Grace's eyes narrowed in annoyance. "Oh, honestly, Jack. They knew you would never let them go to California. You wouldn't even let them go to that slumber party at Mary Jean Watkins's house."

"I had my reasons for that." Jack knew his reply was sharp and testy.

Grace turned to him. "Look, Jack. The whys of this situation are not really important right now. What is important is that two very young girls might have made their way all the way to Hollywood, California, to Celine Rosen's home. We need to learn if that is so. If you have any contact information for Celine, we need to locate it."

She gave him an exasperated look. "And you need to get up and search around these girls' rooms and see if any of their clothes and belongings are gone. You should be able to tell if some of their clothes are missing, Jack. And you should know if they have a suitcase or duffle they usually take when they are going on a trip. We need to see if those are missing, too."

Jack seemed to wake to action then. He strode down the hall to search in the storage closet to see if the girls' duffle suitcases were still there. They weren't. In searching their drawers, he found pajamas and favorite clothes missing—plus toothbrushes and hairbrushes from the bathroom.

He groaned. "Confound it! They've really gone out to California! Grace, I have no current information on Celine. I haven't

heard from her in four or five years. And I know she's moved
since then. There was some TV show on one night talking about
fancy spreads in Hollywood that the stars owned. Celine's was
one of the ones they mentioned. They showed some palatial
Spanish mansion with walls and security all around it. In Beverly Hills, I think."

Grace gave Jack a sympathetic hug. "I'll go search on their
little computer to see if they saved any other information about
this trip . . . or if they left any other notes around." She started
toward the girls' desks. "You'd better call Sheriff Walker. See if
he can help you get any contact information through the police
department in Los Angeles. After all, these girls are in your custody. And Celine didn't get your approval for this trip."

Jack grimaced. "I wouldn't put it past Morgan to have told
her I said it was okay."

"Even so," Grace reasoned, "Celine should have talked to
you to confirm that you'd agreed to let the girls fly out. There's
no excuse for her encouraging those girls in a trip like this at
their age—and alone!"

Jack headed downstairs to find his phone. The next hour
proved to be a difficult one. There was tight security around Celine's home, and it wasn't easy to gain any contact information.
Sheriff Walker finally dropped over to tell them he'd made a
connection with a detective in Los Angeles willing to help recover the girls. Twenty minutes later the detective called Jack.

"You need to fly out here," he said. "We've found record of
the girls arriving on a direct flight that came in earlier today.
The stewardess saw that they were picked up. She said they
were met by a security guard from Celine Rosen's staff—who
showed the flight attendant identification. That's the last that's
been seen of them."

The detective paused. "My feeling is that the twins are at Celine Rosen's place. But in case there's an attempted kidnapping
involved, I think we shouldn't alert her before we go over there
to retrieve the girls. And I would hate to go in there to get those
little girls alone and frighten them. I'll be able to get through her
security, but I think you should be with me."

"You're right." Jack agreed. "I'll get the first flight out that I can and go with you."

"Call me as soon as you get that arranged. I'll post a couple of officers to watch the house until then, to make sure the girls don't leave." Jack heard him shuffle some papers. "My name, again, is Cole Strader. I'll meet your flight, and we'll go over to see if we can find your girls as soon as you get here. We'll have backup in case we need it, but it may be that she simply wanted to see the girls. You say she hasn't seen them since they were born and that you think the girls contacted her. She might have just been curious. Everything might be okay."

"Then why haven't she or the girls called me?"

The detective grew quiet for a moment. "I don't know that, Mr. Teague."

Jack hung up the phone and turned to Sheriff Walker and Grace. "I'm going to fly out to California. This detective and I will go over to Celine's place when I arrive. He can get me in past her security. He thinks it's best we don't alert her first." He sighed. "Just in case it might be a kidnapping—and in case she might try to hide the girls in another location before I get out there."

Offering a hand to Swofford Walker, he said, "Thank you, Swofford. I appreciate all your help. I'll keep you posted as I can."

The sheriff nodded and turned to leave. "Want me to go by to talk to anyone for you?"

"No." Jack shook his head. "I'll call Bebe and my mother after I make my plane reservations. They'll tell anyone else."

"And get folks to praying." Swofford hitched up his pants. "Be sure someone calls the minister. Me and the missus—we'll sure be lifting this up."

"Thanks." Jack saw Swofford to the door, and then came back to slump into a chair at the kitchen table, a phone book in his hands. He opened the book to the airlines' numbers. "I know the Internet is faster, but I'm going to look up some phone numbers, too, in case I can't find what I want online."

He glanced up at Grace. 'You can go on home now. I'll call you as I can and let you know how things are going."

Grace crossed her arms. "I'm going with you, Jack. You might as well book for two."

Jack heaved a sigh. "There's no need for that, Grace. My guess is it will be six hours or more getting out there." He looked at his watch. "Even with all the time-zone changes, it will probably be ten or eleven at night by the time I can get to the Los Angeles airport. And I'm sure I'll need to stay over. You don't need to put yourself through all that."

She gave him a stubborn look. "There's no point in arguing with me, Jack. I'm going. And that's final." She sat down at the table and put her hand over his. Her voice softened then. "I want to be a help to you, and I want to go for the girls."

He wanted to argue, but as he looked into her eyes, he knew it would be of little use. She had that determined set to her mouth that he'd come to recognize.

Jack shook his head and shrugged in resignation. "Well, let's see what flights we can find."

CHAPTER 21

They couldn't get a direct flight. However, Jack was fortunate to find an evening flight with an airline going out of Knoxville and connecting through Memphis before heading straight on to Los Angeles. It was a six and a half hour flight. They wouldn't arrive in California until nearly eleven p.m. Pacific time, even with the time change from East to West.

Grace walked home to pack a bag for herself and to let the dogs out, leaving Jack to pack and make some necessary calls to his family. She felt grateful she had no guests coming in this weekend to the bed-and-breakfast. The one family scheduled had cancelled earlier this morning.

Margaret had already left on her date with Vince. Grace wrote her a note rather than calling her. She hated to call Margaret in the middle of their dinner. Grace looked at her watch. She would call her later before the plane left. Grace smiled to herself. She also didn't want to give Margaret the opportunity to try to talk her out of going.

After changing into some comfortable clothes for traveling, Grace picked up a small picture of the girls to look at while she waited for Jack. Lord, she hoped those girls were safe and well. She knew they'd hardly been out of the valley here in Townsend except to go to the beach or to Disneyworld in Florida once.

When she heard Jack's knock at the door, Grace dropped the photo of the girls into her purse. They might need it later to show to someone. And Jack wasn't the sort to carry family pictures around in his wallet.

His face looked strained as he let himself in the house.

"I made some coffee if you want a cup." Grace smiled at him.

He glanced at his watch. "I'll get some at the airport if we have time. I think we'd better go on. I don't want to take any chances on getting bumped off this flight."

She nodded, and then moved forward to slip her arms around his waist and lay her head against his chest. "It's going to be all right, Jack. I know it. I've been praying here while I've been waiting, and I believe everything is going to be all right."

"Ah, Grace Conley, you are such a comfort." She felt him relax a little against her, his lips wandering over her forehead and into her hair.

He stood still for a few minutes, as if drawing strength from her, and then he pulled away. "We'd better go."

Jack reached down to pick up her small travel bag. "Is this all?" He seemed surprised.

"Yes. Except for my little carry-on bag here. I've traveled a lot, Jack, and learned to travel light."

They stayed quiet on the way to the airport, saying little. Once there, they checked in and then went through security to the airline boarding area. There they sat, flipping through magazines, until their flight was called.

To Grace's surprise, Jack led her to the first-class section.

He actually grinned at her as they sat down. "I got a Y-Up deal, first class at coach prices because I bought at the last minute. Sweet, huh?" He leaned back with pleasure and crossed his long legs.

She smiled back at him, glad to see that devilish grin—for whatever reason. "It is certainly nice." She looked around in admiration.

"Did you and your husband travel first class?"

"Very seldom." Grace answered his question honestly.

She enjoyed seeing another of Jack's smiles. She wondered if he would always compare himself with Charles—and want to know how he stacked up against Charles. Maybe it was a guy thing.

Nervously, her thoughts slid to Celine. A young movie star—and very beautiful. Would Grace look dowdy and old to Jack after he saw Celine again? It seemed inevitable they would see her. Jack had once loved Celine very much. Grace felt uncomfortable at the thought.

Jack played with the seat, looked around the compartment with interest, and explored the brochures provided by the airlines. Then he glued his nose to the window and watched the movement on the runway. Grace smiled to herself. He was like a kid—excited to be on an adventure, even if it was an unhappy one.

As they lifted off, Jack took pleasure in peering down at the scenery below as it grew smaller and smaller. "Problems seem a little less significant from this perspective, don't they?"

"Yes, they do."

Jack leaned back and heaved a sigh. "You know, I thought at first that Crazy Man might have taken the girls. I've worried that his next step might be to hurt someone ever since he followed Margaret. His old pattern of staying hidden seemed to be changing."

"I can't help but wonder what sort of twisted thoughts are in that man's mind to cause him to do the things he has done."

"Well, he certainly isn't operating on all cylinders."

"Has Swofford Walker come any closer to learning his identity? Found any clues?"

Jack shook his head. "None that we don't already know about."

Grace flipped open a fashion magazine she'd brought with her and paused to study a dress that caught her attention.

"That would look good on you." Jack pointed to the dress. "That length of skirt and that swirly kind of material are flattering to you."

She smiled at him. "Not many men notice those sorts of details about a woman's clothes."

"I told you I've always liked women." He grinned. "Liked

looking at them, enjoyed watching them, liked being around them. I've always noticed things about women—more so than most men."

"That's flattering to women—when you notice what they wear, what they like, the scents they use."

He leaned toward her. "You always have that musky floral scent on. Pleasures. Your husband was right to say it suits you. It does."

Jack leaned over to kiss her full on the mouth.

"Jack!" She pushed him back, feeling a blush steal up her cheeks. She looked around furtively to see if anyone had noticed. "We're in a public place."

He traced a finger over her lips before he sat back into his seat. "I'm glad you came with me, Grace. It will be a long six hours. I'll be glad for some company. It will keep me from worrying so."

"Do you think Celine would really hurt the girls?"

He shrugged. "Not maliciously, I don't think. But she's self-absorbed and not very responsible. She wasn't the best mother even for the short time she was with our girls. Hated to get up in the night with them. Got cross and agitated when they cried. Resented it when they were needy when she was engrossed in a movie. Always wanting to get a sitter and go out."

"I don't see much of that character in the girls."

"Thank God for that."

"And they look more like you with their brown eyes and dimples."

"Their hair has a touch of red like their mother's. They didn't get the Teague black hair." He ran a hand through his own hair. "I'm starting to turn white-headed like my mother. My father, too."

"It's very attractive." She looked at the threads of silver gray running through Jack's hair.

He studied her. "You're not graying at all yet. And you're about the same age I am."

Grace laughed. "I've only seen a rare gray hair so far. And I plucked it out as soon as I did."

Jack chuckled in reply. "If I did that, I'd soon be bald."

She looked over at him with warmth. "I love the way you look, Jack. And I like looking at you, too."

His eyes darkened. "Don't flirt with me, woman. It feels intimate in this plane, and it will be growing dark soon. You might give me ideas."

Grace studied her hands, feeling shy—but as always enjoying his compliments.

"I'm not sure you should have gotten linked up with a man like me, Grace. But I'm glad you did."

They sat back in silence for a few moments.

"Tell me how you met Charles," Jack asked.

Surprised at the question, Grace's eyes flew up to Jack's.

He met her gaze. "We've never talked about it. And I've been curious. I told you about how I met Celine. Got fascinated by her and squired her around when she did a movie in the Townsend area. Ended up marrying her."

Grace nodded and searched her memory for where to begin her story about Charles. "You remember I told you that I modeled part-time while in college. Well, the agency I worked for in Nashville sent me over to Conley Carpets one day for a shoot. Charles was there, of course. He was older than I, already graduated from Vanderbilt, and helping his father to run the business."

A faint smile played on her lips. "I knew he found me attractive. I could tell by the way he watched me. We talked at the break. Later, he invited me to lunch. We found so many things to talk about then. Enjoyed each other much more than we expected to. It surprised us both, I think. He began to call me after that. To take me out."

"Margaret said he was a good man."

Her eyes lifted to his in surprise. "Margaret talked to you about Charles?"

He shrugged a shoulder carelessly. "We were both talking about losing a parent one day. I wasn't probing, Grace. She painted a nice picture of her father."

"He was a good man. Hardworking, ambitious, bright. He

truly loved the business—and loved the socializing that went along with being a major business owner in the Nashville area." Grace paused. "Charles liked having money, liked knowing people with money and doing things that moneyed people do. Much more than I did. I hadn't been raised in society. My roots began in a small town around simpler people. Sometimes, I thought we were the most different in that."

"Because he had money?"

"No. Because it mattered so much to him. That he ranked and rated people by how much they had. I felt uncomfortable with that."

"He left you well-to-do?" The statement was a question.

"Yes. Several generations of Conleys had built the business by the time Charles inherited. He left me a generous income and left a lot to the children, too, in trusts. And, of course, he left the boys the business."

Jack reached down to scratch his ankle, shifting in his seat, already restless before even an hour of their flight was finished. "Are the boys coming around about your having moved over here?"

"A little, although Elaine and Margaret seem to understand more. I think the boys still feel they lost an aspect of control that was their due. They are very much like their father in that. He was a bit chauvinistic."

"And you were okay with that?" Jack looked surprised.

Grace considered his question. "It was flattering at first, I guess. Charles was older, and he had a very strong character. It was easy to let him take the lead, easy to just follow. I suppose it became a pattern. It's easy to get into patterns, you know—even if they aren't the best for you in every way."

"Tell me about it." Jack's words were sarcastic, but touched with humor.

"Then with four children, all their involvements, my civic groups and volunteer work, and all our business and social activities—my time was full. I didn't feel really suppressed or unfulfilled, except at odd moments."

"And how did you feel at odd moments?" He was watching her, sincerely interested.

She smiled at him. "Like I was only someone's wife, someone's mother, someone people always called on to head committees, to bring a dish, to plan an event. In odd moments, I wished I could be someone on my own."

Grace leaned back in her seat, remembering. "Sometimes I would meet a woman who had really accomplished things beyond being a good wife, mother, and civic leader. I'd envy her— so polished, confident, sure of herself. And, then, of course, like a typical woman, I'd find a way to tear her down in my mind— to try to make myself feel my choices were better than hers. That my life was the richer."

"Why do women do that? Compare themselves against each other that way?"

"You don't think men do?" She lifted a brow.

"Not in the same way. And I don't think they're as vicious."

She shrugged. "Maybe it's from being a minority group for so long. Men have never had to strive for their identity like women have. Men have always had a clearer life path, clearer expectations. But women, they've always been torn—wanting and needing two things and finding it hard to do both of them well."

"Hmmmm. I guess I never really saw that struggle very much in my mother. She seemed to always realize she needed to be involved in the business. And Bebe always seemed happy at home, taking care of Roger and me, doing the home thing."

"Well, I felt some conflict. Many women do."

Jack turned to look at her. "I think Charles contributed to that, Grace. I think he wanted you to stay at home, tending to him, second to him, dependent on him. Some strong men are like that. And they have subtle ways of discouraging a woman from seeking more, from finding her own success, her own way. I'm not saying that they belittle her, but they have subtle ways of encouraging her to stay right where they want her."

Grace raised her eyebrows and turned to look at him. "Funny. My mother said the same thing. She said she felt Charles and his mother had kept me from developing. And that she worried that I'd lost something of myself over the years in the process."

Jack picked up the magazine off Grace's lap and flipped its pages. "And do you think you've found the real Grace Conley now?"

Grace's face flamed. "Don't tease me, Jack. And, yes, I do think I've found myself in a sense, come into my own more. I like who I am now." She raised her chin.

"So do I. And I didn't mean to tease you." Jack gave her a roguish grin and leaned over to kiss her unexpectedly. "I like who you are *very* much, Grace Conley."

Caught off guard, Grace struggled with conflicting feelings, not knowing how to reply. He'd gotten her to reveal much more than she'd intended to.

Jack held her chin in his hand for a moment and looked at her with an intense gaze. "I like strong women, Grace. They don't threaten me one bit. You can keep becoming all you want to be with me. I'll enjoy watching it happen, enjoy celebrating all your successes with you. I'll never try to hold you back."

"Thank you." Grace wasn't sure what else to say.

He leaned closer to her and gave her a slow grin. "In my experience, strong women are very passionate in bed. I like thinking about that."

"Jack Teague!" Grace looked around to see if anyone was listening. "Watch what you say! Are you always thinking about sex?"

"No. But it comes up a lot in my mind." He gave her a wolfish smile. "Especially when I'm around you."

She blushed. "We're supposed to be on a rescue mission, thinking foremost about your little girls."

"I know. But you've given me a pleasant diversion. And something else to think about—instead of just letting my stomach churn up in knots with worry. I thank you for that." He gave her another quick kiss and patted her on the leg, much too intimately and much too high on her thigh, his fingers trailing into the dip between her legs.

Grace felt herself respond to his touch, and pulled her legs together tightly. She saw Jack smile before he sat back in his seat.

Their whole flight was like that. They talked and shared about their past, and, in between, Jack made passes at her. Flattered her. Teased her with small intimacies. As darkness fell outside and the plane flew through the evening hours toward California, it seemed the sense of intimacy between them heightened.

Grace had thought she would spend six hours with a man torn up with anxiety and worry, talking constantly of the problems that might lie ahead. That she'd console him and comfort him, be his strength and try to calm his anger. It's what she'd always done with Charles when he got upset, she realized. He'd have worried himself all the way to California, imagining all the scenarios that might occur, being angry and annoyed over all the factors he couldn't control. Looking back at what he might have done to prevent the situation in the first place. Talking about how he'd handle things differently in the future. But here, Grace found herself in new waters. Jack was a very different man. And Grace found herself a very different woman when she was with him.

They were both quiet and resting now as the plane flew through its last leg toward the huge Los Angeles airport. Jack had let his arm drift off the armrest onto Grace's leg, and Grace had allowed herself to lean up against Jack's shoulder. They'd drifted into an hour's sleep like this. Back in Townsend, it was well after midnight now.

Grace sighed. "I hope Morgan and Meredith are all right."

"We'll be there soon." Jack breathed deeply.

"You won't be too hard on them, will you, Jack?"

He looked over at her with sleepy eyes. "You can't always know what you will do in a situation until you get there and see how the land lies, Grace." Jack squeezed her hand. "Try to get some rest. We might have a long night ahead."

Shortly before eleven p.m. Pacific time, they finally arrived in the Los Angeles airport. Grace regretted they couldn't look down on the city as they descended. All she could see from the plane window, when she leaned across Jack, was a sea of city lights.

They both were stiff when they stood up to depart. Grace watched Jack roll his shoulders and neck to get the kinks out. Her knees felt stiff and sore. Jack took her hand as they walked off the plane, and Grace thought it a sweet gesture. The airport was crowded with throngs of people everywhere as they made their way out of the arrival area.

A man separated himself from the crowd as they looked around and came toward them with a hand held out. He gave them a slight smile and a nod. "Cole Strader here, LAPD. You must be Jack Teague. Swofford Walker gave us a pretty good description."

Jack took his hand in a strong grip. Grace watched them assess each other quickly as men often do. Detective Strader was tall, of medium build, balding a little on the top of his head. He wouldn't stand out in a crowd until you looked at his eyes— strong and compelling, revealing a depth and intelligence not evident at first glance.

Jack introduced her. "This is my neighbor, Grace Conley. She's very close to my girls. I thought we might need a woman's touch." He grinned then. "Plus, the woman was determined to come with me."

Cole let a small smile turn up the edges of his mouth. "Women can have a strong mind about things sometimes."

It had been a long time since Grace had been in the Los Angeles airport. She'd forgotten how large it was—and how culturally diverse. Cole Strader led them through the airport with ease and efficiency to get their bags, and on to his car. It was waiting at the front of the airport, another officer driving. The officer was introduced as Officer Parks. He stood shorter and paunchier than Detective Strader, with a warmer, more congenial face.

"What have you learned?" Jack asked Detective Strader as soon as they got into the car.

The man frowned. "We've had some men watching the place, but they haven't seen any sign of children. Cars have been going into the place all evening. Report is that there is a big party or gathering going on of some kind. Lots of limousines and money. Lots of glitter and glamour. They can hear a band from outside. Celine Rosen is evidently having a big 'to-do' tonight. It's Friday in Hollywood, after all."

"No one has gone in yet to look for the girls?" Grace asked this.

"We've waited for you." Detective Strader stated these words matter-of-factly as Officer Parks eased his way into the line of vehicles heading for the exit.

The detective turned around slightly to look at Grace and Jack in the backseat. "As I told Jack earlier—in case there is some kind of kidnapping plan going on or some attempt to try to keep the girls from you—our department thought it would be better to wait until you arrived before we approached Ms. Rosen. To the best of our knowledge she has the girls. We know they were picked up at the airport by one of her security people this morning, and we were able to find a witness who saw them driving into the gates at her place earlier today."

"What do you plan to do?" Jack asked.

"We'll go in, now that you're here—you two, myself, and Officer Parks. Hopefully, we can locate Celine Rosen readily—and the girls. You have the legal right to take the girls if we find them there. And we'll stand behind you in doing that. If there is trouble, we still have backup outside the house. We can call in more support, if it should be needed. But I'm hoping this will go easily."

He looked at Jack directly. "How long has it been since you've seen or had contact with your ex-wife, Mr. Teague?"

"Four or five years, at least. Ms. Rosen, then Mrs. Teague, left me and the girls when they were babies to come back to Hollywood. She wasn't much interested in being a wife or mother. Wanted another life. Wanted to try to become a big star."

The detective nodded. "Looks like from the size of her place and what we've been able to learn about her, she made her wish good."

They were quiet as the car made its way into the freeway traffic of a big city.

The detective took a call on his radio, and after a while he spoke again. "It's still my belief that maybe Ms. Rosen just wanted to get a look at the girls. And thought maybe you might not agree to their coming out here. Decided to take things into her own hands to see them."

"I can't say, Detective." Jack's reply was quiet, but Grace could feel his tension building now that they were here. He knew a confrontation lay ahead.

Detective Strader nodded. "Well, we can hope for the best. Parks here has got a nine-year-old girl, and neither of us likes to think of girls that young traveling so far on their own. It's dangerous. You can certainly file charges against Ms. Rosen for aiding and abetting that, Mr. Teague—even if she is a big movie star."

"One thing at a time, Detective. Right now, let's just find my girls."

CHAPTER 22

Jack was reminded of how much he hated big cities as their unmarked police car made its way along the congested freeway overpasses and underpasses leaving the airport. Everyone seemed to drive at lightning speed, and there was a hurrying, stressful, self-absorbed spirit that seemed to hang in the very air. An impersonality.

As they sped up the freeway in the dark, all Jack could see were buildings, lights, cars, and people. It was late, too—moving toward midnight. In Townsend, people would be in for the night. Here, it almost seemed as if people were just coming out.

Officer Parks swerved and honked at a car filled with teenagers that had strayed over into his lane. He grumbled. "Dang kids. Probably already doped or boozed up."

Jack saw Grace grimace and then felt her lean toward him. He put a hand on her leg affectionately, but was too restless to leave it there, to enjoy the feeling. He was thinking ahead now to what he might find at Celine's.

They passed signs for Santa Monica, Hollywood, and UCLA before they finally turned off the San Diego Parkway toward Beverly Hills. Out the window, Jack could see palm trees along the streets, even in the dark.

"Been here before?" Detective Strader asked.

"A time or two," Jack answered. "But not in a long time."

"The motto for Beverly Hills is 'the garden spot of the world.'" Detective Strader turned around to offer a crooked grin at them as they turned off the main boulevard and started to wind down a posh suburban street where many of the homes sprawled on large properties tucked discreetly behind high fences and walls. "The median house price here is $2,613,000."

Jack gave a fleeting thought to the Realtor's commission on a house like that.

The detective turned back around in his seat and made a radio call to the unit near Celine's house.

As their car rounded a corner and started down another street of wealthy estates, Officer Parks began to slow their vehicle. "There's our unit up ahead." He gestured to a police car parked along the side of the road.

Detective Strader talked on the radio to one of the officers in the unit as Parks pulled up in front of them. Then the policemen all got out of their cars for a few moments to confer.

Jack recognized the street name they were on from the slip of notebook paper he'd found in the girls' treasure chest.

"I guess this is it." Jack reached over to pat Grace's hand. "Do you still want to go in with us? You don't have to."

Her steely look was answer enough.

Detective Strader and Officer Parks rejoined them in a few minutes, and then Parks pulled their car out from the curb to begin the approach to the security gate of the mansion where Celine lived. A high stucco wall surrounded the estate, and an ornate Spanish gate led into the driveway. Strader got out to talk to the security guards as Parks stopped at the gate. Jack saw Strader flash his badge and gesture to him and Grace in the back of the car. There was some nodding and conversation Jack couldn't hear.

"There's a big party going on," Strader announced as he got back into the car. "There was some kind of awards event tonight in Hollywood for daytime television programs. Seemed a good time to host a celebration afterward, I guess."

The gate swung open. Strader nodded at the burly security man as they passed through. "Another security officer will meet us at the front when we get to the house. He'll go with us to try to locate Ms. Rosen in all the crowd." His gaze flicked to Grace.

"These parties get a little risqué, Miz Conley. You can stay behind if you're not comfortable with it."

"The girls may need me." Grace's reply seemed answer enough, and Strader turned to watch their approach to the sprawling Spanish-style mansion at the end of the drive. There were cars everywhere, and the noise of laughter, talk, and the sounds of a band floated out to them on the night air.

A short time later a handsome, young security guard led them through throngs of people to help them locate Celine Rosen. The guard had shrugged when asked about where the girls might be. "I didn't know there were any kids here. I just came on tonight to help with Ms. Rosen's party. Takes a lot of us when she has a big event like this."

He raised his eyebrows knowingly to the officers as if they understood exactly what he was talking about. "You're not here to bust anybody, are you?"

Strader frowned. "Not unless they become a hindrance to why we're here."

They found Celine Rosen at last, out by a sumptuous kidney-shaped swimming pool set amid palms and exotic landscaping. She had on a long, slinky dress in shimmering silver with a deeply plunging back. Her red hair, piled on top of her head in a riot of curls, shone in the outdoor lights. Her laugh floated across to them even before they made their way around the patio to her.

In the pool were several scantily clad and naked people. In one dark corner of the water, it looked like one man was in the act with one of the women. No one seemed to even be noticing. A band blared from a tent set up at the other end of the pool, and couples writhed to the music there, many groping each other and sipping from drinks between their movements.

Jack felt embarrassed for Grace to see all this decadence. There were drunk and obviously drugged people everywhere. The mood was totally self-indulgent. At this late point in the night, all the music and the people were too loud, and Celine's guests long past the stage of being of sound mind.

Grace grabbed Jack's hand as a man flopped down onto a lounge chair by the pool and ran his hand right up the dress of a young woman. She giggled riotously while he groped her.

"Mercy, Jack. Where are the girls amidst all of this?"

Her words only echoed his thoughts. His anger grew as they approached Celine and her group of glittering friends.

She looked toward them in surprise as they approached, trying to place them. Her eyes settled on Jack and widened.

"Jack!" She moved forward to reach him and then leaned in to give him a kiss on the cheek. "Gracious, you're as handsome as ever—even after all these years."

She made an effort to press herself closer to him, an arm moving around to slide up his back with affection.

Jack pulled away. "I'm here about the girls, Celine. Where are they?"

"Oh. The girls." Her voice sounded flippant and annoyed. She paused, somewhat vaguely, to try to corral her thoughts. "Upstairs somewhere, darling. Probably gone to bed."

She grinned at him, flashing familiar deep green eyes to his. "They've turned out very cute, Jack. And are really very sweet. I've enjoyed having them here."

Strader stepped forward. "Miz Rosen, I'm Detective Strader with LAPD. It's my understanding that you didn't gain permission from Mr. Teague to have his girls fly out here to you. Is that true?"

Celine looked at Strader in surprise, her eyes then moving to Officer Parks. She turned dramatically pained eyes to Jack. "You've called the police, Jack? Really, darling. I'm surprised at that. Surely you know I wouldn't hurt the girls. This really wasn't necessary."

Jack's expression hardened. "I couldn't even have gotten into this place tonight, Celine, without them. What did you expect?"

"Oh, well," she replied on an airy note. "I meant to call you earlier—after the girls sort of let it slip that you didn't know they were here." She giggled. "But I had the awards to go to. My hairdresser came, and Demetri had to dress me, of course.

There was *so* much to do. And then all my friends began to arrive, and the time just slipped away." She gave them all a charming smile.

"You really didn't need to come out here, Jack. I planned to call later, and everything would have been explained." She waved a hand dismissively as if there were no problem at all with this logic.

A man came up to lean in and kiss her, offering her congratulations, before he moved on.

She gave them all a practiced, radiant smile then. "Our soap placed very well tonight. Won three awards. And I won one—for best supporting actress. Quite a coup!" She raised a toast toward them.

"I want to see the girls." Jack's voice was harsh. He leaned forward and grasped Celine by the arm. "This is no place for nine-year-old girls to be, Celine. What were you thinking? Look around you! These girls are innocents."

She glanced around the pool area with indifference. "Everyone's just having a good time, Jack. You know about good times."

"Little girls don't need to see these things." Grace stepped forward. "And it might be dangerous for them here. Some of these men are drunk—or drugged. Something might happen to the girls. How do you know someone hasn't tried to hurt them already? You don't even seem to know where they are. Or if they are safe."

Celine seemed to notice Grace for the first time then. She ran her eyes down Grace slowly, as if assessing her. "Who are you?" she asked at last.

Jack answered. "This is Grace Conley, my neighbor and a close friend of the girls'. She came with me because she was concerned about them."

"I see." Celine shrugged casually and turned her glance away from Grace, as if dismissing her as someone of no consequence. It angered Jack.

"Where are the girls, Celine?" He moved closer to her, making eye contact with her. She had been drinking, that was a fact.

She still held a wineglass in one hand. But her eyes were too glittery for only alcohol. She'd added a party drug to the mix.

In an airy way, she replied. "Well, I'm not sure, really. I gave them the west suite bedroom, the blue one at the top of the stairs and down the right hallway. Last door on the left near the end. The room has a lovely little balcony I thought the girls would enjoy." She gave Jack a pouty look. "I wish you'd let them stay a little longer. I had hoped to enjoy them some more. It's been a long time since I've seen them, after all."

Detective Strader took a step forward. "We'll be taking the girls with us tonight." His voice was an authoritative, no-nonsense one. "Mr. Teague has legal custody, and he wants to take the girls back home."

"Oh, so you've said before. No need to get disagreeable about it." Celine waved a hand at him and puffed out a lower lip prettily. "None of you are any fun at all. This was a great adventure for the girls, coming out here to meet me. I don't see that there was anything wrong with my flying them out. They are my daughters after all. And they said they wanted to meet me."

"You should have asked me first." Jack's voice was steely.

Celine leaned toward him, rolling in her shoulders to display a long expanse of cleavage. "And would you have said yes if I had, Jackie?" It was an old pet name she'd called him long ago when she was coming on to him.

"No." His answer was short and direct.

"Well, then." She shrugged dramatically. "You see, I thought that might be your answer. And that's why I decided to wait and talk to you *after* the girls had arrived." She gave them all a bright smile as if that explained everything.

"Mr. Teague could bring charges in this instance, Miz Rosen." Detective Strader stepped closer to Celine. "And for several good reasons from what I've seen here tonight."

Celine offered them another pouty look. "Would you do that, Jack? I only wanted to get a look at the girls. Surely you can understand that."

Jack felt his anger flame.

Beside him, Grace moved up to put her hand on his arm.

"Jack, we need to find the girls. That's the most important thing. They're not safe here."

He nodded—checking himself, knowing Grace was right—and then spoke through clenched teeth. "Celine, why don't you take us up and help us find the girls?"

She shrugged indifferently and turned her eyes to the young security officer who had led them in. "Benny here will take you up." She flashed a smile at him and ran a hand up the young man's arm suggestively. "He knows the house and where the bedrooms are."

Out of the corner of his eye, Jack saw Grace recoil—as though she had just seen a snake or a nasty spider. He shrugged. Perhaps she had.

"I'll take all of you right up." Benny stood to attention and was rewarded by a brilliant smile from Celine.

"They'll be a little something extra in your paycheck, Benny, if you cooperate with the officers here in every way you can." She flashed a smile at them all. "And, now, if you'll excuse me, I have guests I need to attend to. You know—the charming hostess and all that."

She walked off from them then, as if they were just a few pesky fans whom she had now dispensed with. Jack felt his hands clench into fists. He took a step forward, but then felt Grace's hand tuck into his arm.

She caught his eye. "Let's go with Benny, Jack. We need to find the girls."

Jack reluctantly conceded, while seething at letting Celine get away with playing that final scene as she had. It felt all too achingly familiar to countless past scenes Jack had once endured with Celine when they were married.

Grace's hand slipped into his, helping him to turn and follow along with Detective Strader and Officer Parks as they made their way back through the crowded rooms of the ground floor of the mansion to the grand stairway leading to the upper floors.

Bits of the party had flowed upward onto the second floor of Celine's house. A drunk sat against a wall in the upper hallway, passed out with his head slumped over. A group of glitzy, young starlets sat in a circle in one of the upstairs lounges, obviously passing around a joint among them. Behind several of the bedroom doors that Officer Parks opened, as they made their way down the west hall, couples were sprawled on the beds, taking pleasures or sleeping after.

Jack began to feel sick.

"I hate to say it, but this is real typical of Hollywood parties among a certain element of the rich and famous." Detective Strader gave them an apologetic look. "Not much we can do about it, really. We can't just come in without cause onto their private grounds."

They found the blue bedroom at last, which Benny thought might be the room Celine had been talking about. "There's more than one that are blue," he told them apologetically, shrugging. "And with a balcony. I think the fricking place has thirteen bedrooms. It's big."

As Jack walked into the room, he saw evidence on one of the beds that the girls had surely been here. He saw Meredith's duffle on a chair by the window and Morgan's jacket flung carelessly over the end of the bed.

Seeing the signs, also, the detective and the officer began to look through the large suite. They did not find the girls.

`"I don't see them," Detective Strader said.

Jack's heart sagged. He turned to leave, deciding that they would simply have to search further. The girls had to be somewhere.

Grace caught Jack's arm before he left. She stood, indecisively. Then she called out. "Morgan! Meredith! Are you here anywhere?"

A muffled sobbing sound was heard in reply. "Ms. Grace, is that you?"

Jack's heartbeat quickened. It was Morgan!

Grace heaved a relieved sigh and answered. "Yes, dear. Where are you? It's safe to come out. Your father and I are here."

Jack heard some shuffling noises from a closet across the

room. He walked quickly to the door and opened it. And then Morgan shot into his arms to bury her face against his neck. Meredith followed, after climbing out from under a rack of clothes at the back. Tears were streaming down her face.

"Oh, Daddy!" Her sobs nearly broke Jack's heart.

Jack dropped to his knees to hold them, his own tears of relief joining theirs.

"How did you get here?" Morgan asked, pulling herself away from Jack's neck for a moment. She had been crying, too. Jack could see the tear streaks down her face.

"I flew here, like you did." He gave Morgan a reproachful look then.

"Oh, Daddy, I'm sorry! We didn't know what she was like. We didn't know!" Morgan began to cry. "Meredith found her e-mail address in a movie magazine, and we wrote to her, and she wrote back. We were curious."

Meredith's tears were soaking Jack's shirt, but he didn't care. It felt so good to hold his girls and to know they were safe.

He pulled the girls off his neck to look at them. "Are you girls all right? Has anyone hurt you?"

Morgan shook her head, understanding what he was asking. "That's why we hid in the closet, Daddy, and locked the closet door. There were these two creepy men following us after we went out looking for Celine and then started back to our room. We had to give them the slip and then come and hide in the closet here."

"We were afraid to come out." Meredith's voice was a wail. "There were bad things going on at Mommy's party. And we couldn't find her. We were so scared."

Jack looked up to see tears streaming down Grace's face. As if noticing the direction of his glance, Meredith ran to launch herself at Grace then. "Oh, Ms. Grace, I'm so glad to see you! We have had a bad time."

Morgan went over to give Grace a hug, too. "I'm glad Daddy brought you, Ms. Grace." All three cried as they hugged each other.

Jack moved over to join the huddle. "Grace insisted on coming. She was worried about you."

Meredith looked at Morgan. "I knew Ms. Grace was nice from the first day we met her." She looked at Jack with accusing eyes. "You didn't tell us our mother wasn't nice, Daddy."

Jack winced.

Morgan scowled at her. "Well, Mer, we should have figured it out by now from how she dumped out on us when we were only little babies."

Jack noticed that the two officers and Benny had politely stepped into the hall when they had found the girls, giving them some time alone with the girls in reunion.

Meredith looked at Grace and spoke in a shocked whisper. "Our mother swims naked in front of men. That's not nice at all. She said we could, too, if we wanted. But Morgan and I wouldn't."

Grace rolled her eyes at Jack.

Morgan looked thoughtful. "She does have a cool pool and a really big house. And she had her cook fix us anything we wanted for lunch. She wasn't mean to us or anything, Daddy."

"She said we were sweet, and she was nice to us when we first came." Meredith seemed to be trying to think of something good to say, too.

Morgan scowled. "But she told this man who was here fixing her hair that it was a shame we hadn't inherited her beauty. That we were a little plain. And she knew we were right in the room. That wasn't a very nice thing to say."

"If Aunt Bebe were here, she would have told our mother that wasn't nice and made her go sit in her room." Meredith said this emphatically.

Jack laughed. "Aunt Bebe probably would have done just that."

He looked up to see Grace suppress a smile.

Detective Strader stepped into the room. "Mr. Teague. The party here is accelerating. I think it might be a good idea if you pack up the girls. It would be best if we leave right away."

"Who's that?" Meredith asked, shying behind Jack as she spoke.

Morgan studied him. "Are you a cop?"

He nodded.

"Wow." She looked at him. "Then how come you aren't arresting all these creepy people for all the bad stuff they're doing?"

"I'll give some thought to that." His mouth twitched in a smile. "But let's get you and your sister out of here first."

"Right." Morgan ran over to dig her duffle out from behind a chair and began to pack up her things. She looked at Grace. "You might want to help Mer, Ms. Grace. She's been kind of upset."

Jack saw Grace smile at that and start over to pick up Meredith's duffle off the chair. Grace motioned to Meredith to come and help her.

Detective Strader pulled Jack aside while the girls packed. "Did they say anybody did them any harm?"

"No." Jack frowned at how close they might have come. "They used their wits and locked themselves in the closet there and hid in the back of it."

"Bright girls." Strader scratched his head. "From what I saw here, it's good they hid. Some of these Hollywood types are kind of kinky."

The detective gave him a direct look then. "You want to press charges?"

Jack shook his head wearily. "Not really. But I'd like to issue some kind of warning. I don't want this happening again."

"I'll go have a little talk with Miz Rosen. See what I can do in that area." Strader turned to walk past Officer Parks. "Parks here will stay with you and see you out. I'll meet you at the car."

Strader looked at Benny then. "Go see if you can get traffic cleared out in the front so we can leave without any problem."

Benny nodded and turned to go.

A short time later, the girls were snuggled into the backseat of the police car, heading out the driveway of Celine's home. The sounds of the party followed them into the night.

Meredith leaned up against Grace. "Do you think our mother will be mad we didn't go down to say good-bye?"

Jack answered that. "No. She knew it was time for you to go."

"Past time," muttered Morgan, with her usual wisdom.

Meredith sighed. "Well, at least we know what she looks like now. And what she is *really* like."

"I hope I am *never* like her." Morgan bit out the words. "She is selfish and vain and really full of herself. I don't like her at all, even if she is our mother."

"We need to be Christian and forgiving." Meredith gave her a pious look.

"Maybe tomorrow." Morgan scowled. "But not tonight."

She leaned her head against Jack's arm. "I'm really sorry, Daddy. We caused you a lot of problem and worry. It was wrong. Celine said she would call you, but I know now she didn't."

Jack gathered Morgan up under his arm and leaned down to kiss her head. He leaned over to kiss Meredith, too. "I'm just glad you're both okay. I love you, you hear. I want you to remember that. We have each other, and that's enough. I don't want you worrying about your mother anymore. She has her life, and we have ours. We have to accept that."

"Okay." Meredith reached up to hug Jack fiercely. Then she leaned over to hug Grace. "And we have Ms. Grace. She's a good kind of mother."

Jack looked across at Grace and watched a little blush steal up her cheeks. "Yes, she is." He passed Grace a smile.

Morgan looked out the window. "Are we going home tonight? It's really late, isn't it?" She yawned.

"We're flying home tomorrow. I figured we all would need a little sleep before we made the long flight back." He yawned, too. "Especially me."

"Where are we staying?" Morgan asked.

Grace answered. "At a nice little bed-and-breakfast here in Beverly Hills. I thought we would like that better than a big hotel. Your father called earlier to see if they had rooms for us. I stayed in it once years ago, and it's charming."

Detective Strader turned around. "If you'll give me the bed-

and-breakfast name and address, we'll take you right there. And we'll have someone pick you up tomorrow and take you back to the airport when you're ready."

Grace told him the name of the bed-and-breakfast in Beverly Hills.

"Nice little place. I know it." Strader offered her one of his partial smiles. "The former owner of the place—before it became a bed-and-breakfast—was a furrier to some of the great stars: Garbo, Monroe."

"Yes." Grace smiled at him. "It has a nice ambience. And I thought a quiet place would be good tonight for the girls—rather than a big hotel like the Beverly Hills Hotel or the Four Seasons"

"Yeah. I'd say they've had enough of glitz and glamour for a while." He caught Jack's gaze then. "I had that little talk with Miz Rosen. We sort of came to a little agreement—if you agreed not to press charges. I told her I'd be writing up a report and filing it, and if anything like this happened another time, we'd pull it and offer her a little jail time. She agreed that might be unpleasant and that she'd mind her ways in the future."

He chuckled to himself. "She also agreed graciously, with a little nudging, to cover your airfare and expenses for this unnecessary trip you had to make out here to California."

Jack saw Strader offer the first genuine smile he'd seen—a rather smug one.

He raised an eyebrow at Jack. "I thought that was the least she could do, considering the circumstances. You get a copy of all the receipts to me later, and I'll go get you a check."

Jack grinned. "Thank you, Detective. That was thoughtful of you." He meant it, but he wished he had been the one to wrangle this cooperation out of Celine himself.

Grace leaned forward impulsively and kissed Strader on the cheek. "What a nice gesture, Detective. And I want you to know if you or Officer Parks ever want to come and visit the Smoky Mountains in Tennessee, that you will have a free place to stay at my bed-and-breakfast in Townsend."

"Well, hey, that's real nice of you," Officer Parks chimed in. "I've never been east. It might be a real treat to come one day."

"It's nicer there than it is here." Meredith said this emphatically, causing them all to laugh.

Later that evening, Jack slipped through the adjoining door in their two-bedroom suite to check on his girls. They could have slept with him or with Grace, but they'd opted to sleep with Grace at this point. Jack could hardly blame them. He'd liked to have done the same thing. Especially after seeing Grace in that pair of black silk pajamas.

The girls lay piled up in bed with Grace now, and she was telling them a story. It was a nice sight.

"Come jump in with us!" Morgan moved over to pat the bed beside her.

Jack came over by the bed considering it. Morgan had opened him a nice spot between her and Grace. It was tempting.

"Daddy tells good stories," Meredith announced.

"He tells *really* good scary stories." Morgan's eyes brightened as she said this.

Meredith shook her head. "I don't want any scary stories tonight. This has been a scary enough time. I want a happy ending story."

Morgan grinned. "Okay. Daddy, tell us the story about when you and Uncle Roger went skinny-dipping in the creek and then were afraid to go back and get your clothes because of the hornet's nest. That's a good one! Grace will like it."

Jack watched a little half smile curl the corners of Grace's mouth as she tried not to smirk. "Yes, that would be a good one to hear." She looked up at him with dancing eyes.

It really didn't take much encouragement then to urge Jack to climb into the oversize king bed with them to join in the story hour. It was a wonderful feeling to be here safe and sound with his girls, knowing they were both out of harm's way and well. It wasn't a bad feeling to have Grace's warm, silky body so close to his, either.

He leaned over to give all three of them a kiss as he snuggled down between them. "I'm a lucky man to find myself in bed with three such beautiful women!"

"Oh, Daddy. We're not beautiful," Meredith argued.

"Oh, yes you are, pumpkin. And when you and Morgan grow up, I'll bet you're both going to be as beautiful as Ms. Grace."

Meredith looked at Grace wistfully. "I hope so."

"What I hope," Morgan added thoughtfully, "is that we grow up to be as *nice* as Ms. Grace. I've decided being nice is better than being beautiful or rich or famous. Or anything."

Jack saw a blush steal over Grace's face.

"Well, that is a very good lesson to learn." Jack reached over to tweak Morgan's cheek.

"I wish our mommy had been as nice as you, Ms. Grace." Meredith's little voice was wistful.

Jack was sorry his girls had been hurt by Celine. He certainly knew the feeling, and he felt a lump in his throat as he began his story.

CHAPTER 23

The girls held a glorious reunion with Bebe, Althea, and the Butlers when they got home. What had been somewhat of a nightmare became a big adventure to share after all the chastisements and apologies were past. After all, the girls had traveled to Hollywood, had met a real Hollywood star—who happened to be their own mother—and then had watched their mother receive a big award on a television screen that took up a whole wall.

Grace had gone with Jack and Bebe to take the girls home, and then Jack drove Grace back to the Mimosa while Bebe stayed with the girls. Grace found Margaret and Vince there—ready to welcome her back—and both unusually starry-eyed.

The couple insisted on hearing about the whole rescue adventure, and then Margaret leaned forward from her seat on the couch with an excited gleam in her eye. Grace noticed that she looked to Vincent for encouragement. Something was up.

"Mother, Vincent and I have decided we don't want to wait until I graduate next May to get married. We want to marry in early September."

Grace couldn't seem to find any words.

Margaret gave her a bright smile. "It's really sensible if you think about it. We already know we want to get married. Vincent has a nice house. And all the family is coming over, anyway for Labor Day. It's perfect, really. Everyone will already be here."

She paused to take a breath. "Vincent has asked Reverend Hartwell to come back to do the ceremony for us. He was thrilled. And Vincent's parents can come at that time, and his sister can come, too. So, you see, we have everything worked out."

Her eyes sparkled. "I thought we could have the reception here at the Mimosa. It would be beautiful if we set up a few tents in the backyard. You know, like we did for Elaine's wedding. Vince and I don't want anything too fancy—just family and friends."

Grace gulped. "Margaret, that's only a few weeks away! It takes time to plan a wedding. To find dresses. To do invitations. To plan a big reception."

Margaret reached across impulsively to hug her mother. "But that's what makes it so perfect. You've planned events a million times. And Grandma and Grandpa Richey are here. And Aunt Myra is tickled about helping me with everything now that you and she have become such friends. I've already been over to the store in South Knoxville and found the most gorgeous bridal dress and one for Elaine she'll absolutely love. She's going to be the matron of honor. And I'm having Vince's sister, Laura, and Mike's wife, Barbara, and Ken's wife, Louise, as bridesmaids. Plus my best friend Rachel Day. She owes me big time since I had to fork out huge bucks for that sequined bridesmaid's dress I wore to her wedding in Nashville last summer."

She stopped to grin at Grace. "Won't it be fun? Your very first wedding here at the Mimosa—and it will be mine!"

Grace was stunned. "But, Margaret . . . couldn't we at least wait until Christmas? To allow some more time to plan?"

Margaret looked at Vincent and giggled. "We seem to be having a little problem with waiting."

Vincent turned a bright red.

Grace felt Jack sit forward a little aggressively then.

Vincent waved a hand. "It's not like Margaret makes it sound." He cleared his throat with embarrassment. "It's only that we're . . . uh . . . rather eager."

Margaret giggled. "Vincent always has the nicest way to put things, doesn't he? None of those crude words like most guys use."

Vincent's face grew redder, and Grace heard Jack chuckle beside her.

"Yeah, I like the term . . . eager." Jack grinned. "It's a nice word."

Grace turned to give Jack a stern look. "Don't encourage them, Jack Teague. This is a very sudden announcement."

Jack patted her knee. "Think of it this way, Grace. If they're getting . . . uh . . . rather eager, it might escalate and cause some embarrassment for our preacher here. After all, he's supposed to set an example for the young people in our congregation about how to purport themselves. In how to exercise restraint."

"Yeah." Margaret agreed. "And we're not doing very well with restraint, Mother. I don't think we'll make it to Christmas."

Jack burst out laughing then.

Vincent twisted his hands nervously. "I do think it would be good if we married now, Grace. We're both very sure. And I will be very good to Margaret, I promise you. Plus you will be able to be right next door for this first year of our marriage to be a help to her." He smiled tentatively at Grace.

"See? That's really sensible, Mother." Margaret chimed in once more. "You know that I don't know doodley about cooking and all that domestic stuff. I've always been too busy at the piano. I'm going to need *lots* of help."

Grace began to mentally calculate the days left in the month of August. "What day exactly are you considering for the wedding?"

Margaret flashed another glowing smile. "Well, everyone will be coming in for my piano recital early Friday evening on Labor Day weekend, so we thought we'd do the Rehearsal Dinner afterward and the wedding Saturday at 2:00 pm. With Monday a holiday because of Labor Day, Vincent and I can sneak in a short honeymoon before I need to be back at classes Tuesday."

Vincent joined in then. "A friend in the church has offered us their rental cabin in Gatlinburg for our honeymoon nights. It's in a gorgeous location on a mountaintop with wonderful views."

"So, you see everything's worked out!" Margaret chimed in

again. "Vincent has already started all the arrangements for the church. Grandma Richey said she and Grandpa would take care of the flowers with the florist they know. And with it only being family and friends, we'll be mailing announcements rather than invitations. There's really not that much to do!"

Grace tried to catch her breath. "Margaret, as I said before, Labor Day weekend is only a few weeks away!"

"I know! Isn't it great!" She flashed another smile at Grace and let a hand rove intimately over Vincent's thigh.

Grace sighed.

"Might as well accept the inevitable," she heard Jack mutter near her ear.

She flashed him a look of annoyance—even knowing he was right.

"Well, I guess we have a lot of planning to do." She tried her best to offer Margaret and Vincent a charming smile.

Jack reached a hand across to shake Vincent's. "Congratulations, man. Guess I'll need to dig out my best suit and get it cleaned."

Grace suddenly felt overwhelmingly weary.

Seeming to sense it, Jack added, "Grace is pretty bushed from the long flights back and forth to California and from all the excitement with the twins. I think she might need to get some rest before she starts planning a wedding or any other event tonight."

"Oh, well, sure." Margaret jumped up solicitously, leaning over to give Grace a kiss on the cheek. "And I'm going to go open the bottle of champagne Vincent and I got to celebrate right now. Vincent and I made dinner, knowing you would be tired. We'll all eat a bite together and then share a toast to the girls' getting back safe and to Vincent's and my wedding plans. After that, you men can say good night, and I'll tuck mom into bed early for a good long rest."

Jack stood up and reached down a hand for Grace's. He smirked at Margaret. "What did you cook? Is it safe?"

"Stuffed ziti. I can cook *some,* Jack Teague." Margaret swatted at him playfully. "Vince helped me make it. It wasn't too hard. We have a Caesar salad and a good French bread, too."

The four shared a nice evening, but Grace's mind raced in a whirl the whole time, thinking of all she had to do in the next weeks to prepare for a wedding at the Mimosa. She would need to plan the menu, order the tents, tables, and chairs, buy invitations and announcements, decide on beverages—naturally, there would be no alcohol. She would need to find a dress for herself and be sure Margaret had gotten the correct sizes for Elaine's and the bridesmaids' dresses. There were tuxes to think about and boutonnieres. Did Margaret even say who the best man and the groomsmen would be? Surely Vince had decided that.

She sighed to herself. There was so much to do. Even with the florist chosen, there were decisions to make about what flowers they would use and where. There were decisions to make about where everyone would stay. And, on top of everything else, she had to worry about whether Jane would come and how she would act.

"One person I *don't* want to invite," Margaret said, as she raised her glass for another toast, "is Crazy Man."

They laughed, but their laughs held an edge to them.

Vincent gave Grace one of his intense gazes. "Margaret will be safer with me, too, Grace, with Crazy Man still not found. You know that."

It was one point Grace had to concede.

The subject of Crazy Man was on the table a week later as Grace scolded Margaret at the breakfast table for taking off the previous day on her own with no one with her.

"Oh, for heaven's sake, Mother! I had to go over for the final fitting on my wedding gown at Richey's." She gave Grace a pouty look. "Besides, I'm tired of governing my life, worrying about that stupid little man."

Grace frowned at her. "I doubt Sheriff Walker would consider him only a stupid little man after all the problems the sheriff has had with him."

As if on cue, Grace looked up to see Swofford Walker at the back door. Behind him, as Grace unlocked the door to let him in, were Jack and Vincent.

Grace put a hand to her throat. "Has something else happened? Don't tell me someone has been hurt!"

"Well, we had an incident." The sheriff took his hat off and laid it on the sideboard before he sat down at the kitchen table. "But it's resolved now. And we've caught our man."

"Oh, my!" Grace sat down herself then.

Jack and Vincent went to pour themselves and the sheriff cups of coffee.

"Hey. Can we eat some of this banana bread on the counter?" Jack's voice floated over. Grace nodded at him dismissively. How could he even think of food at a time like this?

"Tell us what happened?" she asked the sheriff.

"Who was it, Sheriff Walker?" Margaret added this as she pulled out a chair at the table for herself. "And how did you find him?"

"Crazy Man is Beecher Webb," Jack put in. "Can you believe it? Jerrell Webb and his boys Beecher and Cecil have been mowing our yards and doing all our landscaping around here on the River Road for ten years or more. Who would have thought?"

The sheriff took the coffee cup Jack offered him with annoyance. "Now, who's telling this here story, Jack, you or me?"

Jack sat down, chastised, and bit into a piece of banana bread.

"It was, in fact, Beecher Webb." The sheriff affirmed this with a deep nod. "I'd never have thought it would have been him. Fine family, the Webbs. But Lora Jean Johnson came forward to talk to me yesterday, and she sort of put a finger on him. We'd had another incident involving her this time. She and her little girl Janelle live not far down the road from the Webbs—up off Sugar Loaf Lane. Janelle plays with Beecher's little boys. Lora Jean says she's felt right sorry for them since their mother died. And she told me Beecher hadn't been quite right ever since Ira Nelle got murdered."

"She was murdered?" Grace knew her voice sounded incredulous.

"Yeah, and a brutal murder, too." The sheriff took a long drink of his coffee after stirring cream and sugar into it. Then he cut off a piece of banana bread and put it on one of the plates Vincent had brought over from the sideboard.

"Beecher's wife Ira Nelle came to town one night to listen to a little bluegrass band at the Riverside Restaurant down on the Little River, but she never came home." The sheriff shook his head. "It took dogs to finally find her. She'd been raped and stabbed. Pretty brutal thing."

"Who did that?" Margaret asked.

The sheriff scratched his head. "Well, that's the worst of it. We never did find the killer. Sad thing, that. Makes it hard for a man to get peace in his mind and soul when the killer of his wife isn't found. Must have been that fact to push Beecher over the edge. Got him to acting nutty."

Vincent picked up the story while the sheriff dug into his piece of banana bread. "I wasn't living here then, but I remember the retiring pastor told me a lot about what had happened. Said it had been hard on the family. Ira Nelle was the only woman who lived up there with all the Beecher men—with Jerrell, Cecil, Beecher, and their two boys Harley and Hixon. Twins—and real close to their mother. Plus, Ira Nelle sang with the family in the Webb Creek Band—and could play a fiddle right well, from what I've been told."

"But why all the notes?" Margaret asked. "And why, particularly, such a focus on me?"

"You look somewhat like Ira Nelle." The sheriff smiled. "Blond, pretty, and about the same height. There was a resemblance with Grace, too, and with several of the other women who received notes of warning. Lora Jean got a note a few days ago after she had a date with the Statton boy who works at the River Rat tubing company. Told her to beware of bad men."

Grace felt confused. "But those Statton boys are all fine young men. And Lora Jean isn't even blond. Plus that doesn't explain why Jack got notes, or his girls—or Samantha and Roger about their Ruby."

The sheriff looked irritated. "Well, now, I'm getting to it all if you'll just give me enough time. It took a while to make sense of it, and it takes a while to tell it."

Grace shook her head slightly at Margaret who was preparing to jump in with an undoubtedly critical or impatient comment. Grace knew patience wasn't one of Margaret's long suits.

Margaret rolled her eyes—but bit her tongue.

You see," the sheriff continued, "Beecher got himself eat up with guilt because he didn't protect Ira Nelle better. Seems she wanted him to go down to the Riverside with her that night, and he didn't care to go. They had a bit of a snit over it, and she went on down on her own. So that was the first problem. Then, of course, the second was that we never did find the man who murdered Ira Nelle."

The sheriff took a drink of his coffee. "The best clue we had was that Ira Nelle was seen talking for a little while to a trucker passing through. We didn't find her body for three days. By then any truckers going through this area were long gone. It's hard to track without any description of the truck or the trucking company. We did our best."

He looked apologetic. "We even hired a retired detective living in the area to help us on the case, but no one could find any good clues."

Jack spoke up. "I can vouch that the sheriff and his department did everything they could to find Ira Nelle's killer. No one liked to think a brutal murderer was lurking around our town."

The sheriff shook his head. "See, that's the kind of thinking that started turning around in Beecher's mind. He'd helped with the investigation as he could, questioning people, trying to learn more about who Ira Nelle saw that night. Later, some of the things he learned started to fester in his mind."

Jack looked up suddenly. "I had stopped by at the Riverside earlier that evening. I actually spoke to Ira Nelle."

"You did." The sheriff bit into another chunk of banana bread. "So did Roger, if you'll recall. The Statton boy was there, too."

Jack pivoted to look directly at the sheriff. "Beecher got to thinking it might have been one of us."

The sheriff nodded. "You three and a few more. I heard Beecher got fixated on some of the people who last saw Ira Nelle. Felt like he needed to watch them and to watch folks who spent too much time around them. Especially felt he needed to watch out for women and girls they might get too close to."

Grace looked up thoughtfully. "He began to think he might take care of other women and girls like he didn't take care of Ira Nelle."

"That's about it." The sheriff played with a spoon on the table. "It started out with little things and little warning notes here and there. But it got worse. Mental problems sort of escalate like that sometimes."

"Why did he follow me that day?" Margaret asked this.

"Well, you look so much like Ira Nelle—young and blond. And musical." The sheriff grinned at Margaret. "He heard you playing the piano and singing when he was out working in the yard. And he worried that you spent time around Jack. Also, that you walked around so much on your own. Plus the day he followed you it was because he saw the Statton boy talking to you outside of the Hart Gallery. He thought you might be in danger. He meant to follow you for a while to see you got to your next stop safely."

Margaret sighed. "That's really sad."

"Yeah, it is. He's going to need a lot of help to get all this sorted out." The sheriff pushed his chair back and crossed one leg over his knee. "The medical folks seem to think he can be rehabilitated."

Grace leaned forward. "How did Lora Jean know it might be Beecher?"

"She wasn't sure it was." The sheriff reached over to get his coffee cup. "But when she got her own little note, she got suspicious. You see, the Webb boys had been down at her house the day before playing a card game with Janelle. Lora Jean heard them, offhand, fussing that all their cards were messed up because some of them kept getting lost."

"I bet she got her note on a playing card," Jack said.

"That she did." The sheriff grinned at Jack. "And it got her to thinking. She also remembered picking up Janelle from Scouts the day Margaret got followed. She remembered Janelle and the girls talking about Crazy Man's driving a black truck with a headlight out and wearing a cowboy hat. Beecher and all the Webb men always wear cowboy hats. And Janelle remembered Beecher had run into a fence post up at the farm and busted out a headlight last month. She'd noticed it when he came down to pick up the boys one day."

Margaret leaned her elbows on the table. "Did Beecher Webb admit it right away when you went to confront him?"

"Nope. Wouldn't say a word for a while." The sheriff leaned down to scratch the dogs' ears; they'd come padding into the room. "But he broke down and snapped after a while. Said if I'd done my job he wouldn't have needed to protect other women from getting hurt like Ira Nelle did." The sheriff shook his head back and forth. "Made me feel real bad to hear that."

"What will happen to Beecher now?" Jack asked. "This must be hard for Beecher's boys, after losing their mother only a year ago."

"Well, the boys' granddad is helping with that." The sheriff looked at Vincent. "And it would be right fine if you went over to counsel with the family some. Maybe prayed with them and gave them some spiritual help at a bad time like this."

Vincent nodded. "I'll go today."

"I'll go, too." Margaret reached over to take Vincent's hand. "I want them to know I hold no hard feelings. Beecher was sick. I don't think he would have ever hurt me. He just meant to protect me."

Jack slanted the sheriff a sharp glance. "Why do you think Beecher sent that note to my girls about their mother? That doesn't seem to fit the protective picture."

"Well, yeah, it does." The sheriff scratched his nose. "You see, Beecher thought you the most likely suspect among the ones he watched—what with your past reputation with women and all."

He sent an apologetic look to Grace. "When Beecher was working in the yard at the Mimosa one day and heard the girls in the gazebo—wondering about their mother and wishing they could know about her—he got to thinking maybe they would be safer and better off to be with her. He'd heard the old rumors about Jack's having run his young wife off long ago, and it all rolled around and mixed in with his twisted thinking."

"Dang it!" Jack pounded a fist on the table. "I liked that man. Always talked to him whenever he mowed our property. Asked about his boys."

Grace leaned over to put a hand on Jack's arm. "He wasn't well, Jack. You can't take it personally when Beecher wasn't well. His mind was all twisted."

Margaret sighed deeply. "Well, I for one am surely glad we found out who this man is. I'm sick and tired of always needing to have someone with me whenever I go anywhere."

Vincent grinned at her. "Well, maybe not *always* sorry to have someone with you."

She giggled. "Well, maybe not *always*."

The couple passed some looks Grace didn't even want to try to analyze. Perhaps it was a good thing the wedding date wasn't far away now.

The sheriff stood and picked up his hat. "I'd best be getting on now. I just wanted you folks to know we'd found our man and that things would be safer around here now."

"Where is Beecher now?" Margaret asked the sheriff.

"Staying in a mental health facility of some sort for a spell. But then the doctors think they can work with him as an out-patient. He's already saying he needs to give a lot of folks some apologies— and they say that's a real good sign."

Jack got up, too. "I'll walk you out, Swofford. I need to go on to the office. I have a closing in twenty minutes."

"I need to go, too." Vincent stood up. "The florist is coming to look at the church at nine thirty."

Margaret jumped up eagerly. "I'll go with you, Vince. I want to talk with them about tying some roses on each of the pews with white ribbons."

Grace cleaned up the kitchen and then took the dogs outside into the backyard. She walked down toward the river as the dogs played with a stick and chased each other through the yard. She thought about all she'd learned about Crazy Man as she walked down to the tumbling mountain stream and out onto the swinging bridge. It felt nice to stand here on the bridge, looking down the river, hearing the creek rushing over the rocks below. Enjoying a moment of quiet after such a busy sweep of days.

Grace stood in the same spot again a few weeks later—savoring the quiet once more. It was late evening with a full moon floating in the sky overhead. Margaret and Vincent were happily married and off on their honeymoon. And this morning Grace had seen the last of her family and houseguests out the door and then spent the day cleaning, stripping beds, and doing laundry. The house felt suddenly lonely after being full with family and friends for so many days.

Grace sighed and leaned her arms on the bridge rail, looking down on the river below. She could see the moonlight flickering over the top of the water as it rushed on its way downstream. Late fireflies flickered in the shrubbery by the riverside, and the soft sounds of tree frogs kept the night from being totally quiet.

Hearing a footfall, Grace looked up to see Jack coming out onto the bridge toward her. He came to stand beside her, leaning his arms on the rail to look up the river, too. They stood there quietly, enjoying the evening for a time before either of them spoke.

"You were watching for me, weren't you?" Grace said into the darkness.

Jack's voice came back, husky and silky. "You know I was."

Grace felt herself shiver. She waited, expectant, knowing Jack would soon touch her or kiss her. Her body stirred with expectancy.

But Jack only stood looking up the river, quiet.

A little thread of alarm skittered up Grace's spine. Jack was seldom quiet like this, and she could feel a tension coiled in him. Humming. Troubling him.

She waited, wondering if she should ask him what was wrong.

Grace moved one of her hands to cover his on the rail, but he jerked his hand away from hers. Stepped back from her a little, too.

"I need some space to say what I came to say tonight, Grace." His voice sounded strained. Tight.

Grace heard him take a deep breath.

Had he found someone else? She wondered. Did he want to stop seeing her? A barrage of thoughts and doubts assailed her. She had never been sure about Jack's feelings for her.

He looked toward her with a troubled face. "I'm in love with you, Grace Conley."

Relief swept her. She tried to reach for him again.

"No." He backed way. "Let me say what I need to say. It isn't easy for me to say words like these. I've only said them once in my life to a woman. And I was a fool then for saying them. I didn't think I would ever say them again to any woman."

Grace saw his hands gripping the railing of the bridge.

"I haven't been a good man for much of my life. You know that. I've enjoyed a lot of women." He stopped and took a deep breath. "When I met you, I knew I was attracted to you. But I also knew there was more. I kept waiting to grow tired of you, for the fascination with you to wear off. It usually did, Grace. My interest in any woman never lasted for very long before I found myself noticing another one. I'm not proud of that, but it was the way it was."

He moved restlessly on the bridge. Grace felt tense, waiting for what else he had to say.

"You got to me in a way no woman ever has before. I knew that for a surety not long after you moved here. I lost my interest in other women. I thought about you more than normal for me. Wanted you. Fantasized about you. But also began to like you. Respect you. That was new for me. I enjoyed your company. I liked sitting next to you, talking with you, being with you. I liked the different sides of you I learned about. One of my first thoughts when I met you was that you had a lot of layers. That I would enjoy peeling them back. I have, and I'm still enjoying that. I don't think I'll ever stop enjoying it."

Grace reached to touch him again, but he pulled away once more, held up a hand to her.

"I need to say this without touching you, Grace." He took a deep breath again. "I don't know when I realized I was in love with you. Maybe after that trip to California. I just looked at you one day, and I knew. It scared the crap out of me. I've almost been glad you were so busy the last few weeks. It gave me time to think. Gave me time to decide what to do."

He turned to her with anguished eyes. "I'm not good enough for you, Grace. You deserve a better man than me. But I can't bear to think of letting you go to find a better man. I have no right to speak to you of love and commitment when I've lived the way I have. But I have to take a chance and offer. It isn't much of a deal for you. I'd understand if you didn't even want to consider it."

Jack took a deep breath, almost shuddering. His eyes looked dark and troubled. It wasn't an expression Grace was used to seeing on Jack's face.

She started to reach out a hand to touch him again, but then stopped herself.

Instead Grace looked up into Jack's eyes in the moonlight and saw the love—swimming with the fear and tension. It wasn't easy for a man like Jack to admit to love.

She smiled at him. "I'm waiting for the question that's supposed to come at the end of all this talk of love and commitment, Jack."

He gave her a pained look. "You're going to make me step all the way out on the plank, aren't you?"

"Absolutely." Grace looked at Jack with honest, warm eyes. "And I want the romantic memories to go with the moment."

Jack groaned, and then dropped down to one knee and took Grace's hand. "Grace Conley, I love you with all the heart I have. With all I have to offer, which is much less than you deserve, I offer you myself. My love, my protection, my caring, my passion." He grinned. "And I have a lot of the latter."

Grace tried to stay serious and hold back a grin.

"I'd like you to consider being my wife. I'd like you to consider taking on the job of being a mother to my girls. I hope you will love them and love me. As you've already seen, it won't always be easy. We'll have the teen years ahead, God help us. But we'll have each other, too. Every day. In every way."

Grace gave Jack a serious look then. "I want to be the only one, Jack. I want you to be sure of that—that you're ready for that."

He took her other hand in his. "I stopped thinking of anyone after meeting you, Grace. I stopped wanting anyone after you. And then, the Lord up there has been doing His work on me and changing me more. I bonfired all my Playboy magazines last month. They held no interest for me anymore. He's changing me from the inside out; you've been changing me. I'm different in my skin. But like you told me on the plane, I like who I am now. I like who I am today a lot better than who I was. You should understand that. People change. People *can* change."

"Yes, they can." Grace smiled down at Jack, still on one knee.

He waited, looking at her.

"Oh, Jack Teague, get up from there and kiss me. Surely you know I can't say anything but yes. I've fallen in love with you, too. You've gotten into my heart and under my skin. I don't know what I'd do without you in my life. . . ."

He kissed her before she could get another word out. Kissed her deeply and passionately and with all of his being. Jack was never a halfway kind of guy—and Grace could feel the force of his love and joy all the way down to her toes.

Pulling Grace into his arms, Jack ran his hands down her back to rest on her hips. He pulled her against him as he traced his lips over her mouth and down her neck. Grace had known love before, but this love she'd found with Jack was new and different. And she felt new and different with him—stirred, overwhelmed, and touched with the wonder of having discovered love a second time. Of having found someone like Jack who gave her life such joy.

"Do we have to wait until we're married since we've both been married before?" Jack purred out these words against her ear.

Grace pulled back and put a hand to Jack's face lovingly. "We've waited this long, Jack. We can wait a little longer for everything to be right. You know we should."

He gave her a wolfish grin. "I did before I started kissing you and holding you. And before getting your scent into my senses and into my head. And thinking all sorts of delectable things."

Grace leaned in to kiss him again.

"Remember what Vincent said?" he whispered against her neck. "That he thought he and Margaret should get married soon because they were eager."

Grace giggled. "I remember."

"I'm eager, too, Grace. Do you think we could get married soon?"

"It might seem kind of sudden to everyone with Margaret's having just gotten married." She slipped her fingers into Jack's hair while his hands explored intimately up under the back of her blouse.

Grace sighed against him. "Perhaps it should be soon. Like Margaret said, there's no point in waiting once you know you've found the right one."

Jack held Grace back from him and looked down into her eyes tenderly. "I'm the right one for you, Grace. We'll have a good life, and grow old together. And every time we walk across this swinging bridge over the river, we'll remember how we declared our love out here to each other."

"And how you got down on one knee and proposed?"

He gave her a wide grin that lit up his dimples. "You said you wanted a memory."

"So where's my ring, Jack Teague?" she said, meaning to tease him.

He reached into his pocket and pulled out a ring box.

Grace was speechless. This hadn't been a spontaneous moment for Jack. He had planned this in advance.

He opened the box to show her. Nestled inside was a dazzling ring with a round, white diamond set in a circle of smaller diamonds.

She caught her breath.

"Here's the symbolism." He gave her a suggestive smile. "I intend to circle you with love and to always keep you in the circle of my love."

"Very romantic." She was touched.

"Wait'll you see me act it out." He gave her a devilish grin and began to illustrate his ideas until Grace decided the upcoming wedding date they'd been talking about might have to be *very* soon indeed.

&PILOGUE

Five years later, the phone rang in the Mimosa Inn. A tall, lanky teenager, with reddish hair caught up in a careless pony-tail, swung around from the stairs she'd just tripped down to pick up the phone in the entry hall.

"Mimosa Inn, this is Morgan Teague. May I help you?"

"Very professional," a voice responded.

"Daddy!" Morgan's face lit up in a smile. "How is Margaret? How is Vincent? And how is the baby?"

Morgan got the report she wanted from her father and then hung up to race down the hall to share it. Her Aunt Bebe and her sister Meredith were in the kitchen fixing sweet breads and putting together a Saturday morning breakfast casserole for the houseguests expected at the Mimosa that night.

Bebe looked up. "Who was that on the phone, Morgan?"

"It was Daddy." She grinned at them and pulled a kitchen chair around to straddle it.

"Is the baby all right?" Meredith asked. Her hair, longer than Morgan's, was braided down her back to get it out of the way while she worked in the kitchen.

"Daddy says he's great. And Margaret and Vincent are fine, too. Daddy and Grace are going to stay at Montreat until next Thursday, and they wanted to know if we'd be all right handling things for them until then."

"I hope you told them yes," Bebe replied.

"Of course." Morgan grinned. "And I made Daddy promise

to send us pictures on the Internet today. We want to see Joshua Jack Westbrooke, too."

"It's an absolute marvel that you can send photos like that over the Internet today," Aunt Bebe said with a shake of her head. "I never thought I'd live to see the day."

Meredith rinsed her hands and dried them on a dishcloth. "I still can't believe Margaret and Vincent only *barely* made it back into the Asheville airport before the baby came. Daddy said Margaret was in labor on the plane—with Vincent and her doing breathing exercises the last twenty minutes of the flight."

Morgan laughed. "Golly, I'll bet everyone on that plane was freaking out, thinking that baby would come right there on the plane in front of them all."

"Morgan!" Bebe gave her an admonishing look.

Morgan shrugged.

Meredith caught her lip in her teeth thoughtfully. "You know, they wouldn't have been coming home from that convention—where Vince preached and Margaret played that new piano piece she'd written—if that woman hadn't called Grace. What was her name?"

Bebe looked up from pouring pumpkin-bread batter into two tins. "That was Zola Devon. She has that little shop in Gatlinburg, Nature's Corner."

Morgan pulled at her ponytail. "How did she know Margaret's baby would come early and that she needed to come home?"

Bebe smiled. "Zola has a gift for knowing things. Some people do."

"Like a witch?" Morgan's eyes lit up.

"Good heavens, no!" Bebe turned to put her hands on her hips. "You get that kind of disrespectful thinking right out of your mind, Morgan Teague. Zola Devon isn't some kind of fortune-teller. She gets things as she's given it—and for good purposes."

Meredith sat down on a kitchen stool, considering this. "Grace told me the name of our inn came from Zola. She saw that Grace should come and live here."

"Well, pooh!" said Morgan. "So did we."

Meredith smiled. "Yeah, we did. We knew she was nice even from the first day."

Bebe interrupted. "Well, she's not going to be so nice if she gets back and finds out we didn't take care of her guests. You girls get to work. I can't stand on these old legs for as long as I used to."

Morgan went over to give Bebe a kiss on the cheek. "Don't worry, Aunt Bebe. Meredith and I will take care of everything. We're going to live here and run the inn one day."

The trio settled in then to get ready for the Mimosa's guests. It looked like it was going to be another busy weekend down by the river.

Down by the River

Lin Stepp

About This Guide

The suggested questions are included
to enhance your group's reading of
Lin Stepp's *Down by the River.*

DISCUSSION QUESTIONS

1. Middle-aged and widowed for several years, Grace Conley is at a turning point in her life, trying to decide on the next direction to take. What decision does she make for her future while visiting in Townsend? Have you ever found yourself at a turning point in your own life? What new direction did you take?

2. Life changes are exciting, but also hard. What did Grace Conley's family, especially her children Mike, Ken, Elaine, and Margaret, think about her decision to buy the bed-and-breakfast in Townsend? What were their reasons for not wanting Grace to move and make this change? What did you think about their attitudes?

3. Realtor Jack Teague doesn't have much confidence in Grace Conley's ability to run a successful bed-and-breakfast either. Why? Do you think people often underestimate the abilities of women who have not been consistently in the paid workforce? What plans did Grace's family have for her that were different from her own desires?

4. What were your first impressions of Jack Teague? What were Grace's first impressions? How did your original impressions about Jack—and Grace's original impressions about Jack—change as the book progressed?

5. Besides Grace's own heart attraction to the bed-and-breakfast for sale in Townsend, several other factors influenced her to decide to buy the business. What were these? Do you believe God sends helps, or what pastor Vincent Westbrooke termed confirmations, when we are struggling with decisions about new directions in our lives? What did you think about Zola Devon as a helper

to Grace? How did her words influence Grace's naming the bed-and-breakfast the Mimosa Inn?

6. Grace Conley and Jack Teague are attracted to each other from the start. Why do they both not want to encourage the attraction between them? What changes through the book bring them closer together? How is Grace's relationship with Jack different from the relationship she had with her husband, Charles?

7. Secondary characters in a book are often fun—and can often greatly enhance book and life stories. What did you think of Ashleigh Anne Layton? Did she make you think of anyone you know? Did later events in the story change your opinion of Ashleigh in any way?

8. What changes did Grace make to the Mimosa Inn? How did she change and begin to develop as a person as she began to run the inn? How did opening the crafts shop at the Mimosa begin to change Grace's perception of her talents? How had Grace's gifts as a crafter been discouraged by her family?

9. Grace's return to the Mimosa brings her back near her own family in South Knoxville, her father and mother Mel and Dottie Richey, her brother Leonard, and her sister Myra. Why has Grace been estranged somewhat from her family—and especially from her sister Myra? What part did Charles's family, and especially his mother, Jane Conley, play in this? How did you feel about the impact Jane had on the Conleys' life and especially on Grace's and Margaret's lives? Have you ever experienced difficulties like these with your family?

10. Jack's girls, Meredith and Morgan, played strong character roles in this book. How did the twins first meet Grace and how did they influence her to come to

Townsend? How did the developing relationship between Grace and Meredith and Morgan impact Grace's relationship with Jack? As the book progressed, what did you learn about the twins' mother? What caused the girls to later fly out to California to meet her, and what happened in that visit?

11. There are frequent contrasts between the lifestyles of women in this book. What are some of these? How do differences in finances, personality, and inherent beauty impact the women's lifestyles—as with Grace and her sister Myra? How do life choices, such as whether to pursue a career or to stay home in a homemaking role, create differences? In what ways do Jack's aunt Bebe Butler and Jack's mother, Althea Teague, portray warmly how both of these different lifestyle choices can be healthy and good ones?

12. Just as Grace is settling into her new life in Townsend, her daughter Margaret shows up. Why has Margaret come? When Vincent Westbrooke meets Margaret, he believes he's been given a sign from God that he should marry Margaret. Why does this seem unlikely to Grace? What changes occur in Margaret's life during her visit in Townsend, through her interactions with the church pianist Jo Carson, Vincent, and her mother?

13. When Althea has her heart attack, how does Jack handle the news? How does this time of stress cause him to fall back into old familiar behaviors he is trying to leave behind? How does Grace become involved in finding Jack when he leaves the hospital but doesn't return? How does this event affect Grace's feelings for Jack?

14. Faith can impact and change lives. How is this shown in many ways throughout this book? In particular, how are Margaret and Jack impacted by a faith decision in their

lives? Why had Margaret and Jack not been in a strong place of faith even though they had both attended church and been raised in Christian families?

15. What did you think about young pastor, Vincent West-brooke? How had he become a minister? What was different about his beliefs from what you see in many church pastors? Margaret becomes angry in the book when she learns about a new facet of Vincent's life. What is this? What factors eventually bring Vincent and Margaret together?

16. At one point Margaret tells her mother, "I feel different here, Mother. It's as though all the rules I've lived by don't seem to apply. It's sort of unsettling." In what ways are Margaret's and Grace's lives—and the lives of others in the book—changed dramatically by their move to Townsend? Do you think moves to new places can facilitate changes in people? Have you ever experienced extensive life changes through moving to a new place, meeting new people, or encountering a different culture?

17. The mysterious stalker in the book, who is termed Crazy Man, causes many upsets and problems spying on people and leaving little notes and warnings. What were some of these? Many of his interferences caused only annoyance, but others were more frightening. How did his note about little Ruby upset everyone, and why? How did a later event when he follows Margaret frighten everyone? How did his leaving a note for Jack's girls cause even more problems and upset? Who does the book finally reveal that Crazy Man is? What reasons were given for why he did the things he did?

18. What did you like most about this book? Which character was your favorite? What aspects of this story seemed most surprising—and most satisfying?